FOR AN EXILE'S HEART

Ancient Songs
Book 2

LAURA STRICKLAND

ARE YOU SIGNED UP FOR DRAGONBLADE'S BLOG?

You'll get the latest news and information on exclusive giveaways, exclusive excerpts, coming releases, sales, free books, cover reveals and more.

Check out our complete list of authors, too!

No spam, no junk. That's a promise!

Sign Up Here

www.dragonbladepublishing.com

Dearest Reader;

Thank you for your support of a small press. At Dragonblade Publishing, we strive to bring you the highest quality Historical Romance from some of the best authors in the business. Without your support, there is no 'us', so we sincerely hope you adore these stories and find some new favorite authors along the way.

Happy Reading!

CEO, Dragonblade Publishing

ADDITIONAL DRAGONBLADE BOOKS BY AUTHOR LAURA STRICKLAND

Ancient Songs Series
For a Warrior's Heart (Book 1)
For an Exile's Heart (Book 2)

The Three Sisters MacBeith Series
Keeper of the Gate (Book 1)
Keeper of the Hearth (Book 2)
Keeper of the Light (Book 3)

Do our ancestors journey with us
In the choices that we make?
The longings of our dreams,
An aching of the heart?
The hint of a tune long remembered.
Is there a surer way for spirit to travel
Than via homesickness for what has been?

~ Finlay the Bard

*A*T THE HALL *of a Scottish chief, deep in the western Highlands, a bard entertains those who are gathered, singing and telling tales while accompanying himself on the harp. He weaves his tales in praise of his host's ancestors with a rare talent that keeps his listeners enthralled, from the highest to the lowest. Amid the leaping torches and the flickering candles, there is magic encircling the great chamber this night.*

Already he has told one tale, but the hour is not yet late, and his audience longs for another, a journey back through the mists of time to a place both so distant and so magical, it calls to them.

Finlay smiles to himself. This journey he has taken many times, but never once has it been so significant as this night. A hint of enchantment sparkles in his green eyes as he sweeps the room, touching upon his audience. Or does he search for but one face there?

The second tale he tells begins:

Once long ago, when this land we love so well was still called Dalriada, settled by the very boldest of the chiefs from fair Erin, Alba remained a mystery. An Erin chief had three sons, and he sent them hence in turn to accomplish his will. The first son, who was the boldest and his heir, failed in his mission. The second also did not accomplish what his father wished, so the chief sent the third and youngest of his sons, he with the charm upon his tongue, whom everyone loved. For if he was loved, surely he would accomplish the deed, no matter how difficult. Let me sing ye this song for an exile's heart...

CHAPTER ONE

Dalriada, Scotland, the fifth century AD

ADAIR MACMURTRAY PARTED reluctantly from his friends when his father's message found him. A fine day it was at the very beginning of summer, and the group of them—some warriors newly released from the training field, a number of musicians, and a flock of lovely young women—had been enjoying far too fine a time. Young Forba, she with the red hair and the wide brown eyes, had been instructing Adair on the harp. That took him wondrously close to her and offered an apt opportunity to steal a kiss.

But Father had sent the most disagreeable of his advisors, Donnar, who bent such a look of stern disapproval on Adair that he could do naught but make his apologies and go.

They hurried at a fearful pace down the skirt of the hill where the scent of wild thyme danced in the air like the notes of Forba's harp, where the larks circled as if to catch the laughter from below, and the water of the stream sparkled like a band of beaten silver. Adair began to wonder, not without trepidation, what his father wanted, and a hint of foreboding bit at the pleasure that filled him. He had not much time to contemplate it, though, for Donnar led him through the settlement to the big, dusky roundhouse where his father, as chief of the clan, resided with his wife—Adair's stepmother—his three sons, and his two young daughters.

After the bright sunlight outside, the darkness of the interior made him blink. Carved pillars soared to a lofty roof and the stones underfoot were worn smooth by the passage of many feet. Adair's people had held this land for countless generations. As his father never ceased with reminding him, they were descended from one of the greatest warriors Erin had ever known, and thus entitled to their place.

They were, so, meant to achieve great things. And they had a duty to the land that superseded anything so paltry as personal desires or intentions.

Adair had a love for the land deep and wide as the sky over the brae, rooted like the oaks from which these pillars had been stolen. A truth he often thought Father failed to see.

"Ah, Adair. There ye be."

Gawen MacMurtray was a big man, broad in the chest and brimming with life. In his younger days he'd been a fine warrior, and still took the field from time to time if the need came about. Adair could remember his going out often when he and his brothers were still young, all dressed for battle and wearing the torc that denoted his status as a high chief.

Mother would plait his wild red hair ahead of time—because this had been before she died in childbed. And Adair's two older brothers had looked on in sheer longing, because they too wanted to go out and fight.

Adair acknowledged now, approaching his father, who sat in his great chair with but two of his advisors in attendance, that something had changed after Mother died. A measure of Father's laughter had deserted him, though he still led with strength. He'd taken a second wife, far too soon to Adair's thinking, but he'd never regained the joy he'd once carried within him.

"Father," Adair said, coming to a halt in front of his sire.

Gawen shot an exasperated glare at his man, Donnar. "It did take ye long enough to find him."

"He was up the mountain, my chief. With his friends."

The look Adair's father turned upon him was unmistakably disapproving. "Again? Is it all ye do, son? Play in the heather?"

"Nay, Father." Adair shifted on his feet. "I spent all morning on the training field, and part o' the afternoon. 'Tis a grand day, though, and—"

Gawen snorted. "Most o' your days are grand, or so it seems. No matter. I have not the time to chastise ye now. Come sit down. We have serious matters to discuss."

Adair glanced at the two advisors—three now, with Donnar there—before taking a place on the rug at his father's feet. Old Fergal, who had been alive so long he carried the very history of the clan in his head. And Anlon, who advised Father on matters of war.

Ah, Adair did not like the frowns on either of their faces. Serious business indeed.

Father said without further fanfare, "Your brother has returned."

"Aye, so." Adair had seen him, his brother Daerg, that was the middle of Gawen's three sons. He had been away for some three months, having left home at the very end of winter just after the seas calmed enough for him to sail. Off on Father's implacable mission. "I saw him arrive." Though Daerg had not paused to speak with him, and Adair had not lingered either.

"Your brother," Father announced very harshly indeed, "has failed in the task he was set."

"Has he?" Adair raised a brow. Surprising indeed, for Daerg rarely failed at any assignment, especially one set by his father.

Gawen nodded. He looked like a man who had a bee stuck in his mouth, and Adair realized he struggled with his disappointment, or perhaps the desire to curse.

"That makes two o' them." Perhaps unwise for Adair to say so. Indeed, surprise made him speak. Both his older brothers had Father sent in turn to Dalriada, the land over the water in Alba, to try to claim the share of territory there he believed he was owed.

First his oldest son, Baen, last autumn. Baen had been gone so long that they had all believed he'd been successful and stayed to settle the portion of lands that had been promised to Gawen long ago.

But Baen had returned upon the icy blasts of early winter with tales to tell, and defeat in his eyes. Kendrick MacCaigh, the chief holding the lands in Dalriada and brother to Adair's own dead mother, had refused to keep the agreement he'd made with Father long ago, and surrender the promised lands.

So Dacrg had been sent. Daerg, with his hair as red as Father's, his staid and sonorous sense of duty, and his somewhat dogged nature. Only to return also, so it seemed, in ignoble defeat.

"Ah, I am sorry," Adair said. The claiming of the Dalriadan lands meant a great deal to Father. "This must be a sore disappointment."

Gawen MacMurtray got to his feet. "Daerg said Kendric sent him home. He said his uncle could no longer stand the sound of his voice in his ears, and that if he did not at once board his boat and leave those shores, he would be forced to end his own nephew's life."

"He was jesting, surely," Aye, hotheaded the members of the family might be at times, but they did not slay those of their own blood.

"I am no' so certain. Daerg was no' certain, which is why he left. Though," Gawen said heavily, "it broke his heart to bring a defeat back to me."

"No doubt." Gawen MacMurtray did not easily accept disappointment, especially from his sons. And they'd felt that, all three of them, their lives long. It had made of Baen, the eldest, an exemplary warrior rivaling their famed ancestor, Ardahl MacCormac. It had made of Daerg a son so dutiful, he would roast himself alive on searing coals if his father asked it.

And it had made of Adair—what? A man who avoided such duty and the striving for such perfection. Who instinctively avoided the things with which he knew, to the bottom of his soul, no one could match up.

Gawen took an impatient turn around the floor, watched carefully by everyone else in the room. He had a temper that, in his younger days, had sometimes got away from him. His beautiful young wife, Adair's mother, had helped him tame that. It rarely escaped him these days.

But Adair could see that he fought for control now.

"I ha' spent most the day speaking wi' Daerg. I do no' blame him. I do no' blame him for failing in the task I set."

Adair wondered if that was true, if Daerg believed it was true.

"Kendrick MacCaigh proves stubborn and, according to your brothers, deaf to all forms of reason. He refuses to yield what is owed to me."

What was owed—land.

Back in the old days, years ago, when both Father and Kendrick had been young men, Father had sponsored his new wife's brother in a campaign to the land over the water. A place of opportunity, it was said to be. The agreement being that if Kendrick founded a settlement there, half of what he held would belong to Gawen.

Kendrick had never returned from Alba, though tales had come of a rich settlement. Now, with three grown sons, Gowen wanted his portion.

He'd sent Baen first, even though he wanted the portion in Alba for his second son, Daerg. Baen would inherit the lands here, in Erin.

This place Adair so loved.

"Father, 'twas a long time ago, that. Perhaps Kendrick feels since 'twas he who fought for the land, set up the settlement, and has held it all these years, he has a right to it."

Gawen glared at Adair. "I do no' doubt that is what he thinks. But there is such a thing as honor. We had an agreement."

Aye, but a man seeing a young nephew he did not know arrive, seeking claim to what was hard won, might no longer see it that way.

"Where is Daerg now?"

Gawen waved his hand. "I sent him to rest. I do no' blame him, nay, but I will admit I am sorely disappointed in him. I suppose I should have known better.

"I expected Baen would be the one to succeed. He is strong and competent, and carries my authority. And then I told myself it should be Daerg, since the lands are meant for him. But"—Gawen resumed his seat, facing Adair—"Daerg is not a persuasive man."

The big room fell into silence. Gawen stared at Adair meaningfully. Adair gazed back at his father, sensing a hovering significance.

"Ye are."

"I am what, Father?"

"A persuasive man." A slight grimace of distaste crossed Gawen's face. "Ye do not apply yoursel' as ye should on the training field. Ye are certainly not first among my warriors. Ye prefer whiling away the time wi' your friends, playing at draughts and listening to music. But by all accounts, ye do possess a silver tongue that could charm a flea from a hound."

Adair, with dawning horror, saw where this was going. He did not speak. Glancing at the other occupants of the room, he noticed they exchanged glances.

"It seems," Gawen said heavily, "it is what I need—someone with a silver tongue and the ability to talk Kendrick around, and make him see he does not want war."

War?

"Perhaps I should have sent ye in the first place."

"Nay." Adair's legs unfolded beneath him. He rose to his feet.

Gawen stirred to anger. "Ye will no' speak that word to me. Am I no' only your father, but your chief? Have ye no' sworn fealty to me?"

Adair had, not long after he turned thirteen. But that had been a formality, one that had not affected him overmuch. He had two older brothers to serve and carry the duties required.

"I—am no good, Father, at negotiating. I will be no use in Dalriada." That dark land over the water that could be glimpsed from Erin on a clear, beautiful day. A place of risk and danger.

"Ye will be of every use." *For the first time in your life*, so Gawen's tone implied.

It made Adair flush with something akin to shame. "If Kendrick has denied Baen—no mean talker in his own right—and Daerg, who has a stake in Alba, why should he listen to me?"

"Because ye will not come at him with demand. Ye will come in kinship. Make him see ye in a good light. Tell him ye wish to stay there in Alba."

"Stay? Ye are sending me awa' for good?"

"To be sure, not. 'Tis Daerg who will go there to hold those lands for me. But ye can win Kendrick over, see. Make him think ye are the one who wishes to stay." Gawen's gaze flicked over Adair, not without a measure of disdain. "He will see no harm in ye."

"But—" Dismay swept through Adair, full and strong. "I cannot leave here." The land of his ancestors. He lived for Erin, his bones the rock of this place, the waters his blood. Each breath he took, the kindly breeze. How could he make his father understand that?

"Ye can and ye will." Gawen once more rose from his chair. "Mayhap 'tis my own fault. Ye were so young when your mother died. Little more than a babe, and wi' the look o' her about ye. I found it hard to discipline ye the way I should, though, by the gods, I was firm enough wi' your brothers. Adair, ye will do this thing. Go and pack your belongings. Be ready to leave by dawn."

Adair stared at his father, aghast. "So soon?"

"The season is upon us; there is no time to waste. Baen does not know it yet, but I ha' negotiated for him a fine marriage that will expand our holdings here. He will one day be a powerful chief in Erin. Daerg's holdings must be secured as well."

His gaze once more flicked over Adair. "When ye have secured Daerg's claim in Alba, ye can come home."

"And if I too fail?"

"Ye will no'."

How could he be so certain?

As if he'd heard the question, Gawen leaned closer. "Ye will no' fail as your brothers have done. And ye will no' come home till ye have secured our portion of those lands."

CHAPTER TWO

A DAIR FOUND HIS brother, Daerg, in his own quarters, sitting on the floor with a jug of ale beside his knee.

It had taken him some time to chase Daerg down. No one had seen him, which seemed strange. If he, Adair, had been away a matter of months, the first thing he would do was visit all his friends. But the fellows in the warriors' hall had no idea where Daerg might be.

At last a young serving girl said she'd taken him a jug of heather ale at his quarters.

Daerg, clearly sunk into an unsounded depth of misery, barely glanced up when Adair came in. So dim was the chamber, it tamed the fire of Daerg's flaming red hair and beard and washed his complexion to gray.

Adair hunkered down next to him, noting that Daerg still wore the stained and crumpled clothing in which he must have traveled. He'd come to his brother for information. Now concern moved to the fore.

"Brother, are ye unwell?"

They were not close, the three brothers—not so much as it might seem they should be. Too different in spirit, perhaps, for that. Yet Adair could not behold such misery without striving to lift it.

Daerg did not speak, merely tucked his head down more closely between his shoulders and squeezed his eyes closed, the gestures of a man shutting out the world.

"Come now, Daerg, it cannot be all that bad." Daerg, after all, had come home, while Adair faced leaving Erin, the place of his heart.

Perhaps, aye, Adair should be angry with Daerg for his failure to secure his own lands. If he'd succeeded, after all, Adair would not have to take up this unwelcome duty.

"Speak to me," he urged, sitting on the floor beside his brother.

"I ha' failed Father."

"Aye, well, 'tis not the worst thing on the face o' the world, is it?"

Daerg's face lifted. He was not the most comely of Gawen's sons, having a stark, freckled countenance and eyelashes so pale it put one in mind of a fish. Usually he schooled his emotions well. Now devastation rode him hard.

"It is my place and my duty to please Father in all things."

Well, and that was pure foolishness. No one could be pleased in all things. Adair did not say so.

"Moreover, this was my chance. To achieve something Baen could no' do. He is a hard man to follow, is Baen."

So he was. Their faultless elder brother with his fair hair and far-seeing hazel eyes, his competence on the field and nearly nonexistent sense of humor, was—

Well, faultless.

Adair wondered what Baen would think of his upcoming marriage. Who was she?

And would Father one day choose a bride for him, also? Would some far-flung marriage alliance be the way Gawen finally made use of what he considered a near-useless son? The prospect made Adair writhe. He thought of the bonny Forba, with her clever fingers that could coax music from wood and a bit of string, and do even more amazing things on a man's body. Did he mean to marry her? He hadn't got that far in his head. Now he would not have the chance—at least until he accomplished his impossible mission.

"Ye ha' no need to compete wi' Baen," he told Daerg a bit lamely. "Ye are your own man."

Daerg's searing look of scorn told Adair what he thought of that advice.

"Here, have a drink." Adair took up the jug, which splashed nearly empty. "Did ye drink all o' this?"

"What else is there to do?" Daerg once more lowered his head to his hands in despair.

Adair cursed low, under his breath. "Come, man, it cannot be all that bad."

"I have disappointed Father." Daerg seemed stuck on that.

"And will he no' get over his disappointment? Take it from one who knows. I have disappointed him scores o' times."

Daerg directed a bleary look at him. Adair could now see half of Daerg's trouble was a state of mild intoxication. "Fine for ye, Adair. Ye being the favored one."

"Nay, that is Baen again."

"He never asked much from ye, though, did he? Never pushed ye very hard, either."

That was true. Father had never asked much—till now.

Adair shrugged. "I was the youngest."

"He always liked ye the best."

"Least. I do believe he despaired o' me."

"It does no' matter. The worst part o' failing him is, they were my own lands I was going to claim. What manner o' man cannot claim his own lands?"

"What is it like there—in Alba?"

Daerg shivered. "It is a dark and terrible place o' black lochs and dark mountains, won awa' from the savages who still inhabit the interior. The settlements o' our people are held by mere fingertips upon the coastal lands. Kendrick's settlement is a mad place. He has sons—two o' them—who want it, all o' it, for themselves and ha' no liking for an interloper from Erin. And a stepdaughter and a wife no better who tells him what to do. No one there, I tell ye, is right in the head. 'Tis a terrible place to be."

He glanced into Adair's face, and must have glimpsed something there. "Why d'ye ask?"

"Father is sending me there. In your stead."

"You?" Daerg lost all his misery at least temporarily, in astonishment. The look he directed at Adair was not complimentary. "You?"

Adair grimaced. "Aye. I tried to tell him what a bad choice I am. He would no' listen."

"But—you are no sort o' statesman or negotiator." Daerg took up his cup and drank. "Worse even than me."

"Father seems to think where ye and Baen failed in your duties, I might charm Kendrick out o' his lands with my talk and my merriment."

Daerg swore with deep feeling. "When d'ye leave?"

"In the morning. On the same boat, no doubt, that brought ye home."

"Well and I must say, Kendrick will no' be pleased to see ye. Nor his sons."

"Tell me everything, Daerg. All I need to know."

Daerg looked him in the eye. "I suppose 'tis best to be forewarned."

WHEN ADAIR LEFT his brother's quarters some time later, his head buzzed. Daerg had given him what might be too much information, much of it disjointed and out of order. None of it good. He seemed to feel Adair's mission was doomed before his feet left the soil of Erin. Which would not be so bad, if Adair did not agree.

And that was the other thing. His feet did not want to leave the soil of Erin, to go to some dark and terrible land such as Daerg had described. His heart did not. Nor his spirit.

He did not sleep that night, instead spending it packing his belongings, the things he thought he would need in order to court a man—an uncle—who would not welcome him.

He wanted to make the rounds of his friends, to bid them all farewell, but by then it was the middle of the night. So he roused only his good friend, Oisin, and bade him make explanations to the others on his behalf.

Including Forba.

"Why di'ye no' go and see her yourself?" Oisin suggested.

"'Tis the middle of the night."

"She will no' mind." Oisin looked Adair in the face. "Especially if 'tis farewell for a time. I know fine she fancies ye." He grinned reluctantly. "Of course, most o' the clan's young women do. Makes it hard on the rest o' us. Mayhap 'tis no' a bad thing ye will be awa' for a time. Might make it easier on me."

"I trust I will no' be gone long." Adair's hope was that Kendrick would take one look at him and send him straight back home.

"So I trust," Oisin said more seriously. "Ye will be sorely missed."

"Ye say my farewell to Forba for me." A mischievous and beautiful young woman. He had no real idea why she or indeed any of the young clanswomen might favor him. Being a younger son, he had not much to recommend him.

His own father had as much as told him so.

At dawn, he climbed high up the side of the hill and looked out, as the sun rose, upon the land he loved. The land for which his ancestors—including the legendary warrior Ardahl MacCormac—had fought and suffered. The land for which his very heart beat.

On a clear day from up here, one could see the ocean and sometimes glimpse the coast of Alba lying like a sleeping blue dragon to the northeast, their own shore not afar. This, though, did not promise to be a clear day. Clouds gathered over the top of the hill like a white blanket and dulled all the distances.

They would have rain on their journey. No matter, this land

still looked bonny to him, and every part of him rued being torn away.

Surely, he promised himself, surely not for long. Below he could see his party readying to leave. They would journey upon the short trail to the coast where lay Father's boat. Passage to Alba would not take long. As for the journey after they landed there—

Adair did not know. He had never bothered to inquire. He traveled into the unknown.

For some reason, he shivered. He must go down and take up his duty, as never before. But he whispered to the gods and to the land itself before he did, "Please. I was not born to be an exile. Please let me come home soon."

CHAPTER THREE

Bradana MacCaigh left her stepfather's roundhouse and went out into the rainy afternoon. Behind her, Kendrick—said stepfather—still argued with her mam, their words becoming so wild and ferocious that Bradana could no longer stay to listen.

What they argued over this time, she could not say. Their relationship was a tempestuous one, and they quarreled over matters as small as what Mam served for dinner, to as big as whom Kendrick had arranged for Bradana to marry.

Not that she intended ever to go through with any marriage. She would be quite willing to die first.

She blundered out with such force that she nearly bumped into her stepbrother, Toren, on his way into the roundhouse.

They both paused, and Bradana rolled her eyes at him. "I would not venture in there, if I were ye."

He grimaced. Of her two stepbrothers, Toren and Kerr, she liked Toren the better. Kerr had a prickly and devious mind. At least with Toren, one knew fairly well what to expect.

They were nearly of an age, Kendrick having had two small sons when he married Bradana's mother, who had Bradana, no more than a toddler at the time. Both of them widowed.

Bradana could not remember a time when her mam and Kendrick had not argued. And made up so passionately that it had caused no end of embarrassment to their offspring.

Indeed, embarrassingly—and shockingly—Mam was now great with child. At her age.

"I am wet from head to foot," Toren pointed out unnecessarily. So he was, his fair head drenched and even his hide boots sodden. "I need dry clothing."

They all lived here in the great roundhouse that dominated the stretch of coast facing the Erin Sea.

"By the gods! Where ha' ye been?"

"On the shore. And I ha' news for Father. One o' the lads there thought he saw sails coming in. 'Tis raining so hard, no one else can catch sight o' them."

Bradana's heart fell. "No' that awful drip o' a cousin coming back?" Daerg MacMurtray was not, in truth, her blood cousin, but cousin to her two stepbrothers and nephew to Kendrick. He'd come to try to talk Kendrick out of his lands but had been woefully unequal to the task.

The first emissary Gawen MacMurtray had sent from Erin— his older son—Baen, had not been so bad. At least he'd had a bit of pride and backbone, and had not been ill-looking.

Not that Bradana ever noticed such about any man.

"I hope to all the gods not," Toren growled.

"Who else could it be?"

Toren shrugged. "Might be fishers. Or invaders." His mud-colored eyes met hers. "No need to think aught else. Now, let me by."

"I am no' holding ye." She stepped aside.

He brushed past her and was gone. She could still hear the echoes of raised voices behind her. Her parents' anger made her—well, angry in turn. Could they not strive to get hold of their emotions? Just as the rest of them had to do.

She looked out at the gray world. It did not merely rain. Water crashed down from the sky as if the sea itself had moved inland on the arms of low clouds.

How anyone could see a boat out there in such weather, she could not imagine. Surely the lad, whomever he was, had been mistaken. She did not want to go down over the rocks to the shingle on the shore to see. Already she was so wet, the chill reached her bones.

Early summer in Alba. One day sodden, the next so beautiful it made her heart ache.

She decided to go and visit her friend, Maeve. Maeve was used to Bradana turning up when she could not tolerate remaining at home. Often they would go off into the hills, a ready escape. Not on a day such as this.

But when Bradana reached Maeve's hut, safe within the arms of the stone wall Kendrick had built around the outermost part of his settlement, she was not there. She had gone to care for an aged aunt who was unwell. Her mother invited Bradana in to sit by the fire, but she declined.

By the time she returned home, a stream of people came up from the shore, all hurrying toward the roundhouse. All as wet as she.

"What is it?" she asked an older man standing by.

"A new arrival. From Erin."

By the gods, no.

She followed the runners inside to the great chamber where Kendrick held his meetings and received his people. The settlement had been a mere fingerhold when Kendrick founded it as one of a number of adventurers, mostly second sons, who had come from Erin to claim this place they called Dalriada. A Celtic settlement on the fringe of a new land.

According to Kendrick, he'd had to fight for every bit of it back then. In the years since, he'd come to some agreements with the wild tribes who'd lived here when he arrived. And of late, the settlement had grown, new children being born by the score who were neither of Erin or Alba, but something else.

Bradana had herself been born in Alba, her father being one of those second sons who'd tried to settle farther north. He'd failed and died in the fight. Mam had called upon her fellow Erin chief, Kendrick, to help. He had brought her and Bradana here, and annexed her lands.

Bradana's own inheritance, those lands should have been. But like everything else in the area, Kendrick had swallowed them up.

He did not gladly give up land.

Kendrick and Mam, as Bradana discovered when she stepped into the great chamber, had ceased their arguing. Mam remained standing, her arms wrapped around the bulk of the child she carried.

Mam, a beautiful woman, was tall and slender, with dark red hair. She had a face Kendrick often said belonged to a goddess. Unfortunately, she had a temper to match.

Bradana had inherited little enough of her beauty, taking strongly after her father by all accounts—he she could not remember. Fair-haired and blue-eyed, with an unfortunately strong nose. Not that she cared whether she could attract any man. Better by far if she did not.

She sometimes wished she could take her harp—for a facility with that instrument was one of the few talents she possessed—and disappear into the wilds of the land. Become a shanachie, a bard, trudging from dun to dun with no roots at all.

As if there could be anything more absurd than a female bard.

She tiptoed in, listening to the news the runners had brought.

A boat had indeed landed on the shore. From what the runners related, that boat was a familiar one, having departed there only days ago.

Bradana moaned inwardly. Had that sad and overly earnest fellow, Daerg, returned so soon?

Kendrick grumbled and rose from his chair. "Is it Daerg come back upon us?" he asked, nearly echoing Bradana's thoughts.

"Nay, Chief Kendrick." The runner, a young man named Cullen, shook his head. "Another young man it is, with two attendants. Them, I recognized. The young man is on his way up here now."

"Eh?"

"Chief Kendrick, the new arrival says his name is Adair Mac-Murtray. He says he is brother to the one we just saw off."

"Eh?" Kendrick barked it this time.

"Brother to Master Daerg."

A terrible, if brief, silence fell.

Kendrick swore low and bitterly. "By all the gods! What will it take to dissuade my Erin relations?"

Bradana's mother stepped forward. "Gawen MacMurtray has no right to anything we hold here, does he?" When Kendrick did not answer, she added, "Ye said he has no claim."

"I will walk out and meet this lad. See if I can send him straight awa' again."

"But"—Mam hesitated—"there is such a thing as hospitality."

"Any hospitality we owe was worn out by the last two visitors. By Lugh's spear, they are a tiresome lot."

He marched out. Bradana should not have followed. Indeed, her every instinct bade her clear out of the hall and off in another direction, any direction besides the shore.

Well, perhaps not every instinct, for when Kendrick and the runners left, she did follow.

Curiosity, only.

It still rained hard, making the afternoon noisy with the raindrops striking the ground. From the dun, located above the shore, she could look and see the boat—aye, an all-too-familiar craft with the gray sea heaving beyond.

She had never been to Erin, though she understood it did not lie afar off—not much farther than the islands that clustered like protective arms around the shore, like gray-green beasts sleeping in the deep water.

She was, aye, daughter of a man from Erin yet felt no connection to it, being all a part of this place of high hills and bottomless lochs. Alba was in every breath she drew. In the music she loved and played. In the blood that rushed through her.

This settlement, clinging to the rough stones at the edge of a great, mostly unknown land, might be naught to what their new visitor knew back home. Who could say?

She could see him now through the rain. See a party of three, two of the men trailing the first. Kendrick reached the place where the path led down to the sea and paused. Any folk out and about—few enough in such weather—also paused in their tasks to stare.

The visitor looked tall, slender, and ordinary enough as viewed through the rain. He wore a gray cloak, leggings, and boots, and she could see not much else through the blur of raindrops except a mane of brown hair.

Ordinary enough, aye, only—

At the sight of him, a hum started up in Bradana's blood. One such as she'd never experienced, unless she could call it akin to what she felt when she was alone up in the hills. When the wind spoke to her, and the ground stirred beneath her feet, and an eagle rose with a rush of power. A feeling of being caught in the grip something much greater than herself.

She must be going mad. For he was but another accursed cousin from Erin. Not even her blood relation.

Yet the world, the very world, seemed to pause and draw a breath. The raindrops froze in the air and glittered, glittered before all resumed crashing down.

The young man approached and Kendrick stepped forward reluctantly to greet him.

CHAPTER FOUR

THE SETTLEMENT LOOKED smaller and far less grand than Adair had expected. It perched upon the rocky rise above the sea and, from what he could see through the rain, had only a rough hold upon it. The main building, a stone dun with a reeded roof now dripping water, was of a goodly size. But fewer huts than he had anticipated clustered round its flanks, and the stone enclosure wall looked only half finished.

No matter; he was heartily glad to be here and anywhere besides that boat. The crossing had not been a good one. The rain had seemed to drive them from behind—away from Erin. They'd almost overturned rounding an island in furious seas. He'd rarely been so wet.

The climb up from the shore was steep. He could see several people waiting out front of the main dun. Was that Kendrick foremost among them? Impossible to tell.

The men who had helped pull their boat up onto the shore had not been welcoming. Neither, it appeared, was the man standing at the top of the rise.

As Adair reached him, one of the waiting figures stepped away. Another, a woman, emerged from the dun.

"Chief Kendrick?" Adair called, only to swiftly correct himself. "Uncle Kendrick? I bring ye greetings from Gawen MacMurtray in Erin."

"Aye?" The man who faced Adair, almost barring the way, barked the word. Of goodly height and broad with it, he had fair hair darkened by the rain and an air of toughness he wore like the cloak over his shoulders. A wide, craggy face seamed by care betrayed his years, some two score of them. He wore a torc around his neck very similar to the one Father wore back home.

"And who, by Manannan's eyeteeth, are you?" Nay, not welcoming at all.

"I am Adair, son to your brother, Gawen of Erin."

Kendrick's lips stretched in a terrible grimace. "By all the gods, another one? How many sons does the *nathair* have?"

"I am the third and the last," Adair told him, somewhat taken aback.

"Gawen MacMurtray is no' my brother, but was brother to my sister, who is long gone. But I suppose ye'd better come in. I canna leave ye standing in the rain."

The interior of the dun was dim, smoky, and far from grand. Maybe half the size of the hall back home, it lacked the carved pillars and the dais where Father usually sat. A poor fire smoldered in the central hearth, struggling against the damp air.

Still, it felt warmer than outside, and Adair shivered as he took up a stance and looked around.

He could not compare this place with what lay back home. That had been built over generations. This outpost had been here a mere score of years or so.

Kendrick did have a chair, a roughly carved thing at the head of the fire. He plopped down onto this and glared.

"Ye two, I know," he said to Adair's companions, Nolan and Flynn. "Ye will be housed where ye were before—but no' for long. Do no' get too comfortable."

The men went out again, accompanied by a servant.

Adair shot a searching look at Kendrick. He bore only a faint resemblance to Adair's brothers in the stark bones of his face and their strong build. Adair could not remember his mother well enough to glimpse a likeness.

"I thought I'd got rid o' the last of ye," Kendrick spat at him. "Yet here ye be."

Adair did not know how to reply. Father insisted he'd been blessed with a clever and agile tongue, and mayhap that was true. He'd never, though, met with such an uncomfortable situation.

He glanced at the other occupants of the room, hoping for some cue. A woman, tall and slender, stood back from Kendrick's chair. She gave off both an air of beauty and a disagreeableness similar to Kendrick's, and was visibly heavy with child.

"My wife, Tavia," Kendrick said, catching Adair's look.

Adair bowed to her. "Mistress Tavia."

She moved forward, her hair, which hung down over one shoulder, gleaming red gold in the dim light. Eyes of clear blue, set at a slight angle, met his.

"Master Adair. Pray, sit. Ye will want something hot to drink after your journey."

He gave her his best smile. "'Twould be a godsend, mistress."

Kendrick grunted as the woman fetched a ewer from the embers at the edge of the fire and poured a mug full. Adair sat on one of the rugs facing Kendrick.

His uncle waited till he'd taken a drink to ask, "So what brings ye? Nay, do no' tell me. The same thing that brought your two brothers before ye." He grimaced. "Gawen is persistent, I will give him that."

Adair hesitated. He supposed he could try to play this circumspectly, but given the temperature of his welcome, he did not believe he'd succeed.

"To be perfectly plain about it," he told Kendrick, "Father thinks I can charm ye out o' what he believes ye owe him."

"Ah." Fierce eyes bored into Adair's. "And what do ye think?"

"I suspect he may be wrong."

"Aye, then ye're no' so foolish as ye look."

Another silence fell, angry on Kendrick's part, and embarrassed on Adair's.

"Ah well, we will talk further anon. Till then, I gather I maun offer ye houseroom. There are guest quarters of a sort behind this place. Ye will stay there."

Adair got to his feet and bowed, then aimed another bow at Mistress Tavia. "I am grateful, Uncle."

"Off wi' ye now. Change into dry clothes—if ye have them." Kendrick raised his voice. "By the gods, where is that lad?"

A slim, dark-haired boy appeared silently.

"Take Master Adair to the guest quarters. See he has all he needs."

The boy bowed, then indicated that Adair should follow him. Back out into the crashing world of the rain with the gray ocean spread so wide. Separating him from all he loved. Around the side of the dun, he could feel eyes upon him. A deep awareness like fingertips on his skin.

But aye, the inhabitants here would be curious about another arrival. Another unwelcome one.

The hut, built of stone, offered little comfort. The interior felt damp with the rain, the hearth cold. Only a low sleeping bench piled with furs offered any hint of warmth.

The dark-haired lad dropped immediately to his knees and kindled a fire from materials laid to one side. Adair set down his belongings and said to the boy, "Thank ye. What is your name?"

The boy did not answer. He had a scar on one cheek and could not be more than twelve or thirteen.

A dismal feeling settled over Adair, one that penetrated clear to his bones. He found himself far from home, separated even from the men who had brought him here, without friends.

He sat on the edge of the sleeping bench as the flames grew higher in the hearth, fighting to draw against the heavy rain. He tried to imagine Baen and Daerg here before him. Baen with all his calm confidence. Daerg, no doubt feeling as hopeless as he.

Father had no idea what this place was like, or he'd never have sent any of them. Daerg—Daerg had tried to warn Adair about the nature of Alba. A dark and terrible place.

Adair could feel that now. The great land lurking beyond the door of his hut like a monstrous wolf waiting to leap upon him. A great, barely perceived threat.

If he could tell his father one thing, it would be *Ye do not want this place, this Dalriada. Not any part of it.* Erin was home, and Erin was all.

The lad got to his feet and turned as if to leave.

"Wait," Adair said. "Ye have no' told me your name. How am I to call for ye?"

The boy turned back. For the first time, Adair got a glimpse of his eyes: narrowed and nearly blank.

"Torlag," he murmured, barely above a whisper. "I will bring food as soon as it is prepared."

"And am I not to be brought to the main hall, to sup?" Was this to be guest quarters, or Adair's prison?

The boy said nothing.

"See if ye can bring me something to drink first," Adair requested. "Mead or ale."

Torlag went out hurriedly.

He did not return.

NEVER BEFORE HAD Adair been away from home for more than a night or two while hunting, and that out in his own hills. Forests he knew right well, with views he'd seen since birth. He'd taken solace always in the land around him, soft and green, a congenial companion.

It had been a long while—many generations—since the men of the clan had gone out to war. Aye, they still trained, as they were subject at any time to being called upon by the high king. Father had been a strong warrior in his day, and Baen was yet. Adair himself was no mean hand with the sword when, as Father put it, he applied himself.

Being descended from the great Ardahl MacCormac, they had warrior in the blood.

Yet he was unfamiliar with the savagery he sensed in this

place. And he'd seldom experienced such misery as beset him that night.

Since the young servant did not return, no food was brought. No summons came for him to take a meal in the hall. He might have gone out seeking his unwilling host, but the rain came down still harder, making that an uninviting prospect. He kept the fire going with the fuel at hand, and at last wrapped himself in the blankets and slept.

CHAPTER FIVE

W HEN ADAIR AWOKE the next morning, he did not know
where he was. Sunlight poured through the smoke hole
at the center of the roof above him. The fire had long gone out.
Very close at hand, surely up in the thatch, a bird sang a heart-
breakingly sweet song.

Slowly it all returned to him. The wicked crossing from Erin
and the climb up from the shore in the rain. His cold reception at
the hands of his mother's brother.

The lonely night.

He sat up with a groan and took stock of himself. Hunger and
the desire to use the midden beset him. A land—a world—
awaited outside.

Last night before taking to the bed, he'd changed into clothing from his pack, only slightly less damp than those garments
he'd had on. He'd draped the others to dry, but they proved still
wet to the touch now. He straightened what he had on, ran his
fingers through his hair, and stuck his head outside.

What he saw made him emerge from the hut.

So this was Alba.

The large bulk of the great hall stood before him. Built of
rough stone, it looked somehow unfinished in the raw morning
light. The rain had flown while Adair slept, rolling inland over the
rise he could see beyond, where the land clawed its way up from
the shore. The sea…

Stepping out and around the dun, he got a good look.

A great, restless, ever-moving world.

Deep combers raked at the shingle shore where he'd disembarked yesterday. In fact, he could see their little boat hauled well up there above the water, in addition to several other small craft also securely beached.

The sky, fresh-washed, pale blue, stretched limitless toward home. Not far. Surely he could sail there on his own if need be, though he could not imagine his two companions wanted to stay here any more than he did.

A cluster of huts spread haphazardly over the shore and turf as if they'd grown up there and perched wherever they could get a hold. The partial stone wall encircled all. Others were up before him. He could see men on the shore, and a few women hurrying about. A pen off to one side contained some cattle. Beyond, a number of ponies and what might be one or two chariots.

As if anyone could run a chariot over this stony ground.

At home they were within an afternoon's walk of the sea but did not live like this, hard upon the shore so the hiss and rush of the waves remained continually in the ears, and one could pick up its restless mood. From the heights of their home hills, they could glimpse it like a field of blue.

Just south and west of here, not so very far.

Standing there with longing pulling at him, he wondered how many days it might be before he could decently leave off trying to persuade his uncle and take himself home.

His father had told him not to return, not to come home, unless he had a promise of the land. But he would tell his father, when he arrived, *Ye do not want any part o' that place. It is wild and unwelcoming. Leave it go as a bad bet.*

He heard voices raised and what might be laughter. He walked around to the front of the dun.

Two young men approached the building from the direction of the field that held the ponies. Very alike they appeared, of a height with fair hair and lanky builds. Dressed in kilts and cloaks, they sniped at each other, half laughing in a manner Adair recognized.

Just so did friends beset one another back home. Or relations.

As he stood watching, one of the young men shoved the other in a companionable fashion. They both laughed.

Adair stepped out.

The pleasant, teasing expressions the young men wore disappeared the moment they noticed him, replaced by something hard and disagreeable. As one, they changed their course toward the door of the dun and came to meet Adair.

They had to be related, brothers, far too alike to be anything else. Somewhere near Adair in age, they had broad foreheads and narrow, light brown eyes. Wide mouths with lips now also narrowed into hard lines.

Their manner in approaching Adair could not be considered aggressive; neither was it friendly.

"Here he is," said one. "The next o' the Erin cousins bent upon stealing our lands."

Their lands. "Ye must be my cousins." Kendrick's sons. What were their names? Aye, Kerr and Toren. Adair stepped forward. "Guilty as accused. Adair MacMurtray. Ye be my Uncle Kendrick's sons, aye?"

They exchanged glances. One—he on the left—stepped up, all confidence.

"Toren MacCaigh. This is my brother, Kerr. We thought we were rid o' you lot."

"So I gathered from my reception yesterday."

Kerr stepped forward, a glower heavy on his brow. "These are our lands, ye ken. Clawed from the wilderness and fought for. Bad enough having to battle against the local savages without ye lot back in Erin."

He said the last word with utter scorn, which put Adair's back up, though he did not let it show. Seldom did he lose his temper. This did not seem a good time to begin.

"Erin is a fine place," he declared equitably enough. "Ha' ye ever been there?"

"Nay, and no wish to go," said Kerr, who seemed the more irascible of the two brothers. "No need to be anywhere save here."

Aye, so they would have been born here and knew nothing else. They were not, as Adair knew, the sons of Mistress Tavia, whom he'd met yesterday, but of Kendrick's first wife, whom the chief had brought with him from Erin.

"Well," Toren said, "I suppose ye had best come in for breakfast."

Adair barely heard the grudging invitation. For someone else stepped up, and as he turned to regard her—for aye, it was a woman—the light streaming in from the east hit him full in the face and dazzled his eyes.

At least, that was what he later told himself. In truth, he was never really sure, save that a brightness took hold of him, one he felt sweep through him from his head to his feet.

A woman, aye, a young one. Tall for one of her sex, she had hair the color of dark honey, tawny with strands of gold, that hung in waves over one shoulder, bound round with green bands. She wore green also—a plain underdress with a cloak over, and hide boots not far different from his own. Her face…

But her back was to the light and he did not get a clear look at it. He did not need to. The impression she made pierced him through.

Indeed, he could have sworn that everything, the world itself and all the rush of the morning, paused. The birds ceased to sing, the waves to rake the shore. His very heart stuttered in his chest.

She had a hound at her heels, a big gray one that rushed forward, breaking the spell. Everything, including the blood in Adair's veins, began to move again.

The hound thrust its great head at Adair. The best welcome he'd had thus far from anyone.

He stepped toward its mistress. "Adair MacMurtray," he said.

SHE'D NOT GOT a good look at him yesterday—no more than a glimpse when he'd come up the slope soaking wet, and when Torlag led him from the great hall after. Now he stood revealed to her in the clear light of the morning.

The impressions came hard and fast. Brown hair hanging down, a rich color that had threads of copper woven through, picked out by the sun. A clever, charming sort of face, the kind made to smile, though he was not smiling now and looked, rather, as if he'd been struck a hard blow. A good body of more than average height—making him a bit taller than she—but with fine, broad shoulders and narrow hips that made a woman think about... Well.

Lithe, that body would be. Fine to the touch.

Shocked by her own thoughts, she called the hound to her, struggling to look away. "Wen, come."

The hound, usually so obedient, disregarded her. He liked the new arrival, as shown by his great plume of a tail sweeping back and forth.

"Good morn, Bradana," Toren called. "This is our new guest. Yet another one from Erin."

Aye. She knew that. She should speak, say something courteous in the face of Toren's sarcasm.

She could not say anything at all.

"This is our stepsister, Bradana. Bradana, this is—" Toren turned to the man in mock confusion. "What did ye say was your name, again?"

"Adair MacMurtray." He stepped forward, his gaze fixed upon Bradana as if he sought to memorize her.

By all the gods, he was pleasing to look upon. And the force of him—the essence—struck her in a wave that froze her where she stood.

"The last of Gawen's three sons," Kerr drawled, "who he

sends to try to steal our lands. As if the first two were no' bad enough."

Still Bradana—usually so unhesitant with her tongue—could find nothing to say. That tongue seemed to be stuck to the roof of her mouth.

He had green eyes. Grayish green, at least, pale in that clever, tanned face.

"Mistress Bradana," he said as if he memorized her name as well as her face.

She wanted to touch him, wanted to reach out and clasp one of his hands as, surely, a polite woman might do in greeting. Only she was not all that polite, as a rule.

Having been greeted by Kerr and Toren, he must think them all savages. And why should she care what he thought?

Fortunately, Wen deserted him then and returned to her side. Instead of reaching out to the stranger, she buried her fingers in the hound's fur.

Adair smiled. "That is a fine hound. My brother has one at home called Lir. I tell him 'tis not a very original name."

"Better than Cu." Was that her voice? It served her at last, shaken loose perhaps by the force of that smile. Men were not supposed to be beautiful, were they? He had a beautiful smile. "Welcome to Dalriada."

"Thank ye."

The smile again. It did not flash so much as light him from within.

"Come to breakfast," Toren said. "Ye will see soon enough, we may be a rough sort o' family, but we do stand together when need be."

Against one such as you, he did not state, but implied.

Adair shrugged in an affable manner. She'd seen both his brothers in turn, one after the other. He appeared nothing like either of them.

And naught like any man she'd ever known.

But then why, she wondered as she and Wen followed him into the dun, did he feel so very familiar?

CHAPTER SIX

H E ATE AS if he were half starved, did Adair MacMurtray, and listened to their breakfast conversation as if they were all mad. And Bradana supposed they were. At the very least, they had their moments of madness.

He had beautiful manners, despite how eager he was for their food. And she liked his voice, somehow softer than these others in her ears, as if it carried a hint of Erin's mist.

She liked everything about him, which terrified her a little. All too often, she tended to focus on the flaws inherent in the men she met. Not that she met many, other than Earrach and his crew from their holding farther north.

The man she was set to wed, even though she did not want to.

She dismissed that from her mind as an unwelcome future event—akin to death—and returned to watching Adair without being obvious about it. Her mam, who was quite observant, might notice.

But she watched his hands, broad-palmed, long-fingered hands, as he ate, as he stroked the fur of Wen, who had once more deserted her for his side. She watched the light come and go in his face as he spoke. In his eyes. The way the smile hovered there from time to time.

She said little, not wanting to draw attention to herself—even though, in some curious and unprecedented way, she wanted all this man's attention upon her. He did glance at her frequently, and when he did, an intent look came to those gray-green eyes.

He was nothing like his two brothers, no. The first, Baen, had been all Erin dignity and behaved, as Toren so rightly put it, as if he had a stick up his arse. The other, Daerg, had been a sad sort of specimen who could barely put two words together.

Adair spoke readily but not effusively. He listened to what was said with apparent interest. He fairly oozed charm.

Clearly, he was quite dangerous. Apparently, Kendrick's former wife's brother, in Erin, had saved his best weapon for last.

Not that Kendrick would ever surrender the merest shred of the lands he'd won here in Alba. Aye, Bradana knew how the story went. After listening to Baen and Daerg, she should.

Long ago, Gawen of Erin had funded the bid of his wife's brother, Kendrick, to establish a settlement here in Alba, the agreement being he should have a share of what was claimed.

Gawen called in the debt now for the sake of the second son, Daerg, who would not inherit the settlement back in Erin.

And what of *this* son? What would he do with himself?

She stared down at her breakfast in order to keep from gazing at Adair. She was no green girl to fall victim to a giddy attraction. She knew very well it took far more than a smile or the turn of a head to make a good union.

Had she not watched her mother and Kendrick all these years? Wildly attracted to each other, they were. It did not keep them from battling constantly.

She selected a tidbit from her bowl and held it out to Wen, luring him back to her, then listened as Adair slowly won the room.

His brothers had failed to do that, and Baen had stayed with them a long time. But now, telling amusing stories, Adair had Kendrick listening to him, and even Toren gave a surprised laugh a time or two, though Kerr just continued to glower darkly.

At the end of the meal, Adair looked Kendrick in the eye and said with great sincerity, "Uncle, I would like the chance to speak with ye at length."

"To plead your case, eh?" Kendrick returned, but without rancor.

"Not my case," Adair replied, "for I have naught to gain."

Kendrick gazed at him thoughtfully. "Mayhap anon. Today, Kerr and Toren are going hunting. Ye would by chance like to go wi' them and see more o' Dalriada?"

Did a shiver touch Adair's frame? If so, it was swiftly gone as he smiled. "I would like that full well."

Like it he would not. Bradana knew her stepbrothers, and Adair would have a rough time, if they had aught to say about it.

KENDRICK'S TWO YOUNG bucks, Toren and Kerr, took Adair in hand directly after they finished breakfast. As alike as two pups from the same litter, they were, so much so they might have been twins. Indeed, casual conversation, engaged when they started off on the backs of three stout ponies, indicated they were not, though they'd been born less than a year apart.

Both had broad foreheads like their father and rather sharp chins. Heavy eyelids over eyes that could stare dangerously.

Indeed, Adair, who had something of a knack for sensing what lay inside those he met, could feel their hostility lurking behind the occasional smile they offered him. They did not necessarily mean him well, and he wondered if he erred in going off alone with them into the heart of Alba.

The wild, dark heart.

He thought about asking one of his own men to accompany him. But they had been given berths down near the shore and he sensed a kind of challenge in the invitation Kendrick's sons issued him. One to which he needed to rise.

They wished to see of what their Erin cousin was made, did they? He would show them.

The pony he'd been provided was a sturdy one and the day

fine. Toren, who seemed to be the brother who did most of the talking for the pair, asked him if he was good with a bow.

"Tolerably so," Adair returned. "What are ye after this day?"

"Meat for the table. Whatever we find."

The land rose in a steep slope up and away from the sea. Adair turned his head to look back several times, thinking how small and perilous the settlement appeared, perched there at the very edge of the water. When they entered the trees, he could no longer look back.

A dark and heavy sort of wood it was, one in which Adair could not see an end ahead. No trail or path ran here. Toren, who rode first, seemed to choose his way at random. Kerr followed Adair in silence. Adair could feel the man's glare between his shoulder blades.

What if they take me out here and kill me? Send word after back to Erin saying I suffered some accident. Father would never know different.

To break the silence and chase off such dark thoughts, he asked, "How much territory does my uncle hold here?"

"He has managed—*we* ha' managed—to carve out a fair swath. Shall we take ye to the farthest reaches so ye can see all?" Toren asked over his shoulder.

And leave me there, no doubt, Adair thought.

He knew the woods and the hills back home, had run them all his life and hunted there often. Just thinking on that, he felt a tug of longing for the land he loved so well. Nothing like this place where the wood made night of the broad day, shutting out the sun.

Father could scarce have done anything crueler than sending him here.

"Ye ha' other neighbors who came from Erin?"

"Aye. MacDonough to the south o' us and MacGillean to the north. Bradana is set to wed wi' Mican MacGillean's son."

"Is she?" A new spear of feeling pierced Adair's chest.

"Aye, to make firm our alliance wi' them. That will keep us stronger, see. We have had to fight for this place against the tribes that were here—Alban tribes—when Da arrived. Mayhap your father back in Erin does no' understand that."

Perhaps he did not. Adair could not be certain what Father imagined when he pictured Alba. Not this.

He began to think Toren led them in deliberate circles. Not much time had passed before he knew himself hopelessly lost. The land climbed gradually and then it did not. He could no longer hear or see the ocean, only the birds that sang.

Abruptly, they emerged into an open space where sunlight slanted down so brightly that it made Adair blink.

"There," Toren said.

A small herd of deer grazed on the far side of the clearing. They raised their heads at the appearance of the men and ponies but did not flee.

"Would ye like the honor?" Toren asked, and passed Adair his bow. A single arrow.

Another test, was it? And not a difficult one. Accepting the weapon, Adair dismounted from his pony and blinked again to clear his vision. Nocked the arrow and raised the bow.

A sudden flurry. A flicker of light and darkness as if a cloud had passed over the glade. The deer scattered without seeming intent, as if they dispersed by magic. Suddenly gone.

As were Adair's two companions.

Gone.

He breathed out a puff of air. He should have known. Kendrick's two sons had not brought him out here to hunt but to be rid of him. Whether with Kendrick's knowledge or not, he could not say.

He stood still and listened.

He should be able to hear them. Passage through so thick a wood would not be silent. Only, he could hear nothing.

Even the birds had stopped singing.

Another shiver, brother to the one he'd felt when this jaunt was suggested at breakfast, quivered through him. He could not hear the deer moving away or the men and ponies.

It did indeed reek of magic.

"Where are your fellows?" he asked the pony. It should know how to find them. It would most likely know the way home.

Its ears twitched, but it gave no other sign of being willing to help him. A fine joke, this, on the part of Kendrick's sons. Fine at least here in daylight. But once the dark came down, he would be stranded here in country he did not know. With only the knife he always wore, a bow, and a single arrow for defense.

He could wander for days without finding his way.

He swore long and bitterly, and the pony's ears twitched again.

The trees did not allow him to search for a horizon. If he might get a glimpse of the sea, he would have his direction. Or if he might follow the slope of the land down.

But they had climbed and descended several times.

Aye, he should have known what they were about.

He stepped away from the pony and slowly, methodically, searched for signs. Plenty of deer scat here. It must be a favorite place for the beasts to graze. Not so much as a single hoofprint from his companions' ponies.

He'd need to climb a tree for a glimpse of the sea. Tall pines surrounded him, dark and silent. In fact, it felt as if they watched him.

Something watched him.

Did Kerr and Toren lurk nearby, hidden, to see what he would do? Was that why he hadn't heard them moving off?

Would they call an end to the prank, or did they indeed intend to lose him out here, and leave him to die?

An ill fate for one who had never wanted to come here in the first place.

He selected a tree and began to climb.

CHAPTER SEVEN

WHEN KERR AND Toren came home without game and without their Erin cousin, Bradana feared the worst. Indeed, she'd been uneasy about their jaunt ever since the three of them left. She knew her stepbrothers, understood all too well that any show of hospitality on their part must be false and rotten.

She now admitted to herself that her uneasiness had kept her hanging around the dun most of the day. She had other things to do. She'd neglected those things.

Kerr and Toren came riding in at late afternoon, as casually as if they were missing nothing.

"Where's the Erin cousin?" she asked, planting herself in front of them.

They exchanged a telling look before Toren dismounted from his pony. "Out o' our way, Bradana. We are bound for the pony sheds."

"But where is he?" A terrible, icy feeling poured over Bradana. "Have ye killed him?"

Kerr gave a ghastly grin, revealing his big, square teeth. "Not us."

Realization hit her an equally icy blow. "Ye left him out there."

"It seems," Toren said with great satisfaction, "our poor cousin from Erin got lost. He should no' put his feet where they do no' belong."

She stared at them, aghast. A hundred thoughts flooded her mind before she chose one. "What will your father say?"

"I do not know wha' he may say"—Toren wagged his head—"but he should be grateful to us."

"Aye, grateful," Kerr echoed.

"We got rid o' this one far quicker than they other two."

"By Lugh's spear," Bradana swore. "How far out did ye take him?"

"Far enough that he will no' be coming back."

"And the pony?"

"A shame, that," Kerr admitted. "'Twas a fine pony."

They moved off toward the pony sheds as if they had not a care in the world. Bradana stood and considered several options.

She should go to her stepfather. He, at least, must be concerned, if only because he would have to send word back to Erin if Adair MacMurtray was lost.

Lost. And a terrible shame that would be. All that warmth and brightness disappeared into the wild.

Surely Kendrick would send out a search party. Or—an entirely mad idea—she could go herself.

She knew the hunting grounds well enough. No one was so mad as to venture far into the interior, which was just trees and more trees. Here in Alba, most travel was done along the coast by watercraft.

But Toren and Kerr had deliberately led their cousin off.

She might never find him. Kendrick might not. Adair could well wander and die out there.

Alone.

And why should that bother her so? Aye, he was bonny. He was also trouble, and no one to cause this tug at her heart.

He meant nothing to her save an object of unexpected—and unwanted—attraction. Admittedly, a strong attraction.

She turned her back to the sea and eyed the land.

Would Alba be willing to surrender him?

THE SCRAMBLE UP the tree, a dark and bristling specimen, proved hot, sweaty, and painful. Worse, it did Adair little good. Though he climbed as high as he could, risking life and limb on the possibility of a fall, all he could see in any direction was more trees.

Not a hint of the sea. Not a breath of it. Not the rise of a mountain that would mark the farther interior.

He slithered back down, garnering several more scrapes and abrasions.

He could still feel someone watching him.

All right, if they were out there silently sniggering at his plight, he could wait them out. He sat down with his back against the tree and tried to think.

Would the pony lead him back home? It stood placidly, not trying to graze, as clouds fluttered overhead blocking out the sunlight. The fine day fast flew.

After a time, he realized he would have to do something. He got to his feet and called out.

"All right—ye've had your fun. If ye're still there, let's have done with this."

A rustle, very faint from the far side of the clearing. Had they been there all the while? But it was neither of his cousins that stepped out into the glade.

"TOREN AND KERR ha' gone and lost the cousin from Erin."

Kendrick looked up sharply. He and Bradana's mother were in the family quarters of the great dun—for once not arguing. Kendrick got slowly to his feet.

"Eh?"

"But they've gone hunting," Mam protested mildly.

"They took him out under the guise o' hunting and abandoned him, ye mean," Bradana declared roundly. "They've just come back wi'out him."

Kendrick swore.

"Is he gone, then?" Mam asked almost innocently. "Good riddance. Though he seemed a nice enough young man."

"Tavia!" Kendrick chided her. "We canna just leave him out there. Where are those two rascals?"

"Off to the pony sheds," Bradana replied.

Kendrick marched out as he was, in tunic and kilt, no weapons. Bradana followed.

"They should no' ha' done that," Kendrick seethed. "I would ha' got rid soon enough, like the twa others."

He hurried so that Bradana had no breath to reply. They met her stepbrothers coming the other way.

"Wha' is this I hear?" Kendrick demanded of them.

They glared at Bradana.

"The cousin from Erin went astray," Toren replied.

"He went astray?"

"Aye, lost his way there in the forest. After a boar, maybe."

"And ye did no' look for him?" Kendrick roared, never for a minute believing it had not been deliberate.

"Aye, we cast about for a bit, then gave it up for hopeless."

"Where were ye when ye lost him?"

"No' certain." Toren wrinkled up his face. "I doubt we could find the place again."

"And wha' will his father say when I send word he's no' to be found?"

Kerr drawled, "I suppose mayhap he may say 'twas a poor thing he did in sending the bugger here."

Kendrick puffed out an annoyed breath. "Go fetch more ponies. At least five o' them. We maun go out and search for him."

"Aye so," Toren said, "but I do no' think we will find him."

"Ye will search as will I, if we have to look all night."

"I will come also," Bradana heard herself say.

All three of them stared at her in surprise.

"Nay, nay," Kendrick said. "No' a good idea. We mean to spread out."

"Aye. Do I not know the woods as well as these two? Plus I ha' Wen. He may help find the cousin."

She *would* find him. Bradana did not understand quite why she felt so convinced of it. It was as if she had an arrow beneath her heart, straining toward him.

As if she could feel the man.

Kendrick glanced at the hound that hugged Bradana's side.

"Ye saw what a liking Wen took to him."

"Well, so. But I do no' want ye venturing far, lass. If ye become lost as well, yer mother will have my hide."

"'Tis fixing to rain," Toren said with some satisfaction. "If it does, I do no' believe we will ever be able to find him."

THE FADING LIGHT dappled the hide of the stag that emerged from the cover of the trees, alone this time without the rest of his herd. Moving with great and near-silent dignity, he raised his head, displaying a magnificent rack of antlers.

He and Adair regarded one another.

For that one long, incredible moment, Adair did not breathe. The stag's eyes, very dark and full of mystery, spoke to him. Silently did the message come, and Adair's heartbeat thundered.

This place is mine. You intrude upon my land.

Aye, indeed, and so he did.

Slowly and carefully, he backed off a step. Not far, as the tree stood close behind him. Softly he called, "I be here through no choice o' my own."

His pony flicked its ears. The stag did not move. It continued to watch Adair the way Alba seemed to watch him, with a hint of silent threat.

More than a hint.

Perhaps fifty paces separated him and the beast across the clearing. Adair understood how swiftly a stag of that size could cross the distance. Would he defend his territory?

Might Adair seize his pony's bridle and lead him off into the trees? Give the king his distance.

But he did not feel sure he should do that. There was some magic in this encounter, and it held him.

He had left the bow on the ground. He now lifted his hands as he might to a man he wished to reassure, showing them empty of weapons.

And stepped out.

Madness, aye. The very opposite of what wisdom dictated. Quite possibly, he should go back up the tree. Wait for the beast to leave. Yet that was not what was meant.

Another pace and he waited, the pony now behind him.

The stag snorted and stepped out also, toward him.

"By Lugh's spear," Adair muttered. A thrill coursed through him from head to toe. And louder, "Can ye give me my direction? I will leave ye then, leave ye to your kingdom."

The stag tossed his head. As if to a signal, all the light went out of the clearing, blotted by clouds streaming above. It abruptly grew dark as night.

This, as Adair knew—as he felt to the very marrow of his bones—was a moment of magic. In a place of magic.

Alba was not Erin.

"Show me, I pray," he whispered.

The stag moved, turned to his right and Adair's left. Started across the clearing.

Hastily, Adair grabbed his pony's lead and snatched up the bow.

At the edge of the clearing, the stag paused and turned to look at Adair once more. They were now so close, Adair could smell the beast's heavy scent and, despite the fleeing of the light, see each separate hair of his hide. The animal breathed out a gust of air and Adair nodded.

"This way?"

A great swirl of wind entered the clearing and chased around it. All the trees nodded at once, bending their dark boughs.

As if bowing.

"Thank ye, master."

Another snort and the stag gathered its hooves beneath it. Leaped away, leaving great gouges of earth behind. It disappeared into the trees, leaving Adair blinking, no longer certain of what he'd seen.

Had that truly taken place? Had the beast given him a direction back to the settlement? Or would it send him off into the vast wilderness of Alba's heart?

Dare he believe? Dare he not?

He remained unsure till he and the pony had walked some distance, for he led the animal by its reins, and the ground began to slant down gradually. Not even then did he mount and ride. He wanted his feet against the ground and no chance for the pony to take him astray.

He caught no glimpse of Toren or Kerr, and no longer felt as if anyone watched him.

CHAPTER EIGHT

I T GREW DARK as night. A storm moved in from the sea with the speed so often employed, turning what had been a lovely day into windy wet.

Bradana did not consciously choose her direction. Her foray out to seek Adair was not about anything so rational as conscious thought. It seemed more a pull, and so she let it pull her.

She could hear the other searchers for a time until, as Kendrick had said, they spread out. He'd sent out many of the men who habitually went hunting. Kerr and Toren had, in the end, been left behind.

She did not fear getting lost. She knew these woods too well, being in the habit of going off by herself when things at home became unbearable. Besides, she had Wen.

The hound ranged ahead of her and from side to side, but he always came back and, as if checking in with her, gazed into her eyes. She had not brought a pony but went afoot, and took a more northerly track than the others had.

All around her, Alba spoke. It did so in the rustling of the bushes as the wind blew in from the sea. The flight of birds, the sound of her footsteps on deep loam. To her, this land was not so much a place as a living being, one that held an ancient kind of magic as aware of her as she was of it.

Dark, aye—especially now—mysterious and somehow loving. Such was her Alba. So she whispered to the land as she went, speaking in her heart. *Take me to him.*

A hawk arose with a great flapping of wings and flew northeastward. She veered to follow it.

The first drops of rain came slowly, making a pattern of sound, here, there, great splotches like hands striking a bodhran drum.

Wen raced back to her side then darted off again, looking back at her over one furry shoulder.

Again, she followed.

He appeared through the trees walking slowly and leading the pony. He looked like a vision—one of the gods, perhaps, loose in the world. Indeed, it took Bradana an instant to recognize him even though her heart knew. Her heart knew at once and leaped ahead to him.

His step did not falter when he saw her; he merely corrected course slightly so he could meet with her. He did not pause till they faced one another.

"Mistress Bradana."

"There ye be, then. Everyone is out looking for ye."

One brown eyebrow rose. "So ye have found me."

"So I have." She performed a swift inspection of him. Brown hair tangled. Boots covered in pine needles and loam. Tunic opened at the throat, allowing her a glimpse of what lay beneath. "Are ye hurt?"

He shook his head.

"Those two scoundrels Kerr and Toren deserted ye?"

"Your brothers, aye."

"They are no' my brothers," she informed him swiftly. "My mother merely married wi' their father."

He gave her that lightning smile of his. "Fortunate for ye."

"No' so fortunate, since I have had to put up wi' them all these years." She turned. "Come along. 'Tis raining harder."

But he was busy caressing Wen, who had greeted him enthusiastically, rubbing the hound's neck and ears. Bradana imagined those beautiful hands touching her own body and flushed with heat.

She did *not* want that. She did not want him. She had never fallen into the weakness of wanting a man.

"Are we far from the settlement?"

"Not too far. Ye nearly made your own way back. How, I canna imagine." They moved off.

The smile came slower this time. "If I told ye, ye would not believe me."

"I might."

But he only shook his head and stole a look over his shoulder. "'Tis a strange place, this Alba."

"'Tis a wondrous place. A magnificent place. A fierce and ancient one."

"Ye love it."

"Down to my bones," she admitted. "As, I will suppose, ye love Erin."

"So I do."

It rained in earnest now. The drops hit Adair in the face and ran down—struck all four of them hard.

"Then why did ye leave there?" she asked him.

"I did no' want to. I was sent."

"D'ye always do as you're told?"

"Nay. D'ye?"

"Very seldom do I do as I am told." She thought of Earrach, and the arguments Kendrick had put forth for her to wed with him. Whether or not she would prove obedient in that—well, they would have to see.

"Come along." She hurried now, but not because she wanted shed of Adair's company. Nay, not that.

When they emerged from the trees, the settlement lay before them to the south. The sea stretched out angry with big, dark blue combers rolling in. The buildings seemed to huddle against the storm.

"Come," she urged again, and reached out to snag his hand.

The instant their fingers met, skin to skin, she received a vision. Swift and hard it came, blotting out all that lay before her and allowing her to see instead—

A man—nay, not this man, but another just as beautiful in his way. A mane of auburn hair and a pair of hazel eyes that anchored her soul. He leaned in and kissed her softly, bestowing the caresses first to the palm of each hand, then at either corner of her mouth, both cheeks, and her forehead. A blessing.

"Mistress Bradana? What is it?"

She had stumbled. Adair's grip kept her from falling.

"Naught. It is all right." Only it was not. Something grave, terrible, and wonderful came at her. From him? From the past, mayhap.

Other figures emerged from the forest also on their way back to the settlement, fleeing the hard rain. They included Kendrick and one of his advisors. The chief looked immensely relieved to see Adair.

"There ye be!" he cried, as Bradana had. "By the Dagda, I did no' want to have to send word back to yer father that ye were lost. Anlon"—he turned to his companion—"take the pony, will ye, and see him tended."

"Aye, so." The man moved off.

Kendrick fixed Adair with a hard eye. "Ye can come wi' me."

MISTRESS TAVIA HAD a good fire burning, and Adair availed himself of its comfort. His uncle's wife bustled about, giving Adair a cup of warmed heather ale. He drank while keeping an eye on Bradana.

He figured she would leave now, go off to at least change into dry clothing. Her things clung to her, and her hair hung down, dripping and turned amber-dark with the wet.

He did not want her to leave. Just as he had not wanted to let go of her hand. But she had cast his fingers off as soon as Kendrick appeared from the forest.

Mayhap she stayed because Wen, also very wet, had hunk-cred down beside Adair, as close as he could get.

Adair did not know what to make of what had happened out in the forest, the sense of communion with the stag and the aid it had lent. Meeting with Bradana after and that terrible, powerful moment when she'd seized his hand. The emotions that had come at him then, rising up seemingly from nowhere.

Nay, not from nowhere. They had a source. One he did not comprehend.

Had she felt that also? He watched her even as he pretended to center his attention on Wen, so close beside him.

The hound, out of all these here, seemed to favor him.

"Wha' happened?" Kendrick asked, taking a seat also by the fire. "Tell me now before my scamps o' sons arrive."

Adair squinted at his uncle. Would he welcome the truth? Some men did not wish to hear ill of their kin, and especially their sons.

A bit ruefully, Adair said, "My cousins took me up through the forest. It seemed we did no' take a direct route but circled round some. But then, I do not know the land. At length we came to a clearing, a good place for hunting, so I thought. They left me there."

Kendrick huffed out an unhappy breath. "How did ye—"

Before he could complete the question, Kerr and Tolen came in. They crashed into the chamber noisily, shedding water, and Mistress Tavia, who'd just sat down, stood up again with a cry of dismay.

"Och!" said Tolen, stopping just inside the door. "So ye found him, then."

He did not sound particularly pleased about it. Adair reckoned he was supposed to have perished out in the wild.

"Wha' happened?" Kendrick cried. "Your cousin was in your care."

"No' our fault," Tolen said quickly.

And in a dour voice, Kerr repeated, "No' our fault."

"How not? Ye took him hunting and were meant to look after him."

"He went astray," Tolen claimed with a hard look at Adair that cursed him for failing to remain so.

"So," Kendrick barked, "ye did no' leave him out there on purpose?"

"Is that wha' he says?" Tolen demanded with scorn. "Nay—he took a fright, so he did, when faced wi' our wild country. I reckon he is used to the soft fields o' Erin."

The scorn in Toren's voice made Adair shift uncomfortably.

It was Bradana who replied. "He did find his own way back, though, mostly. Wen and I met him up in the trees no' far off."

Tolen's hard glare scorched her. He said nothing.

Kendrick roared, "My sons have embarrassed and disappointed me. There is a law o' hospitality. 'Tis as good as a geis. This law ha' ye broken."

Both young men looked angry, neither of them ashamed.

Mistress Tavia waved her hands at them. "Go. Go. Ye be shedding water everywhere."

Seizing the escape she offered, they went. A silence fell in the room, during which Mistress Tavia once more sat down, cradling her belly.

"Kendrick," she said at length, "I am no' fit to tolerate this nonsense."

"Nay," Kendrick agreed, apparently abashed even as his sons were not. He lifted his eyes to Adair. "I apologize for my sons' actions. They are strong-headed and it leads them into trouble from time to time. Ye maun forgive their boyish antics."

Adair must forgive nothing, but he did not say so.

"Boyish antics!" Mistress Tavia exclaimed. "They are men full grown."

Kendrick ignored her. "Nephew, perhaps 'twould be best for yoursel' and all concerned if ye went back home as soon as possible. As soon as this rain passes, mayhap. It should clear by morning."

For reasons unknown to him, Adair looked at Bradana. Their gazes met and tangled for the briefest moment before she looked away.

"Uncle." Adair returned his attention to Kendrick. "I cannot leave wi' my father's business unspoken."

"In the morn," Kendrick declared. "There has been enough, nephew, for one day."

"As ye wish."

Bradana left soon after, saying she must change into dry clothing, taking the hound with her.

Though Adair sat till his own clothing dried, she did not return.

CHAPTER NINE

"I THOUGHT YE would want to know," Kendrick said heavily, "I ha' spoken wi' my twa sons. Last night, after ye went to your bed."

Morning had arrived. Contrary to Kendrick's prediction, the weather had not cleared. Instead, a heavy mist cloaked the settlement and the rocks of the shore.

When Adair had walked out from his quarters, it collected on his hair and clothing like so much light rain.

Not at all a good day for travel, if Kendrick dismissed him.

He had not slept well last night—too many things crowding his head, and scenes that replayed continually. His two accursed cousins. The encounter with the stag. That incredible moment when Bradana snagged his hand.

He was able to ponder out what two of these meant. His cousins wanted shed of him. He'd somehow encountered the magic of Alba, there in the clearing while facing the stag.

But Bradana? He could not imagine.

She meant nothing to him. A chance encounter here in a strange land. She was not even of his blood. Beautiful, aye. But she meant naught to him.

Still and all, he half hoped she might be at his uncle's fireside when he arrived. Not that he needed her there. He *wanted* her there.

She wasn't present, though. Rather, he found Kendrick alone, with breakfast laid out before him.

"Uncle."

"Come. Eat."

Adair did, his appetite ferocious. He listened as Kendrick once more made excuses for his sons. Heard of their chastisement. "And did my cousins admit why they tried to strand me in the forest?"

"Admit?" Kendrick did not like the word. "'Twas accidental, they say. One moment ye were there, the next gone. They thought ye stepped out after game. They called to ye—"

Adair looked Kendrick in the eye. "Uncle, they did no'."

"Are ye calling my sons liars?"

"Are ye calling *me* one?"

Kendrick visibly considered making a fuss of it, and then backed down. "Aye, well, an unfortunate occurrence and no mistake. Ye will no' go out alone wi' them again."

"I will not."

"In fact… I think, ye being a reasonable young man, ye will agree that, as I said last night, the very best thing ye can do is go back to Erin."

"I cannot, Uncle. No' before presenting my father's arguments for his claim."

"Do so, then."

Adair ordered his thoughts rapidly. "Ye will agree that when ye were both young men in Erin, when ye had just married my father's sister, he did gi' ye the means to come here and strake a holding in this new land."

"He did so." Kendrick spoke thoughtfully. "I was a second son, see, and would no' inherit there in Erin. Your da and I were friends. 'Tis how he met your mother, my sister, through our friendship.

"Others were after talking about sailing to claim lands here in Alba. How the land just sat for the taking. They did no' say," he added weightily, "we would have to battle for every length we got or that it would be won from the tribes living here in blood."

"Still and all, Father had a share in it. 'Twas your agreement."

Kendrick's eyes flashed. "He gifted me a few boats, aye, and supplied the venture. Funded some weapons. He shed none o' the blood."

"Yet the agreement—"

"Lad, listen to me. I ha' explained all of this to your brothers before ye, and I do no' understand why Gawen has sent ye in turn, that I maun explain it all again.

"What aid your father gave me was long ago, and I do consider he gave it in both kinship and friendship. 'Tis I who have clawed my way to a large holding here, which will grow still larger when my stepdaughter marries the son o' the chief who holds the lands to our north. This is all my doing. And 'tis meant for my sons.

"I do no' intend to leave all this to only the elder, which is Toren. My sons will each inherit a big swath of that for which I have fought so hard. They know this full well."

He hesitated before he asked, "Is it so surprising they should want shed o' ye?"

Strange emotions swirled through Adair. Indignation on his father's part. Anger on his own.

"Ye admit it, then—your sons did no' wish for me to return from yon forest."

Kendrick shrugged. "The best thing ye can do, as I say, is leave. I wish ye no harm, lad. Ye seem a nice enough boy, which is why I gi' ye this advice. Ye can sail today, if this accursed mist lifts. But by morning—"

"Nay."

"Wha' did ye say to me?"

"Ye ask me to understand your position. I ask ye to understand my father's in turn. He wants only a measure of land for Daerg, a second son just like ye were. Could you no' afford that, and your nephew could live here wi' ye, side by side, an ally and a trusted neighbor."

Kendrick raised a brow. "Ye argue well. But what about ye?"

"Me?"

"Ye be a third son. Ye say your father worries about his second. What will *ye* inherit?"

Adair shrugged. "I have no ambitions for mysel'. As a warrior, I suppose I will stay and serve Baen. In truth, I want only to go home to Erin. That is the land I love."

Yet that was no longer all the truth. He wanted to go home, aye—he was not, though, so certain he wanted to leave Bradana. Bradana, set to marry an Alban lord to the north.

Kendrick snorted. "Gawen must have been desperate, to send ye."

"He thought I might succeed where my brothers had failed."

"Ye will no'. Be sensible, lad. Consider leaving when the mist clears. Tak' your answer from me, and go."

"HE THINKS ME lacking in honor, does this nephew from Erin. He supposes I owe his father somewhat." Kendrick spoke restlessly to the family at large, late that afternoon. They had met for a meal, Bradana stopping in merely because her mam had been feeling unwell earlier in the day, and spent much of it in her bed. The child she carried, no doubt. She was no longer a young woman to be bearing a bairn.

Now Tavia sat pale as milk beside the fire and listened to her husband rant while Bradana performed the duty of serving the meal.

Adair had not joined them. Indeed, Bradana had not seen him all day, though she must admit to herself that she had looked. She had even paced the settlement with Wen from the shore to the heights. Hoping? Nay, she would not go that far.

Not even her hound had sighted the man.

Kendrick seethed in a defensive sort of way, "He has angered me."

Bradana knew her stepfather. She should, after no many years spent under his roof. Despite his many quarrels with Mam—small tiffs over equally small annoyances—he was not a man easy to anger. Waspish rather than violent in his disfavor. When he did express anger, it was often because in his heart he felt himself in the wrong.

Did he sit here now wanting someone to comfort him? To assure him that an old debt did not matter?

Mam said nothing, pushing her food around on the platter. Toren and Kerr exchanged glances. They had been well chastised for the hunting episode. Wisest, perhaps, to keep their mouths shut now. But neither of them had ever been particularly wise.

"The MacMurtray needs to be showed what's what," Kerr stated, "and sent on his way."

Kendrick sent him a glare. "I want no more japes like the last, hear? Ye will keep awa' from him. I will persuade him on his way in good time."

The two brothers exchanged another look that Bradana felt did not bode well for Adair.

"Where is he," she asked, "this cousin from Erin?"

Kendrick shrugged. "Somewhere about, I do no' doubt."

Kerr suggested, "I do no' suppose he will venture far out o' the settlement again."

Toren offered, "I saw him this morning standing staring out over the ocean like he thought he could fly back to Erin."

Bradana experienced a pang. Did Adair want that so badly? What of when he did go? Naught to her, surely. She was due to wed before long and move away to the north.

And yet—there was something between her and Adair, was there not? What had that been yesterday, when she touched his hand? When she'd received a glimpse of another man whose bright hazel eyes had anchored her soul.

She could not explain it. But she wanted quite badly to see Adair MacMurtray.

She asked, "Has no one thought to behave hospitably toward the man? Show the place off a wee bit. Prove we are civilized people."

Kendrick took offense all over again. "I *am* a civilized man."

Toren hurried to say, "The last thing we want to do is show the place off and make him want it more than he does already."

"Nay, nay," Kendrick said. "We do no' want him going back to his father and saying what a prize we hold here. But he *will* be going."

Bradana said nothing more. She fed the better part of her food to Wen and helped her mother tidy away before she went out, the hound at her side. From the doorway of the dun, she looked down to the sea.

The ugly weather was beginning to clear and a kind of calm spread out over the water, a slant of light from a passing goddess. Down off the rocky point of land a few boats rode, including the one in which Adair had sailed from Erin. The beauty of the late afternoon beckoned her like open arms.

Something else beckoned still more strongly.

"Wen, find him." How many places in a settlement this size could a man hide?

The hound looked at her, then moved off steadily down the slope toward the shore.

They found Adair aboard the little boat with the two men who had sailed with him from Erin. At sight of them, Bradana's heart leaped. Did they prepare to cast off? Perhaps he had taken Kendrick's advice to heart after all.

"Master Adair?"

He looked up, saw her balancing on the rocks that fronted the pier. Light flooded his eyes, and he scrambled over to the side of the small craft.

"Mistress?"

"Are ye leaving?"

For answer, he splashed ashore, moving lightly, and joined her on the stones. He stood there with the soft light washing over him, and Bradana's world suddenly came right.

Everything came right.

CHAPTER TEN

"YOU DID NOT come to the hall for supper," Bradana said.

Adair shrugged. "I did no' think I would be welcome."

"Are ye leaving?" she repeated, since she needed quite desperately to know. She glanced at the sailboat again. The two men had their heads down. For all she could tell, they slept.

"No' yet." He gave her a wry smile. "Do no' get your hopes up. Mistress Bradana."

She drew a breath. "My hopes—my hopes have naught to do wi' it."

A lie. Her hopes were all in a tangle. She hoped he'd stay. Quite possibly never leave these shores.

"We were but playing at draughts to pass the time. Flynn and Nolan, 'tis the third time they have been marooned here. They are sick o' the place."

"Ah, I see." Did she? "Your father must be a persistent kind o' man."

"He can be stubborn when he feels he is in the right."

"And ye? Can ye be stubborn?"

He shook his head. His gray-green eyes met hers, and a sharp thrill passed through her. She wanted to know this man. All of him.

"Walk wi' me."

He shot her an inquiring look and left off patting Wen, over whom he made a fuss.

One should not be jealous of one's own hound.

"Ye have seen very little o' what we have here, Master Adair, save the forest. Let us go up the shore. Is this very different from Erin?"

"Gey different, aye. We live a short distance from the coast. I have no such views as this." He gazed out to sea. "We are in the hills surrounded by swaths o' soft green and a river that marks the boundary o' our lands." He gave a grimace. "Much blood has been spilt into that river, in days gone by. Were it no' for the valor o' our ancestors, we would have nothing."

"Ye love it there." She could hear as much in his voice.

"I do. Mayhap precisely because our ancestors gave so much for it. Their love is my love. Carried in the blood."

"It must have been hard for ye to leave."

"I did no' want to come, and fought my father over it. What can I hope to accomplish that my brothers could not?"

"Kendrick has fought hard here too, and spilt blood to hold this place."

"I understand that."

"A word of advice—insulting or questioning his honor will no' get ye what ye want."

He stopped walking and faced her. "What will? For I cannot leave till I succeed."

"Is it what ye want, to go back home to Erin?"

"It *was*."

Again his eyes met hers, and it felt as if he touched her, touched her the way the man had in that glimpse of vision. A kiss in both palms. Both corners of her mouth, her cheeks, her forehead. She began to tremble.

"Now," he said softly, "I am no' sure what I want."

"Sit wi' me."

They had reached a place where large boulders backed the shingle. They sat side by side there, the waves nearly at their feet. Wen lay down within Adair's reach.

"Erin is no' far, is it?" Bradana asked.

"No' far at all. But I begin to think 'tis a very great distance."

"Tell me o' yoursel'."

"What d'ye wish to know?"

"Everything."

He laughed softly with surprise but said, "Ah, there is no' much to tell. I am a third son. I have trained most my life as a warrior, though we have few enough disputes wi' our neighbors these days. I help in the fields when needed. None o' us in Father's house are above our fellow clansmen."

"D'ye have a wife there? A lover to whom ye are promised?"

"Promised? Nay."

"Why not?" She could scarce imagine it. A man who looked as he did, who spoke as he did, with a cadence like music. Women should be following him in droves.

"Baen must wed first. Someone o' benefit to the clan, as he will be chief. Father has been busy arranging it."

"I see."

"Then there is Daerg."

"Say no more." The very idea of that wet specimen coming back here and battling to hold lands in Alba... Well. "Will ye no' be allowed to choose your own wife?"

"Me? Aye. I do no' matter much." He gave her another wry smile. "I supposes I ha' not yet met the right woman."

"Choose carefully," she told him, "since ye may. Having one's choice made, and one's future destined, is no' a good thing."

"As yours has been?"

"Aye."

"D'ye know him well, this man who's been chosen for ye?"

"Nay. I have met him thrice. Briefly." Bradana thought about Earrach MacGillean. A dark, glowering sort of man, though not ill favored. In each of their encounters, he'd spoken but a few words to her.

"What is his nature?" Adair asked.

"Dour, from wha' I can tell. He is no'—"

He is not you. But she could not say that, could she?

"I am sorry," Adair told her softly. "'Tis a hard thing."

It was. She did not want to go and live among strangers.

"The things we are sent to do are sometimes difficult to bear. If we could only choose—"

"What would ye choose?" she asked him.

Adair huffed out a breath. "Mere days ago, I would have said I wanted only to go home." He looked into her eyes. "Now, as I say, I am not so certain."

Her hand lay between them on the stone. He took it in his, did so softly and carefully, as if it were something precious. And the feeling came, it came again as it had in the forest. No vision of the other man this time—she saw Adair quite clearly. But the warmth, the sense of inestimable belonging. The desire…

This man was hers. And she was his in a way she could not hope to explain.

"Knowing what we do no' want is easy," she said. "Knowing what we do want is harder."

But she knew. Her heart could not doubt. She threaded her fingers through his and held on tight. Just like this should they be, flesh to flesh and life to life.

"You will go home to Erin," she said. "Eventually ye will, with the agreement ye seek or otherwise. Ye will forget me."

He shook his head. "Never. Ye have a rare beauty, Bradana."

Men rarely told her she was beautiful. Aye, they might compliment her hair, eye her breasts, speculate over the length of her legs. They said only that she was *formidable*. Too strong. Her stepbrothers' friends were cretins.

"I will no' forget ye either, Adair. But we are like two o' these pebbles cast up on the shore. They might lie beside one another for a time. The next great wave that comes tumbles them and moves them far apart. We have many great waves coming."

"But here, in this moment, we have peace." He cradled her hand against him, and a kind of serenity reached out from him to embrace her. He turned his gaze back out to sea and she became lost. Lost in how beautiful he was, and the sweet strength of his spirit.

Examining her own feelings, though, she found she did not want serenity. She wanted him to take her in his arms. Kiss her. She wanted the fire and madness she instinctively knew would rise between them. She wanted the violence of loving him and gifting him her soul in a rush of passion.

Yet she sat with him because he asked it, and she breathed him in there in the peace of the dying afternoon, absorbing his feel and his presence.

Storing it up for whatever the future might bring.

Not till nightfall did they part, retracing their steps back up the shore, where they paused and faced each other.

"Will ye no' come in and tak' somewhat to eat?" she beseeched, loath to part with him.

He made a face. "Nay."

"Ye must be hungry."

"Flynn and Nolan shared with me earlier. Anyway, I still do not think I would be welcome at your stepfather's fireside."

"Mayhap not."

"Sleep well, Mistress Bradana."

He leaned toward her. For one blinding, glorious moment, she thought he meant to kiss her. But he only gave a nod and drew his fingers from hers. Abruptly, the last of the light faded from the day. She could no longer feel his heartbeat.

"And you."

She watched him walk away from her toward his quarters, her devastation all out of proportion. Would she not see him come morning?

"Come, Wen," she told her hound, who seemed as disappointed at parting from Adair as she.

❦

CHAPTER ELEVEN

VOICES INTERRUPTED BRADANA'S sleep, partly muffled and accompanied by a burst of laughter. She opened her eyes to the close dark of her sleeping chamber. Morning had not yet arrived, yet someone—quite clearly not the guard—bumped along outside the dun.

She'd been sleeping quite well up to this point, better than she'd expected. She thought she might lie long thinking about all that had passed between her and Adair, might flail and struggle over the impossibility of what she felt for him. But she'd dropped off instead to the memory of him holding her hand, and dreamed of the two of them lying together so in a far-distant place, fingers twined, hearts yearning.

Now she thought she recognized her stepbrothers' voices.

Accursed fools, she thought. They must have sat up late drinking and bragging with their friends, as they tended to do, and be on their way back to their beds. Kendrick would not be pleased if he found out.

She rose at the bidding of her annoyance, went out into the corridor and to the nearest door. Wen followed her, his great head cocked and a growl sounding low in his throat.

The night air struck cool against her body, clad only in a thin sleeping gown. She could see the settlement mostly asleep, and the forms of two men, little more than shadows, moving past her.

She was about to step back and return to bed when Wen ran out, the growl increasing to a rumble.

"Wen? Come back."

Rarely did the hound disobey her, but he did so now, heading off around the side of the dun and down the slope toward the shore.

She should not follow. She wore too few garments and, as the sky had clouded over, could barely see her way. But the hound's behavior worried her, and a bad feeling rose from the ground upward.

"Wen? Wait for me."

A dark gray hound was not easy to follow on a dim night. He'd stopped growling, so she could not track him by the sound. She caught mere glimpses. A hint of fur, the plume of his great tail.

They went down the path to the shore and bore right along where the men worked to repair their watercraft and sometimes gathered to drink. It grew cooler as she met the air off the water, and she shivered.

With both cold and foreboding.

Wen stopped so suddenly, she almost fell over him. He began to whine and nose about the supplies stacked along the shore above the waterline. Piles of skins and bent hazel for making curraghs. Spars and sails.

"Foolish hound, what is it? Come awa' back to bed."

Wen ran back to her before darting forward, his message clear. Dread flooded through her and pooled in her gut. She stood and listened but could hear nothing besides the hiss of the waves and the tumbling of the pebbles.

We are like two o' these pebbles cast up on the shore.

She moved behind the stacks of broken wood, trying to spare her bare feet as much as she could. Wen whined and snuffled around a dark shape lying there.

Bradana swore, invoking the gods, for perhaps it was a prayer.

He lay in a heap, huddled on his side, but she knew him. Even before she touched him, she did. In an instant, she was on her knees and sweeping the hair out of his face.

Blood. The first thing she saw. A sob rose to her throat even as she sought to turn him over onto his back so she might get a better look.

"Help me." A definite prayer now. "Help me help him."

Wen heard and came to her assistance. Between them, they nudged Adair over onto his back. Bradana caught her breath.

Blood on his forehead and in his hair. His face had been battered. She could see little more but did not doubt his body had suffered similar treatment.

Two of them against one—or more of them, if Toren and Kerr had enlisted the help of their friends. Drunk, no doubt.

"Adair? Can ye hear me?"

No response. She clasped one of his hands and lifted it. The fingers were also battered and bloody. He'd given as good as he got. Mayhap, she hoped, the connection between them would recall him from wherever he'd gone.

But nay. No response yet. Was he breathing? Dead?

She leaned close. A hint of breath fanned her cheek. "Adair, please."

What to do? She certainly could not lift him or drag him up the slope. To try might cause further injuries. She needed to go for help, even though everything within her protested leaving him.

"Wen, guard."

She scrambled up, her intention to run back up to the dun. She thought better of it, though. Adair's own men were closer.

She ran along the shore, no longer noticing the bite of the cold air or the pebbles against her feet. Adair's men were camped along by their boat. She found them sleeping soundly.

"Come," she called, and they sat up, groggy. "Your master is hurt. He needs ye."

They followed her back along the shore, with her explaining breathlessly as they went.

"He's been waylaid and beaten. Did ye hear naught?" Such a

struggle would not have been silent.

"Nay, mistress."

Wen stood over Adair, who now lay sprawled on his back like a man slain. Indeed, Bradana had to bend down and once more assure herself he still breathed.

They went in a terrible train, Bradana first, the two men carrying Adair, and Wen behind. Bradana led them straight into the great hall, where she lit the torches, making no attempt to keep quiet.

Kendrick and Tavia both came, Mam with her hair hanging down and Kendrick gasping in disbelief.

"Wha' is this?" he asked.

"The handiwork o' your sons. Ye had better hope they ha' no' killed him."

Kendrick stared in horror from the beaten man to Bradana's face. "How d'ye know this was the work o' Kerr and Toren?"

"Because I heard them on their way home from it."

Kendrick turned to his wife. "Ha' the servant bring the healers as quick as ye can."

ADAIR CAME TO even before the healer arrived, while Mam was making a bed there beside the fire, and his men eased him down onto it. He regained his senses, swearing, but Bradana didn't care. She was far too relieved to see him with his eyes open.

One eye open, that was. The other had already started to swell shut.

Improper as it was, Bradana went down on her knees beside him.

"Adair? Adair, d'ye know me?"

"Aye."

She wanted to reach for his hand, ached to reestablish the connection they'd shared on the shore. But Kendrick was there and her mam, and Adair's men. All hung about with worried faces. And she dared not let them see…

Kendrick moaned, "If this be the truth, that my sons ha' done this, 'tis a terrible breach o' honor."

Bradana tipped up her face and looked at him. "Honor? Ye are worried for that?"

Kendrick turned to the nearest servant, several of whom had entered the room. "Go bring my sons."

Bradana puffed out a breath. If this kept up, the hall would be crowded. "By the gods," she said, "let the healer see him first."

"I am all right," Adair murmured.

He was not, though Bradana hesitated to argue it. The power of what gripped her—a kind of protective wildness—shocked her. At that moment she would have fought ten marauders to keep him safe.

Instead, she looked at him. "What happened?"

Adair clearly had trouble speaking, one side of his mouth torn and bloody, the other swollen. "I was walking. Before bed. Thinking." His gaze met Bradana's, and she knew exactly what he'd been thinking about. "They waylaid me."

"Who?" Kendrick asked.

Before he could answer, the healer came hurrying in. He nudged Kendrick, Bradana, and Wen aside and performed a grim inspection.

"Ye'll live, young master. Pray," he told the rest of them, "gi' me some room." And to the servants, "I will need water, warm if possible."

Mam already had the fire lit. The rest of them moved to the door, where the cold air spilled in.

"Ye found him?" Kendrick asked Bradana.

"Wen and I did."

"How?"

"I heard Kerr and Toren returning from…doing that. Wen led me down to the shore."

"Ye be certain 'twas Kerr and Toren?"

"I do no' doubt Adair will tell ye so himsel' when he is able."

"Why would my sons do such a treacherous thing?"

"Ye know full well why. They are sick of relations turning up from over the water to take their lands. They wanted to make sure he'd go home."

"Still and all."

"They left him there in his blood." To die? Bradana did not know. Adair was young and strong. Still, it was a shameful deed. "There behind the scraps o' wood and all where the boats are repaired. He might no' have been found till morning."

"Aye, well. Your hound saw to that."

Would Kendrick have been happier if his nephew had perished? Bradana could not tell. No doubt it would have solved a problem for him.

And hatched out another with his relations over the water.

The healer, with the help of one of Adair's men, was shifting him on his makeshift bed. Bradana fought the desire to return to his side.

Blood on his hair. On his hands. A muffled groan.

"Father, wha' is it?" As soon as Toren came in the door, closely followed by Kerr, Bradana knew he meant to play at innocence. She sneered inwardly.

"Where ha' ye been?" Kendrick demanded.

"In our beds." Toren peered past them into the hall. "What is happening, then?"

"Our guest has fallen foul o' someone."

"Ye do no' say. Is he all right?"

"Has he accused us?" Kerr asked.

Bradana rolled her eyes and snorted. "Look at their hands. 'Twill tell the tale."

Kendrick towed his sons outside, followed by Bradana and Wen. There he inspected their hands. Even by the dim light, the torn and bloodied knuckles could be seen. Both of them also carried abrasions to their faces, and Kerr's cheek had begun to swell.

Kendrick nearly spat with aggravation. "What were ye thinking? We are under a geis of hospitality."

"He needs to go," Toren said.

"Aye so, but no' wrapped in a shroud. His father is a powerful chief back in Erin. D'ye want him and a force o' men here wi' an axe to grind?"

"Nay." Toren remained sullen. "But we will no' lose our lands to him."

"Get out o' my sight," Kendrick said in disgust. "Let me try to put this right."

His sons left with alacrity. Kendrick went back inside, but Bradana stood for a moment, drinking in the cool air.

Adair would live. Precisely why that mattered so much to her, she could not tell. But it did, och aye, it did.

CHAPTER TWELVE

ADAIR'S CHEST HURT every time he drew a deep breath. The healer, a brusque old man with anything but a kindly touch, informed him his ribs were likely bruised or broken. He had a battered head, a lacerated eye, and bruises down low on his back, of a worrying nature.

"Do not be surprised," the healer said, "if ye see blood when ye pass water."

A cheerful thought that did nothing to raise Adair's spirits. Most of what he felt was anger, mingled with a goodly helping of frustration. He'd given as good as he got, but there had been three of them—Kendrick's two sons and a stranger—and he hadn't been able to finish it.

Now his hosts had stowed him in his quarters, brought him food and drink, and abandoned him to recover alone. Flynn had sat with him for a time and brought up the subject of returning to Erin. Clearly his dearest wish.

"When ye're able to travel, I mean."

Adair could travel now if he wanted to. Not that it would make for a pleasant journey, but a man who was determined enough could accomplish most anything.

If only it did not hurt quite so much to breathe. He'd never realized till now just how frequently one was required to draw breath.

He wanted to take Kerr and Toren apart with his hands—one at a time, preferably, in a fair fight. He remembered their faces, gleeful and snarling, and the other man, a big brute who had mostly held him while the others used their fists. And feet.

He shifted uncomfortably on his bed. The door curtain had been tied back and the sun came streaming in, the day having cleared and turned fine.

It would kill him lying here this way.

A shadow stirred in the doorway and his heart leaped. Would *she* come?

He'd seen the look in her eyes, there in the hall last night. He'd felt her emotions.

Surely she would come.

But it was a gray form that slipped in through the door.

"Wen."

He peered behind the hound, expecting the beast's mistress, but Wen had come alone.

"Kind o' ye," he told the animal as it lay down beside him. He reached out to stroke the gray fur and got a good look at his hands. Knuckles and nails torn.

Once the healer had finished work with him, Kendrick had approached and asked him outright, "Was it my sons who did this to ye?"

But he knew. The look in his eyes, half ashamed and half abashed, said he already knew.

Given that fact, Adair had replied only, "'Tis a harsh kind o' hospitality, is it not, Uncle?"

Now they quite possibly meant to ignore him. Pretend, perhaps, that he did not exist. Kendrick would likely hand out some nominal punishment to his sons. No more than that because, in truth, they all wanted him gone.

Even Mistress Bradana?

He did not know what it was she felt for him any more than he understood what he felt for her. Just that it was powerful, far more so than it should be. They were strangers. Only, inexplicably, they were not.

And aye, she was bonny. She did not play at games of flirtation like many of the lasses back home. What drew him to her was far subtler than that. And though she had lovely hair and beautiful eyes—and, by the gods, beautiful breasts—it went far beyond all that.

Back home, it being something of a closed society, they courted as they danced, changing partners with naught serious behind it. He had never been in love, not even with the lovely Forba.

This, that he felt, now was not love. Too quick, and too instinctive.

It was need, rather than love.

That thought startled him so, he blinked at the hound, who edged closer and laid his chin on Adair's bed. Adair ran his hand over the rough gray head and down the beast's neck.

"Tell me about your mistress," he bade, wishing the animal could.

Wen edged still closer, looking at Adair with canny hazel eyes. Any nearer and they'd both be in the bed.

"Is she patient? Valiant? Loving? She loves ye, that is certain. Is she clever and wily and—"

"Why d'ye no' ask her for yoursel'?"

The query came soft from the open doorway. Bradana stepped in, her back to the light so Adair could not see her expression. But his heart leaped and the feelings came streaming in, victorious gladness and a grateful relief he did not want to show.

"I should ha' known if Wen were here, ye could no' be far behind."

"I ha' been looking for him. Ye ha' stolen the heart o' my hound, so it seems."

"I am certain he loves no one more than ye. He has merely taken pity on me in my loneliness."

"Are ye lonely, then?" She stepped in farther. "I supposed, as must everyone else, ye would wish to sleep."

"I would, if I could."

"Is the pain too great? Allow me to send for the healer, who will mix ye a draught."

"Nay. I do no' wish him back."

What he did wish was for her to sit beside him like her hound. And then the wish came true as she approached the bed and sat down, folding her legs beneath her skirt gracefully.

Reaching out to touch Wen, she said, "I must apologize for my stepbrothers."

He raised an eyebrow at her. "Why must ye?"

"Because they will no' apologize for themselves. They are fools. Did they think they could get away wi' such a deed? That ye would no' fight back and mark them?"

"I do no' suppose they cared in the heat o' the moment."

She gazed at him steadily, and he could feel the emotions rushing through her as if they were his own. "They want ye gone. For yer own safety, it might be best for ye to give them what they want."

"Well, I might do. I could sail home having failed in the task my father set, even as my two brothers did. But now, I am angry."

"Ah."

"I ha' a right to be here, do I not? A right of blood, even if the debt Kendrick owes my father is disregarded. Should I let his sons chase me away? Besides—" He broke off.

"Besides?"

He hesitated before finishing softly, "You are here."

That made her look away from him for the first time. She turned her eyes down to her hands, which lay in her lap.

"I will no' be for long. Soon enough I will wed and move awa'. Better, perhaps—" Now it was she who hesitated.

"Better?"

"If the break be made clean now."

"I see." That was what she chose, was it? A merciful parting, a distance of sea between them forevermore.

"But what of this?"

He reached out and took her hand. For an instant it fluttered in his grasp like a wild bird. Then the feelings came rushing in—those feelings he could only begin to define. Warmth. Belonging. A sense of rightness so strong, it overmastered every other consideration.

Her fingers eased in his. The terror fled her, replaced by something else that fairly screamed aloud.

"But," she whispered, "it is hopeless."

"Is it? Look at me, Bradana. Look at me."

She raised her eyes. Gazed at him in wonder.

"Bradana, there must be a way."

"A way?"

"For us to be together."

She caught her breath. "It is madness. I do not know ye. Ye do not know me. How—"

"I do not understand it either. But if I stay here, even though it means another beating, or half a score more, I can remain near ye."

"For a time, perhaps."

"A time is better than naught at all." He gazed down at their hands—hers smooth and unmarked lying in his, scraped and torn. He whispered, "Stay wi' me."

"I cannot. I should not."

"Would ye toss a glorious gift back into the face o' the gods?"

"'Tis a cruel gift. An unwelcome one."

"Do no' say that. Bradana—"

She made to rise. "I maun go."

He held her there with the strength of his grip. "Nay."

"Adair, do no' do this to me, I beg."

"I do naught. Naught more than ye do to me." But he let go of her hand.

She sprang to her feet, then turned and faced him. "I canna stay. Ye maun see that. 'Tis impossible. Wen, come."

The hound did not stir from his place beside Adair.

"Wen! Please."

The hound tipped up his head and looked at her but refused to move.

"Och!" She gave a choked cry and hurried out, the last Adair saw of her a mere flicker of shadow against the sunlight.

CHAPTER THIRTEEN

BRADANA WALKED FAR up the shore past the rocks where she'd sat before with Adair, and onward. Her favored walk, this was, when she felt trapped or angry or aggravated with those around her. Now her emotions carried her like a storm, and she tried in vain to sort through them.

It seemed strange not having Wen at her side. He was her shadow and near-constant companion. But he had abandoned her for Adair.

Why?

She'd raised the hound from a pup. He preferred no one to her, ever.

She did not feel hurt by his defection so much as bewildered. *All* of this bewildered her.

Aye, Adair MacMurtray possessed a rare brand of charm. It lay in his courteous manner. In his smile. In the amusement that so often sparked in his eyes.

It should not affect a hound.

Best for him to go, she determined before she'd walked a hundred paces. Though she could not agree with Kerr and Toren's methods, their instincts were true. Kendrick should load Adair, injured as he was, onto his boat. Bid his men sail away with him.

Let them all return to their ordinary lives, what had been before—before whatever he was to her had occurred.

She did not care whether Adair's father ever got what he was owed. Did not care if Adair returned to disgrace for having failed in his mission. She needed these outlandish and incomprehensible feelings gone, and if he went, he just might take them with him.

Or he might not.

She stopped walking abruptly and looked around herself. A wild place indeed, she had reached. As wild as her emotions.

Her mother often told her to master her passions. *Get hold o' them, lass, for they will betray ye in the end.*

Did Mam regret having wed with Kendrick? They argued a terrible lot, but aye, the quarrels invariably ended in passion. Bradana had learned young that when the curtain of their sleeping place was tied shut and certain sounds came from within, she had best keep away.

Mam's relationship with Kendrick was not an easy one. Could Bradana go to her for advice? Nay, for she could not explain in any sane fashion what she felt for the man from Erin.

Besides, Mam had said, "'Tis best perhaps, Bradana, that ye go to wed a man wi' whom ye ha' no emotional ties as yet. Feelings may grow between ye, which will be easier than investing the whole o' your heart."

Bradana sat down on the trunk of a tree that had washed ashore and faced the sea. The vast, seething and restless sea that reminded her all too much of what she felt inside.

Was it really better to go and live her life with a man she did not and might never love? To keep her heart clasped tight?

What if it was too late? What if she'd already lost her heart?

Absurd. She did not know Adair MacMurtray. She did not believe in love at first sight. That was attraction. Lust. And aye, she might well feel that for Adair, but…it took a rear position to the rest of it.

Bitterness touched her. She did not need this agony. Had she not enough to dead with? The oft-times stressful situations here at home. The fact that she must soon wed and leave all she knew behind.

Everything but Wen. She would not go without Wen.

At that thought, she felt a powerful pull. She wanted to get to her feet. To hurry back as swiftly as she could.

To the hound?

Or to the man he guarded?

Why had she not realized Wen had assigned himself to guard Adair? When no one else would. Because a knife in the dark could end it all quite swiftly.

End everything, save what she felt inside.

In a rush, she went back down the shore. The sea spoke to her as she went, hissed and gurgled and chuckled around the stones.

Two pebbles. The two of them together for only a short while.

Gods, let him be safe when she reached him.

ADAIR DOZED FOR a time, the hound's great head in his lap. But the pain in his chest roused him again and again. Eventually he had to get up and use the pot behind the curtain in the corner. He thought of venturing out to empty it, but hoped Nolan or Flynn might turn up to inquire how he was, and take up the task.

No one came near him. Not his men nor any of Kendrick's household. Not till the afternoon had dragged on did Nolan come to check on him, bringing a measure of what Adair suspected was his own food ration, and taking the pot away with him.

Some time later yet, Bradana slipped in. She came like the afternoon shadows that stirred beyond the door. Adair's only notice was the sweep of the great hound's tail on the floor just before she appeared.

The sight of her brought relief. He hadn't been sure she would return to him.

She spoke, however, to the hound. "Ye may go now. I am here."

Wen went out—no doubt to relieve himself and find something to eat.

"He's been guarding me?" Not till then did Adair realize it.

"Aye."

"Ye think they will try to finish me, then?"

"I do not know. Ye ha' yer knife?"

"To be sure." A man always had a knife. But it would not help much against attack by a man wielding a sword. Or if they came while he slept.

Bradana sat down beside his cot where Wen had been. "D'ye feel any better?"

"Aye." Only a half-lie. He felt much better now that she had returned.

"Can I get somewhat for ye? Food or drink? Another bolster—"

"Mayhap by and by. Just… For now, just stay wi' me."

She did, her hands folded in her lap and her eyes resting on him. Her eyes were perhaps her greatest beauty, large and fringed by brown lashes. If one did not count that glorious hair. Or those lovely breasts.

No matter what she looked like, he had a powerful attraction to her, now alive in the chamber.

"There is somewhat I must say," she told him. "I feel, in duty—indeed, in decency—bound to do so. For your own good and for the sake o' your safety. Adair MacMurtray, go home."

His heart fell. Even though returning to Erin was the greatest wish of his heart—almost.

Steadily he asked her, "Is that what ye wish, Bradana? To see me away?"

Her clasped fingers tightened till they turned white. "Better to ask me what I do no' want. I do no' want to see ye beaten so, and I do no' want to see ye lying dead."

He looked her in the eye. "Ye think they will go so far as to commit murder?"

"I think my stepbrothers are sometimes very wrong in the

head. They might well think they can solve a problem by stabbing ye in the back and tossing ye in the sea."

When Adair did not reply to that, she went on, "The visitations from your twa brothers caused much consternation. Those here were happy to be rid of them. Only for ye to arrive."

"They are out o' patience."

"I fear so."

"And"—his lips twisted in a wry smile—"should I then take a failure back to my father? He already thinks me good for little more than telling amusing stories and singing songs."

"Better he should receive a failure than a corpse."

A longer silence fell between them. Adair pulled at the rug that covered his knees. Bradana sat quietly, though her clenched fingers did not relax. Outside the open doorway, a whisper of wind stirred. Evening came on, breathing the coming dark.

Adair lay and fought his impulses. So strong were they that even though he knew better, he could not keep from speaking.

"And, Mistress Bradana, what about ye and me?"

Slowly she lifted her eyes to him. "There is no ye and me."

"There should no' be, perhaps. Yet there is."

Quite clearly, he heard the breath catch in her throat. "There is no ye and me," she repeated. "Have I no' told ye there canna be?"

"Ye have told me, aye. Ye are set to wed a northern chief, to leave here and go to live with him. Despite that, I find that somewhat does exist between us."

"It cannot."

"I understand that. Yet can ye deny it does? Bradana, 'tis as if somewhat"—he struggled almost violently for the words—"somewhat existed between us even before we met."

She could have denied it, or tried to. Could have used the word *ridiculous*, or called it fanciful. Naught more than imagination embellishing attraction. Instead, she said nothing.

"If I go home," he said unsteadily, "and you wed to fulfill this alliance, we would quite likely never see one another again."

Still she did not speak. Her whole body had now tensed.

"Is that what ye want?"

"Nay." The word came as if torn from her. "Nor do I wish to see ye lose your life."

"Some things, Bradana…some things are worth the risk."

Her eyes widened, her lips parted, and a flush rose to her cheeks. "Ye would court death, for me?"

"For this thing I feel between us, aye, I would."

"Adair." She barely breathed his name. Much as the hound had done earlier, she shuffled closer till she reached the side of his bed. Reaching out, she captured his hands. "'Tis a powerful foolishness, that."

"It is a powerful feeling."

Slowly, he lifted her hands one by one and planted a kiss in each palm. Gently, he drew her to him, tenderly planted a kiss at each corner of her mouth, upon each cheek, and at the center of her forehead.

She melted. It took but an instant for her to ease down against him, to slide her hands up his chest and around his neck. Carefully, so as not to hurt him, she held him tight.

He felt no pain, likely because the other feelings came flooding so strong and bright. Not just desire, though aye, he felt a rush of that. But warmth also, and rightness. Belonging so deep that it eclipsed them all.

His lips hovered over hers. Aching to meet.

Madness, because the door of the chamber stood wide and anyone could look in. And he should not be found kissing his host's daughter, step or otherwise. The consequences would be dire indeed. This kiss, ache for it as he might, could happen only in his imagination.

No impossibility, that, for he knew how she would taste…familiar. For they had done this before, though certainly they had not. A thousand images flickered through his mind—firelight and a tiny sleeping place, blue eyes embracing him with steady devotion. A young woman who both was and was not

Bradana standing with a sword in her hands. A washing place out in the sun.

Bradana sighed into his mouth, and he took her breath, made it part of him, even though their lips did not actually meet. One person they should be, out of two. One life.

"By the gods, by the gods, by the gods," she whispered as she pressed her forehead to his. Or mayhap it was he who said those words. Who could tell?

"Bradana, my beautiful lass." He cradled her face and gazed into her eyes. They brimmed with tears.

"Do no' leave me," she begged. "Do no' ever leave me."

Were they her words or those of another? No matter, for they lay rooted in his heart.

"Bradana, darling, I will not."

⬥

CHAPTER FOURTEEN

ONCE MORE, BRADANA ranged far up the shore, this time early in the morning. She had remained with Adair all the night long, speaking little, feeling much. She had gone out to bring him food and drink, then watched him while he ate. They played at draughts to pass the time.

She had avoided touching him again, because touching him was too powerful. Too wondrous and devastating and—

Well, she had no fit words for any of it.

When Wen returned at dawn, she left the hound to once more stand guard while she escaped, an effort to discipline her emotions.

It took her only a short distance up the shore to discover these feelings could not be mastered.

Och, what had she done? Begged him to stay with her. The very opposite of what she'd intended when first she went in there.

A milky morning it was, the sky all white and the sea pale blue, dead calm. She stood staring out at the ocean and blinking furiously. Very seldom did she weep. A strong woman did not indulge in such weakness. Yet now tears burned her eyes.

Hopeless, it was. Even if he stayed—*especially* if he stayed. Her betrothed, Earrach, was due to arrive within the fortnight. Better, far better if her parting with Adair came ahead of that.

Yet she'd begged him to stay.

They had not kissed lips to lips, even though she ached for it.

In truth, she'd been afraid to kiss him. The feelings and the impulses incurred in kissing him might be too powerful to endure. She'd wanted to, aye—och, she *wanted*. She wanted more than kisses. To be one with him, a part of him. To belong to him, soul to soul.

Mayhap she already did.

That thought startled her. It terrified her. But aye, mayhap 'twas what all of this meant. She had belonged to Adair Mac-Murtray before she met him.

Impossible. A child's tale. She did not believe in such nonsense.

Then what was this she felt?

She made her way back up the shingle and to the great dun, wherein she found her mother and stepfather at breakfast.

"Good morn," Kendrick told her affably. "Will ye join us to break your fast?"

"Nay, thank ye. I do no' want to eat. Indeed, Kendrick, I would ask a word wi' ye." She glanced at her mother. "Alone."

Mam glared at her, affronted. "Wha' is there ye canna say before me?"

Aye, Mam proved disagreeable these days, carrying the bulk of her child.

"Never mind," she snapped before Bradana could answer. "I may well be banished from my own hearthside. Genna," she called to the servant, "ye had better come too. They no doubt wish to discuss matters o' state."

When the two women had gone, Kendrick rolled his eyes at Bradana. "Pray, sit down. If ye can tell me how to handle your mother these days, I would be well pleased."

"I doubt there is a way." Mam could be prickly at the best of times. "It's about Adair MacMurtray I wish to speak."

That did make him look surprised. "Wha' is he to ye, that ye should so concern yoursel' wi' him?"

A good question. Bradana could not admit the truth. She did not even comprehend the truth.

She sat down. "Ye maun keep him alive, at least until ye can persuade him to get on that boat o' his and sail awa'. If Kerr and Toren tak' things a step farther, ye may have a blood feud on your hands."

Kendrick eyed her far more sharply. "Ye ken fine what Kerr and Toren are. One worse than the other, and they urge one another on. Nay, I do no' want a blood feud wi' relations in Erin. By the same token, it might be argued Gawen was foolish to send the lad here after the first two returned to him empty-handed."

"Perhaps he believed Adair more persuasive."

"He's likeable enough, I'll give him that. Even I like him, though he's a right pain in my arse. I do no' want to see the lad killed."

"Then harness your sons."

This time he narrowed his eyes at her, a far less pleasant expression. She had lived here in his dun from a wee lass. In truth, he had been a father to her, providing as generously as for his own sons. He considered her his daughter—only witness the marriage alliance he'd made with Mican MacGillean.

They shared familiarity, maybe even a measure of affection. She had never before attempted to tell him what to do.

Before he could kindle in anger, she went on, "They will listen to ye, if ye put your foot down. Ye may no' think so, but they will. Right now, they think they ha' your tacit approval to get rid of their cousin."

"Nay, Bradana, they want rid o' him because his father threatens to strip awa' lands that will one day be their own. Lands that they ha' helped me to hold. In truth, who can blame them?"

"So ye are fine wi' one o' them planting a *sgian-dubh* in Adair's back and ending his life?"

Kendrick sighed. "Nay. But the lad and his father should ha' known he entered a perilous situation. Verra well. Since ye ask it, I will speak wi' the lad."

"With Adair? No' with Kerr and Toren?"

"I will speak wi' all o' them. Now awa' wi' ye and let me

enjoy my breakfast." He waved his hand. "And by the gods, if the child your mother carries be anything like the three o' ye, 'twill be a sore trial."

She went off as ordered, not particular happy about the encounter. She collected breakfast for herself, her hound, and Adair, and hurried to his quarters—only to find him up and on his feet.

"What are ye about?" she asked sharply.

He turned and gave her a look. But half clad he was, as she'd caught him changing to a clean tunic. All the bruises on display could not disguise so fine a body—lithe and sculpted with broad shoulders, the chest smattered with fine brown hair. His gray-green eyes gleamed at her, holding an expression she understood all too well, and she went a bit weak in the knees.

"I could not lie here." He tossed his head so the mane of brown hair slapped his back. "I thought I would go mad."

"Aye, so. Here, let me help wi' that."

She laid aside the food she'd brought and stepped up to him. Struggling into the clothing with a set of battered ribs had to be agony.

The fine hair felt soft when it brushed her fingers, the skin beneath warm and supple. Aye indeed, he was a beautiful man.

Standing so close to him made her feel very odd indeed. He was tall enough that his chin was level with her nose. A perfect height for kissing.

How was it that being in his presence made her feel mad and wild and sane all at once? As if her world, slightly amiss all her life long, suddenly came right.

To distract herself, she smoothed the tunic down carefully. Avoided gazing into his eyes. "How d'ye feel this morning?"

"Better. I ventured out to the midden."

"Did ye!"

"Lying in that bed—with or without the company o' Wen— makes me far too vulnerable."

"Sit wi' me and eat. I have brought enough for all three o' us."

They shared the food companionably. Sitting there with him, Bradana had to admit their relationship had changed.

A woman could not beg a man to stay with her, lest it meant something.

"I spoke wi' Kendrick this morning," she told him. "He canna say he can keep those two sons o' his from attacking ye again. And I do no' believe he will ever part wi' a portion o' his lands."

"I ha' been thinking about that." His gaze met hers again. "Ye ha' asked me no' to leave ye."

She had. *She had.* Whatever that might mean.

"And yet"—his gaze clung to hers—"empty-handed or no', I will eventually ha' to take an answer home to my father."

True, she thought.

"Why do ye no' come with me, Bradana?"

She stared. "With ye?"

"Aye, to Erin."

"Och, nay."

"Why not? Ye would be welcome there, ye and Wen both. I ha' lived somewhat o' a feckless life, 'tis true, but I would put all that aside. Take myself in hand. Train hard for a place at the head o' my father's men. I will no' inherit the land. That does no' mean I could not make a good enough war chief."

Bradana's thoughts blurred. She might be with him so. In a foreign place.

"Ye would ask me to leave Alba? I could no'. 'Tis part o' me, deep inside, born and bred, just as I imagine Erin is a part o' ye."

Slowly, he nodded. "'Tis the land I love. A land I would hate to lose. Yet..."

Yet she could not ask him to stay with her, to give up all for her, and remain unwilling to do the same for him. Did it matter which of them sacrificed for the other? Who gave up what, for the sake of...

Love.

Did she love this man? Or did she, on some heretofore unperceived level, merely need him? That, she had yet to determine.

"Let us, Adair, not make any rash decisions just yet. Both of us have heavy obligations we are sworn to fulfill. Let us spend these days together, as we may."

He smiled at her. He did not mention it, that her begging him to stay with her had been a rash and mayhap unfair action. He merely reached out and brushed her hand with his battered fingers.

"Aye then, Bradana. I have no quarrel over spending my time with ye."

CHAPTER FIFTEEN

DAYS PASSED AND Adair healed. Everyone left him alone, save Bradana and Wen. Despite what Kendrick had told Bradana, he did not make an effort to talk with Adair. Whether or not he did speak with his two wild-headed sons, Bradana could not tell him.

Bradana. She filled his days and haunted his nights. He did dream of her, lying alone in his narrow bed—of kisses they'd not yet shared. Of other pleasures as yet untasted. How could he know how it felt to kiss her, when he never had?

It was as if he'd lain with her already, even though he had not. His body knew the heat of hers, the willingness with which she would come to him. It had him in a state of near-constant arousal.

But he did not touch her and she did not touch him, save for the merest brush of hands when they passed one another a cup or played at draughts. In truth, Adair felt afraid to touch her, the response was so bright.

He only guessed she felt the same.

They grew acquainted with one another on a far more ordinary basis during those days. He learned what made her laugh, how swift and clever was her mind, and how well she guarded her emotions with everyone but him. They sat long together and, as he healed, walked far up the shore. She showed him her Alba, the land she loved.

She played the harp for him.

The first time she brought the instrument to his sleeping place, he thought it looked odd in her hands, a harp being so often a man's instrument. Save for Forba, back home, he had never known another woman to touch one.

That was before she began to play.

She possessed a rare talent, did Bradana, one that transported him. From the first gleaming notes, she lifted his heart and his spirit. As if the music gave him wings that carried him to another place and time, he traveled.

"I did not know ye played," he whispered after that first time, unwilling to break the spell she had woven. "In Erin—"

"In Erin?" She lifted a brow.

"I was learning to play because I so loved the sound."

She put the harp aside. "Is that not an odd thing for us to have in common?"

"I do not play a touch as well as ye. 'Tis magic when ye touch these strings."

"I play Alba," she confessed. "The hiss and chuckle of the water. The wind in the forest. The very heartbeat o' the land."

"It has a heartbeat?"

"Och, aye."

How could he thus ask her to leave here with him? Become an exile from her beloved land for his sake? Even though it had become the dearest wish of his heart.

"I began playing many years ago because my mother fancied it. 'Tis one o' the few things to please her when she is in a foul temper."

"I can see why. 'Twould please me to lie here so wi' my eyes closed and listen for as long as ye will play."

"For ye, Adair, I would play as long as ye wished—till my fingers bled."

He opened his eyes and looked at her.

Before the feelings could grow too intense, she asked far more lightly, "Who was teaching ye to play, back in Erin?"

"A lass called Forba."

"Och, aye?" Bradana crooked a brow. "And should I be concerned about this Forba? What is she to ye?" She lowered her voice. "Ye said ye had no lover."

"I did not." Though indeed, Forba might have wished to become that. "I was seeing her, but there was naught in it."

"Good thing I am no' a jealous woman." She reconsidered that. "I never *was* a jealous woman."

"Ye ha' no reason, Bradana. None at all."

Serious now, all the teasing flown, their eyes met. She caught her breath. "Well enough."

"Make a song for me," he challenged her in another effort to keep things light. "A planxty. 'Tis what the best of the shanachies do."

"I am no' a shanachie."

"Ye play as well as any I've heard. And the songs ye make…" He had no words for them.

She gave him a long look. "I will have to give that some thought. I am no' at all convinced I could express my gratitude for ye, or that mere music could capture all ye are to me."

"Your music might. So, what am I to ye, then?" He should not ask. That was dangerous ground.

"Och—quick and bright. Witty and charming. With the soft green o' the hills at the heart. 'Tis in your eyes, that green."

He sobered instantly. "To be fair, I am no' sure I could capture all ye are either, in words or song. What ye are to me."

"Well then. Give me some time and I will work at it."

But they had not much time. The days passed swiftly. One morning Bradana came to him and said, "I will ha' to absent mysel' from ye this afternoon."

"Why?" He lived for each moment she spent with him.

"My mother insists upon it." She avoided his gaze. "Earrach arrives in two days' time."

Earrach. The man she was to wed.

"Mother wishes to fuss over me," Bradana hurried on before Adair, appalled, could speak. "She has had her women making me not only one but twa fine new gowns. She mentioned something about my hair—"

"I love your hair." He should not say so, which was evidenced by the expression in Bradana's eyes when she looked at him. "'Tis perfect already."

"Ah, but she insists I must look just so when my bridegroom arrives. She insists a man treats a woman better when he finds her beautiful. All her life, she has traded in beauty, ye see. And she wants for Earrach to treat me well."

Dismay and anger hit Adair in a furious blow. He did not want Earrach anywhere near Bradana. Not for any reason.

"Bradana." He caught her hand, forgetting all his intentions to keep from persuading her. "Leave here with me. We can sail tonight."

That made her gaze at him long. Did she consider it?

"Ye cannot go off to live with Earrach." He squeezed her fingers. "Ye cannot."

"I know," she whispered. "But ye can imagine the breech it would cause if I break wi' this agreement."

"I understand." She was a strong, intelligent woman and he must let her make her own choice. Without the pressure of what he felt for her.

What *did* he feel for her?

He pondered that later when she was off preparing for her marriage. She'd left him the hound, and the two of them wended their way up the shore whence he had walked so often with Bradana. And he comprehended just what this place meant to her, for he could almost feel her there with him, sense her heartbeat in the thump of the waves and her voice in the cries of the gulls.

Could he ask her to give up what she was and go away with him? Could he forsake in turn the land of his birth, where he ached to return?

It did not matter, because Earrach was coming. Earrach, who would claim what should belong only to Adair.

What already did belong to him.

He would not leave her. Not till she dismissed him and sent him off. Given the pressures of all that rested on her, that day might well come.

MAM DID NOT feel well. Bradana could see that much as soon as she entered the hall, where the two of them were alone, save for Mam's woman, Genna. Though she bustled around the place, Mam's movements were not brisk. She looked pale, and new lines had appeared around her mouth and eyes.

"Mam?"

"There ye are. I have sent Kendrick off about his business and barred him from coming back a while, that we may ha' some peace."

"Aye, but—" Bradana exchanged looks with the serving woman, who shook her head. "Mayhap we should do this another day."

"There is no' another day." Mam tossed her hands in the air. "Mican and his son will be here in two days' time."

"Still and all. Pray, sit down. D'ye need somewhat to drink?"

"I canna take anything on my stomach, be it food or drink."

"Ye ha' not eaten this day?"

Mother shook her head and sat, easing down the bulk of her child. "I ha' no' slept. I keep having these random pains."

Bradana stared in dismay. "But ye are no' due yet."

"Nay, but I am thinking I miscalculated. Look at the size o' this babe."

"Aye, so." Bradana sank down beside the place her mother had settled. "Mayhap ye should rest now." Her mother and she did not always get along easily and often enough butted heads. She did not know whether they were too much alike, or their ideas were too different. But Bradana did not want to lose this woman, one of the few people who had been present all her life.

"This wedding is mistimed. Can we no' put it off till after the birth o' the child?"

Mother's eyes widened. "Nay, 'tis too long to wait. Listen to me. Ye ha' not had much congress wi' men. One thing ye must learn is, they want what they want, when they want it. They are happy when they get what they want, when they want it, and 'tis often gey important to keep a man happy."

Bradana experienced an inner stab of rebellion. "Wha' if what my husband wants is no' what I want?"

Mother made a face. "Often it is so. A woman has her duty."

"Mother, I will sell my soul and my will to no man." Though Bradana would gift her soul freely. Indeed, she might well already have done. A terrifying thought, for how could a woman live without her soul?

"Listen to me," Mother said again, gripping Bradana's hand hard. "A man who's displeased is difficult to live with. He can raise his hand to ye and use other cruelties to make your life a misery."

"Mother, if ye think Earrach is such a man, why d'ye countenance this marriage?"

"Your father was such a man." Their eyes met. "I was sent young to him, in marriage. My father, who loved me dearly, did not suspect what lay behind his smile, and I did not know wha' to expect. I would no' have ye endure the same. I learned late that my beauty alone spared me some o' his wrath."

Bradana stared, stricken. She did not remember more than vague impressions of her father, and Mam but rarely spoke of him.

She whispered, "He raised his hand to ye?"

"He could be a violent man. Mostly he did not direct that violence toward me. As I say, I made mysel' pleasing. But there were quarrels every time I tried to stand up for mysel'. I told ye he died in battle? 'Twas a quarrel wi' a neighboring chief that took him."

"I am sorry ye had to endure that."

"I did no' love him. And I learned much from the union. That is why when Kendrick came along—well, I fell for him hard. I was a widow and could choose. I made certain that in my second marriage, I had a voice. But it has no' been an easy match either. Though he has been good to ye."

"He has treated me like his own."

"Now he and I quarrel as I never dared quarrel wi' your father. I learned to speak up for myself. So perhaps the way things are now is my fault."

"I think your experience taught ye that ye need to stand for yoursel'. And so do I."

"Aye." Mother touched Bradana's face. "But be careful. I would no' wish to see ye hurt or harmed."

Before Bradana could frame a reply, or say that being sent away into this marriage would harm her terribly, Mother rushed on.

"Speaking o' which—I could no' help but mark ye have been spending much time wi' yer cousin from Erin."

Bradana's whole body came on alert. "Adair? He is no' my blood cousin. And I merely keep him company some afternoons while he is healing. Keeping him occupied until he can be sent on his way. His treatment at the hands o' this family has been shameful."

Once more, Mother's gaze met hers. "Are ye certain that is all? He is a very good-looking young man wi' a lot o' charm and a ready tongue. Do no', daughter, let his charm beguile ye. He will soon be gone, and ye ha' far more important things to occupy yer mind."

A flush rose through Bradana's body, one she hoped her mother did not see. "Do I seem the sort o' woman who might be beguiled by any man?"

"No' in the ordinary way, no. But as I say, Adair MacMurtray is remarkably attractive."

He was the sunlight of her world. Though she could scarcely say so.

Whereas Earrach—aye, he was dark and brooding and looked always displeased. To be sure, she did not know the man, and one could not judge merely by appearances. And yet…

"Be careful wi' your heart," Mother whispered. "Sometimes 'tis a woman's only possession. Now, try on your dresses and let us decide how best to arrange your hair for your wedding."

CHAPTER SIXTEEN

M ICAN MACGILLEAN AND his party duly arrived two days later with a certain amount of fanfare, despite the fact that it was raining. Bradana tried not to take the weather as a bad omen. She had worries and distractions enough already.

They had advance notice from their outlooks that the party approached, and despite the downpour, she, Kendrick, and Mam were standing outside when the MacGilleans arrived. The group was not a large one, just Chief Mican himself with Earrach, another, older man who looked like an advisor, and a company of three guards.

They dismounted swiftly in front of the hall, where Kendrick had lads waiting to take the weary ponies away.

Bradana could not help but look at once to Earrach. The man she was to wed. When they had met before, she had managed to dismiss that eventuality from her mind. At least, she'd told herself it did not yet threaten her. Now it had crept up on her, full force.

Much as she remembered him did he appear. He was perhaps of an age with Adair, but a bit taller and more broadly made, with heavy shoulders and a build that argued a large allowance of muscle. His dark hair, nearly black, lay upon the shoulders of his fine cloak in a wild mane. His heavy brows made him appear to be always scowling.

He turned his dark gaze to her also, almost at once. Eyes black as the wing of a raven made a swift inspection. Did he approve of what he saw? Was Mother right, and such approval might ease her way with him?

"Mican, my friend!" Kendrick exclaimed. "We are honored to ha' ye here. Come in out o' the rain."

They went together with Mam in the lead—Kendrick, Mican, and the older man. Earrach hung back so he could follow Bradana, and she could feel his gaze at her back.

"Welcome to our home," said Mam, once they entered the hall.

"Mistress MacCaigh." Mican gave her a bow before turning to Kendrick. "Aye, man, and I see ye ha' been keeping busy. Like mother, like daughter, eh, Earrach?" He turned to his son. "Ye will soon ha' the daughter in a like state."

An icy silence fell.

"Forgive my ready words," Mican said to Mam, not to Bradana. "We are a rough and ready lot up north. We maun be. Do we no' hold the northern gate against the savages?"

Savages. Bradana was being sent to live among those who called their neighbors savages.

"Will ye no sit down?" Mother invited him sweetly. "Warm yourselves. Bradana, please serve the heather ale."

Bradana shed her cloak and hurried to serve. She wore one of her new gowns, soft green—a color that reminded her of Adair's eyes.

But she could not let herself think of him. Could not compare anyone else to him.

"Aye, well. Thank ye." Mican gave Bradana a frank look as she bent to pour his drink. He had the same dark eyes as his son and a broad, heavy face.

"She is a beauty, Earrach, and no mistake. Cursed if I would no' take her mysel', if it were not yer place ahead o' me. I am a widower, ye ken," he said to Bradana's bosom.

Mother and Bradana both stared at him in affront.

Kendrick, with a quick glance at Bradana, cleared his throat. "I scarcely think that appropriate talk, Mican. Our agreement concerns the young folks. My daughter—"

"Aye, aye, the agreement stands. Can an old man no' admire a bonny woman?"

"Well, so." Kendrick did not look happy. But the rules of hospitality forbade him offering a guest—even one who commented in such a frank manner—anything but welcome.

Bradana bent close to Earrach in order to pour his drink. He too looked at her boldly, an openly assessing stare. "A bit more ale, woman," he said. "Fill it up."

Ah, well, it was to be that way, was it? He thought he would give the orders and she would meekly obey. He would soon discover she was not the woman to be treated thus.

Bad enough to lose her home—to lose Adair. She would be cursed if she lost herself also.

Yet as the meeting continued, her distress only grew. She remained silent, refilled the ale cups, and helped Genna distribute food and other comforts. She sat and listened to the things the men discussed—the state of their holdings and the situation with the Caledonian tribes in the north. Fighting there. How firm a grip Dalriada had here in Alba.

Once, she had believed—aye, if in a distant sort of way—that she could do this. Wed this man, make the sacrifice for the sake of home and family, and live with Kendrick's agreement. She would have preferred not to marry at all. But she had been raised to accept that it was what a woman did.

All that, though, had been before Adair MacMurtray.

How could she marry Earrach when she loved someone else?

Sitting there with folded hands, playing at obedience, following the conversation that expanded to include her two stepbrothers when they came in, she acknowledged it in full for the first time.

She was in love with Adair.

The truth of it made her go hot and cold in turns. She became a mere shadow of herself, rushing to serve food and drink, responding when someone spoke directly to her, all with her heart somewhere else.

In Adair's keeping.

How could she do this thing? How could she go away to live somewhere without her heart?

"Our Bradana is quite talented," she heard Mother say suddenly.

"Aye, so," Kendrick agreed. "She rides a pony as well as a lad."

"She knows this land better than we do," Toren put in.

"She will put a knife in your back if ye are no' careful," Kerr told Earrach.

Mother glared at him. "She plays the harp most beautifully. Bradana, go and get your harp, and play for our guests."

Bradana froze. She played, aye, often at gatherings. Of late, it had become an intimate thing, one she did only for Adair.

She recalled the expression on his face, one of almost pained bliss, as he listened to her play, eyes closed, captured in spirit as her fingers wove magic upon the strings.

"Go," Mother told her gently, with desperation in her eyes.

Bradana left the hall for her own quarters, where she'd left her harp. In the corridor she leaned against the wall, feeling every bit of her strength drain away. She could hear the rain crashing down outside, could hear voices from beyond. She could feel Adair in his own quarters. How was it she could *feel* him?

She fetched the harp, brought it back to the hall, and sat with it on her knee. At least this gave her leave to sit a little apart, as a harper tended to do. But her fingers felt wooden, too stiff to play. Indeed, the first few notes came clumsy. And her heart... When the music came, it filled to bursting.

She might be here in this chamber with strangers, but she played for Adair still. Every note destined for him.

No one paid her much heed. She became part of the background, like the ale and the rain. Kerr began to bait Earrach about something—how many ponies his father owned or some such. The conversation heated.

"Come, come," Kendrick said at last, with a reproving look at his son. "We are allies, are we no'?"

"We should fight it out," Kerr suggested to Earrach, "if only for fun."

"Fun, is it?" Mam questioned.

"My son will defeat you," Mican told Kerr disparagingly. "He is a warrior before whom few may stand."

Was he?

"We will spar tomorrow," Kerr, always the more aggressive of Kendrick's sons, promised Earrach.

And what if they do? Bradana wondered. What if things grew heated and incautious, and Kerr did her the favor of killing her bridegroom? Would she then be free of this terrible destiny laid upon her?

The man Chief Mican had brought with him was, so it seemed, their clan elder, who would perform the handfasting here before the entire settlement, two days hence. Tomorrow would be a grand feast. Following their joining would come an even more elaborate one. She would depart here for the north as Earrach's bride.

And would he claim his rights as her husband here, even before they left? No doubt. She would be as a sacrifice to him.

She eyed him as she played, fingers now moving by rote. He ignored her and seldom glanced in her direction.

What would it be like, to be touched by him? Taken by him? Prey to those hands and those lips.

She plucked a sour note. No one noticed, save perhaps Mam, who rose and came to her.

"Lay the harp aside for now," she bade. "Come and speak wi' your betrothed."

"There will be time for us to talk together in the morning."

"Now will be better. Ye maun get to know him."

"Mam, I feel unwell. May I be dismissed?"

Mam's gaze met hers. "I fear not, love."

So she went and sat beside Earrach. He did look at her then.

"Pray, Master Earrach," she said as the others talked around them, "tell me o' your settlement."

"'Tis a vast place, mistress." He glanced around the hall. "Perhaps no' so grand as this. We are too busy fighting off the natives—even after all these years—to spend time on niceties. But I hope to someday make it the strongest holding in the north, for my sons."

"A fine ambition," Bradana said. His sons. The ones he expected her to bear. "Is it beautiful, your land?"

"I think so. Worth fighting for, and won by blood. Ye will learn o' men, true men." He held her gaze even as he drank from his cup. "I am no' afraid o' a fight." He cast a brief look at Kerr. "I am no' afraid to tak' on yer brother."

"I ha' a pony and a fine hound, Wen, whom I mean to bring wi' me."

"We ha' plenty o' hounds. Best to leave yours behind and choose a new one there."

"I am bringing him." She met his gaze with determination.

"You will do as ye wish, I am sure. But our hounds are fierce and may no' accept him. Would ye bring him only to see him savaged?"

"He is most important to me."

"Then leave him here wi' yer brothers, that he may survive."

"Wen comes wi' me, or I do no' go."

Earrach looked interested. His dark eyes latched on to her face and something dangerous moved in them. "I was no' told ye were stubborn."

"Master Earrach, I am giving up much to wed wi' ye and move awa' from my home. I will no' give up Wen."

"Ye gain much also. Many fine hounds. A hall o' yer own. A husband who will die, and kill, for ye."

A shiver chased down Bradana's body from head to toe, precisely as if an evil wind moved through her. An omen of things to come.

"Ah, but," said Earrach, his eyes still pinning her, "let us no' talk o' death at a time o' such joy, eh?"

Aye, but Bradana found no shred of joy in her heart.

CHAPTER SEVENTEEN

THE RAIN CEASED later that night. Adair heard it taper off as he lay on his cot, trying not to think or to imagine what went on beyond his narrow quarters.

He knew very well that the party from the north had arrived. He had heard the stir earlier and even gone to his door, the better to listen, catching the telltale sounds above the crash of the rain.

Bradana had dreaded this. Though she'd said little enough about it, he'd felt the terror growing in her as the days passed. As he healed. As they grew closer to one another in friendship.

Impossibly close.

He knew her now. Knew what would make her laugh and what it meant when she looked at him a certain way—she thought about kissing him, though she never did—and when the worries that filled her head threatened to overwhelm her. She was a woman who often appeared calmer than she felt.

A woman possessed of much composure. Would it hold now?

She had left Wen with him for company, so she'd said, but the hound proved just as uneasy as Adair. He paced the small space and whined, which Adair had never before heard him do. He went repeatedly to the door and stared out at the rain.

"Aye, so," Adair said to him then. "She is out there. Neither o' us can be with her now."

Adair struggled to pass the time. At late afternoon he donned his cloak and went out to the midden, taking the hound with him for a break.

They stopped by the communal kitchens and picked up their supper, then returned to their lonely vigil.

Adair sat and wondered what had become of his life. Back in Erin, his days had been full, his nights enjoyable. Not much to trouble him. Baen took care of matters of state. Daerg—the gods help him—was there to take up what Baen could not. Adair went through his days without a great deal to disturb him. Aye so, as a warrior he must answer at any time to the call of the high king. He drilled most every day along with his brothers.

The rest of it was laughter and song, his deep love for the place where he dwelt.

Now there was Bradana.

She had changed everything about his life. Sharpened and focused it. Made it count for something. He would have said he lived for Erin.

Now he drew breath only for her.

She came long after nightfall. Adair had fallen asleep by the time she quietly entered his quarters. The hound's greeting roused him, Wen's great tail thumping a beat. She whispered, "All right, then, lad. I am well enough."

Only she was not. Adair felt that at once. She brought a desperate energy into the small space with her, like a rush of ill wind. Even her voice failed to sound like her own.

"Adair? Are ye sleeping?"

"Nay." He sat up.

"I am sorry to disturb ye so late." She came and sat on the edge of his bed. "I had to come."

He reached out and drew her into his arms.

He did not need to ask what was amiss. She'd been with the man she was to wed in two days' time.

She clung to him, his strong and dauntless lass did. She trembled down to her bones.

What comfort could he give? They had both known this would come. So he said nothing and only held her while she burrowed in tight, and tighter.

Wen stood close by, whining. They two who loved her best did not know how to alleviate her pain.

He loved her. Loved and needed her, both beyond measure.

She did not weep. For many long moments she did not speak, just held him in a manner that argued she would never let go.

"There, now," he murmured into her hair. Meaningless words. The scent of her engulfed him, made him dizzy with a thousand emotions.

At last she spoke. "I canna do this, Adair. I canna."

Hope stirred inside him, victorious hope. Would she refuse the union? Could she? Impossible.

"He is a hard man, a vicious man, I do fear, and I like naught about him. He wants to take me awa' from all I know, and 'tis a life sentence. He says I may no' bring Wen with me because his hounds will savage him and—and I love ye."

The words came at the end of a rushing breath of others, but stood out stark and bold.

She repeated them as if she could not prevent herself. "I love ye, Adair."

"I love ye also, full well," he whispered into her hair. "I swear by all that is holy, I do."

"Och, Adair! How am I to leave ye to go off wi' him? How am I to leave ye at all?"

A hard question, and a hard fate. A fortnight ago, Adair had not known she existed, nor she he. So swiftly had she become someone without whom he could not live.

"Bradana, is there any way Kendrick will change his mind? Allow ye to beg off from the marriage?

"He cannot. 'Twill break the alliance. Mican is no' a man he would want as an enemy."

"What if…" He shifted her against his shoulder, "What if I were to go to Kendrick? Offer him something else of value? A better bargain?"

"Such as what?"

"I will tell him if he breaks off the marriage agreement, I will return to Erin and convince Father he has no further claim here in Alba."

"Would your father agree to that? Surrender his claim to his holdings here?"

"I do not know." Adair would worry about that when he reached it. "I would persuade him." He tightened his arms around her. "Ye would come awa' wi' me, to Erin."

"Leave Alba?" she asked even as she had once before.

"Aye so, will ye no' be leaving the settlement here anyway, if ye go awa' with Earrach?" Yet she would still be in Alba, this land she so loved. He tipped her face up to his and whispered to her, "I will speak wi' Kendrick in the morning."

In answer, she kissed him.

No ordinary kiss, this. No mere press of lips against lips. For days, despite longing on both sides, it had been withheld. Now she reached for him blindly and clung with her whole being as they fused mouth to mouth.

It altered Adair's world. Foolish it might seem to say so, yet he felt it happen, some unsatisfied longing in him leaping to the same longing in her, so that every other consideration fell away. His priorities were altered in the wink of an eye.

Soft lips trembled violently beneath his own. She parted them immediately for him, the better to allow the need to come rushing. Once again he felt he had done this before, even though he had not. All this time he'd been afraid to kiss her, because instinctively he'd understood what it would bring. If touching her had moved him, what must this do?

For she gave herself to him in this kiss, willingly and gracefully, she did. She wrapped herself around him, threw open the door to everything she was.

He flung himself through that doorway. *His*, she was, as surely as he belonged to her. He could kiss her forever, and so satisfy the longing.

"Adair."

Did she speak his name aloud? That must mean she'd ended

the kiss, for he had not. He could not.

She pushed him over so he tumbled back onto his bed with her atop him. She raised her head and looked into his eyes, and they gazed so for many long moments, staring down eternity.

"Let me try that once again," he said.

This kiss went on so long, Adair risked losing track of time. Of reality. He lost control of both body and mind and came up hard for her. Aye, he'd known it would be thus. Better not touched, and yet who could resist this rush of heat and pleasure?

"Och, Adair. Adair, Adair…" She babbled it into his neck when that second kiss ended, sounding like a madwoman. "Listen to me."

"I am, darling. I am."

"It must be ye."

"What?"

"It canna be him. Do ye understand?"

"Nay."

"It maun be ye. I give mysel' to ye, hear? I give myself whole. Body, heart, spirit."

Aye, so she felt the same flash of possessive wonder as he.

He caught her face between his hands, there where she lay atop him.

"Aye," he said. "I am yours and ye are mine."

"And I will lie wi' ye first before I lie wi' him."

Comprehension struck him a staggering blow. True enough, he lay here in a state of arousal as complete as any he'd ever known. And true, she belonged to him in that way as much as any other. But…

"Bradana, lass, I want ye. I want ye more than I can say. Yet there will be consequences to such an act, consequences for ye." He did not care so much if Kendrick or Earrach retaliated against him. Without Bradana, his life mattered naught anyway. But such punishment, such disfavor, might land upon her instead.

"Earrach may have expectations. If ye be—"

"I am untried." She tossed her head with disdain. "I would let no man touch me that way. Adair, 'twas as if I knew. As if I waited for ye."

"Aye so, yet—"

"And now it can be no one but ye. Understand?"

He did. It would be a sacred thing between them. Not something to be wrested, forced, or torn.

He sat up with her in his arms, barely noticing the complaint of his healing ribs. "Let me talk wi' Kendrick first. I will go to him at first light and do my best to convince him. If I can, and ye come awa' wi' me, we can be together at peace in Erin. Forever."

Her eyes, wide and fastened unwavering to his, revealed her emotions all too well. Fear, dread, reluctance and disappointment, desire, and stubborn resistance. Love.

She said, "I want ye now."

"I want ye now also, Bradana. Here. Tonight."

"This moment."

"This moment, aye."

"I never knew what desire was until I met ye. Now it haunts my days, my nights, my every breath. Promise me we will be together."

An impossible promise to give. Yet he could feel what raged inside her, the other half of what raged inside him. So he spoke the words.

"We will." So they must.

"Speak to Kendrick in the morning, aye, do. Use all your powers o' persuasion. Until then…"

"Until then ye must go to your chamber, as I must stay here in mine. Anything else, if discovered, will anger Kendrick, and then how will I persuade him?"

"He will be angered by any road."

"He will."

"Adair, I am afraid. So afraid."

"Trust me." He lifted her hands in turn, planted a kiss in each palm. Kissed each corner of her mouth, each cheek, and ended with a kiss on her brow.

A sigh escaped her, a sound of acceptance.

"I do trust ye with all I am. But I want ye more, and need ye most o' all."

When he spoke with Kendrick, he had no choice but to succeed.

His whole world, and hers, depended upon it.

⸺⟨❈⟩⸺

CHAPTER EIGHTEEN

ADAIR FOUND NO rest for the remainder of the night. At first light he washed, dressed himself neatly, and walked to the main door of the hall, where Mistress Tavia's woman let him in.

"Master Adair," the woman complained, "'tis gey early yet. My mistress is scarce up from her bed."

"'Tis your master I wish to see."

The woman led him in to the hearth, where she'd just been laying the fire, and hurried off to inform Kendrick who came still fastening the ties on his tunic and with his hair tumbled, looking displeased.

"Uncle, forgive me for calling upon ye so early. I am aware ye have guests and important matters to which ye must attend today, but what I need to discuss is of equal importance."

Adair had practiced the words there in his quarters after Bradana left, taking the hound with her. Despite the emotions surging through him, he must remain calm and winsome.

Kendrick waved a dismissive hand. "If 'tis about your father's claim, I have no time for it now. We have a wedding tomorrow and my wife is unwell. Besides, have ye not spent all your words already in that regard?"

"Not quite. If ye will only hear me out now, before the day begins…"

Kendrick gave a tremendous sigh. "Verra well. Sit down. Genna, bring some ale and then leave us."

When the woman had complied and gone, Kendrick took up

the flask with a grimace. "I do no' usually tak' ale before breakfast, but I do no' doubt this day will call for it. Will ye have some?"

"Aye." Adair waited till the drink splashed into his cup before he said, "Uncle, I am willing to return to my father and argue to him that his claim upon your lands holds little value. Convince him to hold to his own lands and quit suing ye for a portion."

Kendrick lifted a shaggy brow. "And why should ye do such a thing? Ah—having seen wha' we own here, the beauty o' it, ye want a share for yer own, is that it? Ye would ask me to grant ye a portion."

Adair had seen the beauty of what was here, aye. "That is not it." Here came the hard part. "I am willing to sail away—today—back to Erin. But not alone."

Kendrick's eyes narrowed.

"Uncle, your stepdaughter Bradana has come to mean a great deal to me, as I have to her in turn. I would spare her this marriage that looms over her head and take her back with me to my own land."

"Ye be jesting wi' me, aye? I am no' amused."

"'Tis no jest. I am in deadly earnest. Bradana is in earnest. She wishes to come wi' me. To be wi' me."

"Well, she cannot. Her union wi' Earrach enforces an important alliance."

"I am aware of that."

"If I am attacked in future, Mican will come to my aid, and I likewise to his. 'Tis my belief that only if we Celtic tribes hold together can we keep our toehold on this land. But why should he spill blood for me unless we share grandchildren? And in the future, how strong might not our grandchildren's holding become, if united?"

"Bradana is not your blood daughter."

"As good as! I raised that lass. I love her. Can ye say the same, who have scarce known her a day?"

"I can."

Kendrick got to his feet with a snort. "I would ne'er do aught to harm her."

"Then, Uncle, why send her awa' to a man she does no' want?"

Kendrick fixed Adair with a hard stare. "She has no' told me she does not want the match."

"She feels she owes ye far too much."

"In fact," Kendrick continued angrily, "she was fine wi' it before ye showed up. Ha' ye used pretty words on her, trying to charm her awa'?"

"I have not." Words had not been necessary.

"I ken fine Mican and his son seem a rough lot. But they are sound allies and will mak' good protectors for the lass. I would not send her otherwise."

"What I can offer ye, freedom from my father's demands—"

"Wha' good to me if they are lands I cannot hold? I need Mican as an ally, no' an enemy. Nay"—he waved his hand again—"the marriage alliance maun stand. And I believe it best that ye do no' see my daughter again."

Adair's heart sank beneath the weight of dismay so great he could scarcely breathe. He had failed. He had failed Bradana. He had made things worse.

"Pray, Uncle," he said, getting to his feet also, "talk to Bradana. Dismiss me if ye will, but ask her of her true feelings about this match."

"Unfortunately, her feelings no longer matter. It is too late and things ha' moved too far. A refusal now would be a slap in Mican's face, an insult from which he might no' recover. There is naught to be done."

"So ye will send her against her will? Sell her for an alliance?"

"'Tis the way o' the world, is it not?"

Angry now, and crushed beyond expressing, Adair turned to the door. How could he ever tell Bradana, after asking her to trust him, that he had failed?

"Nephew, if I were ye, I would head at once back to Erin. In fact, I would board that boat now, this very morning, and begone before ye come to Earrach MacGillean's attention."

"Uncle, is that a threat?"

Kendrick gave him a long look. "I should hope it does no' ha' to be."

BRADANA WAITED FAR up the shore, in the place where she and Adair had so often sat together with the sea at their feet. Here could she watch for him, and here would he find her after winning his case with Kendrick. If he could.

Another murky sort of day. The early sun shone upon the water, but far off, in the direction of Erin, a bank of clouds gathered.

Bradana, who had lived here all her life, girl and woman, knew that meant they would have rain before long. Here on this coast, rain came and went swiftly, as frequent as a grieving woman's tears.

Wen sat beside her, his great tail sweeping the shingle each time she so much as glanced at him. He watched her get up repeatedly to pace. Wet her toes in the foam.

Today would be busy. She was supposed to take Earrach on a walking tour of the settlement—a chance, as her mother suggested, for them to grow better acquainted. After, Toren and Kerr would take him out hunting. It was to be hoped they would not treat him as shabbily as they had their cousin.

Adair. Where was he, by all the gods?

Later there would be a grand feast. And tomorrow…

Tomorrow she would be bathed and brushed and dressed in her remaining new gown, the blue one, and would wed Earrach MacGillean.

Unless Adair came to her with a miracle in his hands. A reprieve.

She gazed out to sea once again, peering past the clouds to the distance where lay Erin. Could she imagine that place, from whence her ancestors had come? Could she imagine a life lived there? A life with Adair.

Despite the feelings she harbored for him, her heart rebelled at it. Alba was her blood and her bone. It had a grip upon her soul.

As did Adair. If she were forced to become an exile in order to be with him…

Och, by the gods, could she?

Turning once again, swamped by impatience, she gazed back up the shore. Why did he not come?

Could she live if she never saw him again? Could she live without Adair MacMurtray's kisses?

His kisses.

Another emotion swayed her then, one she identified as lust. But nay, that was not entirely true, not all of what she felt for Adair. She desired him, aye, most powerfully. She needed his presence far more.

Upon the thought, she caught movement far up the shore. A gleam of red in the hazy sunlight that proved to be highlights picked from a brown mane. He came at last.

She could not keep still and hurried to meet him, so eager was she to hear what he had to say. But she knew by the look in his eyes even before she reached him that the news was not what she'd hoped.

"Adair? Ye were overlong."

He searched her face before bending to greet the hound.

"Adair?"

"Bradana." Straightening, he captured her elbows in his hands, but said nothing.

"Ye spoke wi' Kendrick?"

"I did. Bradana, I ha' failed ye. I was unable to convince him to dismiss the marriage agreement."

All her hopes came crashing down. So violent were the emotions, she drew away from him and bent double, her hands on her knees.

"Forgive me," he whispered. "I asked ye to trust me, and I was unable to persuade him."

"'Tis no' your fault. Not a bit of it." Swiftly she turned back to him and searched his face in turn. If aught could deepen her sorrow, it was beholding the stark grief in his eyes. "I should have known. The marriage alliance has been arranged for a long time. And once Kendrick's mind is set, he is near impossible to talk round. But och, Adair, what are we to do now?"

"I believe ye should talk to Kendrick in turn. He needs to hear from your lips that you do not want the marriage. He says ye did not object to it till I came."

"I *did* object to it. Not to his face, mayhap, but only because in my mind I put it off again and again. I did no' dream you existed."

"Ye must tell him this is not what ye want."

"I will. I will." It would not be easy. For much of Bradana's life, Kendrick had let her be. Left her care to her mother. Bradana did not fear him. Neither did she have an entirely easy relationship with him.

Yet if she wanted to be a woman who chose her own fate, she must step up and do just that.

"Adair"—she caught his hands in hers—"ye will wait for me? Ye will no' leave Alba before this thing is done?"

He hesitated a moment, a swirl of trouble in his eyes before he nodded.

"Then kiss me once for luck."

"And twice," he murmured as their lips met, "for love."

CHAPTER NINETEEN

WHEN BRADANA APPROACHED her stepfather some while later, there amid the morning bustle of the hearthside, he met her with impatience.

"I ha' no' time for ye now, Bradana," he told her briskly, not meeting her gaze. "I am to sit wi' Mican and his man to go over the terms o' the agreement and mak' sure all is set right."

"'Twill be best for us to speak together first."

"And then," he went on as if he had not heard her, "there is a feast to arrange. Since your mother is no' feeling well, all that will fall to me. Unless"—he lifted a brow—"ye will help wi' it."

"I will, aye, but only if ye can spare a few moments for me."

"Everyone wants to bargain, and I grow weary o' it. D'ye no' ken the weight that lies upon me, keeping us all safe, fed, and alive?"

"But I—"

"I shall have a few moments this afternoon while your brothers take our guests hunting. Chief Mican has said he wishes to go along o' his son. But do no' forget, before that ye are set to entertain your bridegroom."

"I do not forget."

Kendrick moved to the door. "Och, and I do believe our other guest will be leaving for Erin sometime this morning." He glanced at Mam, who had just come into the chamber, her shawl wrapped around her body. "He will no' need a grand send-off."

Mam nodded, and Bradana stood still, caught by consternation. Had Adair not told her he would not go? At least, not without her.

An icy feeling crawled toward her heart. What had Kendrick said to him that made him so confident Adair would go? Had there been threats? Did she even now put the man she loved in danger?

Better to wed with Earrach than do that. Better to enter into a lifelong sentence of banishment and misery than be the cause of harm to Adair.

If Kendrick thought Adair the reason the alliance lay in peril, he would be more than capable of removing his nephew. And that did not merely mean sending him off back to Erin. If Adair proved recalcitrant…

Och, what had she done in sending him to Kendrick?

Glancing up, she caught her mother's gaze. Nay, Mam did not appear well. Swiftly, Bradana crossed the floor to her.

"Why do ye not go and lie down? I will finish making the breakfast."

"Och, daughter, do I look so poorly? I did not sleep well. Beset by pains all night."

"Not labor pains?"

"False labor, I believe 'tis called."

"Go back to your bed. If there is aught I can do for ye…"

Mother hesitated. "Do no' make waves. I know, daughter, you are not easy in this marriage. But 'twill be best in the end."

Bradana wanted to cry out at that. To ask if she did not deserve the chance for love. Her mother's pale face caused her to hold her tongue.

She would wait and marshal all her arguments for Kendrick when the time came.

THAT DAY TESTED Bradana. It drew on every nerve and fiber and made her question all she was. She'd always considered herself a strong woman. Uncowed and unflinching. Able to speak her own mind.

Yet it did little good to speak one's mind if no one was willing to listen.

She made the breakfast and directed the servants, headed by Genna, to set up the hall for the evening feast. She checked on her mother, who slept deeply. Before she knew it, Earrach was waiting for her, ready for the promised walking tour.

She'd had no chance to change the gown she'd donned in haste to meet Adair earlier that morning. No opportunity to comb out and arrange her hair. Earrach made her feel the lack as he eyed her from her dirty hide shoes to the locks tumbled in disarray.

"Forgive me, Master Earrach. It has been a busy morning."

He himself had dressed in a fine embroidered tunic with a pin at his shoulder and had tied back his cloud of dark hair, showing some effort. He appeared large, formidable, and not particularly pleased with her.

"Mistress Bradana, d'ye always dress no better than a servant?"

"Frequently, I am afraid," she answered blithely, denying her annoyance. "If ye wanted a fancy sort o' wife, ye should ha' gone looking elsewhere." Maybe she could turn his interest away from her. A wild stab, but worth pursuing at this point.

"A woman as well-favored as ye should mak' the most o' her endowments." His dark gaze lingered on her breasts, making it clear of what endowments he spoke. "Then again," he continued with a wry twist of his lips, "I will no' have to wait long to mak' the most o' those mysel'."

Och, aye, he would strip her naked, would this man, and take what he wanted. His manner made that clear. Even more than his wife, she would be his possession.

She asked sweetly, "Would ye prefer to wait while I change my clothing?"

"Nay, nay, let us walk out."

They did, she and Wen leading him about the confines of the settlement, and farther. He showed interest in the things that interested her not—the numbers of their warriors, how the guard was situated. The armory and the forge. Far less attention did he give to the beauties of the land, the vistas of shore and sea.

The rain held off, but she worried the whole time that she was missing her chance to speak with Kendrick. At last, they turned back, and she breathed out a sigh.

Conversation had been at a minimum. Earrach asked her only utilitarian questions, few personal ones. At length he did remark, "Ye will be looking forward to the wedding."

Looking forward was not a term she would employ. Dreading came closer.

Not waiting for a reply, he stopped walking and faced her. "A kiss, perhaps, to anticipate what is to come."

What was to come. Herself in his hands. Her body, his to claim. She could not.

"D'ye think it proper, Master Earrach? I would prefer to wait."

He did not like that. She could tell by the flash of annoyance in his eyes.

"Verra well, mistress. But I would hope ye will welcome me more warmly tomorrow night."

She had no words in reply to that.

Fortunately, he walked off toward his quarters.

Desperately, she sucked in air. Though she'd kept her eyes lively throughout their walk, she'd caught no glimpse of Adair.

She needed to see him. To ground herself in the strength and safety of his presence.

But not now.

Swiftly she went to the family quarters, where she found Kendrick standing outside the door speaking with Mican and his man.

"Father"—she used the title deliberately—"ye promised me a moment."

All three men stared in affront. "When I am free, Bradana."

"But ye said—"

"Aye, so. I will be along."

She and Wen waited at a distance, unable to catch the words the three exchanged. The fat drops of rain began to fall as they waited.

"Come inside wi' ye," Kendrick called when the other two moved off. "Wha' is all this, then?"

Nothing more—or less—than a bid for her future.

Servants occupied the family place when they went in. She could hear others moving in the great hall beyond.

"Father, I need to speak wi' ye alone."

He looked weary and put out. "If this is about Adair Mac-Murtray, I spoke wi' that young man this morning. All is settled."

"It is not."

He sighed again. "Then come."

They went to an alcove that Kendrick usually held as private, his alone. Cramped and narrow, it held his personal weapons and other belongings along with a bench. He sat upon one end of this and gestured Bradana to the other.

"Well?" He lifted a brow.

Bradana struggled to master her thoughts. She would have one chance at this, and only one.

"Father, ye ha' been good to me all these years," she began. "Like my own father, in truth."

His expression eased a little. "I think o' ye as a daughter, Bradana. And care for ye as one."

Did he? He'd never said so before, though there had been a measure of kindness, aye, and laughter sometimes.

"I hope ye will hear me as a daughter now and understand—I do no' welcome this marriage."

It was what Adair had insisted she must convey to Kendrick, that though she held obligations toward him, she did not approve the match. Something she had never done.

His expression changed and grew stern. "Why is this? For a

year and more ye ha' known o' the match. And ye ha' met Earrach before. Ye expressed no objections."

"'Tis easy to believe we may accept events that remain at a distance. Now it is come…"

His eyes moved over her face carefully. "Now that it is come, it is come. Bradana, this is an important alliance. Your failure to go through wi' it would destroy our good relationship with Mican MacGillean. Not only that, but it would cause great and terrible affront to Mican and his son that could well turn them into enemies."

Dismay poured through Bradana and stole her words.

"Perhaps 'tis just anticipation getting the better o' ye."

"Nay."

"Or—is this about Adair MacMurtray after all?"

Her gaze came up to meet his.

"My nephew is a gey charming young man. Even I like him, despite the trouble he causes me. And when we are young," he said almost grimly, "we sometimes let fancy take hold and get the better o' us. Ye fancy him? Ah, that will pass."

It would not. An unending stream of lifetimes would not put an end to what she felt for Adair. How could she explain that to this man?

"It is a good match." He covered her hand where it rested on the bench. "And I need for ye to go through with it."

Bradana's eyes filled with tears, which she tried to convince herself were born of anger.

She blurted, "Earrach will not let me bring Wen with me when I go north. He says his hounds will savage him."

"Is that what all this is about? Let me speak wi' Mican. Ye will be allowed to tak' your hound. Now go. The feasting begins soon."

She stumbled to her feet, pierced to the heart.

CHAPTER TWENTY

ADAIR DID NOT attend the feast, and Bradana worried for him. She fretted that some other terrible harm had befallen him, perhaps at the hands of her stepbrothers. Or that Kendrick had somehow persuaded him to board his little boat and sail back to Erin. That she would not see him again.

But nay. Adair would not do that. As she felt for him, he felt also for her.

She had dressed again in her new green gown, and her mother's woman had fussed with her hair. Mother still felt unwell even after her sleep, but she had dragged herself up and given Bradana a smile.

"Ye look beautiful, daughter. Will ye play your harp for them this night?"

"I am no' certain the men from the north appreciate the harp, Mother."

"Nonsense. Let them see what they are getting."

Long boards had been arranged down the length of the hall and streamers hung. Despite the rain that fell steadily outside, scores of torches made the large chamber bright as day. So long as the torches did not set the streamers alight and burn the place down.

Bradana almost hoped they would.

The boards groaned beneath the weight of food, and the mood seemed merry enough. As soon as Bradana entered the room, Kendrick summoned her to sit beside him. On his other hand sat Mican, and his son beyond.

Most the men of the clan filed in, many with their women.

Not Adair MacMurtray.

Bradana ached to ask Kendrick where Adair was, if he'd been forbidden to attend or sent off. Kendrick wanted Adair gone and no bumps in this path he'd chosen.

That much became evident when he rose to speak.

"Welcome all to my hall here tonight. And a most hearty welcome to our honored guests. Tomorrow's handfasting will see the forging o' a powerful and important alliance that will benefit not only our two clans, but all of Dalriada. A grand step toward making good our claim to conquer all of Alba. Let us drink to the success of the union, and to many swords raised as one."

His listeners drank with enthusiasm. They stamped their feet until Mican rose in turn.

"I agree wholeheartedly with what my host has said. The only way we will keep hold o' this land is by standing together. We at Clan Gillean feel fortunate to welcome Mistress Bradana, who will bear a new generation o' Albans."

Cheers arose. They did not cheer for Bradana but for a chance to end the fighting, to sleep safe in their beds at night. To own this land they had come to love.

No one expected, nor would they welcome, Bradana getting to her feet and lending her voice to this chorus, even though she was the means to the end they sought, and her body would bear those children.

Her mother, seated on her other side, sent her a worried glance, as if she feared Bradana might indeed arise and speak up.

So much depended upon this. Upon her.

Mother still did not look well. Her skin had a grayish tinge, and she kept placing her hands on her belly. She had eaten almost nothing. How could Bradana upset her further by making a scene?

She leaned toward Mam. "Are ye all right?"

"I only wish this feast would end."

"Are ye still having pains?"

Mother shook her head.

There was music, though, to come. Kendrick's bard, an aged man called Kallen, told a long and winding tale of Kendrick's ancestors. Then Mother bade Bradana take up the harp in turn.

She rose to do so, if reluctantly. Earrach and his sire had showed little appreciation for her playing last time, but the crowd was far larger now. Her own clansfolk would surely listen with courtesy.

She sat between the tables on a stool one of the servants had placed for Kallen and took up his instrument, since it was at hand, and hers was not.

Her mind went blank. Pinned by all the staring faces, including Earrach's dark visage, she could not remember a note to play.

Kallen leaned toward her. "Something simple, mayhap, mistress? Anything will do."

But Bradana could think only of Adair. Of her longing for him. If only she might play for him as she had when he lay so sore hurt in his quarters.

If only she could make a song that expressed what she felt for him.

And all at once, that song came. It arose unbidden from the longing in her heart and wove up through her, a glorious, bright, and lovely shower of notes. It wound through the air of the chamber, dancing with all she felt for the man of her heart—friendship, loyalty, and love.

It wove a spell that touched every one of her listeners, that warmed them and held off the rain. A song of love eternal.

When she stopped playing at last, there was silence. She sat with her head bent, fingers suspended on the strings, and the no one made sound until Earrach began clapping.

He rose to his feet and stood looking at Bradana, a terrible, dark desire in his eyes.

The rest of the feast passed without Bradana marking it. She left while the men still drank and told stories of past battles and helped her mother to bed, made sure her woman was with her, and that she did not need the midwife.

"I will stay wi' ye, Mother, if ye like."

"Nay, I am well enough now. Go back to the feast."

But Bradana did not return to the hall. Instead, she stood in the rain for several moments before following an impulse far stronger than any will and moving forward through the dark.

ADAIR HAD BEEN long alone in his narrow quarters, struggling with dark feelings. Earlier, sometime before the feast began, Kendrick had come to him. Said he thought it best if Adair did not attend.

"After all, nephew, the goings-on here ha' little to do wi' ye, and this wedding in particular." He'd fixed Adair with a stern eye. "Ye will no' be welcome in the hall this night. In fact, the best ye can do is leave for home."

That, Adair could not do. He would not leave Bradana until she sent him away.

And yet tomorrow—tomorrow she would handfast with another.

Halfway through the evening, Wen came to him out of the wet.

"Aye so, ye have also been banished, eh?" he asked the hound. He could hear the sounds of festivity from the hall, music and voices raised in speech.

He wondered what he should do on the morrow.

Might he challenge Earrach for Bradana's hand? Propose a contest at arms, the matter to be settled between them as warriors? He was not a bad hand with a blade, though unlike many men of his clan, he did not focus all his intent upon practicing at arms.

He'd been blessed with swift reflexes and reactions, a goodly measure of endurance, and speed. Was he not descended from one of the greatest warriors his people had ever known?

He could best Earrach, aye, for Bradana's sake. But…

Should this not be a choice she made, and a fight she fought? She was a living, breathing woman, not a prize to be won by dint of swordplay. He might stand beside her, aye, and might well fight to the death for her sake. But it must be at her bidding.

He could still hear sounds of feasting when at last he snuffed out the rushlight and took to his bed. Wen settled on the floor beside him.

He never heard her enter the chamber, though no doubt the hound did. Adair was half asleep when a pair of hands closed on his wrists and a soft body came down upon his.

"Bradana." He breathed her name, for he knew her instantly by her scent, by her feel. By her spirit that embraced him as completely as her body.

"Hush," she said, and made sure of it by pressing her mouth to his.

His brain exploded with desire. It felt the way he imagined the kiss of lightning must, hot and powerful and instantaneous, traveling all along his veins and searing him from within.

Desire, need, love. At that moment he could not tell the one from the other and did not care. Bradana was here, her body in contact with his, her lips wooing his apart as she drank of him, drank even as she gave to him.

His arms came around her without conscious thought. Soft and warm she was beneath the smooth fabric of her gown, trapped between them. He held her tight and tighter while the kiss went on and on and the pieces of his world fell into place.

This, this was what he'd wanted always. While a young man back in Erin growing with his two brothers ahead of him. Searching for a place, for friends, for an occupation. Searching later for lovers and finding many for whom he cared—but not enough.

Never like this. For Bradana answered the yearning that had

driven him, unacknowledged, every day of his life.

Sanity returned slowly, but it did return. He tried to break the kiss, but she would not allow it, winding her arms around him and wooing him back in. At last, very gently, he caught her face between his hands and, with regret, eased her away.

"Bradana, is this wise?"

Her voice, when it came, was no more than a breath. "Did I no' tell ye, I want it to be ye? Ye, and no' him. I want ye this night, Adair MacMurtray."

Well, that was plain and honest. She was an honest woman, was his Bradana. A surge of joy uplifted him before sanity struck again.

"We cannot."

A sob broke from her throat. "All my persuasions to Kendrick have failed. I must—I must handfast wi' Earrach tomorrow. Go to his bed. But I will gi' myself first to ye."

"My darling. My heart." Now his hands, the same that had halted the kiss, caressed her. He felt tears on her cheeks. "There must be another way."

"There is no'."

"I could challenge him on the morrow. Fight him for ye."

She stilled. "Ye would do that for me?"

"I would."

She caught her breath. "And—should ye lose?"

"Bradana, have ye so little faith in me?"

"I believe in ye, above all things, Adair MacMurtray. But he is a hardened warrior. A brute with a high reputation. If 'twere a fight to the death—"

"Then I would kill him, or die. But I would declare before all the world what ye mean to me."

Her tears now fell in earnest. "And should such a contest go badly, a great light would go out o' the world. Out o' my world. I do not think I can live wi' that."

"Bradana"—he wove his fingers into her hair—"All my life has been spent in waiting—waiting for ye. If I spend my hope for a future attempting to hold ye, now that I ha' found ye—will it no' be well spent?"

"Nay. Nay. Adair, I will no' see ye spend yoursel' for me. Let us become one this night—here and now. No one can then take that from us, not even death. If I ha' that memory to hold to me, I believe 'twill be enough. Tell me ye will love me this night."

He gave her the only answer he could. "I will."

CHAPTER TWENTY-ONE

BRADANA ROSE FROM the bed unsteadily. She could barely see the man who lay upon the cot before her, but she had felt him. Long and lean was Adair MacMurtray. Well muscled and lithe, wearing naught more than the short leggings in which he'd lain down to sleep.

The man she loved. How could she go to her fate—her hard and desperately terrifying fate—without tasting him? Without having him inside her, a memory to take her through the years.

She began removing her clothing, untying the laces that secured the green overdress, which, without regard, she tossed aside. She wriggled from the simple sheath beneath. Her shoes came last.

The cool air brought up goosebumps on her naked skin and she hesitated. If they were caught, if she were found here, 'twould be a terrible scandal. They would be disgraced before the clan. The gods alone knew what would be done to Adair.

Was it worth taking such a chance?

Aye, och aye. Because tomorrow she went to the slaughter. Tomorrow she lost herself. And if one thing might help her hang on to the merest shreds of her sanity, it would be having the man she loved inside her, but once.

So she came back down upon him, naked as she was, and breathed his name. "Adair."

His hands received her, and he began to tremble. She understood all too well what it was he felt. The rush of joy. The eagerness. All mixed up with a terrible weight of dread.

He did not speak, did not at once try to argue her out of this decision. Instead, his hands moved over her carefully, as if he could not believe the gift he'd been granted. They slid down her back. Across her buttocks. Up her sides to curve around her breasts.

Och, holy great light o' the gods.

"Bradana."

Ah, here would come the arguments. All those she knew full well already in her head.

But he said, "I love ye. More than I ever dreamed I could love anyone, I do."

A sob rose to her throat even as she lit up with delight. Aye, they should speak it out plain now, if ever.

"I love ye, Adair. I gift ye my heart. My body, yours to do as ye will, this one night."

"Bradana, this is a holy act in my sight, a sacred one." He captured her hands, wove his fingers through hers. "Let us here vow to belong to one another, handfast like this—even if only we two know."

"Aye. I am yours, only yours, till the day I die. No matter what else befalls me."

They kissed on it, their hands still linked, until the kiss became something more and he moved from beneath her, laid her with care upon the bed. Backed off a very short distance.

She thought he looked at her before she realized he untied the laces on the leggings he wore, then cast the garment aside.

"Bradana, ye have never…?"

She breathed, "Nay."

"I ha' no wish to hurt ye."

Better him, who loved her, than Earrach come tomorrow night.

She thrust that thought away from her. It had no place here. "In becoming yours, Adair, I ha' no fear."

Yet she did not know what to expect. Women talked, aye.

Her friend, Maeve, had lain with her lover last summer and given a fairly detailed description. She'd also heard that, like childbirth, it was hard to describe.

She cared for none of that now. And even less when Adair came down upon the cot and began to touch her, ran his hands across her belly and down her thighs, stroking. Softly, softly beneath her breasts.

He was up hard for her, and she could feel the heat of him like the warmth of sunlight on the rocks of this place she loved. What was there to fear? She belonged to him even as she belonged to Alba. He would as soon harm her as himself.

All such thought shattered when he bent and fastened his mouth to her breast.

Never had she known such a sensation. Never guessed it might exist. He drew upon her emotions, called up her arousal from the depths of her being. She wrapped her arms around his head and urged him closer.

Remember every moment of this, she beseeched herself. *Remember, so you may relive it all again.*

The weight of him settled upon her knees. Gently she reached down and caressed him. Sacred, he had said, aye, but something even beyond that, for she felt a great rush of wonder. Tenderness. *Love.*

Was not such love sacred?

He groaned and raised his head to look into her face. "I take ye, Bradana, as my wife."

He kissed his way downward from her breasts across her belly and lower still. He dropped hot, fervent kisses on her thighs and parted them gently, exposing her to his gaze, to his touch. His fingers brushed her there. Lingered. Pressed inside.

She lost the last threads of her sanity.

Remember, she ordered herself again, and yet the feelings came too fast and too bright. A great, raging flame lit inside her. She spread herself wide in offering to this man she loved.

When he feasted on her, she did not question it. He was hers, as she was his to do with as he pleased. She would deny him nothing this night.

And he made her sing. Every drop of blood in each vein, each facet of her spirit, came alive and glowed in the magic he wove.

"Bradana." By the time he moved up her body and whispered her name, she was more than ready for him. He took her gently, moving with care until the spell of it engulfed him. Until the rhythm of the song embraced them both and they moved, moved together in effortless harmony.

So this, Bradana thought foggily as she lay with her legs still wound around him, his face in her neck, was the manifestation of love. The highest place two souls could reach together.

She did not want to let him go. She did not ever want to let him go.

She did not want tomorrow to come.

If only they could remain together so, flying on the airstreams of the night, far up among the stars, the two of them become one.

"Bradana, love." He raised each of her hands to his lips in turn and dropped kisses into her palms. Planted two more kisses at either corner of her mouth, then upon her cheeks. Her forehead. And it felt familiar. Dear.

"Do not move." She clung to him. "Do not leave go of me. Not yet."

He did not say what he should—that were they discovered, the consequences would come swift and hard. That she would pay as well as he.

She already knew.

"Husband," she whispered, and claimed him all over again.

"Most beloved wife."

At his words, she felt her heart break, shatter into a thousand pieces. For she was that, aye, now more than ever. How, by all the gods, could she go to another man?

How had she ever imagined lying with him once would be enough?

Suddenly she was trembling with emotion. She clung to him

and he held her tight, no words necessary because he understood what she felt, and anyway, there was no comfort he could give.

At length, he began to kiss her again, and the magic once more crept over them so they moved, moved together. Their loving, pure and hot as lightning, became the only available refuge.

Bradana shattered. She came apart as even her heart had, but this time she gloried in it. And the words came in a flood.

"I never knew… I never knew lying wi' a man would be like this."

"Like this?" he questioned softly, his voice a mere breath in her ear.

"Och, well"—she tried to think about it—"I imagined the sensations would be enjoyable—though naught to what I feel when ye lay hands to me. And the kisses. The act itself. I never figured on the emotions. How I'd feel for ye after."

She felt him smile against her cheek, where his face pressed. He drew her hair aside onto the bolster. "Or how ye have claimed me, Bradana? Body and soul."

"Aye."

"The way ye gave yourself to me."

"The way I belong to ye and ye to me."

He raised himself onto his elbows in an effort to look into her face. "Naught can change that now."

"Naught can ever change it," she agreed soberly. "And yet…" Should she tell him what she now felt more certain than ever? She could not go to Earrach. Why bring trouble to this man she adored when they had so little time left together?

Terror and victorious bliss tangled together inside her. All her life, she'd looked square at realities, dealt with life as it came. This, though, was different. She had no idea how to navigate what lay before her.

"'Twill likely be dawn soon," she whispered. "I maun leave ye."

"Aye."

"But not yet." She ran her fingers down the crisp hair on his chest, across the muscles of his abdomen, until she captured him between her hands. "Not before I have had a chance to taste ye everywhere."

"Bradana—"

"Do no' tell me nay. I will have ye. And I will remember."

Dawn came more swiftly than it should. The start of Bradana's wedding day. They'd had no sleep, but Bradana thought it a good bargain, for sleep might be had anytime. This man she loved, but for one night.

When at last she rose to put on her clothes, she went cold, missing Adair's arms around her. The world came rushing in on a breath of winter. But he helped her dress, pinning the brooch upon her shoulder with his own hands and slipping the shoes onto her feet.

Then he stood looking into her face. "Ye will go carefully? 'Tis lighter out than I like."

"I stayed longer than I should." Yet in reward, she carried the flavor of him on her tongue.

"Bradana." She'd never seen him look so serious. "I will challenge him this day. I will no' stand by and watch ye wed wi' him."

"Nay." The fear that gripped her near blotted out everything they had shared, so terribly bright was it. "If ye should fall—"

"Ha' ye still so little faith in me?"

"I ha' need o' ye, Adair, that outweighs aught else. If ye should fall…" It seemed an old fear, one that predated all she felt for him.

"What kind o' man would I be if I did not fight for ye?"

"One who breathes," she told him passionately. "One who continues to love me."

"Always."

Before he could reach for her mouth, she pulled away from him. If she did not go now, she would not go at all.

"Husband," she whispered from the door, and went out into the gray morning.

<hr>

CHAPTER TWENTY-TWO

ADAIR PACED THE confines of his chamber, which now felt like nothing so much as a prison. He could still feel Bradana's hands upon him, the slide of her fingers across his skin and the heat of her mouth. Each touch a gift. Each a blessing.

She had given herself to him this night without restraint. Opened herself to him, not just in body but in spirit.

And he had done the same.

Even though she'd voiced her desire for that time together, he had not expected her to slip in through his door that way. Even more, he had not expected any woman ever to claim his heart, his life.

Back home, he'd lived so lightly. Performed his duties and sought out pleasure. Here in Alba—everything had changed.

He'd not imagined a love such as he felt for Bradana, but he should. From the moment he'd seen her, she had pulled at him, spoken to him, sung to him. Called upon the very root of his soul.

And he had just watched her go from him to handfast with another man.

How could he let that happen?

He could not.

The Adair he'd been back in Erin might. He could possibly have turned a shoulder, declared it not his fight.

The Adair who stood here in Alba did not take this lightly. He had iron in his backbone, was a warrior who would not flinch from the battle.

Indeed, Bradana's love had so transfigured him, he scarce recognized himself.

He knew what he must do, and by all the gods, he would do it.

What then? What if he felled Earrach MacGillean? He and Bradana would need to get away. He would have to take her back to Erin with him—her and Wen—whether she liked it or not.

He felt a measure of relief in that. He longed to be in Erin and would not mind having Bradana there with him.

And if it started a war between cousins? One fought across a narrow stretch of the Celtic Sea?

Then war would come. His father would have to understand.

They had trained long and hard for the field, had Gawen's three sons, Adair behind his two brothers. Baen possessed a measure of prowess with the sword. Would he not one day lead the clan? And though they battled not for territory these days, the King of Ulster could call upon their ties of fealty at any time.

Daerg had dutifully gained competence also, Father insisting he stand at Baen's back. What Da truly meant was Daerg must be able to take his brother's place, should the worst happen.

Adair had been left mostly to his own whims, it being assumed both his other brothers would not fall.

But he had liked training in the field. Liked the feel of a sword in his hand. The effortless sensation of working his muscles and, even in play, besting an opponent.

He'd never expected to face some challenger in earnest, especially for such a reason.

What sort of opponent would Earrach make? A fierce and brutal one, no doubt. A big man. Earrach had something merciless about him.

Adair could not leave the woman he loved in the hands of such a man.

When he went out into the morning, the sun just peeked over the eastern rise. No sign of Bradana or Wen anywhere. And there had been no outcry. He could only imagine she'd got back to her room without being seen.

He walked down to the shore where his boat was situated. The small craft had been hauled well up onto the shingle and the two men who had sailed with him, Flynn and Nolan, had made a camp.

They were just rising when Adair arrived. Nolan, the leader of the two, gave him a swift look.

"Young master, are we leaving today for Erin?"

Adair heard hope in the man's voice, and Flynn looked up sharply. They must be bored near mindless here and anxious to go.

"Aye. Be ready to leave by tonight. At short notice, if need be."

"Aye, so. Have ye then accomplished what your father sent ye to do?"

He had not, and facing Father would be hard, especially if he brought retribution on his heels.

"In truth, nay. But there may be trouble this day."

They exchanged a swift look. "What sort o' trouble?"

"The kind that will require a fast departure. Are ye both armed?"

Now they appeared startled. "Aye, but we are guests here, surely."

"Unwelcome guests," he reminded them.

"Aye, but there are laws o' hospitality," Nolan said.

So there were. They extended only so far when it came to bloodshed.

He told them, "If somewhat should happen to me"—if Earrach proved a better fighter than he could handle—"get yourselves away, hear? Do not wait back."

"And go home to your father without ye? His favorite son?"

"I am far from that."

Flynn snorted. "I'd sooner lose me head."

"Still and all." Adair looked them in the eye, each in turn. "I do so order it."

They exchanged another look. "Aye, so, let us hope it does no' come to that."

There was always hope.

TO BRADANA'S ALARM, she found her mother's woman looking for her when she reached home.

"Mistress," cried the distressed Genna, "where were ye? I began to think the worst."

"The worst?"

"That ye had fled." Genna bit her lip. "I have not missed the fact that ye be no' overanxious for this handfasting."

Bradana looked at the woman sharply. What else had she noticed? "I could no' sleep. Wen and I went walking early up the shore."

The woman nodded.

"Why are ye here so early, Genna?"

"There is much to be done—your bath and your new gown to put on, your hair to arrange, all before Chief Kendrick calls for ye. Ye will wish to be perfect today, o' all days."

But Bradana was not perfect, far from it. She did not always keep to her place or guard her tongue. She often chose her own path even if it be a stony one. She went about with dirt on her shoes and tears in her clothing. She was too open, not humble or modest enough. Adair loved her anyway.

Adair *loved* her.

Just as she loved him, without reservation.

There in her chamber she drew a deep breath. Whatever happened during this day to come, she could let no harm come to him. Even if that meant sacrificing herself.

She thought about that as Genna prepared her for a far more tangible sacrifice. As she stripped off the fine green gown, now crumpled, and led her to the bath. Helped wash her hair.

She had believed it would be enough, having Adair once. She'd supposed one night with the man she adored might provide a kind of bulwark against a future wherein her body was no longer her own.

She'd been wrong, woefully so. Having Adair for one night only made her want him more. It had tightened the bonds that held them, one to the other. They had sworn themselves to each other, man and wife.

How could she go to another man?

Her mother came at noontime, when Genna still worked at arranging Bradana's hair in a wealth of small braids.

Bradana leaped to her feet. "Mam, how are ye feeling?" Tavia still did not appear well. Her skin retained a gray tinge, her face a pinched expression.

"I am well, daughter."

"I think ye are not. Have the pains stopped?"

Mam shook her head. "They but come and go. Never mind it now. This day is about ye."

"If ye be unwell, mayhap we might put off the joining..." Bradana clung to it.

"Nay, och nay. There is no putting it off. Let me look at ye." Mam's blue eyes, so like Bradana's own, made a swift inspection before filling with tears. "Ye will be a beautiful bride."

"Mother—"

"Aye, I know ye feel uncertain about the match and apprehensive about Earrach. But ye maun trust it is for the best. Do no' all women go eventually to their husband's bed?"

"Many of those feel love for the man who will be their husband."

"And many do not. Daughter, we ha' spoken o' this. Perhaps I ha' given ye too much freedom while growing and let ye escape your duty far too often. It has made ye headstrong. For the sake o' everyone involved, I ask ye to accept your fate gracefully."

Should she tell Mother she was in love with another man? Nay, for it would not make a whit of difference. Duty was duty.

"Here, let us see how the dress looks. Genna, slide it over her head. Ye can finish her hair then. Ah, here is Maeve."

Bradana's friend slipped through the door, already clad in what Bradana knew to be her finest garb. She smiled cautiously at Bradana before she said, "Ah, I am in time. Mistress Tavia, let me help. Och, is that no' a beautiful color?"

The dress was indeed a wonderful shade of blue—pale and soft, it picked up the hue of Bradana's eyes. Once the women had it on her, straightened and pulled, and tied to their satisfaction, Maeve sighed.

"Ye be so beautiful."

"Is she not?" A little color had come to Mother's cheeks. "Earrach is a fortunate man, and will think himself so when he sees her."

"How soon must we go to the great hall?"

"Soon. There will be speeches and declarations. The handfasting. We will feast the rest o' the afternoon and night."

Bradana's eyes met Maeve's and slid away. She wished she could talk to her friend alone, if only for a few moments.

But Mother had pulled a small packet from her robe, wrapped in soft leather.

"Bradana, this is for ye. My mam gave it to me before my first wedding and I wore it on the day." A pained smile stretched her lips. "I am sure ye were conceived that very night."

"Oh."

"I wish for ye to have it."

"Your blue brooch?" Bradana searched her mother's eyes. "But 'tis one o' your fondest treasures."

"Nay, daughter, ye be that."

The tears did fall then, all around. Mother pinned the brooch to Bradana's shoulder—an elaborate scroll forming a pony, worked in blue metalwork—with hands that trembled.

"There now. Ye shall tak' a wee bit o' me with ye to your new home."

Bradana wanted to collapse into her mother's arms. To weep

and wail. To beg for a way out of her dilemma. She was, however, no longer a wain who wept or begged.

"Thank ye, Mam."

"Ye have all the courage ye will need"—Tavia looked her in the eyes—"to face what will come."

Bradana could only trust that she did, with all her heart.

<hr>

CHAPTER TWENTY-THREE

"ARE YE EXCITED? Frightened?" Maeve asked Bradana as the two of them waited to be summoned to the hall. Mother and Genna had gone ahead, the one kindly supporting the other. Bradana had been declared perfect and ordered not to move, that she might spoil her appearance.

She eyed her friend, wondering what to say.

"He is no' ill to look upon, this husband o' yours," Maeve offered.

That allowed some surprise to filter through the hard hold Bradana had on her emotions. "Ye think so?"

"I do." A faint flush rose to Maeve's cheeks. "I ha' seen him and would consider mysel' fortunate, were he to be mine."

Bradana could not keep from asking, "How so?"

"Och well, he is young, is he no'? Ye are no' going to an old man. He looks strong and fit. A good warrior."

"And those things are important, are they?" Only if a woman weren't in love with another man.

"It canna hurt. Och, and I ha' seen the way he looks at ye. Wi' desire in his eyes."

"He?"

"Master Earrach, o' course."

Of course.

"To be sure, 'tis no surprise." Maeve gave a sigh. "Just see how beautiful ye be."

Aye, Bradana had likely never looked so fine, or so unlike herself.

"Maeve," she told the other girl impulsively, "thank ye for being my good friend." She did not know what would happen this day. Her every instinct told her things would not end well.

"Foolish lass. Our friendship will surely continue."

"It might. Yet I am going awa'. We may not see one another again."

"No doubt ye will travel home to visit."

"Make me a promise? Ye will look after Wen, if I maun leave him behind."

"I will, of course. But—surely you will tak' him with you."

"I will no' be allowed to."

"Then your family will keep him."

"Aye, so." Some misery filtered into the emptiness inside Bradana. "But he is used to ye. Mother will be distressed wi' her babe on the way. Kerr and Toren have never bothered wi' Wen."

"Are ye certain ye can no' tak' him with ye?"

"Master Earrach says nay."

"Oh." For the first time, Maeve looked sympathetic. "To be sure, I will keep him for ye." But her look said Wen would not be happy so, and perhaps not Bradana either.

Bradana reached out and seized her friend's hand. "Maeve, I am afraid."

"Och, Bradana, I am sure any woman would have some uncertainty before she is to be handfasted."

They had time to say no more. One of the girls who helped Genna appeared at the door of the chamber, breathless.

"Mistress, ye are to come now!"

They went, Bradana with one arm tucked through Maeve's, and saw that a large crowd had gathered outside the great hall. Many members of the clan lined the walkway, and in the open doorway stood Kendrick, well dressed and with Mican beside him.

Kendrick smiled when he saw Bradana. "Daughter! Do ye no' look beautiful? Chief Mican, have ye ever seen a lovelier woman?"

Mican blinked at her. "I might fairly say I have no'." He bowed. "Mistress, ye are a vision, and welcomed to our family."

"Thank ye." Bradana's voice did not sound like her own. Thin and breathy, it threatened to fail her. She looked away from the two men, sweeping the crowd for a glimpse of Adair.

She did not see him, but she swore she could sense him nearby, and her heart began to pound. What if he did something foolish?

Kendrick offered Bradana his arm in place of Maeve's. "Allow me to escort ye, daughter."

So kind was Kendrick's manner, and so fatherly, she almost turned to him and asked for another word alone. She might argue and beseech him to break the alliance. But she'd attempted that already, and here, in Mican's company, he would have to save face.

They went inside, and Bradana saw Earrach waiting. He stood straight and tall at the head of the chamber, his black hair tamed by a circlet of red gold and a magnificent cloak hanging from his shoulders. His dark gaze fastened upon Bradana when she entered and did not waver.

She thought, *I cannot do this*. And then, *I must*.

Steadily, head high, she paced with Kendrick down the length of the chamber. The guests outside followed in behind them and took places along both walls. Whatever happened here would be very public.

They reached Earrach and the holy man who accompanied him. Bradana turned to face the room.

Searching, searching. Her gaze touched every face. Looking for one.

Still she did not see him. Her heart now pounded so hard in her ears, it made her dizzy. She swayed where she stood.

Earrach seized her elbow. "Mistress?"

His dark eyes looked curious, concerned. Possessive.

"I maun speak wi' ye," she began. Perhaps this could be done privately after all.

"Eh?" He leaned toward her.

And just like that, Bradana's attention became captured and drawn elsewhere. Someone had entered through the doors of the hall, which stood open to the air.

He had come armed. It was the first thing Bradana saw. He had his hair tightly braided as a warrior might—she had never seen him so. The torches picked out threads of red in the rich brown of his hair. He moved with quiet confidence.

She wanted to shout at him, to tell him to leave. To cry out and warn him off. *Let me deal with this.* Her gaze met his all the way down the room, and she strove to convey the message.

He came on.

She stepped away from Earrach and raised both her hands, warding off the man who walked toward her.

"Pray, hear me! I ha' something to say."

The chamber went quiet. Startled listeners shuffled their feet and the torches crackled, that was all.

Swiftly, swiftly Bradana turned and looked at her stepfather, a glance of apology, before she turned to Earrach.

"I am sorry. I am withdrawing my agreement to this handfasting. I canna wed wi' ye. I release ye from our betrothal."

"Bradana." Mam's voice. Bradana had not realized she was close by. She could not turn away from Earrach, who held her gaze with those dangerous, dark eyes.

"You what?" The roar came from Mican, who stood behind his son. "Ye canna!"

"I can." Bradana raised her chin a notch. "I do."

Mican bellowed, "The alliance is no' yours to make, nor to break!"

"Nay." She swiveled to face him. "But 'tis my body and my life. As a free woman, 'tis my choice whether or no' I will keep to the agreement that was made. Aye, Kendrick?" Now she turned her gaze to him.

Her stepfather stood frozen, the very picture of chagrin. From the start of all this, when the betrothal had been set, he had assumed her agreement with it. Counted on that agreement. Denied her objections. But he could not and would not force her, save by ties of loyalty.

"Bradana, daughter," he said, "I pray ye do no' shame me this way."

She trembled now in every limb. Even her lips quivered when she lifted her chin still higher and said, "Do no' sell me, if ye hold me dear."

"I am not." Kendrick stepped closer to her and laid a hand on her arm, one that silently beseeched her. "This is for the benefit of all."

"Save for me."

He swallowed so hard she could hear it. "Sometimes sacrifices must be made."

Bradana met his gaze. She managed to hold it, despite her fear, when she said, "This one, I will not make."

And the fear sank beneath a surge of triumphant gladness. Everyone there had heard her declaration, one that to her heart paled beside the fact that she had just saved Adair. He had heard—the whole chamber, so quiet, had heard. He would not have to draw his sword and face the man who stood beside her, also armed despite all his finery.

She needed to walk out. Past all the staring faces.

"Now wait a moment!" The angry words came not from Kendrick or even Mican, as might be expected, but from Earrach. He moved forward, and instinctively Bradana edged away from him.

"I am sorry," she said, finding the courage to meet his gaze. "Truly, I am."

She stepped down off the dais. As if the movement prompted them, several other things happened at once. Mican made to come after her, and Kendrick intercepted him. Mam cried out, a cry like a gull felled by a stone, and Kendrick turned back for her.

Earrach, his eyes fixed upon Bradana, reached for her arm.

"Mistress? Mistress Bradana! This is no' done—"

Dodging his grasp, she did not flee so much as sweep away from him. She could see Adair standing halfway down the hall. Waiting for her, so she thought. He was all the goal she needed.

But when she reached him, standing so tall and silent, he stepped out not to join her, but to block Earrach's way.

"Let her go," he said to Earrach. "It is done."

"It is not. Out o' my way!"

"Bradana, go." Adair glanced at her over his shoulder. But she could not take another step. The blood drained from her face as she realized she might not have saved him after all. They could still come to blows.

And she would sell herself ten times over for the sake of this man.

Her vision sharpened, and she saw every separate occurrence, each movement. The snarl on Earrach's lips and the danger in his eyes. Adair's hand resting upon the hilt of his sword.

She seized Adair's arm and attempted to tow him away with her. "Come, please."

He gave her one searing glance from glowing gray-green eyes. The people occupying the rear of the hall fell away from them as they moved, opening the path to the doors.

Earrach followed.

Bradana could feel him like a dark wind, a distinct threat. She could feel his every footstep.

They were in the clear out in front of the hall before Adair pulled her to a halt. The day—so beautiful earlier on—had clouded over, and Bradana thought, *To be sure, Alba knows. This very place shares the trouble gathered round me.*

"Adair, by the gods, please—"

She had time for no more before Adair turned and faced the other man.

For an instant, Bradana saw the two of them with painful clarity—Earrach standing like a bear, large and poised to maul and tear; Adair balanced lightly on the balls of his feet, that gleam of red in his brown hair. The moment would be burned into her mind forever.

"Leave her be," Adair told Earrach. "She has spoken her refusal. Take it like a man."

"Out o' my way," Earrach growled. "This is between the woman and me."

Adair stepped in front of Bradana. "*I* am between the woman and ye."

Fury blazed in Earrach's eyes. "She has made a promise. She will keep it and wed wi' me this day. Unless her father wishes war instead of peace."

"She has made a free choice," Adair answered. "Leave it be."

For an instant, one glorious instant, Bradana thought that would be an end to it. She could almost see Earrach falling back, she and Adair walking away. What would happen next, she could not tell. No violence.

Then Earrach reached for her, another vicious snatch aimed at her arm.

Adair drew his sword.

People were by now pouring from the hall. Not Kendrick. Where was he? Mayhap he could stop this thing.

But nay, naught could stop it, for Earrach's sword came swiftly to his hand, and violence shone in his eyes.

Adair pushed Bradana aside, not too gently.

"Nay," she cried, and flung herself back at him. "Nay!" This, she did not want. This, above all things. "'Tis decided. I have chosen—"

Earrach threw her a disparaging look. "I know not who this upstart thinks he is. But if he chooses to die for your lack o' honor, mistress, I am willing to kill him."

Lack of honor? Because she chose to claim her own life? That thought was swallowed by bright terror for Adair. Should he fall—should he fall because of her…

She must do something to stop this. Above all things.

But both swords were free of their scabbards, and before she could draw another breath the blades met with a clang. So close was she, the reverberation shivered through her.

Hands gripped her and pulled her from the line of danger.

⚜

CHAPTER TWENTY-FOUR

THIS COMBAT WAS unlike any Bradana had ever seen. Quick, sharp, and without mercy, the blades met and struck at each other again and again. If but once that metal should fail to strike metal and instead meet flesh…

Barely breathing, she stood within the circle of Maeve's arms—for it was her friend who had yanked her out of danger's reach—and watched the deadly dance. Those who would have been wedding guests ranged all around them. Bradana still did not see Kendrick, the one man who might stop this madness. But Mican stood at the forefront watching his son with what appeared to be satisfaction.

For, aye, at first glance the battle did not seem an equal one. Though the two men were nearly of a height, Earrach had twice Adair's bulk, and the sheer power of the blows he delivered—in the manner of a smith hammering at the forge—argued naught could stand before him for long.

Adair, lighter, quicker, must soon tire and falter—and one miss at turning back that relentless assault must earn death.

Yet he did not miss. And a glint of green fire came to his eyes as he leaped and dodged, seeming to take his opponent's measure.

They circled as Bradana's ears cried out for release from the crashing, and her heart cried for mercy from the terror of it all. Och, what had she done? She'd thought to save him, even more than herself, by speaking out. Now…

A flurry and an abrupt change in the dance, and a line of red appeared on Earrach's right forearm. The one that held the sword. He tossed up his head even as Bradana's heart bounded, and he came on.

As if the sight of first blood was a signal, the pace of the fight quickened. Someone pulled in close beside Bradana and Maeve.

Kerr, with Toren at his elbow. Both their faces avid.

"He'll ne'er take him down, our cousin," Kerr said. "Earrach is a monster wi' the—"

Another flurry. A second line of red on the monster's sword arm. He shook himself and roared, aye, like an enraged beast.

Kerr swore. Adair's blade had been too quick to follow with the eye.

But Earrach raised his sword above his head and came in howling. Neither man had a shield, and when that treacherous blow landed, it turned Adair's sword aside. His feet shuffled in the grass furiously. He nearly went down.

Heat drenched Bradana and her heart leaped to her throat. He could not withstand many such blows, her Adair could not.

Would she stand here and watch him slain? She must stop this mad dance.

But Maeve's arms enfolded her, and if she ran forward now, the distraction might be enough to give Earrach the advantage he needed.

Upon the thought, Earrach struck again and Adair whirled, barely in time. Earrach's blade caught his shoulder as he spun. Now the blood started upon Adair's tunic.

"Stop this!" Bradana cried, frantic. "Someone stop this!" No one heard. No one listened. She turned to Kerr and seized his arm in both hands. "Stop them."

Kerr's eyes met hers. They had never been what she might consider friends, but they'd grown up together. He must heed her.

"Please, Kerr."

He started forward, but hesitated. How could he move between those whirling, crashing blades? For the pace of the combat had increased again. Earrach, standing firm with his feet planted in the grass, struck faster and harder. Adair danced around him, his braids flying out behind him in a flurry as he searched for an in, an opening for a deadly strike.

One of these two men would fall to the grass and likely rise no more.

Both of them were tired now and sweating heavily. Adair's strikes were perhaps not so bright, Earrach's not so powerful. Their breath came in gasps. All it would take was one mistake.

And then it came. Adair, dancing, whirled around to face his opponent. Earrach turned and his sword came up—not quite fast enough. Adair's blade swooped in to kiss the side of Earrach's neck.

For an instant everything froze. Not a sound pierced the afternoon. No one breathed nor cried out. Even the clouds seemed to pause overhead.

Earrach did not immediately fall. Instead, legs still planted wide, he stared into Adair's face. Not until Adair, poised like a shard of quicksilver, withdrew his sword did the bigger man begin to go down, crumpling slowly as his legs failed him and he crashed to the grass in a shower of blood.

"My son! My son!" Mican bellowed, leaping forward to go down in the grass beside Earrach.

Earrach, who stared at the sky.

Adair did not move a step, merely stood with his blade, smeared in gore, at his side.

"'Twas a fair fight." The words were on Bradana's lips almost before she could think, for all she could think on was him. "Ye all saw, 'twas a fair right."

Toren leaned past Kerr to look at her, an assessing expression such as she had never before received from him.

"Come," he told her. "Quickly."

But Mican had already stumbled to his feet and swung to face Adair. "Ye ha' murdered my son."

Adair's head came up. His nostrils flared. At that moment he looked like a battle pony fit for the charge. There was more to Gawen MacMurtray's third son than even Bradana had guessed.

Toren stepped forward. Bradana still could not imagine where Kendrick was, unless her mother…

By the gods, what had happened to her mother?

Yet to her surprise, Toren stepped up in his father's place. "My sister is right. 'Twas a fair fight. Everyone saw." He turned to Kerr and mouthed, *Take them.*

Kerr grabbed Bradana's hand, yanked her from Maeve's grip. With his other hand he snagged Adair's arm and towed him away out of the crowd. Towed both of them. "Come."

Kerr was not what Bradana would call a man of practical considerations. Yet now, as they left the thronged area and the man lying on the ground awash with blood, he said, "Go to your rooms. Grab what ye need. I will bring ponies. Ye maun get yoursel's away. Understand?"

Scarcely listening to him, Bradana looked back, sure someone—Mican—would be coming after them.

Adair had killed Mican's son.

But no one had left the crowd.

It had been a fair fight.

Toren still held Mican there, talking to him. But aye, he would be coming. A man like Mican would want blood for blood.

"He will be coming," she said aloud.

Kerr glanced at her. "Aye, so I say."

Adair dragged all three of them to a halt. "I ha' done naught wrong. I will stay and face whatever justice your father hands out."

"Ye cannot," Kerr objected. "Father will want to keep the alliance intact. He may—"

"Sacrifice Adair," Bradana concluded.

"Aye, so."

"Kerr." Now Bradana grabbed hold of her stepbrother. "Where will we go?"

"Better," Adair said, light and darkness flickering in his eyes, "for us to take my boat away to Erin."

"The boat is the first place they will seek ye."

"Then I cannot get my belongings—"

"No' from the boat, nay. Only from your quarters. Hurry, for the gods' sake. I will bring the ponies."

Kerr pelted off. Adair looked at Bradana and she at him.

"I need to go back," he told her. "Face my actions."

"Nay. Please. Come wi' me."

Hand in hand, she led him away in a large circle through the settlement. Everyone had been at the wedding, so no one saw when they circled back and approached her quarters. She could hear voices, though. Shouting.

Adair stood in the doorway of her chamber, reddened sword still dangling from his fingers, and watched while she gathered what she would need. A warm cloak. A blanket, which she used as a bundle. Supplies for her monthly. A few things she might barter if she had to.

Wen.

The great hound had been lying on her sleeping bench waiting for her. Like Adair, he watched her preparations with solemn eyes, never a twitch of his tail.

He would come with her. At the thought, a great wave of relief crashed upon her heart. She would not have to leave him behind to go with Earrach. She would not be going with Earrach, to the north.

At the last moment, as she surveyed the chamber, her eyes fell upon the harp. She laid it carefully atop the other items and tied the bundle shut.

"Wen, come."

"Bradana?"

She looked at the man she loved. He who had taken on this burden for her sake.

He told her, "I think I should stay."

Aye, perhaps they both should. She needed to find out if

harm had befallen her mother. And he had done naught wrong. Why should he flee?

Except he had taken the life of an honored guest. For no fit reason Mican could see.

"Perhaps we should do what Kerr says and leave for a time. Just until things settle down."

"'Tis a cowardly way to behave, that."

Mayhap it was. But och, could she take the chance that Mican would retaliate?

"I canna lose ye," she said.

"Aye, so."

It was for the sake of love, after all, that they fled.

CHAPTER TWENTY-FIVE

THE FURY OF the combat faded from Adair's blood but slowly. Only rarely in the past had he taken part in such contests— battles during training or at times when the high king summoned his father's men, when he marched out under his da's banner.

Nothing ever so personal as this. So immediate, when staring into the eyes of his opponent—a man he knew—he saw that man desired, with all his being, to kill him.

Instinct had overtaken him during that fight, an ancient sort of instinct that cast his emotions to the background.

For the amount of time it took him to kill a man.

And now—now that man lay dead, and Adair did not at all know whether they did right to flee. Flight argued he had done something wrong. He had not, only defended the woman he loved.

And yet Mican surely would not see it that way, as Earrach had not. In their eyes, Adair had no right to defend Bradana. Her father might, and her stepbrothers might, but she'd been betrothed to Earrach.

Until she'd dissolved that betrothal. Renounced it. She had that right.

How would Kendrick see it? Part of Adair—a large part— thought he should stay and find out. The rest of him…

Och, the rest of him heeded the look in Bradana's eyes. He had beheld terror there when he challenged Earrach. By the gods, he had felt her fear. He could feel it even now as they mounted the ponies Kerr brought and started away inland, leaving the settlement behind.

She feared she would lose him, and that thought above all others possessed her mind.

So perilous was love.

He could not doubt that she loved him, this woman made up of half beauty and half courage. No doubt that he loved her. Whatever bound them one to the other had been strengthened when they made love last night. Bound to one another tight.

He understood full well why she'd been unable to go to another man.

The world—their world—would not understand it. Nor why he'd slain that man for her sake.

As they started off, their two ponies with Wen alongside heading for the wooded slope above the settlement, he wondered if there was anything he would not do for her sake.

Back there facing Earrach, he'd been willing to die for her. He must now live for her. Was bending his honor any more difficult?

Still, he did not like it, and he glanced back toward the settlement as they climbed the slope of the land, all laid out behind him. He could see his own small boat hauled up on the shore, and hoped Nolan and Flynn would follow his instructions and leave.

In front of the hall the wedding guests still gathered, looking like so many dark blots—perhaps insects. Even as he watched, the blots broke apart and began to spread out.

Discussion over. Would pursuit be far behind?

"As soon as we are safe awa'," Bradana said, "we will stop and look at your shoulder. I have bandages in my pack. Is it bleeding much?"

It was. The right side of his tunic was heavy with wet. He could smell his own blood. "I do not know."

"We will camp a couple nights and then, once tempers ha' cooled and perhaps Mican has left, we will go back, if ye want."

He did want. He'd been taught to stand on his feet and face his actions.

Yet he could hear the terror still in her voice, and when she glanced at him, he could see it in her eyes.

Spending a few nights out on the land was no great matter. He had done so often enough with friends, back home in Erin.

But this was not Erin, the land he knew and loved. It was Alba, deep and dark, dangerous at its heart. A place where the trees whispered and deer gave a man his direction. Where he might lose himself.

Would this place that was not his own accept him? Reject him?

Bradana led the way, her cream-colored pony eager enough to be away. His own mount followed hers, and Wen gamboled alongside. The trees closed around them, and all too soon, just as when Toren and Kerr had taken him hunting, he could no longer glimpse the sea. So fully did Alba swallow them up.

For some distance, they rode in silence. It felt strange and isolated, not knowing what happened behind them. When they came to a small stream, Bradana halted her pony and swung down.

"Here is a good place. Sit there." She pointed to a flat rock. "Let me look at ye."

Adair dismounted, his every muscle screaming in protest. A score of scrapes and bruises had he collected during that battle. Only the one at the shoulder worried him. The steady pain there had passed into numbness. He could barely feel his right arm.

Bradana went down on her knees beside him, bringing her face close. He watched her as she pulled the sodden cloth away from his skin to expose the wound, and he traced the movement of emotions across her face.

Distress. Worry. Terror.

Her eyes came up, wide, blue, and bottomless, to meet his. "'Tis bad, this."

"Aye." He knew it.

"Ye have lost much blood."

Dispassionately, he looked down at himself. Earrach's

blade—the tip of it—had caught him as he turned. His own movement had torn the flesh, removed a chunk of skin and muscle the size of his fist. If that blade had caught a vital blood vessel, he could well bleed to death.

But…

"'Tis slowing now," he told her.

"Ye think so?"

"Aye. Pack it and we will go on."

He could hear no sounds of pursuit from behind them. Could hear nothing but the songs of birds, Wen's huffing, and a kind of curious murmuring from the trees overhead. It seemed as if the three of them had fallen out of the world, to this other place. An endless stretch of rock and forest.

Alba *breathed*.

That thought came from nowhere. He found he could not dismiss it. He must be lightheaded from loss of blood.

"There, now." Bradana made a neat bandage and tied it off. Her hands lingered upon him as if she could not bear to draw them away, and she leaned closer.

The kiss came so sweet that it curled his toes and stirred the desire inside—let him know, all over again, how much he loved her.

Slowly and reluctantly did she pull her lips from his to say, "Adair, I was so afraid. If I lost ye—"

"You have not. Am I not here?"

Her gaze flicked to the bandage, betraying her worry. "Aye."

"Bradana"—he held her with his uninjured hand—"I must go back after a time. Face what I have done."

"After a time." Disconcertingly, her eyes filled with tears. "No' yet. I canna lose ye."

"What makes ye think ye will?"

"Unjust punishments have been imposed before this. Kendrick, aye, is a fair man. But what if he decides to place all blame on ye in order to salvage his ties wi' Mican?"

Wen, who had been lying beside them, suddenly got to his

feet and looked back the way they had come.

Pursuit?

Hastily, Bradana tied up her bundle. "Come—we must ride on."

"D'YE KNOW WHERE we are?" Adair asked as night began to fall, gathering like a gray blanket beneath the trees. Night came late at this time of year. That and Adair's bone-deep weariness told him they had traveled far.

She shook her head. She had deliberately lost them, steering a course through the thickest part of the forest and over stony ground.

He must have faith she could find her way home again. For he never would.

The trees here towered around them, and the ground rose steadily. They had climbed the mountain—no hill this, like the ones back home—and now skirted the summit. He could sense, if not see for the dark, that a drop opened on their right. Wen, who followed him, kept away from it, making a barely visible gray shape against the upward slope.

Traveling near blind in such country was surely madness. When Bradana drew her pony up in the midst of the trees, he felt nothing but relief.

"The animals need rest." She slid down from her mount. "So do we."

So did he, she meant. And aye, as he too dismounted, he had to admit that his strength flagged. He'd lost much blood, and to his dismay, his head swam a little when his feet met the ground.

Instantly, Bradana was at his side. "Come. I will mak' ye a bed."

They had little in the way of supplies. Bradana unpacked it all and spread the blanket out for Adair before urging him down.

"How bad is the pain?"

"No' bad." He did not mention that both his arm and hand still felt numb.

"Ye need water to replace all that blood ye shed. I ha' a flask and can hear water nearby. Let me bring ye some."

He caught her with his left hand. "Be careful, love, in the dark."

"Love?" She froze an instant there in his grip. "So do ye call me?"

"Aye, for surely that is what ye are."

"Until the day I die."

She moved off silently and Wen went with her, which made Adair feel only slightly better. If trouble caught them, what use would he be to her, his sword arm so sorely hampered?

He stretched out on the blanket and listened to Alba breathing all around him. The sigh of it through the trees. The song, aye, of the water rushing nearby. He was half asleep when Bradana returned to kneel down next to him and tip the flask to his lips—cold, sweet water to sustain him.

"Thank ye, Bradana."

"We have nay food," she said starkly. "None for us or Wen."

"No matter."

"I will take the ponies to water and return."

He was far more than half asleep when she came and lay beside him, wound her arms around him, tucking up the side of the blanket about them both. Wen lay down on Adair's other side, a bulwark of protection.

There in the arms of his lover, on Alba's breast, he slept.

⚜

CHAPTER TWENTY-SIX

THE HOUND MUST have left them and gone hunting during the night, for when Adair and Bradana awakened, he had a dead rabbit laid across his paws and looked immensely proud of himself.

Bradana exclaimed and accepted the gift with much praise for her hound. She moved off to the stream to skin and clean her prize, and Adair sat up. He took stock of himself.

He felt better, though far from what he could call well. The pain in his shoulder was considerable, but to his great relief, the feeling in both his arm and fingers had returned.

He rose. He and Wen followed Bradana to the stream, a rill that tumbled, chuckling, down from the slope above.

"Where are we?"

She glanced up at him, her hair in a tangle escaped from the fancy arrangement it had been given yesterday, and her eyes shadowed. "I ha' no idea."

"Are we still on Kendrick's land?"

"Likely not. We traveled far yesterday."

He looked at the rabbit and his stomach rumbled. "Do we dare have a fire?" He would much rather eat his food cooked but would take it any way he might.

She glanced around them. They still could not see down into the glen below, for mist had tumbled from the mountain above and filled it.

"I think so." She looked stricken. "I did no' bring a flint. I usually carry one, but I am no' in my regular clothing, only this." She indicated the blue gown she wore with disdain. Wedding finery.

"Do not fret. I ha' one in my pocket. My da always said, do not be caught without a flint or a knife."

"Aye, so." She looked relieved.

He went off and began gathering deadfall for a fire, feeling better rather than worse for the movement. A few days away, he thought, to give tempers in the settlement time to calm, give Mican a chance to leave as Bradana had said, and they would go back. He would face what he had done. A man had to accept his consequences.

He laid the fire and then found he could not use the flint with only one good hand. He passed it to Bradana when she returned and watched her set the game to roast.

"While that is cooking, let me look again at your shoulder."

He sat stoic and quiet while she peeled away the bloodied bandages, went to the stream and washed them, cleaned the wound as best she could, and covered it once more. Neither of them spoke, but he could see the worry in her eyes.

"Bradana," he said at last, "I will be all right. I have taken wounds in the past."

"So dire as this?"

Mayhap not. The skirmishes in which he'd engaged had resulted in slashes and glancing blows only.

But he did not want her to worry.

He tipped up her chin with a finger and gazed into her eyes. "I will be well, *alanna*."

The breath hitched in her throat. "I canna lose ye. I do not know how I could go on."

"Ye will not lose me. Am I not right here?"

He kissed her because he could do nothing else, and felt some of her fear and tension drain away.

"Do not fret over it," he told her when the kiss ended. "Am I not already better than I was?" More likely, he thought, to worry about what would become of them out here in the wild.

This land, so unlike the one he loved back home, that wanted to whisper to him.

"Aye," she sighed. "Ye be young and strong. Nay need to think the worst."

"Which direction do we head today?"

"East," she said without hesitation.

That gave him a qualm. "Farther away from the coast?" Into Alba's dark heart.

"Aye, for we canna go home yet. And northward lie Mican's lands. We dare not intrude upon him. I thought if we travel inland and circle back toward the south—the chief who holds lands there is neither friendly nor hostile to Kendrick. We might be able to go home that way. But no' yet."

He must leave this in her hands. He must trust her even as he trusted these bonds that united them.

They divided their meal into three strictly equal portions and moved out after making sure the fire was covered with dirt. The mist cloaked them as they skirted the bulk of the mountain and crossed the rill. It swallowed them as they picked their way steadily eastward.

A magnificent sight met them when the sun rose and set the mist aflame. They rode into a great, white-gold sea of light. To Adair, it felt like moving through a magical doorway into another realm.

Another world.

Someone should make a song about it, he thought as his pony followed Bradana's. She should, and play it upon her harp. Though no listener in any hall would believe such a tale of travelers transported from one world to the next, no matter how skilled the bard's words and fingers.

The mist rose before the sun, trailing streamers upward, revealing a scene of such beauty that it made the breath catch in Adair's throat. Below them, far below, lay a glen. The green, shaggy shoulders of the mountains stretched away, following the path of a long, silvery loch that seemed to beckon into infinity. A thousand colors of green there were, all light and darkness, and wild to the heart.

Would this foreign land be kind of them? Already it had guided Adair to the greatest gift a man might receive. And a load of trouble.

He let his gaze rest on the hair, honey fair in the new light, of the girl who rode ahead of him. What he felt for her both sustained and terrified him.

Pray, be good to her, he beseeched the wild, eternal land, *if not to me.*

FOR THREE DAYS they traveled east and then northward, their way south being blocked by a series of long glens. Wen kept them fed. Sometimes the food proved barely palatable, a mangled bird caught by a wing or a limp-necked rodent. Sometimes they dared not have a fire and Bradana nearly choked on the raw game. She remained grateful for every bite.

Adair had placed his life and safety in her hands. She could not fail him. This, despite the fact that she knew not precisely where they were, nor how far they had gone from home. Nor could she tell if they were being followed, though she doubted it.

Who would come after them? Kendrick? Would he send her brothers?

More likely Mican would pursue them out of a desire for revenge. He had been very angry. Not the sort of man to let the death of a son go unanswered.

She thought much on that as they rode into a land big and wild enough to engulf them. It had been a fair fight, that in which Adair had felled Earrach. Everyone there had seen so.

Would that matter to Mican? Quite likely not. She might eventually be able to argue it to Kendrick when they went back.

Not quite yet.

Meanwhile, she must keep Adair safe and out of danger's reach. She dared not travel too far inland, for the kingdom of Dalriada, settled by chiefs from Erin, had but a fingerhold on Alba's west coast, wrenched away from the tribes of blue men who still held the interior.

She could not lead her love from one danger straight into another.

That he was her love, she had no doubt. No mere girlish emotion, this, that made her fingers tingle and caused a flutter in her heart. Though her fingers did tingle with desire when she looked at him, and though everything about him pleased her beyond expression.

This was need, more that aught else. In a curious way, it seemed she'd been looking for Adair MacMurtray all her life without knowing. Missing him without suspecting it.

Was that why she'd never more than given a glance to any other man? Why she had not fought as hard as she should when Kendrick proposed the marriage alliance with Earrach?

She'd wanted no one, had expected she never would. She had not known that she wanted a man she hadn't yet encountered.

Out here, living upon the face of the land with almost nothing to support them, she suspected that they would stumble over each other's faults and fall into disagreements. She awaited it day after day. They were short on sleep, worried, and ill fed.

It did not happen. Adair healed steadily, and she could feel his strength return despite the short provisions. He had a deep well of vitality, and when she felt at her worst—most worried and desperate—she need only catch a smile from him to benefit from it.

And then there were the signs. Curious occurrences at moments when she hesitated over their course or direction. A bird might suddenly fly up with a harsh cry, warning them of a steep drop ahead. Several times, stags appeared and seemed to guide them onward.

"Follow him," Adair told her then.

She could not shake the notion that Alba herself watched over them and also led them, for soon enough Bradana had no hope of guessing where they were.

Or how to get home.

◆

CHAPTER TWENTY-SEVEN

ONE COOL MORNING, as they rode single file, they smelled smoke from a fire. Bradana drew her pony up in a dead stop and raised her head. Adair, in his usual place behind her, lifted his head also and scented the wind.

He had now lost count of how many days they had spent wending their way up and down across Alba's hills and glens. Utterly lost, he'd placed himself in Bradana's hands. So far they'd met no one, and if they barely clung to life—for he was hungry all the time—at least they did so on their own and by the grace of Wen. And though he'd seen worry in Bradana's eyes more than a few times as she'd strained to watch their back trail, he'd as yet caught no sounds of pursuit.

She had told him there were native settlements out here. People she called blue men, for the tattoos that covered their skin, and that the southerners called Picts. It seemed they had nearly ridden up onto one such settlement.

Wen went forward, stepping like a gray shadow through the trees and bracken.

With another wave for Adair, Bradana got down from her pony and followed the hound.

Adair had no doubt that they would not have managed so far without Wen. Like a protective spirit, he accompanied them, guarded them while they slept, and provided for them.

If something happened to the hound...

Quietly, he slipped his sword from its loop. His injury had

improved enough that he could now grip the hilt of the weapon. How he would fare in a battle… Well, he hoped he would not need to find out.

Bradana soon came slipping back and moved directly to lay her hands on his knee.

"We maun turn back. A large settlement. Blue men, I do no' doubt."

Wen came back whining.

"Aye, so," Bradana told the hound. "We are going."

She stepped away from Adair's pony and seemed to take stock of their surroundings. Choosing the best route could not be easy. He could see she did not know.

Help her, Alba, Adair thought. He did it only half out of fancy and half from the odd belief that had lately been creeping over him.

For several moments, nothing happened. Wen whined again. Then a bird came streaming up out of the bracken that clothed the steep drop to their right and flew in the opposite direction.

Bradana's head turned. Their eyes met. She stepped back to him even as he lifted his brows.

"I do no' want to go that way," she breathed. "Father north."

"We cannot go south." He indicated the steep drop.

"And we canna continue east." She bit her lip.

"Surely we are far past Mican's lands."

Clear worry showed in her eyes. "We should be. The last thing I want to do is lead ye into trouble."

"Let us circle north a distance and ye can correct again."

"Aye."

She remounted and they rode on, choosing a stony route up and over the flank of the mountain. It eventually offered them a splendid view of what lay to the east in a pocket on the side of the hill—a large settlement with a round tower at its head, cook fires emitting lazy smoke into the clear air.

A narrow escape.

Bradana seemed more vigilant after that. She led him cautiously and sent Wen ahead to scout often.

Not till that night, when they lay together in their blanket, did she speak of it.

"I nearly blundered back there today." They lay as close to one another as they could get, holding hands, and she spoke in his ear. It grew chilly out on the open land at night, though it did not become truly dark at this time of year. They dared not have a fire. "What if I'd led us right up onto that settlement? If one of their scouts had seen us?"

"What d'ye think they would do to us, these blue men?"

"I hate to think." She moved uneasily and squeezed his fingers. "Kendrick and the other Dalriadan chiefs have been fighting them as long as I can remember. They would know us by our clothing, our ponies. Our weapons. They hate our kind. I fear…"

He did not press her on it. He could feel her apprehension as if it transferred from her body to his.

He said, "We must have passed beyond the bounds of Dalriada."

"Dalriada has no proper bounds. The Erin chiefs, like Kendrick, push it ever eastward. The blue men push back. Once, all this land was theirs."

"Ye cannot blame them."

"Nay. I was born in the north—the granddaughter of another such chief. My mother's sire. He held—holds—territory some distance beyond Mican's."

"Ye have people there still?"

"I do. My mother was already a widow when she met Kendrick at a gathering o' the Dalriadan chiefs. They discussed means o' uniting to fight the blue men through alliances and such. Even then, the wise men among them preached o' marriage alliances.

"But that was no' why Kendrick and Mother married. He was besotted from the moment he saw her."

"Aye," Adair said softly. At one time, he might have scoffed at such a notion. Now he understood what could draw two people together. "Ye must ha' been very small."

"I was. Even then, I did no' want to leave home. I loved that land where the sea—the far sea, I used to call it—came up to woo the rocks, and the hills towered over. Giving dreams, I thought they did."

"Giving dreams?"

She turned to him in the cocoon of the blanket, so close they might have kissed. "Ye will think me mad."

"Never."

"I used to dream o' ye. Well, no' o' ye so much. I did no' see your face." She touched his cheek where the beard had now grown in, for he had no razor. "'Twas more the *feel* o' ye I felt in the dreams. I imagined ye were there somewhere up in the dark hills. But 'twas fancy only and I did no' truly believe in it. Nor that one day ye would come for me bringing… Well, I ha' no words for it."

"Nay." There were no words for what they felt, the one for the other.

"'Twas as if," she whispered, "I had a memory o' ye, even though I did no' know ye yet."

Curious, he thought, for the both of them to feel that way.

"For all that," she murmured, "I did not know ye when first I saw ye. At least"—she gazed into his eyes—"I did, even as I did not. Does that make sense?"

"It does, to me."

"These dreams were a long way in the past when you arrived. And I'd long stopped believing in such a love. One that—that could make me feel whole inside."

"Aye, so." He closed his eyes for an instant, absorbing the rightness of having her in his arms.

"I saw Mother and Kendrick arguing endlessly despite how they were supposed to love each other, and I thought marriage wi' a man I did no' love could scarce be worse. Then ye came."

"Just barely in time."

"Just barely. Adair, tell me, how can this be so right, when 'tis so wrong? When I barely know ye. When it has torn both our lives apart."

"Because it is." He had no better answer.

She pressed her lips to his, crossing that smallest of distances, as she came closer and closer. The night breeze, like a breath, brushed over them as without conscious thought they shed their clothing, touched one another with reverent care. As there, on the breast of Alba, they made love.

"Beautiful girl, *alanna*," he murmured when she held him deep inside her. As it should be, the two of them made one. A thousand things he should say to her, not the least being that they needed to turn back for home. He needed to face the consequences of his actions.

But the enchantment was too strong. He was caught fast in it, in her. For them at this moment, nothing else existed.

He wanted naught else to exist.

"Never leave me, Adair." Her face was wet with tears.

Never leave her? Never go home? Or else persuade her to go away with him, from this land that, in a curious way, held them both?

"As if I could ever leave ye," he breathed, and even as she laughed for joy, he fell into her again.

CHAPTER TWENTY-EIGHT

BRADANA CROUCHED OVER the grassy bank and peered at herself in the pool of still water. A blur only, did she appear at first, with the sun behind her shoulder. A brightness of gold and blue, until she shifted and her reflection came into focus.

She did not recognize the woman in the water. Hair tangled, no matter how times she tried to plait it. Face gone thin. Clad in the blue gown meant to be her wedding finery, now ruined. Dirty and torn and mere rags.

Eyes wild, like those of some feral creature glimpsed in the dark.

Moreover, she did not recognize the woman she had become inside. Had she not been strong and sensible, as she grew? Put away from her sentimental things? Now one man ruled her heart and the need for him ruled her world.

Rarely was Adair MacMurtray out of her sight. Even now while she washed, she could hear him moving around behind her, loading their few possessions onto the ponies.

She knew what she would see if she rose and turned. Adair, tall and slim, for he too had dropped weight. With her fingers, she could count his ribs. His hair, also tangled, hung down in a rich brown mane.

She knew the look that would be in his eyes if he turned to her, gray eyes speckled with green, that held everything, everything she needed.

There was no more to be had than him. No greater joy than

being in his company. No higher pleasure than being in his arms. She did not understand quite the nature of this love that united them, though, aye, she had her suspicions.

She rose and turned.

He stood beside his pony but watched her, his eyes drawn to her just as hers went always to him, and aye, everything else fell away from her, even though they were mired in trouble.

Should she tell him they were lost? That ever since they'd changed direction back at the native settlement, she'd been turned round in her head, following the sun and supposed signs? Everything from a rogue ray of sunlight making a path to the flight of a bird.

She had no notion of where she was, save with him.

"Look at me," she said ruefully. "This gown was once quite grand. No fit attire in which to travel."

"I am looking. I cannot imagine a bonnier sight."

"Ye fool," she chided, but the tears rose hard into her throat. So emotional was she these days, who had ever held her feelings in strict abeyance.

He grinned at her, that wide, beautiful smile that never failed to touch her heart. "A mad fool, 'tis what I am."

She went to him, there where he stood, and looked into his face. Aye, she knew it so well now. Each separate freckle. The way the hairs—redder than those on his head or, indeed, on his body—curled upon his cheeks. "I ha' a confession to make."

"Aye, so. Go on."

"I do no' ken where we are. Where, in all of blessed Alba."

"Ye think I did not know that?"

"Did ye?"

"For days I have known."

"Aye so, but ye placed yoursel' in my hands, and I ha' misled ye."

He put out his arms and tugged her up against him.

"I think," she said, "we have come too far east. And maybe too far north, after. If we turn back now, I am afraid we will cross

Mican's land—the last place we want to be. Yet…"

He lifted a brow. "Yet?"

"Each time I try to turn south, our way is blocked by a loch or a glen. By the land itself. 'Tis as if—"

"Alba is directing us?"

"Aye," she agreed, relieved that he too had felt it. "Yet we canna keep on this way. You are hungry. We all are. Wen is down to fur and bones."

They both looked at the hound, who did not appear bothered by his condition.

"What's to do?" she said. She might wish to go on so forever, just existing with him, but they would run out of strength, and soon.

Adair glanced around as if seeking to read the land. They had spent that night in the shelter of a pile of stones on a broad stretch of moor, where lay the pool. It appeared to go on into a limitless vista of green turf and blue hills, in all directions.

He said, "The sun is far north this time o' year. If we wish to start doubling back southward, we must set our backs to it."

"I am afraid, as I say, to head south. I think we must be northeast of Mican's lands. What if we stumble upon him? Or upon a native settlement. The blue men are everywhere." Indeed, they had seen what they took to be hunting parties in the distance.

"Bradana, my love"—he gazed into her eyes—"ye must believe. Alba has so far protected us."

"Aye, so, but she is wild and capricious. What may she show us next?"

They found out later that afternoon. They had turned to the west—what Bradana took for west—reasoning that if they could reach the sea, or sight of it, they could get their bearings. Yet the land seemed to go on forever, rising and falling beneath the ponies' hooves, and when clouds gathered, Bradana could no longer see the sun.

It was as if Alba now hid her face and her signs. As if she

opposed the change they had made.

Late in the afternoon, it began to rain. They'd had rain before, to be sure. A land of rain was this, brief squalls quickly flown, before the sun flitted through the clouds. Now, trapped on the broad stretch of moorland, they had nowhere to hide as it came in sheets, driving down through hair and fur and clothing.

Somewhere amid the deluge, before nightfall, they got turned around. By the time they stopped in a copse of young hazel trees above a nameless loch, Bradana could not tell north from south, east from west.

Hungry and soaked to the skin, the three of them sat in a huddle beneath the trees, Adair with his arms around Bradana and Wen across her feet. Protecting her, the both of them were, as best they might.

She wanted to weep. There, with the wet coming down, Adair would not be able to tell that she gave way to her misery and despair, but she would not. She would not because she needed to be strong for him.

She'd been placed in the position of leading him from harm. Yet she was fumbling and failing. That terrified her more than anything.

The storm blew through sometime during the night, but it left a chasing wind behind. Soaking wet, they sat and shivered and got no sleep even after the rain ceased.

When they rose, the world lay cloaked in mist. So thick was it, they could see no more than a few steps in any direction. When Wen moved off, a gray shadow in a dim landscape, Bradana feared she would lose him. He returned to them, but without any game.

Despair touched Bradana's heart. Indeed, Alba showed them her hard and merciless side. What were they to do?

"We cannot travel far in this," Adair said, answering the question she had not asked. "Let us scout around to find a better place to lie over till it clears."

They did, though it seemed like stumbling through the dark. Shapes of rocks and hillsides and stunted trees loomed before them. When a much larger shape appeared, Bradana stopped in consternation.

In the gray-misted world, it looked like a monster, hulking and twisted. Malevolent. Reason told her it must be some man-made structure, which she found still more terrifying.

People out here? They must be blue men. Had they stumbled on another settlement?

"Do not go near." She seized Adair's hand.

But Wen ran forward, his great tail a plume in motion. And Adair told her gently, "I think 'tis a tower. Half ruined."

Aye, the blue men built such towers. They must indeed have strayed beyond the bounds of Dalriadan civilization.

"Stay here with the ponies." And Adair followed Wen.

The moment, the terrible moment when he disappeared from her sight, she thought her world wound end. Terror made her disobedient, took her forward to follow him in turn.

The tower was indeed ruined, half fallen and no doubt long abandoned. The top stones had tumbled sideways into the turf, but the side with the doorway still stood.

Even as she came up leading both ponies, Adair emerged from inside.

"I think 'tis safe and will offer some shelter if the rain returns."

"Is anyone there?"

He shook his head. "Abandoned."

"Are ye certain?"

"Aye. Let us rest up here until the weather clears, and we can figure our direction."

Bradana did not feel easy about it. She could not see the land in any direction, and the dark stones of the tower, glistening with wet, lent a feeling of dread.

To be sure, with the top fallen, those who had built it would likely not return. But the doorway looked like the entrance to doom.

Did Alba offer them sanctuary? Or a trap?

She could not tell.

$$\begin{array}{c}\text{\textemdash\textemdash}\diamond\text{\textemdash\textemdash}\end{array}$$

CHAPTER TWENTY-NINE

THEY LEFT THE ponies outside so they could graze. So far, the two animals had fared better than the rest of them, grass being thick and lush at this time of year. They hauled everything else inside, where Adair insisted there was room to have a fire.

"We have no fuel," Bradana protested, standing with her hair, her clothing, and her very spirit drooping.

"I will go out and gather some. Love, if ye do not get warm, I fear ye will fall ill."

She turned and tried to look at him, difficult in the gloom. In truth, she did not need to see him. He was as wet as she, clothing sticking to him and hair plastered down. Beneath that clothing, his vitality threatened to wane. The great tear at his shoulder had healed over but left an ugly, ragged scar he would carry all his life. He must be as hungry as she.

"Is it safe to have a fire?" she asked. Given they could get one lit.

"Aye—in this weather, no one will see."

He had followed her all the way from home, mostly on faith. Together they had followed Alba's signs. Time now for her to follow him. *Believe* in him. If she could believe in anything in this world, it must be Adair MacMurtray.

He left the tower and Wen went with him. While they were gone, Bradana laid out their pitiful collection of belongings. The blanket, sodden. The few items of clothing she'd been able to snatch before they fled. The wet bandaging.

Her harp.

She stood that on a pair of stones arranged together and let her fingers caress the damp wood, hoping it would not be ruined. The instrument had been fashioned from ash, and the sound-board from birch. The strings gave a soft whisper as she drew her fingers across them.

She had no idea what had made her bring it when they fled, save it was among her most beloved possessions. It made an awkward burden and could do them little good.

Would she trade it for a warm, hearty meal?

Nay.

Adair came back in with his arms full of sticks, none of them large and all of them wet.

"I do not know if we will get this lit. If we do, I can fetch more. There is a copse of rowan nearby."

"Rowan?" The tales said it was a sacred wood and not meant to burn. Yet Alba would provide what she would provide. "Where is Wen?"

"I think he has gone hunting." Adair did not add that he hoped the hound brought them something. He did not need to.

Together they laid a fire upon the cleared stone area of the floor and struggled to make a spark take hold. It would not, in the damp tinder, and once more despair touched Bradana's heart.

What were they doing out here? What did she hope to achieve?

Adair persisted with the flint and at last some thin twigs caught. He blew on the fire, giving it his life, and fed it sticks of rowan one by one.

She watched him kneeling there as the flames grew. Her beautiful man who kept the faith even when her belief flagged.

She sat on the floor, telling herself she must be as strong and faultless as he. When he went back out for more wood, she did not demur. And when he returned with Wen at his heels, a hare hanging from the hound's jaws, she took it and went out to clean and skin the offering.

Maybe, just maybe, Alba had turned a kindly eye upon them again.

She was sure of it later that night when they had food—if not near enough—in their bellies. When the misty, damp air of the tower sweetened from the fire. When the blanket dried enough that they might wrap themselves in it and she lay in Adair's arms.

Could she ask more than this? Despite the fear, the hunger, and the uncertainty. Was there more to be had in the world than his arms around her and the sound of his heartbeat in her ear?

"Bradana, let me make love to ye."

They had not been doing that much of late. Och, there'd been kisses and fumbling caresses along the way. But at first, she'd been worried for his wound, and after that, distressed.

Now they'd removed most of their clothing to dry. They lay skin to skin and she had not the power to deny him.

He started with kisses, sweet, plaintive ones planted in her palms. At the corners of her mouth, her cheeks, and at the center of her forehead. Then deep ones that claimed her, that drove the fear from her heart. The terror flew away as they kissed, giving and taking one from the other. He fondled her breasts and a new, insistent tension built low in her belly.

She had been born for this. Even though the physical attraction made up but a small part of what lay between her and Adair, the connection of spirit to spirit, that need came leaping up now even as the fire had, and every bit as sustaining.

"Take me, Adair. Please."

They moved quick and hard, desperate for one another, a fundamental and primitive urge. That, she knew, would not end things this night. Too deep was the need, too beguiling the comfort.

She took her turn and kissed him all over, from the mouth downward. Lost herself over again in the scent and taste of him. This strong and beautiful thing that had been born between them knew no bounds and held back nothing. Whatever he asked of her this night, she would give and would take without modesty or hesitation.

After, they lay in perfect peace, fingers linked in the dark. Up between the stones of the tower where the roof had fallen away, Bradana could see stars, a hundred thousand of them seeding the sky. They were just two small humans and a hound. But if she had a choice, nay, she would ask for no more.

She should say something, mark the significance of this moment when they possessed one another so completely. Tell him what he meant to her.

Were there words?

"Adair?"

"Aye, love?"

"Just…Adair." Her world lay in his name, in him. Terrifying, it was, to give all her welfare to another being. But she could not have recalled her love from him now at any cost.

He lifted their joined hands to his lips and kissed the back of hers. She could feel him smile. "Daft lass."

"I was but thinking, what if your father had never sent his clever third son out from Erin? What if I'd never met ye? What would my life have been then?"

"A whole lot easier, mayhap. Less perilous. Ye would no' be lying in a half-ruined tower in the midst of the wild."

"And I would have lived but half a life." She rolled atop him, gazed into his face by starlight. "And I would never have known—never guessed—what I was missing. Ye are the beginning and the ending o' me, Adair."

"And ye, o' me. Whatever comes."

"Whatever comes," she repeated softly.

His arms tightened around her. "Bradana, what d'ye wish to do, come morning?"

What she wanted was to stay here forever with him. Subsistence living. But it could not be.

"What do *ye* want to do?"

"I ha' been thinking. The furor back at the settlement must have died down by now. If we return to Kendrick, I will accept the blame for what I ha' done. Then return to Erin, if I can."

"Ye want to return to Erin?"

"I will take ye with me, *alanna*. Away from this mad place. Back to the soft, open hills that I know so well."

"The land ye love."

"Not half so much," he told her forcefully, "as I love ye. Bradana, I will not go without ye. But aye, my heart does yearn to go."

And must she, then, lose the land she loved in turn? Become an exile for the sake of love. It seemed one of them must make that sacrifice. And had she not just said she would do anything, give anything, to be with him?

"If that is what ye wish, Adair, 'tis what we will do."

"Aye?"

"Aye. The trick of it…"

The trick of it would be finding a route home, and a safe one at that.

Yet, she thought later when he had fallen asleep, when the sweet sound of his breathing filled her ears, she might have spent all of her life on one side of the silver water that separated Alba from Erin, and he on the other. Their spirits never knowing they needed to span that distance.

She did not think anything could be worse than that. She prayed she was not wrong.

CHAPTER THIRTY

A STRETCH OF good weather followed, soft summer days when Alba showed them a kindly face. Bradana struggled visibly to get her bearings. Adair watched her without comment, not wishing to add anything to the weight she carried.

Something had changed between them during that night back in the round tower, had deepened and strengthened. He had less reason to ask her questions. She did not doubt him. They had thrown their lot in one with the other, wherever the path might lead.

Yet they did struggle. The long trail began to tell even on the ponies, who had fared, in grazing, far better than they. Wen had not the vigor he'd formerly enjoyed. Bradana had become a thin shadow of herself, and Adair felt his own strength ebbing.

Yet they made love more frequently, the both of them sensing that from their joining came their best sustenance. And at night, when they were somewhere secure upon the breast of Alba, Bradana played her harp for him.

She began it one clear evening when they'd shared a woefully inadequate meal, reminding him shyly, "D'ye remember when ye asked me to make a song for ye?"

"I do." He lay stretched out with the dying embers of their fire on one side of him and the limitless sky above. Bradana was no more than a silhouette with the harp on her knee.

"I did no' think I could manage it," she confessed. "How to capture all that ye are in my music? Funny and bright and deep and beautiful—so many things, ye are. But as we have been riding, a tune has been unfolding in my head. I call it 'Planxty Adair.'"

She put her fingers to the strings. A shower of notes, a moment's hesitation, and then the music burst forth. A winding, intimate, and quite complicated tune it was, as magical as the night.

The hound's head came up. Adair stopped breathing, for he had no need for breath.

That—what he heard—could not be *him*.

Naught about him was so beautiful. Besides, he heard Alba in this music, the broad breadth of the sky, the bold sweep of a hillside, the strength of the land at night when they lay upon it. He heard Bradana too, her grace and capriciousness. Her endurance. And Wen, regal and steadfast. Even the clop of their ponies' hooves.

Everything they were, and everything they were to each other, lay in the music. He could have listened to it forever.

And a curious thought entered his mind. If he never had anything more than this, a moment of lying here in the night in Bradana's company and her music in his ears, it would be enough. For a higher state of living could not be reached. A man could ask no more.

When she finished, when her fingers stilled on the strings, a hush fell over the land and upon Adair's heart. He broke it only to say, "Bradana, *alanna*, are ye sure that is for me?"

"My gift to ye." She set the harp aside and came to him, already loosening the ragged blue dress she wore. "And all that I am."

They made love there on the strong earth, and Adair could still hear her music in his head.

After that, she played for him often. They traveled south and west, leaving the open moorland and any Pictish structures behind and once more entering dense forest. They still followed signs—the glint of light on the hide of a deer, the flight of birds—

so Adair could only conclude later that it was Alba who led them astray.

Or perhaps it was the wind, for as they headed down a slope and into an open area, it blew hard from behind them, fooling even the clever hound's nose.

They never heard or had any whiff of the riders till they saw them, a band of five or six men mounted like themselves. They appeared from the trees on the far side of the clearing as abruptly as if they'd materialized out of the thin air. Indeed, Adair blinked at them even as Bradana, still ahead of him, drew her pony to a sudden halt.

All this time away, in the wilds of Alba, they had encountered no one other than Pictish hunters at a distance. These too must be a hunting band, for they had bows upon their shoulders. Adair's shocked eyes also noted a boar, loaded onto an extra pony.

And he recognized the foremost of the riders, a man of middle years, his face deeply seamed by what might be grief.

Mican.

Bradana recognized him also. Her back tensed, and if she had shouted aloud to him, Adair could not have picked up more clearly on her rush of alarm.

By all that is holy. Mican. Here.

That the man—that all of the band—was surprised to see them also, there could be no doubt. Mican knew them in that instant. His eyes grew wide, and it took him only an instant to cry out.

"There! It is she, the false bitch who betrayed my son!" His gaze moved to Adair. "And Earrach's killer."

Wen gave a growl, and Adair drew his sword from its loop. These men, out hunting on what could only be their own land, had come armed with only knives and *sgian-dubhs*, the bows and arrows. Not one of them boasted a sword.

"Come," Bradana said, and pulled her pony around. "Wen, come."

The hound obeyed her instantly. She moved her pony, clearly intending to flee. Adair weighed their chances, then eased his mount over behind her, still facing Mican and his men.

"Adair, come!"

He could stay and take responsibility for what he had done—indeed, it was his first instinct, what he had meant to do all this while, and perhaps the reason Alba had led him to this. It had been a fair fight, that in which Earrach had died.

But he had no reason to believe Mican would see it that way or would hear him fairly. He believed Adair had possessed no right to come between Earrach and his bride. To make off with her.

And if this went very badly, this fight he stayed to face, Adair did not want Bradana to see what befell him. Indeed, his greatest concern at that moment was for her.

Over his shoulder he told her, "Go."

She gave him a stare so incredulous that it needed no words, though she spoke anyway. "Leave ye?"

"Get Wen away. Quick as ye can." Because he knew she would not agree to go without him, even for the hound's sake, he added, "I will delay them and catch up wi' ye." Five men, for he'd now had time to count them. Six horses. Could he take them all? He was, aye, good with a sword, but the odds predicted doom.

The decision was taken out of Bradana's hands when Mican shouted, "Get them!"

The party rushed Adair in a group, the man who led the pony dropping its traces. He heard Bradana wheel behind him and Wen leaping into the fray, snarling and snapping at the MacGillean horses. The men had drawn their knives—long hunting knives—but Adair went in whirling his sword around his head.

This was no battle pony he rode, but one who'd existed too long on short rations. It balked at moving in close upon its fellows, which probably saved Mican from losing his head. Adair got a good look at the man's face, twisted with hate and wearing an ugly grimace.

"Bradana, go! Call off Wen!" For Adair had a premonition that the hound was about to die, either beneath the hooves of the ponies or by arrow, as the men had fallen back from Adair's fury and lifted their bows.

"Wen," she called. And with stark terror, "Adair!"

One of the young men in the party had pressed forward past Mican and lunged at Adair with his long knife. Adair laid the man's arm open and glanced over his shoulder at Bradana.

She did not flee. She would not go without him.

He fell back and turned his mount, the poor beast stamping in confusion. He told Wen, "Come."

They fled into the forest, back the way they had come, and Mican's hunting party came after. Adair could hear them all too well, shouting and crashing through the undergrowth, Mican yelling at his men, "Shoot fire upon them!" Arrows darted through the trees and Adair veered away from Bradana, off to one side. If the hunters meant to take anyone down, it would be him.

It might have been the trees that saved them. Their mounts were in poor condition and soon spent, but no one could move quickly through such thick cover, and the three of them began to gain ground. Adair could just glimpse Bradana to his right, with Wen, a gray shadow, at her side.

Then came a yelp. From the edge of his vision, Adair saw the hound falter and go down.

"Wen!" Bradana howled.

Och, by all the gods, nay.

Adair drew his pony up and leaped down. Bradana had stopped also, staring at Wen—who lay stretched on the ground—in horror. The shaft of an arrow protruded from the hound's right rear haunch.

A shout from behind proved their pursuers had seen them. "Down," Adair told Bradana. "Get down." His own pony was not near enough, and they had not a moment to waste.

She obeyed, her eyes fixed on her hound, even as Adair stretched his ears behind them. He heaved Wen up in his arms and draped him over the back of Bradana's pony, which stood like a rock, too tired to do differently.

"Come," he told her. "Quick." His own mount even now picked its way to him. He seized the lead and told Bradana again, "Come—there, where the trees are thickest."

They went at a dead run, Bradana ahead of Adair with one hand on her hound's hide. She heeded not Adair's muffled grunt when a second arrow, as well aimed as the one that had found Wen, took him in the back of his shoulder, the pain so hot and strong that for a moment he saw only light. He dared not make another sound and delay Bradana. Because ahead, to their left, Alba offered dense cover that seemed to part ahead of them and close behind, like sheltering arms.

Too late, for the damage was done.

They stopped perforce when Wen began to slide from Bradana's pony.

Somehow, before he could reach them, Bradana got the hound down, though he must weigh near as much as she. Tears streamed down her face unheeded as she fell to her knees beside the animal. She did no more than glance at Adair.

"My fault," she was sobbing. "All my—"

"Bradana, it is not."

"I must have led us too far west. We are too close to the ocean. We are on Mican's lands."

"'Tis not a fatal wound." Though whether the hound would be able to run…

Adair fell to his knees beside Bradana. Sometime during the last part of their flight, the shaft of the arrow in his shoulder had broken off against an overhanging limb. He remembered that pain as bright as the first. When she glanced at him now through her tears, she did not mark the injury.

Yet something in his face must have alerted her, for she stopped weeping abruptly, and her gaze moved to the patch of red spreading across his tunic.

"Adair! By the gods!"

"Hush," he told her. "Silent as a hare. They are still out there, looking."

All they could do was hold their breath and hope the danger passed them by.

$$\rule{1.5in}{0pt}\text{❖}\rule{1.5in}{0pt}$$

CHAPTER THIRTY-ONE

B RADANA NOW KNEW how prey must feel when the hunter passed near. The tiny creature, its heart beating furiously while the shadow of the hawk moved over. The rabbit deep in its burrow awaiting the fox.

Alba was their burrow now, this dense patch of young brush all twisted up around them like defensive walls. Where her beloved hound lay and bled. Where Adair…

Och, to see him there giving barely a sign that he'd been pierced through by one of their hunters' filthy arrows, making nary a sound, his gray-green eyes wide in the deep gloom and his skin milk-white. To see him suffering.

It fair convulsed her heart.

But aye, now they must keep still. Silent. For she could hear their pursuers moving through the forest behind them. Hear the crack and rattle of branches beneath the hooves of the ponies. The breath of their mounts. A distant murmur of voices that screamed danger.

Their own ponies stood quiet with their heads drooping, too tired to move. Bradana knelt with her hand on Wen's side, keeping him still, and her gaze on the man she loved.

The man she loved.

She had brought him to this. She had, with her willful disobedience to her fate. With her heart's choice of him. Now he knelt beside her and bled, and she—she had naught with which to heal or comfort him.

But the sounds of the searchers grew steadily more distant. At last, she heard a shout far away to the right. Mican's voice calling.

Were they giving up the search? Was it a trick?

The young trees all around them might be a trap as well as a protection. Yet she remained still. Adair held her with his gaze, lifted a finger to his lips in a cautionary gesture.

She nodded. By some great miracle, they might have escaped notice. They would have to wait and find out.

Her thoughts stumbled wildly as she wondered how she might help these two she loved best in the world. If she lost either of them—

The tears came again and she wept them silently. Wen strained to look up at her and licked her hand.

All her fault, aye. What had she been thinking, supposing she could lead them through the wilds of Alba safely? Adair had trusted her. And now, Mican knew they were out here.

He would not stop looking. He wanted revenge, and without Kendrick here to assure a semblance of fairness, anything could happen if they fell into his hands, here on his ground.

She it was who had brought them to this. She who must save them.

Tears would not help. She choked them back and listened while the sounds of the hunters died away and the silence of Alba took hold all around them.

Only then did she touch Adair's arm, pull him around so she could see the place where the arrow had pierced him.

For an instant, she went dizzy. Black and red dots danced before her eyes, and even though she knelt, she feared she would fall.

The shaft had broken off the span of a man's hand from Adair's shoulder. The iron head was still buried in his flesh—the same shoulder that had sustained the dire wound when they fled Kendrick's lands.

Slick red blood matted his tunic and his hair, all down his back.

Oh, by the gods. By the holy moon—

Adair's gaze caught hers and he clasped her hand. "Whisht, now. 'Tis nay so bad," he breathed, a mere whisper.

"Nay so bad?" Her gaze must have betrayed her disbelief.

One side of his mouth quirked. "I am moving under my own power. Wen is not. We had best take care o' him first."

"But—"

"I can hear water, can ye not? There must be a stream nearby. We will need clear water to wash his wound."

"But…" she said again, stupidly. That would mean her leaving the haven of the copse, for Adair could not go. She looked from his green-specked eyes to the hound stretched on the ground. "Aye." Aye, she would have to call upon every speck of courage. For them.

"What d'ye have for bandaging?"

"Naught. We have used it all." The silent tears came again. She could not stop them.

"We will ha' to use the blanket."

It was all they had. "'Tis filthy."

"So is our clothing. Go now. Take the water flask."

He was thinking clearly. Giving her calm directions. Even though he had a cold iron arrowhead in his back.

Och, she had seen the damage such a projectile could do. Kerr had once taken an arrow in the calf of his leg while out hunting. While in the hands of the healers after, his screams could be heard all over the settlement.

He had hobbled for weeks. But aye, he had survived.

She drew a breath. Scrambled up. "Stay wi' him." To which of her loves did she speak?

She had to battle her way out of the thorny thicket, which made her wonder how they had slipped in when they had. Had Alba truly opened the arms of the bushes and allowed them passage?

Mayhap she had not abandoned them yet.

She found a stream tumbling down the slope and dissecting

the march of the trees, clear, clean water, and she filled the flask. She stole a precious moment to stand listening. Each shadow, each flicker, might be the hunters come back again. But she heard nothing, saw no one.

She stumbled twice on her way back to the copse.

Wen lay where she had left him, so still she feared he was dead. Adair calmly worked at tearing strips from their blanket, which he must have got down from her pony. Her harp, usually wrapped in the blanket when they traveled, stood placed carefully to one side.

"Here, let me do that." She took the knife from him. How could he even move for pain?

The man she loved was strong. Patient. Wise. All that would make her love him more, were her heart not already so full of love for him it might burst.

She must be as strong as he.

"The arrowhead will not pull out," he told her when all stood ready. "We will have to cut it out."

Take the knife to Wen's flesh? She could not.

"Let me." Adair's hand trembled when he held it out for her to pass the knife back. "Ye lie across him to keep him still. Hold a hand on his muzzle. If he yipes…"

Aye. How far might such a sound carry in the quiet?

She threw her body across her hound, her cheek against his. She murmured to him.

He did yipe, though Adair did the deed as swiftly as he could. Bradana flinched at the sound and beseeched Wen to be still, then waited—waited for sounds of the hunters' return.

Those sounds did not follow.

"Here. Ye bandage him." Adair rocked back on his heels, gray-white in the queer light of the copse. His eyes refused to meet Bradana's now.

He knows he will have to endure the same, Bradana thought. *And 'twill be my hand on the knife.*

She could not. *She must.* She could not leave that ugly barb in his flesh.

No easy task, bandaging a hound's haunch. Wen lay panting deeply with his pain, not otherwise moving. When Bradana finished, she used some of the water left from cleaning the wound to wash her hands before turning to look at Adair.

"Help me get my tunic off," he requested, already fumbling at the task.

"We had best cut it."

"I do not want to. I will have naught against the cold."

He had naught. Because of her.

Savagely, she blinked away the tears that came again.

"Let me."

Somehow she got the garment off him, at great cost in his pain. Tenderly she laid it aside. Eyed the wound.

Her head went light again.

Blood coursed down his freckled back. The wound was a jagged tear around the iron arrowhead and what was left of the shaft.

Adair swept his hair aside. "Ye saw how I did for Wen. Ye must free the barbs, cut away the flesh around them."

She had not seen—she'd been holding the hound. Anyway, *she could not.*

She must.

"Aye. Gi' me the knife."

He passed it to her, their fingers brushing.

She rinsed the blade carefully with water. Saw her own fingers move like something in a dream.

Alba, help me.

It got no less dreamlike when she set blade to flesh. As if she watched some other woman from affair, she freed the barbs on the iron head, which she could see. Ignored the blood that flowed. Blood would cleanse the wound.

It took all her strength to withdraw the arrowhead.

Adair made not a sound. But when the ugly thing came free of his flesh, he sank down to lie limp upon the ground, which shattered the spell that held Bradana in its grip.

For one terrible moment she thought he was dead.

"Adair?"

"Clean the wound. Water." His voice came in a croak.

She did, reaching hard for control. His back rose and fell with his breaths. She did a reasonably neat job of bandaging the wound, but she worried. The knife blade was dirty. The blanket filthy.

How might these two she adored survive?

CHAPTER THIRTY-TWO

T HEY SPENT THE night there in the thorny thicket. Bradana did not stir even to lead the ponies to the stream, though they must want water.

Wen fell into a deep sleep, and Adair into a restless one. Bradana, on guard, did not sleep at all, busy listening or checking her patients one after the other for signs of renewed bleeding or fever.

Wen's bandage felt hot to her touch and the hound refused to move much. He did not try to stand. If he could not, she feared he would grow weaker and weaker.

She laid her hand across Adair's forehead often. Clammy and sweaty, but no heat there. Not yet. She could not tell, after a time, whether he slept or had fallen unconscious. Whichever, he stirred often and mumbled words she could not catch.

When dim light began to turn the air from black to gray, she went out again for more water. They could not stay here indefinitely. The ponies would need to graze. Adair and Wen would need food. They had none.

Wen had been their provider.

It occurred to her over again, how deep in trouble they were. They stood, without doubt, on Mican's land. Within trees that obscured their view even as they offered cover. She could only guess at their direction.

Mican would be searching. Would he send out bands of armed men?

She could not get home, to Kendrick's territory.

What to do?

She stumbled back into the copse to find Adair sitting up and Wen whining. She liked the look of neither. Adair had gone pale and sweaty, and she had never before seen her hound, usually so full of vitality, unable to rise.

She gave them both water, cupping some in her hands for the hound.

Crouched beside Adair, she asked, "How d'ye feel? How bad is the pain?"

"Not bad. I will be able to travel if we must."

He lied. No need to challenge him on it.

"Mayhap," she suggested softly, "a day of rest."

His gaze met hers. "Bradana, we cannot stay here."

Mican could be coming. With a band of men.

"Aye," she said miserably. "Aye. But if Wen canna stand—"

"We will load him on one of the ponies."

It took Adair two tries to stand. Getting him into his tunic was out of the question, so Bradana tied her own cloak around him, wrapped her harp in what was left of the blanket, and tied it to his mount.

Together they heaved Wen up and onto Bradana's pony. They fought their way out of the copse.

Sunlight now slanted down through the boles of the trees like shafts of beneficence.

Adair, sweating heavily, stood with one hand on his pony's shoulder and eyed the shafts of light.

"The sun rises far north at this time o' year and to the east. I suggest we ride into it."

She nodded. "Ye mount up."

"But—"

"We will tak' turns at riding." With her pony in such poor condition, Bradana dared not load him double with Wen's weight. "Ye for now."

She pretended she did not notice how Adair struggled to

mount up. She led the ponies first to the stream for water, and then away through the trees.

Following the light.

Throughout that day, she worried. First she worried they would be followed or that an army of men would leap out upon them from concealment in the forest. Neither happened. Then she worried for the condition of her two patients. Wen tended to slide down the pony's back with the beast's motion. She had to struggle and reposition him at regular intervals.

Adair…

Ah, but Adair worried her. He rode with his head bent, and she could not tell if he slept. Far too quiet, though they had an excuse for keeping quiet.

He needed food. They all did. Her own stomach had gone from sick, to aching, to sick again, and rumbled within her.

Grow used to it, she ordered herself, and kept walking. She had no intention of trading places with Adair and letting him walk, but as it was, she set a woefully slow pace. Terrifyingly, she had no idea where she was. The forest just went on and on. Still on Mican's lands? Quite possibly.

When the sun was high overhead, they reached a stream, and Bradana paused. It took both of them to get Wen down, but when they did, he was able to stand on his feet and even wobble a step or two.

So great was Bradana's relief, she felt as if the hard fist clutching her heart had released its grip.

"Let me look at your wound before we move on," she told Adair.

He had bled through the bandaging, which she removed and washed out carefully. The wound looked pink and angry. More blanketing was sacrificed.

He insisted the pain was bearable.

But she could feel his agony when they hoisted Wen back onto the pony. And she ordered him to ride.

"You tak' a turn," he suggested. "I can walk."

She fixed him with a flinty eye. "No' yet."

They moved on, Bradana with her hound on the lead pony, growing dizzy and tired. Long before nightfall, and moving by sheer will alone, she began looking for a place to spend the night. She found it in an outcropping of rock that pierced the trees.

No fit place to lay one's head. It would have to serve.

ADAIR DREAMED. A good and happy dream it started out to be, for he was back in Erin, land of his birth. *Home.*

He took comfort in the sweet roll of the hills, the sweeps of green, and the way the light spilled over it all. He stood high upon the breast of the brae and watched the stretch of river below him, a winding track of beaten silver. Relief flooded his heart. Some terrible ordeal had ended. He was back where he belonged.

And yet another emotion came, stealing up through him persistently. Here in this beautiful land that supplied all his wants and was all he'd ever asked…

He was missing something. Someone. As vital and fundamental to him as his own heartbeat.

"Adair? My love."

The voice came curling softly through his dream like a hint of song. Aye, and there was a song he could hear in the distance, very nearly out of his ears' reach.

"Adair?" Lips touched his forehead. "Ye be dreaming."

He opened his eyes. Saw that for which he'd been longing while asleep.

Her face hung just above his, lined by fatigue, blue eyes shadowed by worry. The most beautiful thing he'd ever seen.

"Bradana."

"Ye were having a nightmare, I think."

"Nay, 'twas a good dream. I was back in Erin. Looking for ye."

"I am no' in Erin."

He knew that. At least, when he was in his right mind he did.

Was he in his right mind? Had he been, since his father tore him from his life and sent him to this land? Since first he'd set eyes on this woman?

"Maybe," he told her, "this is all a dream. Mayhap I've fallen asleep in the warm sun back home and I will soon go back to the hall for supper."

She frowned with concern. "Nay, but ye feel awfully warm. I fear ye may be starting with fever." Disconcertingly, tears flooded her eyes. "I ha' naught to give ye. Nay medicine. Nay food. We are starving."

"Hush. Hush." Her misery pulled him out of himself and snapped the last threads of dreaming. He drew her down into his arms, held her tight and tighter.

She wailed, "'Tis all my fault. If I am punished by losing the two I love most in all the world…"

She loved him.

"Now, now, is Wen not better? He is near back to walking on his own."

"And ye?"

"I am not beat yet."

"Ye are weak fro' hunger, as am I."

"Whisht, Bradana. Trust Alba." Which seemed an odd thing for him to say when he'd just been longing for Erin. "She will provide. Now." He held her away from him a short distance. They had camped in a stony depression in the side of a glen, shelter that, aye, Alba had provided. "Will ye play for me? On your harp. The song ye made for me."

"Someone may hear."

"The music will be trapped here in the stone."

She mopped her cheeks, rose and fetched the small harp, then sat back down beside him and began to play softly.

He fell into her song and, in so doing, knew it for the answer to all his longing.

CHAPTER THIRTY-THREE

THE NEXT DAY they found a patch of wild currants, precious gems of red fruit. It appeared along the side of the hill they crossed, like the answer to a prayer.

The fruit was not at peak ripeness, but they ate all they could and picked the last of the fruits to take with them.

It was a gray day with a lowering, restless sky, promising rain. Wet weather had been their enemy, as they had no shelter, and Adair hoped the clouds would blow on past as they sometimes did. Alba's weather moods proved changeable as the tides.

Not long after they found the currants, Bradana spotted another plant growing and insisted on stopping again.

"'Tis yarrow," she told Adair. "Aye, so, the healer back home uses this for wounds and sometimes for fever. I ha' seen him coming back to the settlement wi' armloads o' it. 'Twill be good for your wound."

Alba was providing, though Adair did not point that out. He let Bradana gather the herb, uneasy at being so long out in the open on the side of the hill. They needed to move on and get beneath the cover of the trees.

No sooner had the thought come to him than a great flock of birds rose up at the near distance, taking flight and flapping directly over their heads. Adair watched them through narrowed eyes, and the urgency prodding at him sharpened.

"'Tis enough. Come," he told Bradana.

She questioned him with her eyes but did not argue it. Not

until they entered the next patch of forest did his anxiety ease, and even then he felt sure they were being followed. He could not put his finger to a sighting or a sound of pursuers, but instinct told him so. Something had caused that flock of birds to rise behind them. A disturbance of the very air.

A warning from Alba?

When Bradana began casting about, locating a place to camp for the night, he protested. "I think we should keep moving."

"But we are weary. The ponies are weary."

So they were. Wen had walked a short distance on his own, as had Adair, offering Bradana his place, but they all needed rest.

She seemed to spy something in his expression, and took alarm from it. "Is someone after us?"

"I've seen or heard no one. 'Tis but a feeling."

"Aye." She drew herself up. "'Tis dangerous traveling at night. There are steep drops, ravines."

Indeed, he was coming to learn the folds in the skin of this land they crossed. Softly he said, "It may be dangerous to stop."

She drew herself up and nodded. "Let us pause just long enough for me to clean and pack your wound, and Wen's. I want ye to have the benefit of the yarrow."

"Aye, but do it quickly."

She did, mashing the plants into paste and cleaning the wounds carefully. Adair pretended he could not see her hands shaking as she packed his wound as carefully as the hound's.

They went on into the soft gloaming when it came. The rain started not long after and lent a darkness the gloaming withheld.

A miserable night, withal. By morning, when the rain decreased to a drizzle, they were all soaked and exhausted.

Bradana edged up to him and asked, "Can ye tell, did we lose them?"

Adair shook his head. The whole world dripped with rain. The raindrops hitting the soft ground sounded like footfalls.

Or maybe there had never been anyone on their tail. He might be mad or fevered. Yet instinct—that which alerted him—persisted.

He looked at the woman he loved. She stood drooping, her wet hair hanging down, her wedding finery past saving. The ponies too stood with their heads drooping, and poor Wen panted his distress. They could not go on this way.

"We canna go on this way," Bradana said just as if she'd heard his thoughts.

"Nay." He thought hard on it. "Bradana, love, 'tis me he wants. Mican wishes to spill his ire on me for the death o' his son. If I turn back, they will likely not pursue ye any farther."

Her eyes widened. "Turn yoursel' over to them, ye mean? Nay, and nay! This is all my fault and my doing. If either o' us should pay—"

"He fell by my sword. 'Tis all Mican knows."

"Ye canna ask me to abandon ye. To let ye gi' yoursel' over to his hounds. I might as well put a dagger through my own heart."

"Love, ye need rest. And food."

"As do ye!"

"If they stop pursuing ye, ye and Wen can make your way home slowly. He is doing much better. Wi' the pony—"

"I will no' hear it!" Her eyes blazed. "I would far sooner starve here wi' ye than leave ye behind."

"*Alanna*, ye are already starved."

"I do no' care. I do no'."

She threw herself into his arms and clutched him as hard as she could. She did not weep now. Her distress went way beyond mere tears.

"I will no' leave go o' ye. Adair MacMurtray. If he takes the one o' us, he takes the both. I did no' wait the whole o' my life for ye, just to part from ye again."

"Bra—"

"We do no' even know for certain we are being followed."

Only he did, as if Alba whispered it into his ear.

"Please, Adair. Let us keep moving. We will go slowly to ease the ponies. We will all walk for a time. Here among the trees, we canna be seen."

He nodded though he was not happy with it. The sun broke through the clouds as they went, showing them that they still traveled roughly north. The cover of the trees, though, did not last long. Even as the sun broke through, they stepped out into a stretch of open hillside where Bradana stopped dead.

She gazed about, letting her eyes absorb what lay before her.

Below them lay a small glen, a narrow river running along it like a thread of living silver through the green. Hills huddled close, including the one upon whose shoulder they stood. Beyond was…

The sea.

They had found it at last.

Adair drew a breath, flavored with salt. The narrow river ran to empty itself into the great, gray, heaving expanse of the ocean. Beyond he could see a scattering of islands looking like sleeping dragons, half submerged in the water. Beyond there—home?

Bradana too caught her breath. "I know this place."

"What?" That made Adair stare.

She turned a wondering smile on him, one the likes of which he had not seen for days uncounted. "I believe this is my grandsire's land."

"Your grandsire?"

"Aye, so. My mother's father, as I told ye. She was born here, and I knew this place as a wee girl. We used to climb up here when we went exploring. Adair, we are no longer on Mican's lands."

Robbed of all words, Adair said nothing.

"My grandsire—his name is Rohracht MacFee—holds lands north from Mican's. I wondered—I did wonder if we might reach him, though I did not know the way. It seems Alba has led us."

"Will we be welcome here?"

"My grandsire has not seen me in a long while, but aye, I will be welcome."

For an instant, Adair went dizzy with relief. *Food. Rest. A chance to heal.*

And then mayhap a boat might be had to take him and Bradana home.

"The dun lies down there." She pointed. "Ye canna see it for the shoulder o' the brae, but it is no' far. Och, Adair"—her eyes swam with tears—"ye were right. We needed only have faith in Alba after all."

CHAPTER THIRTY-FOUR

S O GREAT WAS Bradana's relief as they picked their way down off the brae, she felt as if she walked on air. Her grandfather, so she told herself, would remember her. He would welcome her. Offer the hospitality they so desperately needed.

As unannounced visitors, however, they were first met with suspicion. The settlement not being a large one, they tramped some distance before reaching the first of the outlying huts, guarded by a drystone wall with an open gate. The residents stared. Some went pelting off to summon members of the guard, who came at a run.

The guards raised their weapons, looking at Bradana's party unhappily. She could only imagine how they must appear— injured, filthy, her wedding finery in shreds, with two exhausted ponies and a limping hound.

She made haste to identify herself. "I am Bradana MacCaigh, granddaughter to Rohracht MacFee. Is he here?"

Great confusion ensued. The guards held them at the gate— with wary courtesy—while another man went running. A crowd formed in the almost magical way that happened when such things occurred.

Bradana expected her grandsire to come, figuring the guards had sent for him. Instead, a woman soon came walking up.

A tall woman she was, with red hair gone mostly to gray. She moved proudly and with some confidence, though her clothing appeared plain. She stared at Bradana and her companions with considerable astonishment but smiled as she paused at the gate.

"Mistress Bradana. Do ye remember me?"

Bradana did, and she did not. The woman's appearance rang a distant bell of memory. She had been very young the last time she'd been here, but remembrance came fast.

"My grandsire's wife?" she half guessed.

"Aye. My name is Morag MacFee. Lass, what brings ye here and in such straits?"

"I come seeking refuge wi' my grandsire."

For an instant, the woman's kindly blue eyes clouded. "He is ill, my lass, and has been for some time. But to be sure, ye are welcome here. Come awa' in."

Bradana hesitated. She cast a look around at all the staring faces, avid and curious, and another at Adair. A miracle, this. But she owed these people a warning.

"I maun say—we are in trouble and may have danger on our heels."

"Ah, well." Morag smiled. "There will be a story in it."

"Aye, mistress. A long one."

"I love a good story, me."

MORAG POSSESSED A calm, reassuring manner and seemed welcoming. She had their ponies led away, promising they would be given the very best of care, and exclaimed over the limping hound.

Yet Adair sensed something in her manner and the very air of the settlement—about half the size of Kendrick's to the south—that put him on edge. All was not as it seemed here at Fee.

Mayhap, he told himself as Morag led them to a sturdy if modest roundhouse, it could be placed at the feet of the chief's illness. For surely naught could throw off the wellbeing of a clan more than that.

Still and all, Morag's hospitality seemed genuine. She conducted them to the fireside in the hall and sent servants hurrying with low-spoken requests. *Bring food. Hot water. Bring the healer.*

Bradana collapsed beside the fire, looking as dazed with relief as Adair felt. Morag hastened to pour drinks of heather ale. She drew up a rug for Wen and looked them over carefully.

"Bradana, lass, 'tis plain some terrible misfortune has befallen ye. How d'ye come to be here, so far from home?"

"That, mistress, is the tale."

"How is your mother?"

"She—" Bradana stumbled, no doubt recalling all that had occurred when they left. "I am no' certain. She is carrying Kendrick's child, a late pregnancy, and no' an easy one."

Morag looked concerned. "And how is it your stepfather has let ye travel all this way, to arrive in such a condition? But ah, here is me asking another question when quite clearly ye must recover before ye can tell me aught. Drink up. Rest. The healer should be along soon."

Bradana eyed her hostess. "How sore ill is my grandsire?"

"'Tis bad, lass." For an instant, Morag's calm expression wavered. "So bad, he is no' expected to live."

Bradana took the blow bravely, but could not contain her dismay. Too many and too swift had been the blows of late, and Adair felt for her.

Servants began to return with hot water, cloths for bandaging, and food. As soon as they had washed, they fell upon the meal, and Bradana began to tell her tale.

She stumbled a bit over it, introducing Adair as her stepfather's nephew from Erin and visibly agonizing over whether she should dub him her lover also. She did not, but Morag, hearing the rest of it and being no fool, doubtless did not need the clarification.

She proved a good listener and did not exclaim till she heard the account of the ill-fated attack in the forest, the injuries, and their struggles since.

"A miracle ye ha' reached here," she cried then, "in truth!"

"But as ye can see, we bring trouble wi' us," Bradana reminded her, "and may be followed. Tell me, mistress, hearing all, are we still welcome? If not, I shall surely understand. We will tak' our rest and leave."

Adair spoke for the first time. "Indeed, if ye might spare the lend o' a boat, we could sail home to Erin."

That made Morag's eyes widen and caused Bradana to steal a look at him. Did she not understand that would be their safest course, safest for everyone?

Morag contemplated before answering. She had a gravely ill husband and a clearly reduced clan, but she rallied to say, "To be sure, Rohracht's granddaughter is welcome here always." Her gaze moved to Adair. "All we have is yours.

"But I maun provide ye wi' a bit o' a caution. Our own fate has no' been easy of late. Bradana, your Uncle Darroch perished in fighting last year. He was to take the place o' chief in your grandfather's stead, ye understand, and his son died wi' him. Not much older than yoursel', was Eobhan. We are engaged in clan fighting." Her gaze met Bradana's. "Against Mican MacGillean."

Bradana caught her breath, and Adair's stomach turned over within him, the food he had just consumed so ravenously not sitting well.

"Och, nay," Bradana exclaimed. "Are we to find nay refuge even here?"

"I offer to ye what refuge we have." Morag added dryly, "I must say, 'tis a bit of welcome news to hear that Earrach MacGillean has been taken from the world. 'Twas he who killed young Eobhan."

Again, her gaze flicked to Adair. "Ye, Master Adair, have done us a service."

"And stirred up a cauldron o' trouble," he added. "As if ye needed more o' that."

"Trouble," she pronounced, "is a drink always in abundance. Let us see ye healed and rested, and we shall take stock o' what needs to be done."

"Aye, thank ye," Bradana said gratefully.

"Ye will want to see your grandfather."

"I will."

"I shall tak' ye there myself. But first, let us provide ye with clean clothing and mayhap a brush-up. We do no' want ye frightening the man off to Tìr na nÒg."

"Do I truly look so bad as all that? And is he truly so ill?"

"Aye to both, lass," Morag said. "But there is always hope. And is your arrival here no' proof o' how swiftly things can change? For good or ill."

The healer arrived then, an aged man who wore a grave expression. It altered to one of concern as he examined the filthy wound at Adair's shoulder. Aye, Bradana had done her best to keep it clean, but when even the bandaging was soiled, the task was impossible.

He gave Adair an assessing look before he said, "Well, Master Adair, ye must possess the strength of a warrior, that ye are no' flat on yer back wi' fever o' this."

"I had not the opportunity to give way," Adair told him honestly.

"Well, if ye have lived this long, I predict a full recovery. The arrow must ha' hit bone, for it did no' burrow in so deep as it might ha' done. Ye will heal."

Adair nodded. "So long as I can fight, if I need to."

"Amazing," said the healer, "what a man can do when he must. And"—he eyed Wen, who sprawled on the rug that had been provided for him—"I collect this is to be my next patient?"

"If ye will no' mind," Bradana said softly.

"That is a very large hound. He will no' bite me, will he?"

"Wen? Nay, he is good of nature and wise as any man."

"Wiser, let us hope."

$$\textasciitilde \cdot \cdot \cdot \textasciitilde$$

CHAPTER THIRTY-FIVE

WELL SCRUBBED AND wearing clean clothing, with her hair untangled and plaited at great cost in pain, Bradana followed her step-grandmother into the alcove at the rear of the hall. The place where her grandsire lay.

The space smelled of many things. Tinctures and medicines. The herbs that had been scattered on the floor in an effort no doubt to sweeten the air. And something much worse that lay beneath it all.

Bradana's gaze moved to the figure on the sleeping bench. When last she'd seen her grandsire, he'd been tall and vigorous with eyes as blue as her own, and a son—her Uncle Darroch—to match him.

Now she tried to weigh that image against the new impressions coming at her. The white head on the bolster. The face that had once been strong and handsome, deeply creased by pain.

"Rohracht?" Morag said. "Only look who has come. 'Tis your granddaughter, Bradana."

"Eh?"

"Your granddaughter."

"Bradana?" He fought his way up in the bed, gazing at Bradana in some surprise. Morag hurried to help him. "Granddaughter, is my daughter also here?"

"Nay, Grandfather." Bradana moved forward softly, distressed to see him in such a state. "She is with Kendrick yet."

Well enough, Bradana hoped, though she could not dismiss

the memory of that last image. Had Mother birthed the baby early?

"I brought you this, to prove who I am." In her hand she had tucked the blue brooch Mother had given her before her marriage, and now she held it out. Surely he would recognize it.

His blue eyes came up to meet hers. He smiled. "Lass, I ha' no need to look at that. Ye ha' the look o' her about ye—yer mam, I mean."

In her calm voice, Morag said, "Bradana has traveled far wi' a companion to see ye."

Bradana flicked a look at the woman. Aye, so, Morag did not wish her to worry the man.

"Come here, lass. By the powers, how ye ha' grown!"

Bradana sank down next to the bed and into the embrace of that blue gaze. The evil smell grew stronger as she approached. Aye so, it came from him.

"Grandfather. It is good to see ye. Even though—" she faltered. "Even though it pains me to find ye in such straits."

He studied her face closely. "I ha' been brought low by a wee illness and shall be better soon. It does a clan ill to ha' its chief off his feet. And even more so here in Dalriada, where he maun be vigilant every moment to keep hold o' what he owns."

"Aye," Bradana agreed. The old man still had his wits, at least.

"Ye just wait, granddaughter. I will soon be on my feet again."

Bradana glanced at Morag, whose face remained calm and expressionless. She feared the man deceived himself.

"What a wonder this is," Rohracht went on. "Ye were but a wee thing when your mother took ye from us. Will she be coming to see us?"

"I fear not, Grandfather. Her place is with Kendrick, and when I left she was great wi' child."

"Aye, so. She is happy, then?" He did not wait for an answer. "Sit, lass. Sit and talk wi' me."

Bradana did, occupying a stool Morag brought forward for her. No doubt the mistress used it herself and often. Bradana could almost see her sitting there for great stretches of time.

She spoke to her grandsire of life back home, of her two stepbrothers and the beauty of the place, though she did not mention her marriage agreement or the trouble that pursued them. Morag stood listening quietly, her hands folded at her waist.

"Ye will stay here for a time," Rohracht said when she wound down. "Keep me company until I am well."

"I would like that," Bradana said, tears pricking her eyes.

"Your granddaughter has brought a harp," Morag said quietly. "Lass, d'ye play?"

"I do."

"Then ye must play for me," Rohracht said. "Your grandmother played the harp, did ye know that?"

"I did not."

"Her father was a harper, a shanachie back in Erin when I met her. She played like a goddess. And after I brought her here from Erin, difficult as life was, she claimed she could hear Alba's music, an ancient song that made her fall in love wi' the place. She would play for me—"

He faltered suddenly, as if under a weight of grief too heavy to bear.

"To be sure, I will play for ye, Grandfather," Bradana told him, wondering if a measure of her grandmother's ability had not traveled down to her, in the blood.

"Good lass."

"As I say, Bradana has brought a companion wi' her," Morag said. "A young man from Erin. Ye may wish to speak wi' him as well."

"Mayhap, aye, when I am no' so tired. For now, Bradana, only let me look at ye. Ye ha' your grandmother's eyes. Seeing ye, 'tis almost like looking at her again."

Another love, Bradana thought, that endured beyond death

and parting. She had no doubt her grandsire held great affection for Morag—who would not so value that gentle lady?

But his heart, aye, belonged to his first love.

Would it be that way for her and Adair? Loving one another forever, beyond the bounds of a single lifetime? Aye so, for it felt she'd loved him even before she met him—that moment when her world had paused before the wheel of it began to turn once again.

The aged healer, the same who had treated Adair and Wen, shuffled in through the door.

"'Tis time for your draught, Chief Rohracht."

"Ah, we will allow your grandfather rest, lass," said Morag quickly. "Rohracht, let your granddaughter take her rest also. She will see ye again come morning."

"Aye, Grandfather, I will." Bradana smiled at the old man in the bed. "And I will bring my harp."

SHE AND ADAIR were given a sleeping place together, proving that Morag did indeed understand the nature of their relationship. Full as Bradana's mind was when they retired to it, she did not think it would take her long to succumb to the comfort of such a place after their days of sharing a ragged blanket on the ground.

Indeed, she could ask very little more than to be lying in the dark beneath a secure roof with a full belly and Wen stretched out beside her—holding Adair's hand in the dark.

Yet for a short while, she could not stop talking. She told Adair about her encounter with her grandfather and lamented the misfortunes here, the death of her uncle and his son that rendered the holding all too vulnerable.

"If my grandsire dies—*when* he dies," she corrected herself carefully, "I do no' doubt Mican will move in. 'Tis what he is waiting for, no doubt."

Adair said nothing, just lay with his fingers laced through hers.

"Grandfather told me my grandmother's sire was a shanachie in Erin. And she played the harp, just like me."

"Well, is that no' a wonder? A gift, the things that come down through the blood."

"Just what I thought." Bradana turned her face to him there in the dark, even though she could not see him well. "Did ye mean what ye said back there, to Mistress MacFee?"

"What did I say?"

"That if she would give ye the lend o' a boat, ye would be awa' back there, to Erin." She could not keep the agony from her voice. "Would ye leave me?"

"I said *we* would be awa' to Erin."

"But Alba is my home. Its music runs through my blood."

"Love, I did no' say we would stay there forever. Just to take refuge for a time, until the strife here may die down."

And if he returned to the land he loved, would he ever agree to leave there again?

He raised the hand he held to his lips and planted a kiss there. "Do no' fret for it now. Let us take some rest while we may."

He gathered her in his arms and she melted against him, unable to resist the warmth of the emotions that united them.

But a black cloud remained hanging on her horizon.

CHAPTER THIRTY-SIX

IN THE DAYS that followed, Adair grew familiar with the small holding perched on the edge of the cold sea. His wound healed steadily under the hands of MacFee's healer, and with sufficient food, his vigor began to return.

He could not keep still and so walked the settlement while Bradana sat with her grandsire, often playing on the harp for him. Wen came at his side, still limping but seeming just as unwilling to be quiet.

Adair became acquainted with members of the guard, who told him tales of Bradana's uncle and cousin, both of whom had fallen battling to hold their lands not against the native Pictish, but against Mican and the now-perished Earrach.

To a man, they lit up with approval when they learned Earrach—universally detested—had fallen to Adair's blade, and they swiftly adopted him. They wanted to hear of Erin, from whence their ancestors had come.

Indeed, Adair spent much time thinking of Erin, standing down on the shingle of the shore and staring out in the direction of home. No clear sight line here, for a number of islands lay offshore, huddled like half-submerged, green-backed *cirein-cròin*. But he knew he could find the way home.

He did not mention the longing to Bradana. She was fully occupied with her grandfather's plight.

She believed he would not live long. Whatever illness ate at him had him well in its jaws. When they were alone together at night, she needed Adair's reassurance, not somewhat else to worry on.

So he held his tongue and bided his time, and learned the bones of the place. A settlement in decline, it had once been much more prosperous and could, Adair felt, become so again. With a great deal of work, and a will to defend.

One night as they lay in the sanctuary of their sleeping place listening to Wen's deep, peaceful breaths, Bradana said, "Grandfather does want to meet ye, no doubt because I speak o' ye so often. But though I ha' asked permission again and again to bring ye to him, he does no' wish ye to find him in his sickbed. Instead he insists that tomorrow he will rise from it and come out to the great hall, where we shall"—she hesitated—"feast."

Adair frowned in the dark. Most of the friends he'd made among the guard said they did not expect their chief ever to rise from his bed again. As for a feast—he knew all too well the holding had little means to provide one.

"Can he reach the hall?"

"He seems determined upon it. He says my music has healing properties."

Adair would not be surprised if it did. "Well then. Would it no' be a wondrous thing if your presence here proved his saving?"

"Of saving, I am no' so certain. But may I tell him ye be willing to meet him?"

"Pray, tell him 'twill be an honor."

"And I was thinking, Adair—we might become handfasted here. There is naught, is there, to prevent it?" Before he could answer, she drew his hand to her heart. "That is, ye have surrendered any thought o' going back to Erin, have ye no'?" As he hesitated, she hurried on, "Ye like it here, I can tell. Ye be happy enough here."

"I do like the place."

"Well, then it is settled. After Grandfather meets ye tomorrow, I shall approach him on it."

And if Mican should turn up here looking for them? To be

sure, the possibility was what had pushed Adair to make the acquaintance of the guard in the first place.

It would be far better for Bradana's grandsire and everyone involved that Mican should not find them here, if and when he did come.

In caring for her grandfather, Bradana seemed to have forgotten that. If they were caught here, it could well mean the destruction of the settlement.

"Bradana, love," he told her truthfully, "I would like naught better than to handfast wi' ye."

Before he could finish what he meant to say, she rushed on, "And for Grandfather to witness it before—While he is still with us, aye? To be joined here among family is all I could ask."

Aye, then she would have all she could ask. All he could provide. If Mican came with a horde of men after, well, he would worry about that then.

He leaned in and kissed her. "Handfasted we shall be. Ye know my heart already belongs to ye."

ROHRACHT MACFEE'S EMERGENCE from his sick room turned into a grand event. Adair gathered that the clan had not enjoyed many of those of late, and everyone from the highest to the lowest threw their hearts into it.

Adair himself helped the men arrange the hall—as of old, they told him—with the chief's grand chair at its head. The room was swept and new herbs spread. Flowers were brought by giggling young girls.

Morag and Bradana prepared the chief. Bradana had dressed for the occasion and wove flowers through her hair.

Adair waited, kicking his heels, for the old man to be brought in, wondering what he'd think of Rohracht, and what Bradana's grandsire would think of him.

It took an age. Indeed, everyone waiting together in the great hall began to eye one another uneasily, wondering whether the grand appearance would happen after all. When the chief did come, it was borne in the arms of two stout young clansmen who deposited him with all due care at the head of the room.

If Adair felt shocked by the man's appearance, he strove mightily to keep from showing it. Rohracht had the frame of a big man, now wasted, a crop of white hair and fierce blue eyes in a face lined by pain. His voice sounded reedy when he spoke to his people, clustered around him.

"Well, this has been a long time coming, has it no'? As all o' ye ken, I ha' been laid low by illness and grief since the death o' my son and grandson. But since the coming o' my granddaughter"—he reached out and seized Bradana's hand, for she stood close by his chair—"I ha' been growing stronger. Her presence has done me a world o' good."

Tears ran down Morag's face, and the rest of Rohracht's listeners were visibly affected. The old man's gaze roved the room, touching on many a face fondly before it settled upon Adair.

"Granddaughter, is this your young man? Bring him to me."

Bradana ran to Adair and caught him by the hand, giving him a beseeching look. No need for it; Adair already brimmed with respect for the old man. He went forward and bent his head courteously.

"Chief MacFee."

Rohracht took Adair's measure, eying him from the top of his head down to his hide boots. "Adair MacMurtray, of ye I ha' heard much. Indeed, my granddaughter has fair assailed my ears wi' words o ye, so much I just had to get up from my bed and see ye for mysel'."

"Master." Adair met Rohracht's gaze warily, wondering if he would see approval, calculation, or—worst of all— disappointment.

Rohracht smiled at him. "A fine, braw lad from Erin, so I see.

Aye, well, we will no' hold that against ye. Did no' all o' our ancestors once come from Erin? Wha' d'ye think o' my holding here, eh, lad?"

"A grand place. I like it very much."

"It has fallen, as I ha' fallen. As my son and grandson ha' fallen. Just like me, it may rise again." Was that approval Adair saw in Rohracht's eyes? "Some new blood, that is wha' is called for."

"I am grateful, Chief Rohracht, for your hospitality and the refuge ye have offered me."

Rohracht waved a hand. "'Tis no' refuge when 'tis family. My granddaughter belongs here. So, now, do ye."

True liking flooded Adair's heart. He could grow fond indeed of this generous-natured man. Bradana's eyes brimmed with tears, and Adair had to swallow back his emotions when he expressed his thanks.

"I am in your debt, Chief Rohracht."

"Come, sit beside me while we eat, and tell me o' yourself."

Adair did, sitting at Rohracht's right hand with Bradana beside him, and Morag on Rohracht's other side, helping him to eat. Not that the old man did much more than pick at his food.

Indeed, from somewhere the cooks had provided a feast of sorts. The plentiful food, as well as Rohracht's presence, lifted the mood of the hall considerably.

"I hear," the old man said to Adair, "ye be the man who took down Earrach MacGillean in a fair fight."

"Aye, so," Adair admitted.

"'Twas well done, lad, and I am impressed. 'Twas he who took the life o' my grandson, Eobhan."

"So Bradana did tell me, master."

"Lad, d'ye believe in circles?"

"I beg pardon, chief?"

"I speak o' life's wheel, upon which we travel round and round until events circle us back again."

Adair thought about that. "Aye, master, I suppose I do."

"As do I. It seems the wheel has made a good turn for me—for us—before I have to leave this world."

Adair eyed him uncertainly.

"My granddaughter has returned and brought me a braw warrior."

"And possibly a load of trouble. 'Tis because I slew Earrach that his father wants my head. If he tracks me here—"

"Then we will ha' a battle. 'Twill be worth it."

Adair did not say what he wished. How it might be safest for all if he and Bradana were not here when Mican arrived. That his own circle had begun and might well end in Erin.

There would be time for that discussion later, and he would not ruin this happy moment for the world.

✦

CHAPTER THIRTY-SEVEN

AFTER THAT, BRADANA'S grandsire left his chamber often, always borne in the arms of his two braw clansmen and always smiling. Sometimes he stayed in the great hall but a short while. Other times he sat long while Bradana played the harp for him and all the company. The very spirit of the settlement altered from despairing to brightly enthusiastic. Folk went about their tasks with lighter steps, paused to exchange words, and smiled. Began to carry hope in their hearts.

That Rohracht liked and approved of Adair, Bradana could have no doubt. The two of them sat and talked together long, even laughed together from time to time.

It did her enormous good to see the both of them laugh.

Not that she could fool herself. Her grandsire was very ill, no doubt dying. But new life had been breathed into him, however long it might last.

The late summer days rolled past, and here in the small settlement, cupped in the stones at the edge of the sea as if held in Alba's protective hand, she began to forget there was a world beyond this one. A place of danger, pain, and strife.

She did think often of those she'd left at Kendrick's holding, and worried for her mother, but it was in a strangely distant way.

She and Morag MacFee planned the handfasting with enjoyment. It was to be a simple thing, if only because the settlement could not boast much more, but like the chief's visits to the hall, it became a welcome diversion. The women of the household, from the servants upward, threw themselves into it enthusiastically.

Morag gave Bradana the gifts of a gown that could be altered to fit her—a task that her woman, Ciari, promptly took in hand—and combs for her hair. A broad, silver-colored ribband.

"This," Morag said, caressing it, "is the same as was used to bind your grandfather's hand and mine, when we were joined."

"Och," Bradana exclaimed, "then it is precious to ye."

"Quite precious." Morag raised her kindly blue eyes to Bradana's. "I would like for ye and Adair to use it."

Profoundly touched, Bradana accepted the ribband into her hands. "I will, but only if I might return it to ye after."

"Aye, lass. I ask ye, do no' wait too long for this joining. Your grandfather may seem strong now, but I fear... I fear 'twill no' last. And I do wish for him to see ye wed."

Bradana brought that up with Adair later. She found him standing down upon the shore, where he'd made a number of friends among the young men who kept the boats and went out fishing. When she came upon him he was alone, gazing out over the silvery waters of late afternoon with an intensity that caused her a ripple of disquiet.

For what did he look? For what did he long? The land he had lost over the water? Could such a longing come between them?

He turned and smiled at her, though, when Wen, who was with her, ran up to him.

She joined them where the running tide came up, reaching for her toes.

"Adair, is all well?" Without giving him time to answer, she went on, "Why d'ye stand here so?"

He shrugged, his eyes returning to the water, and her uneasiness grew. She did not doubt she owned this man's heart. She wanted it given free, without reservations.

"I ha' just been thinking," he said.

"Och, aye?" She fixed her gaze on him. "Tell me truly if ye have any doubts about our being joined. For the handfasting is all but set. 'Tis what I came to tell ye."

That made him withdraw his gaze from the sea and the sleeping islands beyond, and focus on her. "Doubts about joining with ye? None." He laid his hand on her back in a gesture of reassurance. "Are we no' already joined in every way that matters? We gave one another promises, did we not? The handfasting is naught but a formality, to my mind."

"Then 'tis well wi' ye if it takes place tomorrow?"

"'Tis very well."

Bradana thought furiously. She knew this man now, knew his every expression. She could feel the very ripples in his spirit. Standing here now, she willed him to speak of anything troubling him.

And he did.

"'Tis after that which concerns me, Bradana."

"After?"

"The handfasting. I think we should embark on a wedding trip. To Erin."

Dismay hit Bradana a fierce blow. Quietly, she said, "I thought ye liked it here."

"I do, all too well. I like these people and the place."

"But 'tis no' Erin." Where part of him did still reside. Mayhap she did not own all of his heart after all.

"It is not. But that is not why I suggest we leave. From the first, I have feared bringing trouble down on those here. If Mican comes—"

"He has not. He may not."

Adair shook his head. "If—when—it comes to him that those here are o' your mother's blood, that ye may have come here to your grandsire, he will want vengeance. He will want me."

Bradana swallowed hard, not wanting to accept the truth of it.

"Better," Adair said almost bitterly, "if he does no' find us here when he comes. It may keep him from destroying this place, which I dread to see."

So too did Bradana dread such an occurrence. "You do no' think this place has a chance of standing against him?"

"I would like to think so. The folk here are fine and courageous, your grandsire especially. But…"

"Aye."

She did not want to leave Alba. The dark of this land and the light, the wild of it, was part of her, woven deep into her soul. Nor could she imagine parting from this man for any reason. Either course—leaving here or seeing him leave—would tear her in two.

With sorrow, he said, "I would no' like to think my presence here caused the destruction of your grandsire's holding. I do no' think I could live wi' that."

And if he did go home to Erin—if she went with him—would she ever succeed in persuading him to return to Alba? Or would she live the rest of her life in exile?

How was it their two hearts, so deeply rooted in different lands, clung so to each other?

Starkly, she asked, "How long? How long will we stay in Erin, if I sail wi' ye?"

"I cannot say. How long d'ye think it will take the desire for vengeance to subside in Mican's heart?"

Forever, mayhap.

"My father will no' be happy to see me returned without Kendrick's promise to cede him what he owes in land, as did my two brothers before me. But if I return wi' Kendrick's stepdaughter…"

"He may decide to send ye back again."

"He may."

"I worry what might have happened at Kendrick's holding. What befell my mother. To leave here without knowing."

"Aye, 'tis hard."

He stood there looking at her with his green-speckled eyes, waiting for her decision. He would not offer her lies or false assurances that they would return, if they went to Erin. For that was not the man he was.

"Let us handfast," she told him at last. "Let us have this joyous time. Everyone is looking forward to it, Grandfather especially. Then…*then* will I give ye my answer."

"Fair enough." He walked to her and captured her hands, planted kisses in first one palm and then the other, at each corner of her mouth, each cheek, her forehead. "Remember ye but one thing, Bradana. Where one o' us belongs, there also belongs the other."

"Aye." She closed her eyes against the strength of her feelings. "And ye remember the same."

THEY WERE JOINED late the next afternoon, out in the open in front of Rohracht's hall, where the sun shone down. Every member of the clan was in attendance. Rohracht's men carried out his carved wooden chair, and he sat there, beaming, Morag at his side, while the holy man spoke the words and the knot was tied.

After, there was feasting, all the settlement could afford, and merriment. And Bradana, who at that moment could ask no more from life, so deep was her contentment, sat gazing about happily. This, *this* must be what the hall had been like when it was first raised. When Rohracht, as a young man in love with Bradana's grandmother, had been full of life and strength. Laughter and glad voices. Love.

Could it not be so again?

Still later, alone in their quarters, she and Adair lost themselves in each other, lips sliding across skin, tongues sampling and cherishing. When she took him inside her, knowing she could never completely let him go, she banished all worry from her mind.

Think about it the morrow, she told herself when she could think at all.

Little did she know, the morrow would come with a weight of sorrow.

<hr />

CHAPTER THIRTY-EIGHT

ADAIR STILL LAY asleep in Bradana's arms when the call sounded from outside the door of her quarters.

It seemed a terrible intrusion, an abomination, for they'd stayed late at their wedding feast last evening and made love for a long while after. It did not seem the morning could already have arrived.

Yet when Adair pried his eyes open one at a time, he saw that aye, light came in around the chamber door.

Bradana lay sprawled across his chest, still sleeping, her breath deep and even and those glorious eyes of hers closed tight. Her hair covered him—his only covering, in fact—and in that moment his heart clenched with love for her, so fierce it hurt.

Surely this was still the tail end of their wedding night. Who would come to disturb them?

"Bradana," he whispered.

Her eyelids fluttered but she did not wake. Aye, they had expended all their strength in loving. And she felt safe in his arms.

A sudden thought occurred to him: he must keep her that way even if it cost him his life.

His life so far—apart from his assignment to Alba and the events that found him here—had been a carefree one. Full of many pleasures and few enough responsibilities. He'd never thought on marriage. Never expected to take on the safety and welfare of another. Yet here he lay with his whole world in his arms.

The call came again, closer now so that he could identify it as a cry of alarm.

"Master Adair?"

It sounded like Morag. If it were, why would she be calling on him and not Bradana? If Bradana's grandsire had taken a bad turn…

He began to wiggle out from under Bradana and she came awake. Great, slumberous eyes opened. She reached for him.

"Not now, love. There is someone at the door."

"Eh?"

She drew up one of the blankets. He, naked, took another to cover himself.

Morag stood outside the door, her face stark white, her mild eyes full of fear. At that moment, Adair felt certain Rohracht's health had failed him.

Behind Morag, he could see people hurrying about. Men at arms. Distress flared within him.

"Mistress MacFee, what is it?"

"I am sorry to disturb ye at such a time, but—"

"Is it the chief?"

She shook her head and stole a look over her shoulder.

"Come in, pray."

The woman did, standing just inside the door with her hands twisted in her smock and that awful look on her face.

Bradana, now sitting up, responded to that look. "My grandsire?"

Morag shook her head again. "A party o' men has been spotted. They approach through the forest—from the south. Mican, it is. Our guards, out on patrol, recognized him."

Bradana gave a soft exclamation of dismay and Adair felt her emotions spike. So well connected were they, he could almost tell the thoughts in her mind.

"How many men?" he asked. "Did the guards say?"

"A goodly number, though no' an army. Heavily armed."

Adair reached for his clothing, the same he'd worn the day

before and which had mostly fallen near the bed. Ignoring the presence of the woman, he began to struggle into it. "How far off?"

"At the border. They must ha' traveled all night."

To be sure, they would have. Or they had camped there, just beyond Rohracht's lands. Mican would want this visit to be a surprise.

As it was.

Adair's mind raced, considered options and possibilities. "The chief will have to receive him." Politely, if the old man could manage it. "It may no' come to a fight. If Mican does no' learn we are here…"

"Aye. The healer is with Rohracht now, trying to get him up. He is very tired after yesterday, and spent."

Bradana made a sound of distress and got up, her hair and the blanket trailing her. "How dare Mican come here and cause Grandfather distress?"

Kindly, Morag told her, "I doubt Mican knows your grandfather is ill. He must have chased down the fact that ye ha' blood relations here, though, lass. He's come looking, I do no' doubt."

Adair froze in the act of reaching for his sword. "Then he cannot find us here. Bradana, we must sail at once. If Mican finds that Rohracht is giving us sanctuary, he may destroy the dun and the settlement."

Bradana said nothing, but her face paled.

"Rohracht asks ye to come to him," Morag told Adair. "At once."

"To be sure, I will. But we must hurry."

"Then go on ahead o' me."

"I will follow," Bradana gasped even as Adair went out.

It was a beautiful morning with clear sunlight flowing over the hills to the east and the sea lying calm in a sheet of silver-blue. The settlement should have been calm also. Instead, the word had gone out. Men scrambled for their weapons, and women gathered their children close.

The very feel of it struck on something deep inside Adair, as if he remembered times like this. He had prepared before for such an attack, long ago—only he had not. His father's lands had never come under attack, not in his lifetime.

Still and all, a feeling filled him, one of determination. Of desperate courage. A man fought in such circumstances. He fought for what he loved.

He came upon the old man still in the act of rising, helped by his faithful manservants and the healer. He groaned as he moved, his wasted form showing beneath the robe they wrapped around him. All yesterday's buoyant strength and happiness had deserted him.

But his gaze fastened to Adair the moment he entered the chamber and did not waver, save to travel swiftly down to the sword in Adair's hand.

"There he is. And aye, ready to battle."

"Chief Rohracht—"

"Grandfather. Ye maun call me Grandfather now."

"I suppose there is no chance this is not Mican coming?"

One of the manservants answered, "None. Dabhor, who has encountered him before, saw him wi' his own eyes."

Adair knew Dabhor, a sturdy, levelheaded warrior of middle years. If the settlement possessed any man who might be considered a war chief, or head of the guard at least, it was he.

Adair's heart fell a little farther.

"I ha' sent men out," Rohracht gasped against the act of moving his old bones, "to escort them in. We shall know much by whether they offer us fight, or come in willingly."

"Aye." Adair thought rapidly upon what he must next say. "Chief—Grandfather—this is my fault. 'Tis my head Mican wants in revenge for the death o' his son. I who have brought this trouble to your door. The way I see it, we have two courses o' action."

Everyone in the chamber eyed him.

Determinedly, his hand clutching the hilt of his sword, he

went on. "I can leave here—Bradana, Wen, and I can at once—by sea. If Mican does no' find us here, he cannot retaliate against ye and yours. Or I can turn myself over to him. 'Tis my head he wants."

"And ye would do that, would ye? Turn yoursel' over to the man? Knowing 'twould mean yer certain death?"

"To save Bradana, and the settlement, I would."

Rohracht stole a deliberate look at his men. "Did I no' tell ye o' what he was made?"

Adair did not know what to say.

"Aye, well, lad," Rohracht said, his voice a bit stronger, "there is—as I see it—one more course we can steer. We can fight."

Adair blinked at the old man, barely on his feet. "Fight."

"Aye, so. Repel the bastards. Mak' sure they do no' again set foot on our land."

It would have been laughable, were the old man not so earnest.

"Master, have ye the men to put up a fight? Men enough, that is."

"Do we ha' the men to fight? Aye, I believe we do. Mican has no' come wi' an army. Just a stout band. I ha' trained warriors and men skilled at farming the land or sea who will down tools and up weapons." Rohracht bent a look upon Adair. "I ha' you."

Dismay momentarily robbed Adair of all breath. "Me."

"Aye. My grandson now. A man who has already defeated the redoubtable Earrach. A man who, if I am no' much mistaken, has the makings o' a warrior beyond compare."

"Master, ye *are* much mistaken. I trained at arms back home, aye, but I am but a third son. 'Tis my brother, Baen, who is the warrior."

"I ha' no' met your brother. So I canna say what sort o' man he is. Whether he has the fire in him. Ye ha' that fire, lad. What I used to have. My men will follow ye."

Adair stepped forward, imploring the old man now. "Grandfather, I cannot help but think the best thing I can do for ye and yours is vacate this place. That way, Mican can find nay fault in ye. He cannot raze your holding and come back wi' an army."

"That is what ye want, is it? To tak' my granddaughter and sail off? To Erin, is it?"

"'Tis no' so much what I want. But it may be the safest for all o' ye."

Rohracht did not reply at once. He fastened the belt at his hips and said to one of his men, "Bring me my sword."

Love for the man—this valiant, wasted man—flooded Adair's heart so that for the moment he could not speak.

"Lad, either ye stand wi' me or no', but I am standing."

"I still feel, master, 'tis an unequal battle."

"Such has been won before now. They ha' been won by heart and by the grace o' the gods."

"Aye."

Rohracht took a step toward Adair and laid a hand on his shoulder.

"Grandson," he said deliberately, "stay and fight wi' me, fight for this holding, and when I die, 'twill be your own. I ha' no heir, save my granddaughter. And now, ye."

"Grandfather," Adair returned, "I am no' worthy."

"Then prove yoursel' so."

Slowly, Adair said, "A man does no' fight for land or for a holding. At least, no' to my mind. He fights for those he loves."

"Then come, and we shall both do just that."

CHAPTER THIRTY-NINE

"I NEED A weapon," Bradana croaked as she finished dressing and bundled her hair into a hasty knot. Adair had gone out ahead of her to join Grandfather, but Morag had lingered, twisting her hands in her smock and looking distraught.

Wen, also still with Bradana, stared up at her and whined.

"I ha' my knife," Bradana went on, still breathless from hurrying. "But if there is to be an attack, I will no' be caught defenseless." Deep was that conviction, and fundamental. She would arm herself, stand with Adair, if she must.

Morag looked sick with fear. But she said, "Come. We will find something."

Outside, the beautiful morning seemed strangely muted. People rushed about—all the men at arms with weapons on their shoulders—heading for the great hall, and women following in a hush.

Bradana and Wen followed them.

"Your grandfather will insist on getting up to fight," Morag told Bradana as they hurried. "He was already at it when he sent me to ye."

"He is too weak."

"Do no' let him hear ye say that. Come."

At the hall, Morag veered and led Bradana around the side to a dusty room clearly used for storage. Here they found weapons—swords and spears, axes and shields—many of them broken. Indeed, one of the men ran in while they stood there, looked startled to see them, and grabbed a sword and shield before darting out again.

Bradana began to search through the weaponry. She doubted she could manage both a sword and a heavy shield. But she would be cursed rather than stand helpless.

"Come," she told Morag, barely noticing that the woman also snatched up a weapon.

Back at the front of the hall, Rohracht had emerged with Adair at his side. The old man wore his light armor and looked pale and unsteady, but determined.

Bradana ran to him. "Grandfather? Is it certain 'tis Mican who comes?"

"Aye."

"Mayhap he wishes only to talk. It may no' mean battle."

Her grandsire looked at her, blue eyes clear in his set face. "If we can kill him now, we may set his clan back on its heels and remove the threat."

Bradana fell back a step. Her gentle grandfather's leap to aggression hit her hard.

She looked at Adair and saw the regret in his eyes. Sudden fear convulsed her heart. They'd not been married a day—need she face losing him?

She asked, "Must this go to battle?"

"Unless ye can convince your grandsire to let us leave, and spare all here."

Rohracht laid his hand on Bradana's arm. "This, as I ha' told him, granddaughter, I will no' do. I see ye be armed. Ye fight wi' us?"

He must be mad, Bradana thought fleetingly. But no madder than she.

"I do."

Rohracht gave a nod. Supported by one of his men, he moved forward.

Adair took his place at Bradana's side. "I do no' suppose there is any sense in asking ye to fall back?"

"Nay. Adair, can we win this?"

"By what the guards say, Mican has come wi' only a small force now. If your grandfather's intention is to run him off, we may prevail."

"He will never survive a battle."

"Nay. That is why I must stand for him." Adair turned and looked Bradana full in the eyes. A look of regret it was, and promise. "My love, I would no' have traded this time with ye for any amount o' riches. If I am to fall—"

"Nay!"

"—know that I will find ye. I will find ye again in spirit. If no' in this lifetime, then in the next."

She had no chance to reply. Two members of the guard came running, both sweating heavily and looking grim.

"They come!"

"Aye." Rohracht stepped forward. "Then let us meet them."

"ROHRACHT MACFEE!" MICAN bawled out as he and his band of men approached, escorted by members of Rohracht's guard. None of them looked happy, and Bradana wondered if there had already been a scuffle between the two forces. The MacGillean men led their ponies, and several of them—for she hastily numbered them at nearly a score—rested their hands on their weapons.

Rohracht called out, his voice sounding reedy despite his best efforts, "Wha' are ye doing, Mican MacGillean, on my land? Ye be no' welcome here."

Mican scowled. He wore an embittered expression, all too visible in the clear morning light, still more heavily lined than when Bradana had glimpsed him in the forest. His eyes scanned the group that had come out to meet him—visibly frail Rohracht with his guard gathered around him. But Bradana had pulled

Adair a step behind. Mican did not at once see them.

"I ha' business wi' ye," Mican called, "and wish to talk."

Bradana's heart leaped. Mayhap they could avoid a battle.

But her grandsire called back, "I ha' naught to say to ye. We were allies once. Your father and I both founded our holdings here in Dalriada within years o' each other. Since his death, ye ha' turned on us and striven to take my lands. Your son killed my grandson. So ye can turn yoursel' right around and begone."

"My son, Earrach, is dead."

"Aye, so, death comes to us all in the end."

"'Tis my belief ye ha' something I want—Earrach's killer. We ha' tracked him here. And I believe he is wi' your granddaughter. Turn the bastard over to me and we shall go awa' without dealing ye any harm."

"Naught is here but belongs here wi' me." Rohracht's voice now sounded steady, but from where Bradana stood behind him, she could see him trembling with strain.

How long could the valiant old man last?

Beside her, Adair stood stiff and tense, his arm like iron beneath her fingers. She clutched him in order to hold him back, even though she knew she could not for long.

Mican scanned the crowd again, catching sight of something that interested him. "That hound—I know that hound. It belongs to yer granddaughter."

Bradana shifted and, too late, sought to draw Wen back by the scruff of his neck.

"If my granddaughter be here," Rohracht called, "wha' is it to ye?"

"I want the Erin-born whoreson who is in her company."

Before Bradana could prevent it, Adair stepped forward. He did it deliberately, and took his place beside Rohracht, standing straight and tall.

"Here I be. Wha' would ye have of me? I battled and took down your son in a fair fight, Mican MacGillean. Have ye so little honor, ye would now come grumping and whining over it?"

Mican's gaze fastened to Adair, and even across the space that separated them, Bradana could see the rage engulf him.

"No' a fair fight!" he seethed. "Ye got between my son and his betrothed, where ye had no business to be."

"I will no' stand by and watch a man abuse a woman, especially one who wants no part o' him."

Mican sneered. "And one ye wanted for yerself. I suppose ye ha' had her now, and filthy she is from it. I ha' no interest in her, but I want yer blood."

Adair spread his hands. They were empty, his sword now thrust through the loop at his belt. "Then take me."

Sickness roiled in Bradana's gut. She stepped forward also. "But ye will ha' to fight me to get him."

For an instant, Mican looked like he wanted to laugh. Before he could, Rohracht said, "And me."

"And me." The man at Rohracht's side.

"And me."

"And me!"

Other members of the guard stepped up.

An ugly look transformed Mican's face into a scowl. He drew his sword. The sound of it whispering forth was followed by that of his men following suit.

They teetered on the edge of a battle. Of death. To the root of her soul, Bradana knew this beautiful morning could be torn asunder in violence and blood.

She heard herself say, "Tak' me instead."

Everyone there stared at her, including Adair, who stood so close she could feel his heat and his emotions.

"Nay," he said, low.

"Nay," Mican said. "'Tis no' ye I want." He pointed at Adair with his sword. "His head will decorate my hall before the sun goes down this night."

Adair drew his sword, which made no sound.

Bradana took another swift step forward. "'Twas I who refused your son and broke the marriage agreement," she told

Mican fiercely, "and I who should pay the price. Take me wi' ye. Punish me as ye will. Leave my grandsire's lands alone."

Better that, so her heart cried within her, than those she loved should pay a high price. Her grandfather who could barely stand. His people who had welcomed them so warmly.

Adair.

She lived to be with him, but she would sacrifice herself a hundred times over rather than see him fall in a shower of blood.

"Bradana, nay." He stepped forward also and laid his hand on her wrist. She could feel the ties that bound them—spiritual ties far older than the ones that had united them yesterday.

"Let me do this," she whispered to him. "Pray, let me."

"Nay!" He sought to step between her and Mican's group of men. But Mican watched her closely and a cruel look came to his eyes.

"Well so, Erinman, will ye let a woman fight yer honor battle for ye?"

"I will not." Adair raised his sword. "I challenge ye to combat here and now. The two o' us one against the other."

For a moment longer, Mican stood, his men all watching him, before he said. "Later, mayhap. I shall return for ye. But first, aye, I will tak' yer woman as ye took my son, and she shall suffer for her treachery. She shall suffer well."

"Nay!" Adair yelled, and leaped forward. The whole of Rohracht's company leaped with him as one, but Bradana evaded them all save Wen, who stuck to her side.

Filled with equal parts raw fear and determination, she stepped to Mican, who promptly seized her by the arm and raised his blade to her throat, even as the nearest of his men wrested her borrowed sword from her hand.

Wen growled and Mican kicked at him. "Get this beast awa' from me or I will kill him."

Bradana begged her beloved hound, "Wen—go." She raised her gaze to Adair's face. Never had she beheld such agony. All his love came rushing at her in that moment. Hers for him kept her still in Mican's grasp.

Let me do this for ye, she begged him silently. *My love, my love.*

Aloud she called, "Hold, Wen! Please!"

"Granddaughter!" Rohracht bellowed, clearly distraught. Mican kicked at the snarling hound again and backed away, hauling Bradana with him. His men closed around them.

"Bradana!" Adair called in turn, and came leaping forward. The beautiful morning erupted in bloodshed.

CHAPTER FORTY

A THOUSAND THOUGHTS crowded Adair's head as he engaged in the fight, but one dominated. He had to reach Mican, to cut him down and end this terrible travesty before the man made off with Bradana.

Naught else truly existed for him. Even though his heart was torn by the desire to protect Wen, who had thrown himself headlong into the battle. To protect the old man who so valiantly fought at his side, nothing came before rescuing his wife.

Why had she done it, delivered herself into Mican's hands? But he knew, aye, even as he battled, his sword crashing into weapon after weapon. Even as he watched Mican, still clutching Bradana, slip away while his men held Adair off. *He knew.*

She could no more bear to see harm come to him than he could see it come to her.

He fought like a wild man, some old skill flooding through him from he knew not where. Mican's men fell to his blade one after the other. But even as he felled them, Mican moved off and away, fighting his own path through Rohracht's guards, who surrounded him. When Mican reached his ponies, he mounted, pulling Bradana up with him.

Adair and Wen both broke through the battling crowd of Mican's men. Wen leaped at Mican's pony and the man danced the animal away even as Adair struck at him, careful not to hurt the woman clutched to his enemy's chest.

Her eyes filled with agony. With regret. With a plea for forgiveness.

Mican dug his heels into his pony's sides and, in company with several of his mounted men, sped off, scattering the remaining ponies out of Adair's reach.

Adair wanted to scream. He wanted to flail and rage. Instead he chased after them till his breath gave out, and he found himself surrounded by those of Mican's men who had followed him.

"Go!" he told Wen then, for the hound had accompanied him on his desperate chase.

Wen took off in a gray streak after the charging ponies, no longer in sight.

Not what Bradana had asked of him. She'd wanted for him to keep her hound safe. But she had done something so terrible.

For the sake of love.

He was not sure he could forgive it.

For the moment, though, he found himself in a desperate fight against no fewer than four of Mican's men. They would like naught better than to kill him and take his corpse—or at least his head—back to their chief.

Winded as he was, distracted as he was, he might not have survived that fight had two of Rohracht's men not reached him and thrown their swords behind his. One of them was Dabhor, with whom Adair had grown friendly. When the last of Mican's men fell, their eyes met, Dabhor's wide with dismay.

"He has the chief's granddaughter!"

"Aye." Adair gasped for breath, his distress weighing him down. "The chief?"

"He survives. Just barely."

Why had Mican taken Bradana when he'd wanted Adair's blood? Because he wanted to cause Adair maximum pain. And he now had the means in his hands.

Adair wanted to retch there on the ground. He wanted to tear something apart with his bare hands. Neither would do the woman he loved any good.

He straightened and said, "I ha' sent Wen after them."

"The hound? Wha' good will that do?"

"Ye may be surprised."

ROHRACHT WAS DISTRAUGHT, though not half so upset as Morag. The kindly woman, when Adair and his companions reached her, stood torn between dismay over the plight of her husband and fear for Bradana.

"He took her! Och, he took her," she kept repeating over and over again. "Whatever will we do?"

Rohracht had collapsed after his valiant stand and had to be carried to his quarters.

"Go after her," he implored Adair, grasping his arm. "That brave, misguided lass—she has done this for yer sake."

"I know."

"He will hurt her. Just because he can."

"Aye. The hound has gone after them. I will need ponies. A few men." A small party would make for a better pursuit. "If I cannot reach them before he gains his stronghold…"

"Aye. Go. Tak' wha' ye need."

"And ye." Adair clasped the old man's hand. "Keep alive till we return. She will need ye."

Rohracht nodded. His wife fell upon him, fussing over the man even before Adair walked away.

With nothing more than his sword, a knife, and the flint in his pocket, Adair left Rohracht's settlement behind. Dabhor had chosen their ponies and did his best to keep up with Adair as he rode off. Quick as they'd been, Adair feared they had lost too much time.

The ground showed evidence of Mican's departure back through the turf and up along the rise from whence Adair and Bradana had first arrived, until the ground turned to stone and the possible trail veered in several directions. Dabhor tried to convince Adair to scout for signs, and further time was lost, all while Adair sweated.

He meant what he'd said to Rohracht. If they did not retrieve Bradana before Mican reached his own stronghold, he did not believe they could succeed in getting her back.

Mad lass with the valiant heart, throwing herself to the wolves that way. He could still see her, stepping up fearlessly. Her thoughts all for him. *Him.* The third son of an Erin chief with little to recommend him.

Save her love. If he ever amounted to aught, it would be her love that made him so.

Still, he thought as Dabhor scoured the ground for sign, he should have done as his first instinct argued, taken her and sailed for Erin. Got her clear away out of danger.

If he was too late…

He closed his eyes against the pain of that thought, and it seemed as if the land spread out before him.

"Alba," he whispered, "lead me."

A bird flew off in a flurry of wings southward, giving a wild cry.

"That way," he told the men.

They went on over stone, across the hill, and through the forest as the day grew strong around them. They passed the site—a fire not long dead—where Mican and his men must have spent the night, waiting for dawn. That told Adair he headed the right way.

All four of them were quiet, searching for signs. No glimpse of a party ahead. No sight of Wen, upon whom rested Adair's greatest hope.

Wen had gone ahead, and the intelligent hound could find Bradana. So long as the valiant animal did not go rushing in and get himself slain.

Help us, Adair said silently to the land itself. This wild and dark-hearted place where he'd been exiled. *Save her for me.*

"Master Adair," said Dabhor, who drew his pony up. "We are

veering too far west. Mican's holding is almost due south from here." Worry stood stark in the man's eyes. "It will no' tak' much to lose them."

"Aye."

Adair scanned the forest ahead of them, crowded with trees and looking nearly identical in every direction.

Again he closed his eyes. "Show me."

As soon as he opened his eyes, a flash of russet brown caught his attention. A deer slipping off.

"That way," he said, desperation rising to near choke him. "And hurry."

⟡

CHAPTER FORTY-ONE

TRUE, RAW FEAR did not set in until Mican had hauled Bradana up on his pony with him and ridden away. Up till that moment she'd been so focused on saving Adair, on doing whatever she must to avoid a battle that could cost his—or her grandsire's—life, she'd spared no actual thought for herself. Had no room for it.

Now, though, galloping headlong farther and farther away from those she loved, she looked squarely at what she'd done, and the terror came rushing in.

She would do the same over again, aye, to spare the man she loved. Only now she had to deal with the consequences.

Could she get away?

She did not think so. Up on Mican's pony with him, held as close to him as could be with his arm across her chest like an iron bar, she could barely breathe. The hurried gait of the pony made every jog an agony. If she did manage to hurt Mican somehow and drop from the back of the horse, the entire group of his men would be atop her.

What might Mican do with her? Aye, that question occupied a great portion of her mind. He would take her back to his stronghold. There, he would doubtless wreak some sort of vengeance upon her. Punish her for the death of his son.

The very thought made her go hot and cold in turn. She could endure much, especially for Adair's sake. But an existence there among strangers who hated her? One of unending misery?

He would not keep her alive that long, she assured herself. Mican would kill her after he hurt her—for it was not she he wanted to punish so much as Adair. He would kill her in some terrible manner and deposit her remains where Adair would find them. Or perhaps use her for bait to capture him.

Och, why had she failed to see that possibility? She might have spared Adair nothing.

For he would come after her. He would, the man she loved— he with the heart so valiant, even he did not see his own worth. If Mican used her as a means to lure Adair in…

She should have warned him. Should have forbidden his coming after her. There had been no time when the mad idea of giving herself up came to her.

He would not have listened. Nor would she, were their positions reversed.

Suddenly she heard his voice in her mind. *I will find ye. I will find ye again in spirit, if no' in this lifetime, then in the next.*

But was that Adair's voice? It must be, for it echoed through her with sacred promise. It filled her heart.

It tried to chase the doubt. Adair, her husband, had made a promise. Yet perhaps they weren't meant to be together in this life.

Do no' think that, she chided herself. *Do not ever doubt him, or our love.*

Mican eased their hectic pace a bit. The ponies could not sustain such flight for long, and anyway, they were entering the forest, where such incaution could prove dangerous.

Bradana strained to look back—hoping, hoping for what she could not see. Back past Mican's men. Through the trees that closed behind them.

Did she catch a glimpse of gray? Or did her eyes, fooled by the flicker of light through the trees, play tricks on her?

"Keep still," Mican growled, and squeezed her cruelly. "Unless ye want a beating. Ye may believe I will gi' ye one—and gladly."

She did believe it. He would beat her senseless. She'd be easier to transport limp over the back of a pony.

Tears filled her eyes. Och, she should have done as Adair wished and sailed away with him to Erin. Left this land she loved while still they had the chance.

"YE KEN," DABHOR said when they paused to let their ponies pick their way across a narrow stream, "if we do catch them, we ha' no' enough men to fight her free. 'Tis a stout force Mican has wi' him still."

Adair glanced at the man. He appeared as worried as Adair had ever seen him.

"I will fight her free," he vowed. "No matter what it takes. Keep your eyes peeled for the hound."

"The hound is far ahead o' us."

"And may well come back for me. They will ha' to stop eventually. If Wen knows where she is, he will lead me."

And what condition might Bradana be in by then? Adair did not want to express that thought. He did not even want a hint of it in his mind. But if Mican took out his ire on the woman who'd spurned his son…

"Hurry," he told Dabhor. "And silent, now."

They continued on through the seemingly trackless forest, and Alba whispered in his ear. She did, with a stirring of air at his cheek. A flicker of light up ahead. The scurry of a fox. The ponies grew weary, the men wearier still. Dusk came late in Alba at this time of year, but at length a kind of preternatural dusk began to gather beneath the trees.

Would Mican try to press on for his settlement, through the dark? Adair believed it was too far, but who could tell?

He must catch them before they reached the settlement. Once inside Mican's stronghold, Bradana was as good as lost to him.

The gloom beneath the trees deepened to night. They stopped perforce.

"You three rest the ponies," Adair told the men. "I am going ahead on foot."

Dabhor protested, "And if ye get lost? Ye do not know this land."

Nay, but he was coming to know it, deep and strong.

"Wait here," Adair bade the men, and hared off before they could prevent him.

Soon enough, the silence of the night forest closed around him. Only, as he swiftly discovered, the silence was not *silent*. It still whispered to him in the movements of small animals, in the rustle of tree branches, and in something more—a low hum that matched the rush of blood through his veins. A soft voice that sounded almost like the music Bradana wove from her harp late at night.

Alba, alive around him. Speaking to him.

He spoke back to her. *Aid me. Let me find her. Show me which way to go.*

When the hound appeared before him, he had to blink for fear he'd summoned up what he wanted to see. Wen was no more than a long, dark shape, but he whined beneath Adair's hands and trembled.

"Good boy, fine lad," Adair breathed, hunkering down. "D'ye know where she is?"

Apparently Wen did. He ran forward, then back to make sure Adair followed.

The next few moments felt like a dream, too fantastical to be real. The hound moved silently, as did Adair. He could no longer feel his feet hit the ground. The trees, seeming identical and endless, blocked his way repeatedly but he wove his way through them, one hand resting on Wen's rough coat.

He smelled a wisp of smoke before he saw the place, and his lips spread in a mirthless smile. So confident was Mican, he'd dared to light a fire.

Wen paused at the edge of a small, stony clearing, and Adair stood stock-still beside him. The hound trembled with eagerness. Neither of them made a sound.

To the left, large, dark shapes and a few restless movements told Adair the ponies had been picketed. The fire slumbered, no more than an orange-red eye on the ground. So did most the men, anonymous, dark shapes wrapped in their cloaks.

Two men stood guard, neither appearing particularly alert. One stood motionless across the way. The other, not far from Adair and Wen, moved restlessly.

To be sure, the man had no notion that Adair and the hound were so near.

Which of the prone figures was Bradana? It was too dark to see the colors of clothing. One body did appear a bit smaller than the others, but naught was certain. Which was Mican?

A knife blade in the dark might solve many problems. But once the sleepers roused, the battle would be intense.

Wen whined softly. Adair pondered what to do. He could follow them and wait for a chance, one that might not come. They would no doubt reach Mican's stronghold sometime tomorrow.

Wen whined again. The guard nearest them turned toward them.

One of the prone figures lifted its head from the ground.

Was that Bradana? Had she somehow heard her hound? Aye, the size of the figure seemed right. But she lay close to the fire, and Adair would be hard-pressed to reach her.

He touched the hound's back again. *Stay.* He slid not his sword but his knife from its loop on his belt, and crept forward.

CHAPTER FORTY-TWO

B RADANA NEVER KNEW what alerted her. Some wild instinct, perhaps, or a rustled whisper from the trees overhead.

She ached too badly and harbored too much fear to sleep, though the men around her did. When they stopped, Mican had dumped her on the ground and growled at her that she should not move. His men had built a fire but made no offer to her of food or water.

She cared little for the former, but would have killed for a cool drink.

She had remained where Mican dumped her as the men conversed, mounted a guard, and eventually lay down around her. Mican lay not far away—within arm's reach. Two men stood on watch pacing the perimeter of the camp. Until the fire died, she could see them clearly. After, not so much, but she knew they would see her if she tried to rise. If she made an attempt to get away.

Mican—arrogant man that he was—had failed to bind her hands or feet. He did not think much of her as an opponent.

If she ran, they would pursue her. She knew not what lay out there in the dark. But she sensed…

Something. Someone.

Aid me, she told the land beneath her, the trees above her, the very air around her.

And then she heard the whine. And she knew who it was that lurked out there in the dark.

Wen had found her. He had.

She lifted her head and tried to see. Impossible.

Please, she begged of Alba, and looked from one guard to the other.

If only one of them would step off into the trees to relieve himself. She could make a run for it. With Wen there to defend her…

But had she learned nothing? Would she want her hound to spend his life for her? Had she not sacrificed herself to keep those she loved alive?

She should just stay where she was. Continue on to Mican's stronghold. Take whatever punishment he wanted to hand out.

One of the guards disappeared. It occurred so swiftly and so silently, Bradana did not see it happen. One moment the fellow pacing the perimeter of the camp was there, the next he was not. She blinked and strained her eyes.

Gone.

She did not understand. If Wen had leaped upon the man and taken him down, she would have heard.

Her eyes moved to the second guard. Had he seen? He stood perfectly motionless and might be sleeping on his feet.

Then suddenly, before she could blink again, he disappeared also.

Bradana sat up, sure her eyes must be deceiving her, or that she slept and dreamed.

Aye, that must be it, for she saw Wen approaching, picking his way across the camp on his big, silent feet, stepping around and at one point *over* the sleeping men.

Bradana scrambled to her feet. Dream or not, she was following her hound.

But she did not breathe as she crept past the sleeping figures. Mican first, who stirred and snorted, making her heart falter in her chest. Two others.

At the edge of the trees, arms enfolded her and gripped her hard. She knew him at once, and her poor heart bounded, but she did not say a word.

Hand in hand, they moved off. Past the guard who lay sprawled on the ground. Led by Wen, who still moved silently and looked like a figure from an ancient tale.

Neither of them spoke, but strength came to Bradana through Adair's fingers. She wanted to ask him a hundred questions, but she already had the answers.

I will find you always.

They walked on and on through endless trees, following the hound and not seeking any other direction. Listening hard for someone to wake behind them. To leap up and begin a pursuit.

No sound came.

Alba closed her arms around them. Bradana could describe it no other way. The trees shielded them. The very earth guided their footsteps. Just the three of them alone.

At last Bradana faltered, and they paused. Her body still hurt, and the effects of her ordeal had her in a fierce grip.

Adair ran his hands up and down her arms, imparting reassurance, and unfastened something from his belt. A flask.

Bradana drank the water greedily. Wen pressed against her side and whined. She dug her fingers into his fur.

"Come," Adair breathed in her ear.

"Which way?"

"I do not know. I am trusting Wen."

But when she would have moved off, Adair seized her, trapped her face between his hands, and kissed her.

All his love lay in that kiss. His fear and his relief. When it ended she clung to him, drawing on his presence.

The trees rustled overhead as a dawn wind rose. It would be light soon. An advantage, and a disadvantage.

Bradana could no longer hear whether anyone came after them. But Wen, who had lain down beside them, looked calm.

She gazed into Adair's eyes. "What now? If we go home they will follow us and may still attack Grandfather. I do no' wish to bring harm to him."

"Bradana." Adair brushed her cheek with tender fingers. So

much emotion brimmed in his eyes, it fair shook her. "If we do no' go back, even if we send word by his men that I have found ye, that old man will worry himself to death over ye. He will no' rest till he sees ye with his own eyes. *Alanna*, ye must learn to let others love ye."

"I—" She had no words in reply to that.

Gently, he went on, "Why did ye do as ye did—turn yourself over to Mican back there?"

"Because…" Her eyes brimmed with tears. She saw him through a haze. But she did not have to see him, for she could feel him, the better part of her soul. "I could no' bear the thought of harm coming to ye. Better anything he might do to me than that."

"Och, lass. Did ye have so little faith in me that ye thought I would not fight like fury itself to protect ye?"

"I thought—I thought ye might fight to the death for me. How could I bear that, Adair? Tell me how."

All at once she was weeping, crying out her terror and relief.

"There, now. There, now," he crooned.

"'Tis just because I *do* ha' faith in ye that I thought ye would spend your life for my sake."

"Aye, so. We are bent, so it seems, on sacrificing ourselves for each other."

"When all we want is to be together. I care no' where, Adair. In a chief's hall, in a hovel. Wi' no roof over our heads at all."

"Aye. And have I not promised ye it will be? Trust my promise."

"I do. I trust ye, but then the fear comes." She dabbed at her eyes. Wen had risen to his feet and looked concerned.

Bradana dropped down and embraced her hound. "Thank ye for helping to save me."

The big hound nuzzled her. When she got to her feet, she had her answer.

"Ye be right, Adair. We must go home. Reassure Grandfather and Mistress MacFee. After that, we will think again."

CHAPTER FORTY-THREE

THE WEATHER CHANGED sharply as they circled northward through the trees and eventually met up with the rest of Adair's party. Rain moved in from the sea riding the tail of that dawn wind, and soon enough they moved through a steady downpour.

Alba, spreading protective wings over them? Bradana could not quite lose the fancy. The men, all highly relieved to be taking her back to their chief without a fight, traded off going afoot so she could ride a pony, and they came at last to Grandfather's holding, where they met up with two soaked and worried members of the guard.

"We do no' ken whether we be followed," Dabhor told them. "If no' yet, they will be after us soon enough. They ha' no need to track us, for they know where we are bound."

"The chief has set up a strong watch," one of the guards said. "Mistress Bradana, he will be that glad to see ye."

He was. Morag came running out to greet them when they arrived, heedless of the rain, and took them straight to the hall, where Rohracht directed matters from his great chair.

Bradana fell into her grandsire's arms. Love was here, she could feel that. She also felt the old man's weakness and pain.

"Granddaughter, let me look at ye. How did ye get free?"

"Adair and Wen rescued me. 'Tis only by their wit and courage that I am here."

Rohracht cast a look at Adair and the hound. "I am that grateful, I ha' no words. But ye, lass"—he cradled Bradana in his arms—"'twas a foolish, foolish thing ye did turning yersel' over that way. Did ye think we would no' defend ye?"

"Just what I asked her," Adair said softly.

"I did no' want it to cost ye," Bradana told the old man, "and cost ye dear."

"Aye, well, one fights for what is precious. Ye maun promise not to do that again, Granddaughter."

"I am not sure I can."

"Stubborn as well as true-hearted."

"Chief Rohracht," Adair told the old man, "he will be coming after us—Mican."

"Aye, no doubt he will. We maun ha' some time, though, for I do no' doubt he will go home first and raise an army. No matter, we will be ready for him."

Would they?

"For now, go and get yoursel's some dry clothing, rest, and take something to eat. We shall have a war meeting anon."

"Only if ye will rest also, Grandfather."

"Just wha' I ha' been telling him," Morag put in.

"I can rest now I know ye are safe. Help me up, Morag."

He went off to his chamber, and Bradana and Adair, with Wen, repaired to their own.

Once she wore dry clothing, Bradana stood at the door trying to listen for sounds of an alarm above the crashing of the rain. They would come from the south. The only question was when.

Adair sprawled on the bed, watching her.

"D'ye think Grandfather is right and Mican will go home for an army? Have we some time?"

"He canna hope to defeat us wi' the number o' men he had with him this time."

Bradana turned her head and looked at him. "Are ye prepared to fight?"

"I am," he answered, his eyes steady upon her.

"Even for this place no' your own?"

"There are good people here. Strong people. They deserve better than to live beneath Mican's thumb. Besides—if 'tis your place, this, is it no' also mine?"

"Aye." She came to him swiftly, put her knee on the bed, and crawled up next to him. "For everything I am is yours."

He gathered her in to lie beside him. Once more, despite the fear and the doubt, her world came right.

"What your grandfather said," Adair whispered after a moment. "Ye must promise never to do that again—sacrifice yourself. Ye have no idea how I felt knowing ye were in his hands and prey to whatever he might decide to do."

Bradana drew a breath. "As I told Grandfather, I canna make that promise. If there's ever aught I can do to spare or save ye, I will do it."

"Bradana—"

"'Tis the other side o' love, is it no'? A love such as we share. Fear. The fear o' loss. Of parting."

Adair did not speak, though once again she could feel the emotions moving through him, surging.

"Morag loves Grandfather so much, but she will lose him. In battle, if Mican returns. Or when he loses the other battle he fights. 'Tis…'tis unbearable. Yet it must be borne."

Very gently, Adair turned her face to his so their lips were only a breath apart. "Would ye, lass, rather not have had me at all than live fearing ye will lose me?"

"Nay. *Nay.*" She kissed him fiercely, with all her love and desperation behind it. She could taste his emotions flowing back at her, wide and deep as the ocean.

So much love.

"Not that," she said when she broke the kiss and clutched him tight. She could hear his heart thundering. Life, to unite them. Such a fragile thread, yet so strong. "It terrifies me how much I love ye, Adair MacMurtray. But I would no' give up what I've found in ye."

They made love slowly and with devotion while Wen slept

on the floor beside them. As Bradana loved her husband, she became more certain than ever what she had to do.

And when a messenger—Morag herself—came to fetch them, Bradana went hand in hand with Adair, her mind already made up.

The meeting took place in her grandfather's chamber with the old man back in his bed, which Bradana took as a bad sign, even though it was a legitimate council of war.

Master Dabhor was there, as were other key members of the guard, who reported that Mican's men had not been sighted.

"And we made a few forays out into the wood, scouting for them," Dabhor said. "Not a glimpse."

Rohracht grunted. "He must indeed have gone back to collect more men. That gives us some breathing room. But he will return."

"He will attack," Dabhor agreed, "and when he does, we maun be ready."

"We shall be." Rohracht sounded much stronger than he looked. "Alert the settlement. Arm all the men. Tell the women, children, and aged to be ready to flee when Mican's army is sighted. They maun go to the hills and wait till the battle is o'er." He looked at his wife. "That includes ye, Morag."

Her brow furrowed. "If ye remain here, I do also."

"To be sure, I will remain here. I mean to fight." It should have seemed absurd, the old man marooned in the bed making such a declaration. It did not. Too fierce was he, and too determined.

Bradana felt a surge of pride. She came of such stock. Yet that pride came tinged with pity.

Gently, the chief said, "Our men will fight all the better if they do no' need to worry for the safety o' their families. That includes me."

Two tears rolled down Morag's cheeks.

Rohracht looked at Bradana. "And ye. I would like ye to go wi' the women—to head the group o' them and shepherd them if ye will."

Bradana shifted on her feet. "I am sorry, Grandfather, I cannot."

"Now, now, I know ye will want to stay and fight beside yer man. Ye and that fine hound o' yours both. But I need ye elsewhere."

Bradana drew a breath. She could feel Adair watching her, feel all of them. He had bidden her to not sacrifice herself again.

This time, though, she would need to sacrifice something she loved—near as much as him.

"I believe if Mican comes wi' his army, he will come for but one reason. Grandfather, he has no real quarrel wi' ye. Wi' your people. It is only because Adair and I are here that he brings strife to ye."

"That is no' true," Rohracht declared. "We ha' battled the man in the past to hold our land. Did his son no' kill yer cousin in just such a battle?"

"Aye, but now he comes for revenge. 'Tis my being here, and Adair, that has brought him."

"Bradana…" Adair began.

She ignored him. Tears flooded her eyes. "I canna stand and see this place ye love destroyed, Grandfather, because o' me."

"Who says it will be destroyed? Ha' ye so little faith in me, Bradana?"

"I do have faith in ye." At that moment, Bradana overflowed with faith in the old man's courage. But the fear stemmed from a place so deep, she could not gainsay it.

"Ha' ye so little faith in your man that he canna help us win?"

"He cannot, Grandfather. He will not be here. Adair and I are leaving for Erin."

CHAPTER FORTY-FOUR

THEIR FIRST QUARREL, and their marriage but a day or two old. They waited till they were back in their quarters to begin, Adair burning with so many emotions that he could barely express them. Anger. Distress. Dismay. Frustration.

He did not want to aim all that at Bradana. Yet as soon as they were alone, but for Wen, he set into her.

"Ye promised me ye would no' do that again."

Bradana turned to face him. She looked impossibly beautiful to him, with her tangled hair all wild around her, face flushed and eyes overbright. His wild Alban love. Determined to leave this land she adored.

"Do what?" she asked, stalling for time because, to be sure, she knew.

"Sacrifice yoursel' for me."

"I am no'—"

He rode over her, a thing so rare he had never before done it. "Sacrificing what ye love, for my sake. This place that is as good as a part o' ye."

"Naught matters to me more than ye. And I did no' promise. I said I could no' promise—"

"Ha' ye so little faith in me that ye think I cannot fight Mican?"

"Ye keep asking me that, and I ha' told ye that is no' why. If Mican comes and finds ye no' here, finds both o' us gone, he will spare the others. All those good people and my brave grandsire."

"Or he may burn down the settlement. Without us here to help them stand." To Adair's own surprise, he was not afraid to fight. Growing up in Erin, he'd been no devoted warrior. True, skill with weapons had come easily to him. But going off to fight for the king's interests had not held much interest.

This situation was vastly different. And his anger refused to lie down.

"Ye do no' want to go to Erin." He made of it an accusation.

And watched a war fought in Bradana's face. She did not want to live her life in another land. Nor did she want to admit that.

"I want to be wherever ye be, Adair."

"That is no' an answer."

"It is!"

Wen whined. Bradana dug a calming hand into her hound's fur.

Fiercely, Adair asked, "And if I wish to stay here with your grandfather and fight against Mican? Will ye be with me then?"

"Och, I beg ye, nay!" She came forward into his arms—an action he found hard to resist. "Please, Adair."

Adair knew how badly she wanted this. He could feel that, just as he could feel her determination at other times, or her desire for him. A stronger wave of frustration swept through him.

"Would ye leave your grandfather knowing ye will likely no' see him again?"

"If doing so may spare his life, this place he loves. Adair, I canna explain it. This fear reaches so deep inside me."

He understood that. Despite the carefree way he had lived his life before coming to Alba, he too felt things deep. It occurred to him, for the first time, that maybe he had chosen to live lightly in denial of those deep feelings.

But now, here in this dark land, those feelings had caught up with him.

"Bradana." He trapped her face between his hands and gazed into her eyes. Eyes full of storm. Of passion. "I do not like to run from a battle."

"Ye are no' running. Merely returning home as ye ha' wanted to do since first ye came here. Was it no' ye who said over and over again, we should sail to Erin?"

His frustration built higher. Before he could speak, she went on.

"I thought we were to be equals in our decision making. Standing side by side."

"Aye, so," he growled. "Then why do ye push this at me?"

In a rush she said, "I am no' pushing the decision so much as agreeing wi' what ye have wanted all along. Adair, d'ye think Grandfather can hold this settlement against Mican's full army?"

Adair tried to consider that rationally, without his anger in the way. Some instinct—as deep as the fear that beset Bradana—told him if he stayed and fought his best, they could withstand aught Mican might bring. But he could no more assure her of that than he could promise life would never part them.

Only that if it did, he would find her again. He would search always, life after life, for this woman's love.

A knock at the door heralded the arrival of a visitor. Bradana tore herself from Adair's arms and went to answer.

Morag slipped in, distress marking her face. She looked from Bradana to Adair and back again. "Ye have been quarrelling."

"Nay," Bradana said. "Merely discussing what should be done."

"I know I ha' no part in it," Morag said, her eyes swimming in tears. "The decision must be yours alone. But if ye are thinking o' leaving here, and suppose the going might spare Rohracht his life…" She wound her fingers together. "Och, I ken fine I am going to lose him. And, man that he is, he might prefer to die in fight than in that bed." She tried to smile. "A heroic end. But one that may steal precious time from me.

"I ha' never asked for much. I stood by while other women married, and I tried to be of help to those I knew. My union wi' Rohracht came late." She glanced at Bradana. "After he lost your grandmother. I waited my whole life for him."

"Mistress," Adair said huskily, for he understood that kind of love, "are ye saying ye wish for us to go?"

"I am." She looked torn. "Though I would no' wish Rohracht to know that I came to ye."

Adair sighed. Had no one faith enough in him to believe he could fight them free?

He eyed Morag. "This is no' what the chief wants."

"Nay. He wants to make a stand. A valiant last stand. His honor and his heart are stronger than the rest o' him."

Adair suggested gently, "Sometimes a man must be allowed to follow his heart."

"Aye, ye be right, young master. But 'tis I who canna bear the cost."

Bradana reached out and clasped the woman's hand in a quick gesture of understanding. United they stood in this.

Heavily, Adair said, "I know not how I will bring the chief this news. He has favored me with acceptance, even a place here if I choose to take it. Am I to answer that with flight?"

"I will speak to my grandfather," Bradana said.

Adair experienced another flash of anger. "I will be man enough to take the whole o' the decision to him."

Curious how he had not wanted to come to Alba. Now, with his whole being, he did not want to leave.

Morag let go of Bradana and seized Adair's hands. "Thank ye, Master Adair. I understand this does no' sit well with ye. But ye shall forever have my gratitude."

It did not sit well with Rohracht MacFee either, when Adair and Bradana went to him just a short while later. They went hand in hand, even though they were not entirely united in will. In spirit, aye, but Adair's emotions still would not lie down.

He saw a reflection of those feelings in the old man's eyes. Rohracht listened silently to Bradana's explanation, into which she launched almost at once, before looking to Adair.

"And ye, young man? My granddaughter has said her piece.

But where do ye stand?"

"I will admit to ye, Chief Rohracht, I am torn. I want the best defense for yourself and those here. Bradana is convinced that means removing us from the settlement, and Mican's reason for attack."

"Ye be no' so certain?"

Adair bowed his head.

"Young man, I ha' accepted ye as a grandson and think o' ye as such. Have I no' said I would like to leave this holding in your hands if—when I pass?"

"Grandfather," Bradana answered before Adair could, "there may be no holding to leave, should Mican strike in revenge."

"Women." Rohracht closed his eyes and seemed to muse to himself. "They look too hard upon their fear and see not the glory."

"There is no glory, Grandfather, in death."

"Aye so, lass, there is if 'tis met in courage." He opened his eyes to look at her again. "Ye ha' plenty o' courage, lass. And the man ye ha' chosen possesses even more. Bear that in mind."

"I will," Bradana vowed. But Adair knew she focused only on getting him away. On her fear, still. "We will leave at once, as soon as we can prepare the boat."

She embraced her grandfather and stepped to the door. Adair hesitated before he followed, bent over the bed, and took the old man's hand in his, a hard grip.

"Forgive me," he said.

"Lad, there is naught to forgive."

There was. He deserted this valiant old man, when his sword should be sworn to his service. It was as simple—and as complicated—as that.

Rohracht's eyes met his. "Remember, ye will always be welcomed back."

---◇—⟨⟩—◇---

CHAPTER FORTY-FIVE

U NPREPARED FOR HOW much it hurt, Bradana watched the shore slip away. Not her last sight of Alba, not yet, for they must sail among the many islands—the slumbering dragons—that lay between this land and Erin. Her last glimpse, perhaps, of home.

She had been born and raised here in Dalriada, a land her Celtic ancestors considered foreign. Dark. Dangerous.

A land she loved quite desperately and was about to lose.

Tears stung her eyes. She'd been doing a lot of that lately, weeping—she, who had always prided herself on being stronger than tears. She could feel the land pulling at her, could feel those she loved calling.

Almost, almost did she tell Adair to turn around.

Wen was not happy about the small craft. The hound had never before been at sea, and he crouched at the bottom, afraid to move and panting wildly.

Neither was Adair happy. She could tell by his silence, and by what she sensed from his spirit.

He would prefer to stay here and die. She shook her head and half echoed her grandfather's lament. *Men.* Reaching for some honorable glory.

She respected Adair's wish to stand beside her grandfather. Indeed, she did. But did he not see the danger of it? That death could part the two of them—a possibility that terrified her beyond measure.

They sailed on, Adair's hand steady at the tiller, and her heart slowly tore in two. Like a leaf borne on the silver breast of the sea, they bobbed their way along, and Adair concentrated on the task of sailing.

He did not look at her.

As inevitably, aye, as a leaf floating downstream, they journeyed toward Erin. What would it be like there? She had heard Adair's fond descriptions during many a conversation. It seemed a kindly land of soft rains and gentle hills. It had birthed the man she adored.

Would she be welcome?

What would Adair's father say to him, bringing home a wife when he was supposed to bring a grant of land?

She wished with sudden, deep longing that she'd been able to discover her mother's fate before leaving. Had she delivered the babe safely? Was she well?

It struck Bradana then. She might never find out. She might never return.

She clung to the side of the small craft and craned to look back.

Dark land. Wild land. *Remember me.*

All too soon, the last glimpses of the mainland and then the islands slipped from sight. Naught but silver water surrounded them. The light began to fade, hanging bright to the north, like a glow of promise. She slept, curled in the bottom of the boat beside her hound.

The next she knew, gentle hands lifted her. The soft dark of summer lay all around. The craft had come to rest at a pier made of stones, and Adair urged her up.

"Come, love—we are home."

Home.

A WEALTH OF sensations flooded Adair when his feet met his native soil. Relief. A powerful sense of homecoming. Regret. His thoughts had been much, during their water journey, with those he'd left behind.

Mayhap Bradana was right. It was possible if Mican came in force looking for them, he would spare his aging neighbor at finding they were gone.

Or he might crush Rohracht out of thwarted anger and spite.

Something deep within Adair—so deep he barely recognized it—protested that. From whence sprang this incipient warrior in him?

No matter now. Erin extended her green arms to welcome him. Bradana was exhausted and her hound miserable. He needed to get them settled ashore.

They would stay here at the coast for the rest of the night. Morning would be soon enough to make the lengthy walk home. Then there would be explanations for his father. A place to make for himself. It was one thing being a carefree third son. Quite another being a man with a wife to support.

He had left Erin one man, and returned another.

He requested beds for the night from the man who had originally sent him, Nolan, and Flynn on their journey to Alba. So weary and bewildered was Bradana that as he helped her to the rough lodging, she asked, "Is this your home?"

"Nay, we must travel some distance inland. We will be there by midday the morrow."

Indeed, they were all of them feeling the effects of their ordeal. As they crept—or in Wen's case, limped—to their humble beds, Adair could think of little beyond holding Bradana for the night. And indeed, as sooner as their heads hit their borrowed blanket, they slept.

Morning came all too soon, the kind of soft, milky morning Adair imagined so often when he thought of Erin. Their host's wife packed them a breakfast for the road, and Adair looked Bradana in the eye before they departed.

"Are ye fit for this walk? 'Twill take us most the morning, but 'tis a good road all the way home."

She nodded, but looked uncertain.

He wished he might borrow a pony to make the way easier for her, but the men on the shore, who dealt mainly in boats, had none to spare. The sun came up behind them as they walked, and the scents Adair loved surrounded him. His heart settled within him, and some of his worry calmed.

It sprang back to life, though, as they breasted the last hill and followed the trail down into his father's settlement. Never had it looked better to his eyes.

How would Bradana see it, though? Old and established, no doubt. Larger than either her stepfather's or grandsire's holding.

She did not say much. He held her hand, though, so he felt her tense.

Members of Father's guard came running and, recognizing Adair, broke into wide smiles. After an exchange of words and some frankly curious looks for Bradana, they were walked on.

Someone must have gone running to Adair's father, for Gawen himself came walking down from the great hall with Baen at his side. Baen spoke furiously to Gawen as they approached. Aye, Baen would recognize Bradana.

"Son!" Gawen called out even before they met. "'Tis well to see ye returned. Have ye good news for me?"

Before Adair could answer, his father raked his eyes over their ragged band, taking in the woman and the hound. "I see ye return wi'out your men—but no' alone."

"Father. This is my wife, Bradana. Stepdaughter to Kendrick MacCaigh."

"Wife?" Father shot a look at Baen.

"Aye, so. Father, there is much to tell, and our party is fatigued. I pray ye let us find rest, food, and drink before I tell my tale."

Gawen seemed stymied. "But at least tell me, where are yer men?"

"Still in Dalriada, as far as I know."

"As far as ye know?"

"They did no' come home wi'out me?"

"No' yet. But tell me whether or no' ye outdid your brothers, given the task I did set ye."

"Nay, Father, I did not."

A new sharpness entered Gawen's eyes. "Ye were no' successful?"

"I was not."

Baen made a hissing sound of disdain. "I am no' surprised. A den o' savages, they are, in Alba." His gaze flicked to Bradana without apology and away again.

"By the Daghda, son!" Father exploded. "I thought sure since ye were gone all this while, ye would come back wi' what I am owed. Indeed, it seems ye ha' accomplished naught for which ye were sent."

Adair stiffened. How had he forgotten his father's—and indeed, his brother's—habitual disdain while longing for home? They might treat him any way they chose, but by all the gods, they would greet Bradana as she deserved.

Stiffly, he said, "Father, I hope ye will welcome your new daughter."

Gawen gave a grudging nod. "To be sure, she is welcome. But there is a tale here I will most certainly need to hear."

"And no one," Baen muttered disagreeably, "tells a tale like our Adair."

"Meanwhile"—Gawen directed a stern look at Baen—"we offer up our hospitality. Adair, will ye require new lodging?"

"My old quarters will do well enough."

"Then settle your wife and come to me as soon as ye can."

It felt like a sentence descending onto Adair's shoulders. He warranted punishment, aye.

He could endure all, for Bradana's sake.

⬥━━━⬥❧❧⬥━━━⬥

CHAPTER FORTY-SIX

NOT UNTIL THEY reached Adair's quarters did he realize just how unsuitable they were for a man, his wife, and her large hound. Too small and cramped, too untidy. The air smelled stale, and he propped open the door, gazing around at the mess he'd left weeks ago before a hasty departure.

Barely room for the two of them, to say nothing of Wen.

"Ah," he said with considerable chagrin, "perhaps this will not do. I will find us better. For now…"

Bradana perched on the side of the bed. There was nowhere else to sit. "If water might be had, for Wen?"

"To be sure. And ye will be hungry."

"I want only to sleep."

She had slept away most of the voyage. Should he be worried?

"Aye, so. Can ye make yourself comfortable? I will see about food and drink. A fire."

"I am warm enough."

Adair went to her, took her in his arms. He bestowed a kiss in each palm, dropped one on each side of her mouth. Both cheeks. Her forehead. She burned to his lips.

"Bradana, are ye ill?"

"Nay. Just…" Clearly she had no words for what she felt.

"I will send the healer."

"Nay. Do not. I wish only to be alone, save for Wen."

And him? Did she want to be with him?

She had seen nothing of the settlement or this land he loved so well. No more than a glimpse of it on their way in.

Once he showed her all that lay here, she would settle. She would be happy.

"Aye," he said again. "I will send someone with food and water for Wen. I must go and attend my father. Make my explanations."

"Go." She kissed him softly, and the glimmer of a smile lit her eyes. "Husband."

He should not worry, he told himself as he stopped by the kitchens with his request, as he headed for the great hall after. Their love would hold them, wherever they might be.

Baen was still with his father when he reached the hall, which made him scowl. He did not want to do this in front of his oft-superior brother.

But aye, Baen had failed in the same task as he. What cause had his brother to find fault with him?

The two men had been speaking avidly, but broke off when Adair came in.

"Sit," Gawen bade him. "Quench yourself. Baen has just been telling me he what he remembers of Mistress Bradana from his visit to Dalriada. He says she was betrothed then to a chief in the north."

"A chief's son, one Earrach." Adair sat down and poured a mug of ale. "Dead now." He drank deep. "I killed him."

"What?" Gawen fair roared the word. He exchanged an incredulous look with Baen. "This was to be a goodwill mission. And ye come home wi' blood on your hands?"

"And bringing your victim's woman?" Baen added.

"'Tis a long story."

"Ye had better tell it, then."

Adair did, to the best of his ability. It made no favorable impression on either of his listeners. Before he finished, Baen got up and began pacing. His father just stared at him in angry disbelief.

"So," Baen said when Adair reached an end, "ye ha' destroyed relations wi' Kendrick instead of bettering them."

"And," Gawen added heavily, "ruined any chance of our gaining our lands there."

Adair sighed and shook his head. "Father, I am not certain ye want lands there in Alba. They would be of dubious worth and hard to hold." *Strange land. Magical land. Wild with beauty.*

"That is not for ye to decide, Adair. Those lands are owed me in good faith. They were to be my legacy to Daerg. I have to say, I expected better of ye."

A spark of anger joined the frustration and worry already in Adair's heart. Despite his weariness, he got to his feet.

"Why? Why should ye think I would succeed where my brothers both failed? Ye never expected much o' me before."

Gawen too sprang up from his big chair. "I never required much o' ye. A lad wi' two fine older brothers need not trouble his head over much, and I let ye run as ye pleased. Mayhap I did not ask enough o' ye. And the very first time I do?" Gawen seemed to choke on his own words. "Ye come home wi' someone else's woman. And trouble behind ye!"

"Bradana is no one else's woman, save mine." Of all things, Adair was sure of that. "If we are not welcome here, we will leave."

"And go where?" Baen challenged. "Have ye not burned your boat behind ye?"

Indignation joined Adair's other careening emotions. "That is not fair—"

"Enough!" Gawen cried. He focused angry, disappointed eyes on Adair. The disappointment, Adair found the harder of the two to bear. "I did not say ye are not welcome here. But what to do now? Kendrick will be furious wi' us—the very man who owes me a share of land. This Mican—a powerful chief, by the sound o' it—will make naught but an enemy if we do achieve a settlement there."

"I have good relations with Bradana's grandsire."

"An old man teetering on the edge o' death, by the sound o'

it, and one whose holding may well be under attack also. Son, I despair o' ye."

He had, so it seemed, fully expected Adair to return in full triumph. For him to prove his worth. Adair's heart sank.

"Perhaps," he said steadily, "'tis best Daerg achieve his own lands. Perhaps 'tis best if I do also."

"Ye, with what army?" Baen growled. "Did your time in Dalriada teach ye naught? It is a hard land, and all that here in Erin is held by old men."

Gawen glanced at him. "Who are ye calling old? Adair, get out o' my sight. Go back to wasting your time wi' your friends and learning to play songs upon your harp."

"I have a wife now. There will be no more playing at games."

Gawen lifted a brow. "Then what d'ye intend to do?"

"I thought," Adair said, surprising even himself, "I might work at training the men for the field." In Alba, his sword had felt remarkably strong and sure in his hand. "Perhaps work wi' the lads coming up." It felt right, that notion, like the echo of something known long ago.

"Surely," Baen said, "that is Daerg's place."

"Daerg is no warrior," Adair returned.

"And ye be that?" Baen shot back.

"Mayhap so."

"Och well," Gawen said, "if that is your choice. Go now and tend your stolen bride."

Not stolen, Adair thought angrily as he left the hall and walked out into the quiet morning. Meant for him, if ever anything was.

She'd merely been awaiting him there in Alba. Spending her time till he could find her. Till they could complete one another's lives.

That was what mattered. Not his father's disappointment or his brother's attempt to cast disfavor.

Yet the very fabric of his world had changed. The whole time he'd been away, a part of him had longed for Erin. For his life here. For the beautiful hills, the soft rains, the glorious afternoons. A piece of his heart had remained here all the while.

Now his place here felt…well, sullied.

He would change that, though. He would work hard and earn a place. He could do that for Bradana's sake.

He would show her this land he loved, and they would both be at home in Erin.

CHAPTER FORTY-SEVEN

B RADANA LAY ON her back in the bed and stared up at the
rafters of the hut, trying to number the days since she'd left
Alba. She failed, for her mind had fallen into confusion. It might
be ten days. It might be a fortnight. She'd spent so much of the
time sleeping, she could not tell.

Sleep had become her refuge and her means of hiding what
she felt from Adair. He had done his best to make her feel
welcome here. He had taken her and Wen on long treks over the
land, sharing his love of this place. He had introduced her to his
friends. He had taken her to dinner in the great hall.

She did not feel welcomed. Not by Adair's father, the chief,
and not by his brothers, both of whom she remembered far too
well from their visits to Alba.

Alba.

The place haunted her. She dreamed of it at night and
thought she was there again, striding over the hills or gazing out
at the sea. She longed for the place during the day, even when for
the sake of pity she took Wen out on her own and began, aye, to
appreciate the beauties of Adair's land.

She could not let Adair know. Could not tell him how the
longing for home beset her, like a sickness. He exerted himself
each day working in the field, making a place here for them both.
She admired him for that and determined she would support him
in it.

But it left her and Wen much alone. Lonely.

Thank the gods for Wen. What would she do without him?

Her nights, at least, were spent in Adair's arms. They made love often, a bit desperately on her part as she sought that deep connection with him. Sought to belong somehow in this strange land.

She sighed and stirred in the bed. Wen lifted his head from his paws and gazed at her sorrowfully.

Aye, one made sacrifices for those one loved. Wen, confined so often to the new quarters Adair had claimed, knew that.

She must find a purpose here. Continue going out and about, if only for Wen's sake.

They did make a daily pilgrimage to the training field where Adair worked. It gave her the pleasure of watching him. Of overhearing the gossip of the other young women who also went there.

These young Erin women wanted no part of her. They gazed at her solemnly and made no overtures of friendship. From what little she had overheard, she gathered Adair had long been a favorite among them, and competition had been fierce to see which he would take for a bride. Forba—she who had once occupied herself teaching Adair to play upon the harp—watched her with cool, unfriendly eyes.

In time, they might come to accept her. At least, that was what Adair seemed to think. She did not want to contemplate a future spent here, endless days stretching to years.

And she dreamed of Alba. She wondered how those she'd left there fared. Whether her grandsire's lands had come under attack or if this bid of hers had saved him. If he lived yet.

"We canna go on like this, Wen." She sat up, her hair swinging behind her. Adair had run his fingers—beloved fingers—through her hair last night. He had kissed her all over. He had been inside her where he belonged.

But now an endless day stretched ahead of her. Without him.

She got to her feet, and the hound pricked up his ears. She dressed carefully, brushed out her hair, and braided it. She took up her harp from its place in the corner.

It had been days since she'd touched it. Travel and the trip at sea had not been kind to the instrument. Though she'd tried giving Adair a song once or twice, the notes sounded sour and so she'd quit.

"Wen, come."

She'd heard Gawen MacMurtray's harper, a man called Caomhán, at practice during her walks each morning, either out in the open at the foot of the brae, or tucked into a corner of the hall. He also played for the company at supper, and when Adair persuaded her to attend, she heard him there.

A man of some talent. And one, so Bradana understood, who had been part of Adair's circle before he left for Alba.

This being a fine morning, she found him at the foot of the hill with his acolytes around him. Most figures of importance here in Erin seemed to have acolytes. Even Adair.

Some of those now gathered in the grass were young women. A couple of them looked up sharply when Bradana approached and she saw with dismay that one of them was Forba.

Wen ran ahead of Bradana over the green grass, and she paused a moment to gather her courage and take in the scene. Aye, this place was beautiful with its gentle rise and Caomhán's students in their fine robes looking bright as flowers.

She walked on.

A man of early middle years was Caomhán, with dark brown hair that showed red in the sun, a quick gaze, and clever hands. She had never before spoken directly to him, save for a word of greeting. He glanced up from his student—a young boy surely no more than twelve—and watched carefully as Bradana approached.

"Mistress." He made to get to his feet.

"Nay, pray, do no' rise."

"Wha' is it ye have there?" His gaze fixed to her harp.

"A clàrsach."

"One made in Alba?" Aye, they all knew who she was and

from whence she'd come.

"Aye. It is no'…no' as fine as your own." He played a beautiful instrument, all carved with the twisted figures of animals and leaves.

"Ah, 'tis the voice o' the instrument that matters." He had blue eyes, and when he looked at Bradana, they appeared kind. "Do ye play?"

"Aye. But I canna of late. She needs strings. I wondered if ye might help."

"She?" He smiled. Setting aside the lad's harp, he got to his feet. "May I?"

Bradana surrendered the harp to his hands. Her most treasured possession besides Wen, it looked small and crude as the man examined it.

"Aye, so, ye are indeed in need of new strings."

"Can ye provide them? I am sure my husband can pay for your service."

His smile widened. "Your husband, Adair MacMurtray. He is a good friend o' mine. I can fit your harp, mistress, and gladly—if ye repay me wi' a song."

"Och, I am sure I do no' play as well as yourself, Master Caomhán."

He ignored that. Stepping away to a nearby pack, half the contents of which had already been spread on the ground, he fished for supplies.

"I have been to Alba, ye know."

"Have ye?" Bradana's heart leaped.

"Indeed, as a young man. A wild sort o' place, is it no'? But I got some wondrous tunes there."

"Aye."

"When there, I did not see any female harpers."

"'Tis no' usual," Bradana admitted. "I had to beg to receive my lessons."

"Och, so. A determined woman, then."

Bradana found herself smiling. "I was gey determined about that."

"Well, we must spread beauty as we can."

She watched as, with quick and practical motions, he replaced the strings on her little harp.

As he worked, he continued to chatter. "I myself have two children. My son already learns upon the harp. I confess, I would not have thought to teach my daughter also. Mayhap ye can change my mind."

"'Tis always good to learn." When he finished stringing her harp, she said, "I thank ye. Adair will be glad of it also. He loves me to play for him."

"Adair possess an excellent ear and might have made a fine harper, in another life. These new strings will need to stretch out."

"Aye."

"But ye owe me a tune, mistress. Why not use my harp?"

"Yours? Och, I could not."

"Why?"

"It is much larger than mine, and it is so magnificent—"

"The harp canna see itself, and knows only its own voice." He walked to a nearby rug, where sat his harp in solitary splendor, and took it up. "Please."

How could she refuse when he had shown her all she'd seen so far of kindness here in Erin?

By now, everyone there watched them, including Forba. Hesitantly, Bradana took a seat on one of the stools and balanced the instrument on her knee. She ran her fingers down the strings and the harp gave voice into the clear, soft air.

It was enough to let the magic take hold, and her doubt fled. She gave them one of the first songs she had learned, finding her way on the strings, adding the embellishments by which it had become her own. She broke then at once into the song she'd made for Adair. The beautiful harp sang for her, and when they finished, there was not a sound.

Not until Caomhán cleared his throat. "I ha' ne'er heard that last tune."

"Because it is one o' my own."

"Mistress, ye ha' a wondrous talent. I hope ye will cultivate it well, for it deserves to be passed down to future generations."

To her child? Hers and Adair's?

She could not see the future, but of a sudden, she wanted to.

CHAPTER FORTY-EIGHT

RARELY HAD ADAIR seen a more beautiful season. Late spring had been easing into early summer when he left home for Alba, and the full of it when he and Bradana returned. Now, Erin bloomed around him as if determined, in all her splendor, to show him everything he loved.

Soft, gentle mornings cloaked in mist that rose with the first rays of the sun to reveal the sweet shapes of the hills and valleys he'd known all his life. Noontimes when he worked at the training field, and the scents of sod and horse and wild thyme filled the heated air. The glitter of the river at nightfall, when the quiet seemed to arise like magic from the very ground, to enfold him.

What man could ask for more?

Not he.

Why, then, did he yearn for something else?

It was a longing that, at first, he did not recognize. He had longed for Bradana all his life, without knowing it. At first when this other wanting began to dog him, he thought it was because he wished to be with her at all moments, even while at work or with his father.

Then it began to haunt him even when he was in Bradana's company. When they walked together with Wen through the woods or over the braes. When they lay together in one bed at night.

He could not understand it. Despite his rather fraught relationship with his father and his uneasiness with Baen, he had all he'd ever sought. Work he enjoyed more and more each day. Time to spend with his friends if he wished. The company of the woman he adored in the land he loved.

Then why did this discontent pull at him?

He could not lay the disturbance at Bradana's feet. Though she seemed quieter than before, and a bit lost, she did not speak of missing home or complain to him. By *her* insistence had he returned to Erin. As the days slipped past, did she begin to find a place for herself in Erin? It seemed so. She once more played for him on the harp. She even began to make new songs.

There could be no greater pleasure than lying at nightfall while the notes from her harp trembled through the still air and shivered around him. Not even making love to her pleased him so well.

He did not speak to her of his discontent and, indeed, only puzzled over the elusive feeling at odd moments.

One afternoon when he finished up with training, he noticed Baen standing at the far side of the field. Adair had taken on working with the youngest of the lads, ages twelve up, and they made a clamor and din, laughing and teasing one another as they started home.

Slowly, with his sword still in hand, Adair walked over to his brother.

"That is a rowdy crew," Baen observed, frowning at the youngsters.

"Aye, and I have worked them hard." Adair also looked at the lads, but with affection. "They have boundless energy, do they not?"

Baen flung him a searching glance. "What has made ye take them on?"

Adair shrugged. "It is as I told ye and Father when I came back—I want to be of service here. And Daerg did not want the job. He said they lacked discipline."

"And so ye, also lacking discipline, thought ye were up to the task?"

Adair narrowed his eyes at his brother. "I may ha' lived lightly before I went away, but I always did focus on my training."

"Is that wha' ye called it? All the times ye were off over the hills wi' your friends when it came time to drill, or when ye had a sore head from sitting in the ale hall most the night? Focusing, was it?"

"It never affected my skill wi' a sword."

"Nay." Baen's lip curled. "Ye were always gifted in that regard, were ye no'? As Donnar always said, only imagine if ye had applied yourself."

Donnar had said that about him? Adair always believed the man approved of him.

And from whence did this aggression on Baen's part come?

"Brother, I would almost think ye do not welcome me working with the lads."

"It is not that. Someone has to take them on, and the gods know no one else relishes the task. They seem to favor ye. Everyone favors ye."

Adair eyed his brother again. Was this jealousy speaking?

Mayhap so, for Baen went on, "Including Father. The favored son returns, is that the part ye play? That is how all the old stories go. Just so long as ye know, it does not wipe out your carelessness o' the past."

"I am not playing a part."

"Are ye not? The bright star who returns from Dalriada with failure and a stolen woman, but nevertheless makes himself out to be a hero."

"I never claimed to be a hero."

"Have ye not?"

"And when it comes to it, ye too failed in your task in Alba."

Baen sniffed with disdain. "I am to be chief here one day. I should never have been sent on so menial a task."

"Ah, too good to fulfill your duties, are ye?"

"As ye have always been."

Adair drew a breath. "Brother, if ye do not want me here in Erin—"

"So long as ye make yourself useful, I have no objections. Just remember to whom this land belongs."

"It belongs to all o' us."

"And that one day ye will swear fealty to me."

Adair said nothing.

Baen began to turn away but swung back. "And be aware, Adair—if the high king calls for warriors, 'twill be ye who leads our forces."

Because he was expendable? That was the implication, and it felt like a slap in the face. Adair's high spirits, earned while training the lads, evaporated in a poof.

He watched Baen walk away and wondered at such ill feeling in a brother. He kept wondering even after he went home and shared supper with Bradana. And later, when he, Bradana, and Wen went walking through the soft, gentle evening.

Bradana glanced at him once or twice as if sensing his mood, but said nothing of it. They spoke in murmurs, relating the events of their days, and watched Wen frolic over the hillside and down to the stream.

Not until they sat together on the side of the brae—a favorite place to watch the sun go down—did Adair ask, "Bradana, are ye happy here?"

He caught her sharp look before she treated him to her profile and said, "I am happy anywhere ye be."

"Aye, so." He knew that, down to his soul. And it had been at her insistence, as he reminded himself yet again, they were here. He would have stayed and fought beside her grandsire.

He would have stayed.

"I do wonder how they fare," she said softly after a moment. "My grandsire and Morag, and all the others. And I wonder, is my mother all right?"

"Aye."

"But I will mak' a place here wi' ye."

She reached out and captured his hand, threading their fingers together tight.

He marveled again at the strength of this thing between them, almost terrifying in its depth and intensity. They sat quietly for several moments while the sun sank in the sky. Peace should have found Adair then. For he was here, was he not? In the land he loved, with the woman he loved. What mattered Baen's ill feeling or the uncertainties of the future?

He had known always he was naught but a third son, if one who received a certain measure of favor. Mayhap Baen was jealous of that. Or mayhap he meant only to use Adair to best purpose when his day as chief came. Adair had no ambitions to reach farther, had he?

Be content, he told himself. Yet contentment refused to come.

CHAPTER FORTY-NINE

GAWEN SUMMONED THE three of his sons, Baen, Daerg, and Adair, one bright summer morning.

Adair had been headed for training with his weapons already in hand. Bradana, with Wen at her side, meant to spend the day with Caomhán, the harper.

And a glorious day it promised to be, sparkling with early dew and soft with fragrant air from the hills. Adair and Bradana were in the midst of parting at their door when a lad brought the message and darted off again.

"I wonder what he wants." Bradana shifted her harp in her hands, looking uneasy. "I ha' a bad feeling, all at once."

"Do not borrow trouble," he bade her, but uneasiness stirred in his own heart. He leaned forward and kissed her. "I shall see ye anon."

"Aye." But worry still filled her eyes when they parted.

He met Daerg on the way to the hall. His brother, since returning from Alba, had taken to spending much time with the priests and had become, if possible, more retiring than before. They could scarcely be more different, Adair reflected as they walked side by side. Baen, so grave and full of duty. Daerg, tentative and restrained. And he—who was he now? Beyond Bradana's lover, he scarcely knew.

He raised his eyebrows at Daerg. "Why d'ye think we ha' been called hence?"

"I dread to think."

Baen was there ahead of them standing with Father in the dusky early morning hall with only servants flitting about. Father, as Adair could see at once, was in one of his moods, brisk and impatient. He got that way at times, when he would act at any cost.

"Come away in," he bade his two younger sons. "We have matters to discuss."

Had they? And did Baen know what this was about? Adair looked at his older brother, but Baen's expression remained cool and indifferent.

"Sit, sit," Gawen invited them. "Will ye eat?"

Daerg shook his head.

"I ate at home," Adair murmured.

Gawen directed a look at the three of them. Adair remembered his doing this all the while they grew, lining them up in a row of the tallest to the smallest and charging them with either some task or some misdeed.

His stomach tightened.

"We must contemplate the future. Last autumn I determined to do just that, and yet my plans have come to naught. Baen, I sent ye to Alba to make a claim upon our lands there. Ye came back empty-handed."

Baen gave no reaction. He stood with his arms crossed upon his chest, the very picture of a stoic.

"And ye." Gawen switched his gaze to Daerg. "I sent to secure your own lands—those that would not only expand our holdings but make o' ye an Alban chief in your own right. Ye failed."

Daerg flushed but said nothing in his own defense.

"And ye." Gawen turned to Adair. "Ye, with the supposedly golden tongue, did worst o' all, for not only did ye fail to make good on our claim, but ye destroyed relations there and came back with a stolen bride."

Pure condemnation, and it stung. Adair had hoped he'd made up for that and earned a place for himself while working hard at training. Now he wondered if aught he could do might wipe out the disparagement he saw in his father's eyes.

Miffed, he began "If I—*we*—are not welcome here—"

"What?" It was Baen who turned on him. "What will ye do? Leave? Where will ye go? The favorite son," he half sneered, "disgraced."

"Silence!" Gawen roared. "The fact remains, Adair, ye have destroyed our alliance in Alba and made it that much harder to stake our claim. That does not mean I will give up. Baen and I have discussed this long."

Baen and he had? But of course. Baen would one day be chief.

"I will not die without seeing all my sons well provided for."

"Father," Daerg spoke up, "ye will no' die for many a year yet. Ye remain strong and vital."

"Aye so, I do for now. But a man may be struck down in many ways, and he must look ahead to the future. Baen will be well prepared to take my place one day. Adair, Donnar and I both think if ye work hard and continue to devote yoursel', ye may one day take the place o' war chief. Perhaps so, ye may undo some o' the harm ye have done." He turned toward his middle son.

"Father, I have thought much upon my future, and may wish to take the way o' the priests."

"Is that so?"

"A holy life might well suit."

"That is no' the road I have chosen for ye."

Father and son stared at one another. Daerg swallowed hard, and Adair felt a flash of sympathy for him.

"Ye will wed," Gawen promised, "and ha' children, and expand my holdings. In Alba."

"But—" Daerg paled. "I had no' thought to marry." He turned wild eyes on Adair. "My brother already has a wife. Let him take my place."

"Your brother is disgraced and cannot return to Alba. Ye will do so. Ye will grow a set o' balls, hear? Ye will claim your lands from Kendrick and set up your future holding there."

"But my uncle will not deal with me. He sent me away. And now, now that Adair has stolen his daughter, will he not be even less disposed to hear what I say?"

"No doubt."

"Father, ye cannot send me back. My life is here. This is my land."

Words Adair might himself have cried, once. Indeed, he likely had. They would do Daerg no good.

"Listen to me, Daerg. If ye think I will surrender our claims to valuable lands in Alba, ye are even more foolish than ye look. Ye must go back—difficult task or no'—and ye be the only one who can. They are to be your lands. Ye foolish lad! D'ye not want the wealth o' them?"

Daerg looked like he'd just been handed a life sentence, as perhaps he had. "What am I to do if Kendrick still will not deal with me?"

"Stay until he will. This does not end, Daerg, until one o' my sons holds ownership o' Alban lands. D'ye hear me?"

"I hear," Daerg acknowledged him miserably.

"Now go out, the both o' ye, and about your business. Daerg, I will expect to see ye packed and ready to leave by tomorrow morning."

They went out as ordered into the bright morning.

"Och, what am I to do?" Daerg lamented. "I had thought—hoped—that after ye returned Father was done with all this Dalriada nonsense. Kendrick will not deal with me. He has no opinion o' me. Adair, what am I to do?"

Adair shook his head. "I cannot help ye, Daerg." Had he himself not been declared disgraced? Fallen irretrievably low in his father's regard.

"Mayhap ye can." Daerg turned to him and laid a hand on his arm. "Ye can go in my place, as my agent. I will pay ye well in a portion o' my lands there, if ye can claim them. Ye, at least, are adept wi' a sword and fit for the fight. Will ye, brother?"

Adair, with lands in Alba? The plea was a sincere one—he could see that in Daerg's eyes. But he shook his head.

"I have already done more harm than good there. I am the last man Kendrick wants to see."

"Och, what am I to do then? Brother"—Daerg's fingers tightened on Adair's arm—"for me is not the life o' a chief wi' a wife. And bairns. By the gods! I have found my place among the druids who study the old laws and search for signs."

"I cannot help ye, Daerg." Adair would do well to keep his own head up after this, knowing what his father—and Baen—thought of him.

Yet as he went off about his day and to his duties at the training field, the thought would not leave him alone. His own lands in Alba. Just what Rohracht MacFee had offered him.

CHAPTER FIFTY

SOMETHING WORRIED ADAIR, eating at him like an illness. That much, Bradana could not deny. What it was, he refused to say.

Though he had fought her on leaving Alba, she had expected him to settle once he returned to Erin, this land he loved right down to his bones. And she could see why he loved it so. It was a bonny place of soft rains and hazy distances, the kind to lend peace to a man's heart.

Adair's heart did not harbor peace. She could feel that when he came home from the field. When they spoke together. When they walked with Wen and even when they made love, a time they were so surely joined, his every thought nearly became her own.

Still, he held what troubled him from her.

His brother, Daerg, had gone off back to Alba at his father's bidding. Was it that which ate at Adair? He felt much guilt about the way things had gone when he was there. He felt guilt over abandoning Grandfather and for stealing her, as his elder brother, Baen, put it.

Did he regret bringing her back here to Erin with him?

She did not think so when he kissed her. Could not believe it when he was inside her. Yet doubt haunted her even as trouble flitted in his eyes.

She came to like Baen less and less. She'd had little to do with the man when he came to Alba. He'd been naught but an

291

interloper there, of whom everyone wanted shed.

Now he appeared to be amassing a measure of power and making his opinions known—to be expected in a future chief. He did not hold back from sneering at Adair. And just what he thought of her, Bradana could only guess.

She had taken to cutting the man dead when they met. But she did not want to make things worse for Adair by showing her antagonism. They would eventually have to live under Baen's rule, and if she showed how she disliked him, he could make it very difficult indeed for them.

And their children.

Even after she became certain she carried Adair's child, she did not tell him. She could not say why, save that he already had enough crowding his head, and she did not know how he would take the news.

He would be glad, surely? Even if his father looked upon the child as just another interloper?

Either way, her child would be born here in a strange land, his or her mother an exile. The very thought made her heart hurt, though she could not tell Adair that, either.

So she gave him what comfort she could. A quiet place to rest when he came home. Long walks with her and Wen. And she played for him on her harp, which seemed to provide him the greatest ease of all.

He would lie upon their bed with his eyes closed while she wove her songs, some of them ancient and some tunes from her own head and heart. He told her that when he listened so to her tunes, he felt as if he could fly. As if, like a bird, he soared out over the ocean and away.

He never said to where he flew, just that her music set him free.

"We are so tied to this earth," he mused once into her hair, after she'd ceased playing and come to lie in his arms. "Tied to those who came before us and those who will come after. Your music, *alanna*, has a magic which takes me beyond all that." And he would drop kisses into the palms of her hands, at both corners of her mouth, her cheeks and forehead. She would dissolve in love for him and vow in her heart that nay, spending her life here in Erin was not too high a price to pay for being with him.

Then came the night he whispered, after she ceased playing, "Perhaps—so I pray to all the gods—our children may inherit your talent. Only imagine if a whole line o' them became bards or shanachies, down into the future."

Bradana shifted in his arms. "Ye would like that?"

"Och, aye, far better bards than warriors. For what does a warrior deal, save death? A shanachie weaves enchantment."

"We may find out sooner than ye think. By the next turn o' the holy wheel into spring, I am thinking."

"What?" He went very still, and her heart faltered. Aye, perhaps he desired children at some time in the future, but not now.

"I am carrying your child."

"Are ye certain?"

"I am." Were he not so distracted by whatever bothered him, he would have noticed she'd missed her monthly more than once.

"Bradana, by the gods!" He kissed her, and in his kiss she felt what he did not say, his love for her and the child they had created between them. He framed her face between his hands and gazed into her eyes. "Are ye well with this?"

"So far, I am well."

"Why did ye not tell me?"

"Because ye ha' had enough troubling your mind. Adair, please tell me what bothers ye. There is something."

"Naught that matters now. This is the best of news."

And indeed, he lit up with the joy of it, like a man transformed.

Before he left for the training field the next morning, he said, "Ye go off to Caomhán. I want our wee one hearing as much music as possible, mind."

"I do not suppose he—or she—can do aught but hear it, when

I play. Adair, my love… This makes ye happy?"

"Completely so."

And who was she to quibble about homesickness when she'd raised the spirits of the man she loved?

A CHILD. ONE created between him and Bradana, begotten of their love. For Adair, it changed everything.

Would he not work ceaselessly for his child? Make a place here that might be handed down? Create security and a sense of belonging?

Then why did he keep thinking of Alba?

The place, or memories of it, had indeed begun to haunt him. Only, the memories did not seem like memories; they were too vital and too immediate. A kind of longing would come upon him in the midst of the day when he sweated on the training field. Or when he and Bradana, with Wen, walked together in this place he loved. Suddenly he would see a rough, dark mountain in place of the sweet and familiar stretch of hillside. He dreamed of Alba—almost believed he was there surrounded by her forests. And she whispered to him in the movement of the wind.

Most beguiling of all, he heard Alba in Bradana's music, in the tunes she made for him and played in the still of the evening. Those had the power to carry him over the water to that place for which some deep and fundamental part of him yearned.

Was not Erin the land he loved?

Aye, but Alba had a claim on him.

Where and how had it happened? At what point during his sojourn there? When the stag led him out of the forest? When he and Bradana followed every sign granted to them, through the wild?

Or even earlier than that, the first time he'd gazed into Bradana's eyes?

Whatever the moment, Alba called to him.

He could not admit to that call, especially now that Bradana had settled into life here. When she'd brought him the wondrous news she had. It had been she, after all, who insisted on leaving Alba. She believed they were safer here, and everyone they had left behind was safer for their absence.

How could he admit to her that he wanted to go back? But he did. With fervor that increased with each passing day, he did.

He said nothing of it, kept a cheerful demeanor with the boys he trained during the day, tried to be grateful for the small favors that came to him, and courteous toward his father and Baen.

At night, in his dreams, he roamed Alba's forests and woke feeling he'd been pierced to the heart.

His old friends, those with whom he'd spent so much time in laughter and games before ever he left Erin, made a few forays into drawing him back among them. But he no longer felt comfortable there. For good or ill, he had changed.

He would be a father by spring. Nothing else mattered. Third son or no, he must make a place here, work as hard as he ever had to establish a standing for those who came after him.

On into the future.

⊰ ❦ ⊱

CHAPTER FIFTY-ONE

B RADANA FELT WELL and strong during the days of that summer, as if she'd been born to carry Adair's child. None of the sickness that had beset her mother in her pregnancy, the weariness or distress. Indeed, as the bairn grew inside her, she seemed to gain in vigor, and Adair told her she shone with beauty.

She wondered often what had befallen her mother and remembered repeatedly her last glimpse of her mam, when everything had broken apart, and she and Adair fled. Had the child been born safely? Did she have a new half-brother or -sister? Had her mother perished?

The two of them had not always got on easily. Mother was a quarrelsome sort of woman, and Bradana herself was strong-willed. But she felt closer to the woman than ever, now.

After Mother had wed Kendrick and they had come south, it was just the two of them, at first. Those days now lingered in Bradana's mind.

The truth was, she wanted to go home. With a deep and fervent urging, she wanted her child to be born in Alba, where she herself had been born.

But she could not say as much to Adair. He worked so very hard day after day to make a place for himself here. To make a place for them. And had she not been the one to insist they come here, to Erin? For the sake of her grandsire and Morag, and all the others.

Adair would think her mad if she changed her mind. Yet she could find no peace.

The only times she felt a measure of it was while lying in Adair's arms, or while playing her music. Caomhán very kindly continued to insist she had a great talent. She knew only that when the music possessed her, she could express all the tangled emotions inside her, the love and longing. She created song after song.

All about Alba.

While Adair worked at training, she often took walks on her own, with Wen. And she came to appreciate the beauties of Erin. The broad sweeps of green stretching to the horizon. The mist that rose from the ground of the mornings and the gentle hills. The rain fell softer here than in Alba. She could walk out through it as if it did not exist. The sun soon came out again, like a woman smiling after passing tears.

Bradana could see why Adair loved this place.

She put her energy into her music and into growing her child, and let no word of complaint cross her lips. Lammas came and went, and Erin's fields began to turn golden.

One afternoon, Adair came home early and told her, "Baen is to become handfasted. 'Twas announced today. A woman from south o' us. Father is hoping 'twill give us a chance to expand our holdings."

"Ah. He has given up on expanding to Alba, then?"

"Nay. But no one has heard back from Daerg. We do not know if he is alive or dead." For an instant, Adair's eyes turned bleak.

"What will she be like, this wife for Baen?" The woman would one day help to lead the clan.

"Who knows? He will, so I imagine, want an heir right quick."

Their eyes met. They had so far not told anyone that Bradana carried what might at present be the heir to the clan.

"That will make your father happy."

"Aye, so. But no matter. I am home early with time to spend. Shall we go walking? Or will ye play for me?"

She came to him, stood close and then closer. She craved this man's company the way she craved air. "I do no' mind what we do."

They kissed as naturally as breathing. She wound her arms around his neck. He smelled of sunshine and the hard work he'd done. He tasted of eternity.

What if she told him she wanted to go home? Home to the land she'd lost.

"Play for me," he whispered when the kiss ended.

"Aye, so. I made a new song today." A song of longing. Mayhap with her music, she could tell him what she dared not say.

ADAIR DREAMED OF Alba. He stood upon the shore at Phee staring out to sea, away past the islands that lay there like crouching beasts. Toward Erin.

There, in the dream, he turned his back squarely upon the place of his birth.

He now faced Rohracht's dun, and the place was under attack. On the rise above him, the hall burned. Men fought everywhere by the garish light of the flames, a life-or-death struggle for possession.

For his heart.

He heard Bradana's music in his ears, one of her sad and wistful laments, a complicated weaving of sound that grew ever louder with the crashing of sword on sword, sword on shield, till the very din of it woke him where he lay shivering.

"Adair?" Bradana stirred in his arms, and Wen lifted his great head from the floor. "What is it? My love?" Bradana touched his face. "Are ye unwell?"

He spoke without thinking, still half held by the power of that dream—or vision.

"I must go home."

"Home? My heart, ye *are* home. Here in your own bed, in Erin."

"I must go back to Alba, where my destiny lies."

She caught her breath. For many moments she did not speak, merely ran her hands down his arms, soothing, and over his heart.

"Are ye certain o' this?"

"Aye, Bradana. I know ye were the one who wanted to leave there—"

"Hear me, and hear me well. I did no' want to leave. I thought it might save ye. My fear o' losing ye is such that I would do anything, give anything, to keep ye from harm."

"Aye, *alanna*, but there is fear, and there is destiny." And a man must endure the latter, no matter what it cost him.

Bradana drew another breath. He felt her pull hard on her courage. "If this be what ye want, love, then I am with ye."

"Ye will return to Alba with me, despite your fear?"

"Wherever ye may be, I am also."

He kissed her deeply.

Would they arrive back in Alba to find the dream's prediction come true? Would they step into battle? Would their time together be cut short?

Life was indeed about the choices one made. Adair hoped he made the right choice now.

THEY LEFT FOR Alba on a day that hinted of autumn, with a bit of a cool breeze from the north. One of Adair's friends, Oisin, was to accompany them to the coast so he could bring the ponies back once their company of three set sail.

Caomhán wept when Bradana parted from him. He made her

promise to keep playing music and weaving tunes, and she whispered to him in parting, "I am carrying a child. Tell no one. Maybe he will be a grand harper someday."

"Be sure and teach him well," Caomhán returned.

Adair did not receive as fond a farewell from his father or brother. Baen said nothing. Bradana got the feeling he was glad to see the back of his brother se. Poised to marry and come into his own, he did not need competition from his father's supposed favorite.

Gawen told Adair only, in parting, "Make something o' yourself. And send word whether or not Daerg is still alive."

"I am naught to my father but a third son," Adair said to Bradana bitterly as they sailed away, "and of no value. They speak o' the son returning home joyfully—he will no' want to see me again."

"Ah, but my love," Bradana said, and kissed him, "ye are—ye are returning home."

<hr>

CHAPTER FIFTY-TWO

THAT VOYAGE SEEMED like a dream, one that ended as a nightmare. The little boat ferrying everything for which Bradana cared sailed with mystical ease over a smooth sea between the sleeping dragon islands. When they approached her grandfather's settlement, Alba lay swathed in a bank of mist, her dark land banked like a fire. A place of magic and imaginings.

Not till they passed through that mist to the shore did the truth become apparent. For the mist cloaked even the din of the battle taking place.

She stared in horror, and Adair abandoned his oars to lean over the gunwale of the little boat. Even Wen picked up his head to stare. Bradana felt the blood drain from her head so rapidly, she went dizzy.

Nay. Nay!

Most of the settlement appeared to be aflame. Indeed, the smoke from the fires mingled with the mist to obscure the horrors before their eyes. Even a few of the boats on the shore burned.

Men fought everywhere. In the settlement itself, near to the hall. On the heights. On the shore.

One thought broke through Bradana's dismay as she took in the terrible scene, her mind flailing. Their departure from this land she loved had spared her grandsire nothing.

Och, by all the blessed gods, where was he? That valiant old man who had been so ill when she left. Did he live or die?

"Mican?" she breathed, and reached to touch Adair, seeking to ground herself. "Are they his men?"

"Aye." Adair did not move, frozen in his dismay, his eyes narrowed upon the throes of battle high and low.

Bradana knew this man now. She knew his heart. He would plunge into this fight.

But for the moment they hung there in their wee boat like the inhabitants of a far dream, no one upon the shore noticing them, though they floated in clear sight.

Wen gave a whine that seemed to break Adair's paralysis. He seized the oars tight.

"We cannot land here. 'Twill be certain death."

He began to pull on the oars. Bradana hung over the side, unable to look away from the settlement as they scuttled past. Her mind would not work right. She half expected Adair to turn them around and row back to Erin.

He did not.

Instead he took them farther up the coast, where he beached the little boat on the stones of the shingle. He and Wen both leaped out, and he dragged the boat ashore.

"Adair—"

They could hear the clamor of it now that their feet had met Alban soil, the terrible screech and cry of attacker and defender.

And suddenly, suddenly Bradana knew what her lover was going to do. She knew that all of their tale, from the moment they'd met to this very instant, had led to the action he would now take.

She seized hold of him and stared into his face. That beloved face she knew so well. Every freckle. Every smile and frown. The eyes that could brim with laughter.

Stark and cool now.

"Ye will stay here, Bradana. Hear me? Stay here where ye be safe till it all goes quiet."

Till the battle ends, he meant.

"I am coming wi' ye."

"Nay."

"Adair, I am always wi' ye! Where'er."

He seized both her arms and shook her gently. "Think o' the child. Ye must think o' the child."

"But—"

"Once it falls quiet, ye must creep close. See whose men are in charge. Right? If they are Mican's men"—his gaze turned still colder—"I want ye to put back out to sea. Can ye do that? D'ye think ye can make it back to Erin, or down the coast to your stepfather's holding?"

Because he would be dead. That was what he told her. He went to fight, and he would not quit till he was either victorious or had spent his life.

"I canna lose ye."

"You are strong, Bradana. Live for our child. I will live on in him." He kissed her. One kiss, fierce and bright as the flash of light on a war shield. "Ye will stay here. Promise me."

She wept now, the tears running down. "Aye," she said, for she could deny him nothing.

He turned to Wen. "Stay wi' her. Guard."

And then he ran with all his might, his sword already in his hand. Straight back down the shore into the dark horror that was, in truth, no dream.

Wen whined. Bradana could feel how he wanted to follow this man he loved. That she loved.

They stood, the hound quivering and the woman weeping till Adair disappeared around a curve of the headland.

Then Bradana looked around herself. Naught but the tiny boat, still holding their possessions. The misted land and the gray sea.

The soft voice of Alba beneath it all.

Alba whispered to her in the shush and draw of the waves. In the breath from the land. In her own heartbeat.

Too much to ask her to remain here while life and death raged just out of sight.

But she must think of the child. Adair's child.

She pressed both hands to her belly, and for an instant prescience poured into her. As if it came from the land itself, from the sea and sky.

If Adair did not survive this battle, his child must live. It was important. The very future depended upon it.

But och, she could not stand here without knowing. Everything inside her longed to find a weapon of her own, to join that battle she could hear, but not see. To fight at her lover's side. To fight for him.

He wanted her to live for him, instead.

With her hound at her side, she climbed up the rough headland that fronted the shingle and through the gorse and bracken, to see.

ADAIR RAN INTO the smoke, the heat, and the horror of the battle. It felt as if he ran somehow back through time to the past, to other battles when strength took hold inside him and he knew no fear.

He could taste the fear now, though. The uncertainty. He remained connected to Bradana and could feel her there behind him. Naught else about the situation was known—who was winning, who losing. Whether he would be required to die.

If he did, at least he would be leaving a part of himself behind.

It was all a man could do.

He had no shield, and the fight swiftly closed around him. Dead lay everywhere on the shore and in the settlement. Some of them wore Mican's tartan. Far more, it seemed, Rohracht's colors.

He met his first two opponents before his feet left the shingle. They came in tandem down the rocky slope that led to the settlement. Mican's men. The fighting here on this stretch of shore was fierce, as if it had tumbled down from the dun.

Adair felt his mind and his emotions flow into a single channel. *Kill or be killed.*

He felled Mican's warriors one, two, without conscious thought. He turned and pelted up the slope toward the dun.

Not a great distance. The settlement was not a large one. It might as well have been half the length of Dalriada, for he had to battle for every step. Here the fighting grew fierce indeed, and the smoke mingled with the mist. Alba breathing fire. Just ahead, he saw men he knew—members of Rohracht's forces with whom he'd grown friendly before he left. No sign of Rohracht.

How could the old man survive this?

At the door of the hall, half of which, though seared by flame yet stood, raged the thickest of the fighting.

There, so Adair knew on a deep and primal level, he needed to be.

He fought his way to it, his sword shedding blood, flesh, and bone, an extension of his arm. His mind directed it without conscious thought. He did not see Rohracht's men, what remained of them, falling in behind him as if he were the head of the spear.

But he heard their cries—of surprise those must be, at seeing him there. A roar came from up ahead, and peering through smoke that stung his eyes, he saw one man fighting amid a knot of others for admittance to the hall itself.

Mican.

With a single thought for the woman he loved, Adair dove in.

CHAPTER FIFTY-THREE

MICAN FOUGHT LIKE a man possessed, with a snarl on his face. Whether he still battled for revenge or for conquest, or just because he refused to lose this fight, Adair could not tell.

It did not matter. For the man stood at the very door of Rohracht's hall. He could not be permitted inside.

A mere two defenders kept him out, and one of them sore wounded. Instinct, unfathomable within Adair, weighed the situation. Bone-deep knowledge took him forward.

He had to fight his way in. The attackers gathered close around Mican battled well, and Adair soon found himself in a fight for his life. Snarling faces turned toward him, as did reddened swords. Well enough, for it took the pressure off the defenders.

Adair did not feel the wounds he took, too busy keeping a far grimmer count in his head. One opponent down. Two. Three. Shedding his own blood now, he leaped forward and placed his back against the scorched door of the hall.

Facing Mican.

The door felt hot, but what was left of it had been shut tight—barred, he hoped—and made of solid oak. Strong.

As strong as he must be.

Mican, blood showing on his face, recognized him at once for the very man who had killed his son—here suddenly within reach of his blade. For one vulnerable moment, his eyes widened and Adair struck. Mican's blade met his, and his face hardened.

Men bellowed and hollered all around them, and the clash of metal on metal and wood was deafening. Adair, possessing no shield, wrapped both hands on the hilt of his sword. Mican still possessed a shield, but it was split. He came at Adair with it, using the edge as a weapon.

The door behind Adair held. His body absorbed the attack.

They were nose to nose now, only the battered ash of Mican's shield between. Hate flared in the man's eyes.

Adair pushed back against that hate, a mighty shove that crashed the shield asunder. Mican threw it aside.

"Ye bastard!" he spat into Adair's face, with no sign of fear. "Ye killed my son. Ye will die for it."

If Adair died, the settlement would be lost. He did not know how he knew it, or from whence the belief came. But he set his back more firmly against the door and raised his sword.

Only one of them would survive.

BRADANA CRAWLED ON her belly through the rough grass and drank in the scene beyond. She could see it all. The scattered fighting on the shore. The clots of men fighting here and there up the slope, and the dense throng of attackers at the door of her grandsire's dun. Where Adair had gone.

She could see him there. Even from this distance, aye, and despite the heavy smoke. She knew him by the way he moved. By the way he used his sword. By some greater, deeper form of recognition she did not question.

She watched from the top of a rough knoll while he gained the front of the hall and took up a stance there, his brown hair swinging behind him.

Her heart convulsed within her, with fear and pride and love. Her entire being wanted to run to him. But for the sake of their child, she must keep away.

If he lost this fight, if his sword could not make a difference in what looked like an unequal battle, Mican would be as happy to kill her as he would Adair.

But och, if she had to crouch here and watch him die, did she want to live on?

She moaned low in her throat, and Wen, flat on the ground beside her, echoed her with a whine.

Was that Mican himself facing Adair, there at the entrance to her grandsire's hall? She narrowed her eyes against the smoke and mist, desperate to see.

He had black hair like Mican. And he moved the way she remembered, with brutish strength—just like his son. The figure came at Adair with the remnant of a shield, which promptly broke. A furious gesture took him forward to where Adair stood with his back planted against the door.

Bradana closed her eyes. She did not pray often, though aye, she believed in the gods and goddesses in a distant sort of way.

She believed still more fiercely in this land against whose skin she now huddled.

Alba, protect him. Defend him for me.

She reached out with her mind, with her very being. A supplication and a vow. *Protect him and I will live for thee—and for him.*

Her desire, even more than her words, went like an arrow to Alba's dark heart. The stones of the shore heard, as did the high peaks of granite. The trees and the strength of oak at Adair's back. Eyes wide and heart aching, Bradana raised her head and watched.

ADAIR BLED HEAVILY, and he began to weaken. Though the battle clamor surrounded him, he saw only the snarl on Mican's face and the hate in his eyes. This fight between them was pivotal, and personal.

Did the question of which of them would win come down to that hate? He was younger than Mican by a generation, and presumably stronger. Mican was experienced in battle, and skilled. Both of them wounded. Bleeding their lives away. It could come down to that—the hate that fueled Mican.

Adair must be fueled, then, by love.

His mind, quite apart from the rest of him now, called upon it. The love he felt for Bradana and that she felt for him. The love he harbored for this land.

It came flooding to him up from the very ground, through the oak planks at his back and into his heart.

One last burst of power.

His blade met Mican's and held. The power filled his legs, his body. He pushed off from the door, pushed, *pushed*. The two swords gave voice as they screeched together.

But one of them held.

BRADANA SCREAMED AS she saw one of the men go down. Even across the distance she could see the bright shower of blood as he fell.

Both of them fell.

She was up and running before she knew it, her feet acting on their own. Breaking her promise. It did not matter, for with the conclusion of that one small battle there at the door, the rest of it crumbled, the individual fights ending and the attackers pulling away, away like a black mist from the land.

Bradana ran, past sprawled bodies of the dead and dying. Past living men who recognized and called out to her. Past reddened turf and stone, climbing, climbing with the breath searing her lungs and her heart disbelieving what she had seen.

His brown head going down.

Nay, nay. She could not live so. She could not endure without him. She could not wait for another lifetime to find him again.

She had no breath when she reached the door of her grand-sire's dun. So clogged was it by the fallen, by the dead, that she could not reach the two men who lay up against it.

"Mistress Bradana!" Men, her grandfather's men, called to her. She ignored them, her gaze fixed on but one form.

He lay facedown, his brown hair a tangle, and the sword fallen at last from his hand. Surrendered in death?

Mican lay almost touching him, face up and eyes wide, a terrible, gaping slash across his chest.

No need to ask if he were dead.

"Mistress. Mistress!" someone else cried.

Mican was dragged aside. Careful hands turned Adair over in the space allowed. Bradana dropped to her knees beside him.

Breathing? Was he breathing?

His eyes were closed and his face, liberally splashed with blood, looked unusually calm. Serene. As if he saw beyond this world.

"Nay," she moaned in her throat. "Nay, nay."

Surely he must breathe. Despite the terrible wound she could see, seeping blood across his belly. Surely she would know if he were gone. Her world would collapse around her and grow dark.

The man kneeling beside her, the one who had turned Adair over, looked into her face. She knew him, a member of her grandfather's guard called Dabhor.

He had tears running down his face.

"He turned the battle. He did. We all fell in behind him and—"

"Aye. Is he dead?" She touched Adair's face, his cheek, and his brow, just where he always kissed her.

"He breathes."

Bradana's blood surged so hard, she went dizzy. The door behind Adair opened.

"Bring him awa' in," said a voice she knew.

Willing hands lifted Adair and carried him into the darkened dun. Away behind, Bradana could still hear someone—her grandfather's men—pursuing the last of Mican's who had broken away.

Blood. There was so much blood. It trailed from Adair's body as they carried him. More blood than one man should be able to shed.

He breathed and he lived, aye, but for how long?

CHAPTER FIFTY-FOUR

A SECTION OF the dun still smoldered, making it dark inside, and a terrible reek of burning filled the hall.

They did not carry Adair there but to the other side, where lay Grandfather's quarters.

Someone took Bradana's arm. She jerked in surprise.

"Morag?"

"My dear, wha' are ye doing here? We thought ye safe awa'."

"We came back." She had no other words. Those said it all, did they not?

"He turned the battle, yer young man. Everyone saw."

"Grandfather?"

"He saw, aye."

"He is alive?"

"We had to drag him fro' the battle."

Suddenly, Grandfather was there, tottering on his own feet, ushering them in out of the gloom. It did not seem real. But none of this could be real, the flames, the presence of those she knew. Adair, bleeding so.

So much blood.

Maybe she was still back in Erin, dreaming it all.

They laid him down upon a pallet and suddenly the healer was there, the same who had treated them before.

Bradana looked into the man's face, which appeared so terribly grave that she had to look away again.

At the man she loved.

Someone put his arm around her. Grandfather, it was.

"Lass, come awa'."

"Nay."

"Let the healer do his work."

"I canna lose him. If I do—"

"Let her stay," the healer said, and his eyes said still more. *It will not be long.*

With a sob, she fell down beside the pallet and took Adair's hand, scraped raw and red with blood. She drew it to her lips.

"Please, my love. Please."

Morag wept. Wen hunkered down beside Bradana as close as he could get and whined.

Bradana's heart wept.

Adair lay like one already gone from her, that look of almost holy ease on his face. She could not wish him back to pain. She should not.

She did.

"Please," she beseeched him again, and dropped a kiss into the palm of his hand, leaned forward and kissed both corners of his mouth, his blood-splashed cheeks.

His forehead.

He did not stir.

THE HEALER TREATED Adair's wound. Not the one on the side of his face or the others, nearly innumerable, that marked his arms, but that most terrible one in his gut that leaked away his life's blood. He had to do it while Bradana still clutched Adair's hand, for she would not leave go of him.

Morag tried to coax her away, as did her grandfather. Not far, they said. Just a few steps to give the healer room.

The healer said nothing, just worked around her and continued to let her stay, which terrified her more than anything else.

The blood on Adair's hand had now transferred to her fingers. He felt very cold. She wanted to lie down next to him, once the bandages were in place, and keep him warm the way he had kept her warm so many times—on the trail out from Kendrick's in Alba's wilderness. In Erin.

People came and went from the room with hushed voices. Reporting to Grandfather about what went on outside. The aftermath of the battle. Prisoners and defenses and the pursuit of those who had fled.

The words floated around Bradana, but she didn't truly hear them. Adair continued to lie without moving. Not so much as a flicker touched his face.

Had he already gone from her? But he still breathed, calm and quiet, and the blood seeping through the clean bandages had slowed.

His heart still beat. The heart that belonged to her.

Her grandfather, his face ashen, stooped and hugged her. "Lass, I maun go out. They are asking wha' to do wi' Mican's body."

"Burn it," she said bitterly. "It should no' occupy the same world as Adair."

"Aye, so." The old man went, moving, it seemed, by sheer willpower.

Time passed. Bradana could still hear the commotion from outside. The healer changed Adair's bandages again and had a whispered conversation with Morag, one Bradana could hear.

"I canna believe he is still wi' us. I did no' think it would tak' so long."

"He is young and strong." Morag's voice throbbed with grief.

"Aye, and his heartbeat sound. Mayhap, mistress, ye should convince the lass to tak' some rest away."

"She will not go. Not until…"

It dropped into Bradana's heart, into her mind, what Morag meant. That she would not stir until Adair was gone.

But she could not see a world for her and her child that did not contain him.

Stay wi' me, she beseeched him silently.

No response showed in the calm face turned toward her.

She wanted to weep. She wanted to wail. She could do nothing but hold on.

"Lass," Morag said a while later, "come awa' and tak' something to eat. The women are cooking. 'Tis near morning. Come get some rest."

Bradana shook her head. She lay down beside Adair and wrapped an arm around him. She could feel his heart beating against her wrist. Low. Low and steady.

She slept.

She woke an unmeasured amount of time later and remembered it all in one jarring jolt that brought her upright. The man in her arms still felt cold, and at that terrible moment she was sure he had gone, slipped from her while she slept most treacherously, a victim of her own weakness and exhaustion.

But he breathed yet. So did the healer, slumped upright at some distance. And Morag, not far away.

"Adair?" she whispered, but he lay without moving. "My love."

No response. But he had stayed with her. She tried to be grateful.

When Morag awoke and found Bradana still holding Adair's hand, she tried once more to persuade her. "Come awa'. Ye will need to relieve yoursel' at the very least. Tak' something to eat and drink."

"Aye." Bradana turned her head and looked at the woman. "I suppose I must eat, for I am carrying his child."

"Rohracht's great-grandchild!" Morag gasped. "All the more reason ye maun tak' some food. For the wee one's sake."

"I am afraid to leave go of him. If I do…"

"For but one moment, lass. Come."

It took all the strength Bradana possessed to let go of Adair's hand. To place it on his chest. To step away, her arm laced with Morag's.

Outside, it was another day. Another time, another world. She relieved herself, which had indeed become urgent. She gazed on the damage to the settlement and wondered how it could ever be put right. She felt Alba beneath her feet.

"When did they come, the attackers?" she asked Morag.

"'Two days before ye returned. Mican had been before, ye ken, demanding Adair should be given over to him. Rohracht turned him away, saying the neither o' ye were here, but Mican did no' seem to believe him. Indeed, he must no' have done. He went awa' for many days before coming back and making the demand again. During that time, we had a messenger fro' Kendrick, come by sea. Mican had been there also, mayhap thinking ye had taken refuge wi' him. He told us your mam had her babe—a wee girl—and though 'twas a hard delivery, they both survived."

"Och, I am glad," Bradana breathed. Another daughter to perhaps provide Mam with comfort.

Morag turned her gaze away from Bradana's face. "When next Mican came, only days ago, as I say, he again demanded the both o' ye. Rohracht told him ye had sailed off to Erin, but he did not believe it and said he would search the settlement. That was enough to start the fight.

"We should ha' known better than to think Mican had given up on the idea o' revenge. Even if he had no' found ye here, I believe he would still have taken out his ire on us instead."

Bradana nodded, staring at the portion of food one of Morag's women had placed in her hands. Not truly seeing it.

She needed to eat if only for the sake of Adair's child. If she lost that part of him…

She tried to choke down a barley cake. Her stomach heaved.

Morag rubbed her back gently. "Yer man is a hero. Everyone says so. If ye had no' arrived when ye did, all would be lost."

And if he died, all would still be lost.

"Ye can be proud o' that, lass."

Proud? What good the best of warriors, if dead?

"I need to get back," she said, and turned to the door. Only to see that Mican's head had been nailed above it. She gasped. "I asked Grandfather to burn him, mak' him disappear."

"And aye, his body will be burned, lass, with the rest o' the enemy dead."

With a shudder, Bradana passed beneath the gory trophy.

"Your belongings ha' been brought up from along the shingle where yer boat lies," said Morag. "Some clothing and your clàrsach."

Her harp.

That made her look into Morag's eyes. "Have it brought, please. Here to me."

CHAPTER FIFTY-FIVE

ADAIR STILL LIVED and breathed when Bradana returned to him, a fact of which she swiftly assured herself by touching his face and placing her hand over his heart. She took up her vigil again with no intention of moving.

For the balance of that day, so it went. The healer made appearances, as did Grandfather. Had Bradana any notice to spare, she would have marked how ill her grandsire looked.

No one tried to call her away again. A pot was brought for her use and food offered. Their belongings arrived.

At the healer's suggestion, they tried tipping ale into Adair's mouth, but it just ran off his lips. He did not swallow.

That night, Bradana again slept with her lover, unmoving, in her arms. She lay so she could feel his breath come against her cheek, and she prayed to the very ground beneath them.

Sustain him.

How much time passed so, she could not rightly say. Nothing existed beyond the small chamber with its smoke-tainted air and its quiet occupants.

Just as she did not measure the time, she never later knew what made her take up her harp. That terrible quiet, perhaps, or the memory of how Adair had loved to lie—much as he did now—listening to her music.

She played for him, only for him. The tunes he loved best. Those he so often requested. Most of all, over and over again, she played the tune she'd made for him, her fingers fumbling over the stings before taking flight.

It was love that loosed the notes into the room. They wove a balm that served, at least, to soothe her own heart.

For days uncounted she played, never ceasing.

ADAIR FLOATED IN perfect ease, wanting for nothing, when the first notes reached him. He seemed to be sprawled on his back in the bottom of a tiny boat upon the sea. A blue sky above him. Naught but water all around.

He wondered if he dreamed. If he had somehow come to be floating here halfway between Erin and Alba. Banished, mayhap. Or perhaps he was caught between the past and the future. Between worlds.

Curious, though, that he should be alone. Someone was meant to be with him.

And then the music came stealing, separate, delicate notes that quivered through the quiet air and set it alight. Strangely, he could see the notes. Silver they were, and so beautiful that he had no words for them. They shivered and gleamed with their own sounds, captured and beguiled him.

They formed themselves into tunes.

One particular song surrounded him over and over again. A bright and complicated series of notes, it wrapped about him, flowed through his veins, and strengthened his heartbeat.

It called to him.

Why did he let himself drift so, between Erin and Alba? There was but one place he needed to be.

He sat up in the boat, which rocked perilously. He found oars near his feet, which he was quite sure had not been there before.

He took them up and began to row.

A hard pull it proved to be, for now the sea became wild. But he followed the music, followed the trail of silver notes until he saw the dark land up ahead of him.

Land of magic. Land of promises. Land of his heart.

Not till his boat grounded on the shore of the shingle did he stop rowing. He had reached the place where he was meant to be. An exile no more.

He opened his eyes.

The first thing he saw was Bradana in profile, with her harp on her knee. Beautiful, she looked, with her hair hanging down all amber-golden and her hands moving on the strings with unearthly grace.

He did not want to interrupt her, to make her cease the glorious song, so he lay quietly until the great hound, lying beside her, raised his head and whined.

Bradana ceased playing, the notes continuing to quiver through the air of the room like living, sacred things. She looked at him.

"Bradana?"

He did not see her move or lay aside the harp. She was just there of a sudden, kneeling beside him, touching his face, his chest, his hands and weeping. Weeping.

Mayhap this was a dream. But nay, for then she kissed him, and he could feel the life in her and taste her tears.

"Why d'ye weep?" he asked when her mouth left his.

"Because ye were far, far from me."

"Did I no' tell ye I would find ye? I will always find ye again."

In MacMurtray's hall, the tale pauses upon a bright shimmer of harp notes. Finlay the bard smiles, knowing that he holds his audience spellbound. His eyes sparkle just like the notes he gives them, with knowing, and memory.

His dancing, skillful fingers leap and accompany the rest of his words, releasing cascades of sound, his voice like singing.

"Adair MacMurtray recovered steadily after that day, and 'twas as

well that he did, for though the settlement also recovered, Rohracht MacFee did not, and soon enough lost his far more personal battle wi' the sickness that possessed him.

"On his deathbed"—a further shower of notes—"he again told his granddaughter's husband, who had once been only a third son, that he wanted him to have all his lands. And"—Finlay's green eyes gleam—"is that no' how our good host, Chief Anders MacMurtray, comes to hold these lands even today?"

The chief smiles with pride and pleasure. Finlay's gaze seeks out but one of his listeners. Is it to her he speaks?

"We come and go from one another. Time after time, and life after life. The dreams that fall between the lifetimes may beguile our eyes and keep us from knowing one another. But"—a still brighter cascade of notes—"a vow is a vow. A promise remains a promise, like that the blessed land of Alba gave to a one-time exile when she took him to her heart.

"He is here still."

THE END

ABOUT THE AUTHOR

Laura Strickland delights in time traveling to the past and weaving deliciously romantic stories for her readers. Her first love has always been Scottish Historical Romance, and her work has garnered her several awards including a RONE. At home in Western New York, she's been privileged to mother a number of very special rescue dogs. Her lifelong interest in Celtic history, magic, and music, along with her mantra of *Lore, Legend, Love* are all reflected in her writing.

Visit Laura at www.laurastricklandbooks.com